Confliction

AMANDA G.

 PUBLISHING LLC

GW Publishing LLC

Paperback ISBN: 978-1-73672-680-8
Hardback ISBN: 978-1-73672-681-5

Cover illustrated by Kaleigh Wyckhouse

PRINTED IN THE UNITED STATES OF AMERICA

This book is dedicated to the memory of
Virginia Sue Rucker Pattman.
You will always be in our hearts.

ACKNOWLEDGMENTS

To move an idea from a thought to a full- fledged manuscript requires time, discipline and faith. It also requires surrounding yourself with people who believe in you. My heart is full to overflowing that my idea evolved into *Confliction,* a labor of many years.

Essential people who cheered me on during this marathon cannot go unnoticed. To my childhood friend, Regina Tholmer, I am forever grateful. You read early drafts and provided invaluable comments. I hope I was a good listener, which is the toughest thing to be.

To my dear son, Nigel Wheeler, who took precious time out of his busy schedule as a father and an attorney to read, critique and provide encouragement. I thank you. I look forward to seeing your books in print someday soon.

To my first editor Barbara Dicks, formerly at Fawcett Books, thank you for having the vision to champion my earlier work. This acknowledgment is late in coming. Sometimes we sprint past angels in our midst.

My mother, Velma Mae Rucker Green, continues to be a source of endless inspiration. Your life, your struggles and your triumphs could easily consume volumes. Someone should write a book about you. Maybe I will.

1

THE BOMB

I believed in "forsaking all others until death do us part" before my husband of twenty-five years almost killed me. "Years ago, when we were living in Detroit, I fathered a baby with another woman." Poisonous words dripped from the dry, cracked lips of my husband, Pastor Phillip Sampson.

Every unholy word proceeding from his mouth, I dissected into syllables. "This cri-sis is God's op-por-tu-ni-ty to man-i-fest our faith. Are you rea-dy to show God we trust Him?"

Is he talkin' to me, the one who snatched his raggedy ass off the streets?

I wanted the nonsense to stop, for him to yell "April Fools", even though it was the middle of a balmy January. Phillip caught his rhythm, droned on in preacher's cadence. A pulsing vein divided his scrunched up forehead. His captive audience of one slumped deeper into the overstuffed butterscotch leather couch. In free fall, unable to catch hold of anything to break the impact, a groan swelled in the pit of my throat and entered the universe as a feeble yelp.

Dizzying pain shot through my brain and radiated every cell of my body. My shattered heart galloped out of my chest. Metal shrapnel from Phillip's word bomb showered me like confetti. Bitter bile erupted in my acid gut.

It was the day after my forty-fifth birthday. I, Aubrey Sampson, First Lady of Trinity Baptist Church, bargained silently with the Lord, "Help me, Holy Ghost. I'm too young to have a heart attack." In my mind white clad nurses shrieked, "Code Blue, Code Blue". Would I make it to the hospital with a discernible pulse?

Phillip's lips moved up and down like a marionette on a faulty string. Maybe it was bad lip syncing. He forgot the lyrics and was testing me, I hoped.

Time and silence were all I needed from the vertically challenged stranger masquerading as my husband. His gray pinstriped suit, starched white shirt stretched tight over a pooching belly, Allen Edmond wing tips and gold, diamond encrusted tie clip looked familiar. But there was nothing familiar about this man who booted me into the twilight zone of fear.

My mind reverted to a place of safety, the precious interlude before the fork tongued preacher stormed into my glass menagerie and shattered it. He found me mind and body at rest, reclining on the couch in the family room, mesmerized by the purple and hot pink bougainvillea climbing a top heavy trellis in the sprawling yard. At the outstretched property line giant bird of paradise flagged on a gentle breeze. Branches of seven foot sago palms reached skyward like protective swords.

The precise moment before the bomb dropped, I gave thanks for an abundance of blessings---a loving husband and son who made me proud every day of the week. In my spirit there was peace, a flowing river of gratefulness. My meditation was soft, baggage lighter since I surrendered to my role as First Lady of Trinity Baptist Church in Yorba Linda, California.

The Bible rested on my lap, open to scripture for Bible study scheduled for the following evening. Phillip dragged in with the dread of a man about to preach his best friend's funeral. Imaginary chains shackled his hands and feet.

I peeked above the rim of my reading glasses and smiled. For the first time in memory Pastor Phillip Sampson was at a loss for words. Free flowing words were the trademark of his thriving ministry. The youth ministry dubbed Phillip "The Rapping Reverend". His ability to deliver sermons without notes and quote scripture faster than fire from an AK-47 propelled him to the precipice of ministerial majesty. Phillip Sampson had words to uplift the downtrodden, rally the sick and bring comfort to those in mourning. He spoke truth to power, disarmed high ranking conservative men and lured them into his social justice army.

Word peddler, Pastor Phillip Sampson, used urban charisma to draw a crowd to his growing church in the bastion of conservatism. With a library of sermons, metaphors and religious clichés he thrived in the midst of affluent Orange County. Left leaning Phillip was an anomaly in the predominantly Republican County with an African American population of less than two percent. A self-proclaimed mover and shaker, Phillip invited the natural enemy into his camp and embraced them.

Orange County, the least likely site for Phillip's firebrand preaching and calls for social justice, welcomed him. Many dismissed him as a fluke while others read The Rapping Reverend for what he was---a miracle. When he got the "call" to Orange County Phillip hemmed and hawed for days. He did not want to leave Detroit where he was an up and coming young preacher, gaining traction with the ministerial elite. Running the rails as a pulpit associate, Phillip had a clear path to becoming HNIC at Tabernacle Missionary Baptist Church in Detroit. The presiding pastor at Tabernacle, Reverend Doctor Kenneth Sheets, was staring ninety up the yang yang. Sheets kept his congregants on edge about the minute and the hour when he would take his last wheeze and keel over in the pulpit.

The lure of the West was hypnotic for me. California meant freedom from the hawk of Michigan winters and more frequent visits to my mother and father less than one hour away by plane. Above all, I was ready to shed the heavy yoke of vigilance each time I ventured into Detroit streets. I thirsted to reclaim the lightness of my joy.

I moved with energizing expectation of westward movement. Phillip moved with dread of re-establishing himself and pastoring a dwindling congregation for the rest of his life. Keep in mind, this was before I knew that his steady supply of Motor City "poontang" was being cut off.

And so I innocently cooed, "What's up, babe?" as he hovered above me. His negative energy bounced off recently painted Dunn-Edwards "pale beach" walls.

Phillip's tongue went in retreat. Two beats. He asked if I was busy. I lied, "Never too busy for my boo. Shoot."

Phillip cleared his throat. "Bree, I've got something to tell you...and it's not good."

I marked the passage, Proverbs 6:26-27(King James Version). "For by means of a whorish woman a man is brought to a piece of bread: and the adulteress will hunt for the precious life." A laminated book mark, featuring a painting by William H. Johnson, slid between the pages. I smiled at smoldering coal eyes of a milk chocolate girl with knock knees. Was it sorrow or glee in the girl's penetrating gaze? I closed the Book.

Phillip's chestnut skin had turned ashy gray. Inches shrank from his compact frame, reaching five feet, seven inches on a good day. Guilt tacked twenty years of hard time on his chronological age of forty-seven. Perennially bright, twinkling eyes cowered under a blanket of fear. A bluish gray haze circled each pupil. When did he get cataracts? I thought to myself.

It took several minutes from the moment he dropped the bomb before I inhaled my first real breathe. I dug out of my slouching, caved chest position, lifted upright and planted heavy feet on the floor. My bones creaked as I stood and squarely faced my husband.

When it finally emerged my voice was tiny and frail.

"How old is the child?"

"Donovan is twenty. You should meet him. He's a nice kid."

Twenty years ago, we had been married for five years. Our son Miles was in kindergarten at Troy Montessori School. Phillip was an associate minister at Tabernacle. I was happy. Thought he was happy.

The story repeated in my head like a broken eight track reel. I'm too old for this shit, I mused.

Phillip's sonorous voice droned in the timbre of an early morning sermon falling on sleep deprived ears. "I had a relationship with a woman in our congregation. Her name was...is Delia Upchurch. I didn't know about Donovan until recently."

"How recently?"

"Six months ago."

"*Six months*! And you're just telling me?"

"The boy...young man, got in touch with Miles."

"Aw, hell no!" Rage shot from my eyes. "You mean my son, our son, knows about this?"

"I tried to protect my family."

"By sticking your dick in a whore's pussy?"

"She's not a whore, just a lonely..."

The Bible cannoned from my hand like a Frisbee. Phillip swayed in fear thickened air. A Tai Chi practitioner. He bent backward, ducked low, mimicking Keanu Reeves in the Matrix. Not low enough. The metal zipper of the whizzing Bible grazed his left brow. Like ketchup squeezed too tightly, blood spurted on his immaculate shirt. A Swarovski crystal vase filled with three dozen long stem red roses, my birthday present, crashed to Brazilian walnut flooring.

"Baby, it was twenty years ago. By the grace of God we can deal with this... and Donovan."

"We? There is no we...Get outta my fuckin' face," I spat at him. Rabid eyes scoured the room.

Phillip's hands shielded his face, fearing more incoming explosive devices.

Simultaneously, our gazes fell on a black fireplace poker with a curved hook.

Phillip moved with the swiftness of a man free of chronic football injuries. There was no spasming back pain as he accelerated into second gear. At a safe distance he pivoted, glanced back at me standing Medusa still.

Phillip slinked into the shadow of the mile long hallway. The master bedroom door slammed. Family photos clattered on the wall. The lock turned, shutting me out, but only temporarily. I was the one who stashed the spare key.

Glued to the spot, I wailed until snot backed up in my skull. My ears clanged, eyes bulged like a victim of Graves' disease.

My world went dark. A blue velvet curtain fell on the wonderful life as I knew it.

2

BROKEN HEARTED

AUBREY

M iles Sampson unbuttoned his Ralph Lauren camel hair jacket and breathed a sooty whiff of midnight Dallas air. The day was long, too long, for a young man who rose with the sun, ran five miles and reported to work at KXAS in Fort Worth Texas by eight a.m. At twenty-five he was a veteran of the news business, having catapulted from UCLA with a mass communications degree to the crime and punishment street beat.

Tonight's breaking news-- a four alarm fire in Pleasant Grove left three people, two of them children, dead and their mother mumbling incoherently in the street.

The KXAS news van kicked up to the curb. Two charred stucco apartments stood defiantly intact, dressed in wide swaths of gray and black from searing heat. The only good news was that the lawn, tangled with yellow vines of crab grass, failed to ignite beyond the two apartments laid to waste. Pleasant Grove, a misnomer for this neighborhood shackled with poverty, was alive with "lookey loos" summoned by screaming sirens to the scene of human misery.

Miles called to his cameraman, Early Hutchinson, hoisting a camera on "traps" mimicking mountains, "Hey man, shoot the other apartments for backdrop." Windows of unoccupied apartments were boarded with plywood. Wrought iron guarded the front doors and windows of occupied dwellings. Two buildings away a floral bed sheet flew from an open upstairs window. A snaggle-toothed woman, wearing a greasy gray doo rag, shined a powerful flashlight into the street.

Miles turned to a camera happy onlooker, "Didn't they evacuate these houses?" The onlooker posed for the camera, flashed a glittering silver grill, "Hey, I'm Fast Freddy. " Fast Freddy wore a bandana tied Tupac style on his head, a white wife beater, baggy jeans cinched mid-thigh and plaid Calvin Klein briefs that saluted the world. "That's Miss Mackabie. She ain't comin' out. Been stayin' in the same spot fitty years. I'mo' be on TV?"

"We'll see," Miles answered, scanning the crowd for the victim's families. The mother of the deceased children was impossible to miss. She paced unabated, back and forth down the short block, praying audibly for a miracle to rise from ashes. Her thin, floor length night gown twisted around toothpick ankles. A starter jacket, tossed over slumping shoulders by a concerned neighbor, threatened to slide to the ground. The mother's mission, to bring her two-year-old baby girl and seven year old son back to life, was impossible.

Miles turned to Fast Freddy, "What's the mother's name?"

"Miss Minnie. Minnie Ingram. Real nice lady. Work hard, mind huh own biz-ness. Dem kids. ..." Fast Freddy shook his head. Waist length dreadlocks swung east to west. "Dey huh life."

Miles hesitated. He was torn between desire to let Miss Minnie grieve in peace and the need to do his job. A van from their competitor, a local CBS affiliate, circled the block. Miles sprang into action. He jogged to the grieving mother.

"Mrs. Ingram." No response.

"Miss Minnie, I'm Miles Sampson from KXAS, NBC News. We're very sorry about your loss. Are you willing to talk with me?"

Miss Minnie breathed like an angry bull gored by her tormentor. Her sighs escaped in wheezes and snorts. Tears were sparse. Sweat beaded above her top lip. A single pink sponge hair roller jutted from her head scarf. Her feet shuffled bare against cracked pavement littered with broken glass, cans and metal pop tops.

"Somebody please get this lady some shoes. It's freezing out here. She needs shoes," Miles begged.

"She sho' do." A stout woman with a lazy eye, Ruby Dean, replied in a raspy voice. Ruby held up an unopened package of fuzzy pink house slippers and shook her head. "It's all I could do to get her to take the coat. She woke up with a fire ball chasing her. Neighbor over there, pulled her out." Ruby nodded in the direction of a sixty something wiry man with Popeye arms. "He had to fight to keep her from going back in for the kids. They were sleeping in the back room. Minnie sleeps on the front couch. That's the only thing that saved her."

"Miss Minnie, you're about to be on television. I know you don't care how you look, but your neighbors are trying to help out. Will you let them help?"

The wall of confusion trapping Miss Minnie came half way down. Ruby wiped Minnie's nose with a towel draped over one arm, then removed the hair roller and head scarf. Minnie slumped to the curb and sprawled with her knees flared out. Ruby squatted deeply and pushed the house shoes on her neighbor's feet.

Miles removed his jacket and draped it over Miss Minnie's knees. Jacket sleeves dusted the litter strewn gutter. For the first time that evening Miss Minnie turned her back to the remains of the fire.

Miles sat next to Miss Minnie. It was an unusual angle on the story, a reporter and his subject camped out on a curb. Later that evening the station manager hailed Miles as a hero for capturing the essence of this exclusive interview that would become the lead story on Channel 5's six a.m. news.

Miles did not feel like a hero. He walked away from the scene of the fire with shoulders weighted down by the still unfolding tragedy. Interviewing a distraught mother in the midst of denial that her babies were gone struck a nerve. Where was the line between the news and breach of privacy drawn? When Miss Minnie Ingram touched his hand during the interview his heart melted. Miles fought to keep his composure. His human instinct said, drop the mike, give Miss Minnie a hug. Instead he squeezed her hand reassuringly. He reminded himself: A reporter's duty is to report the story, not become the story. Sometimes, like tonight, lines blurred.

Early climbed into the news van, eagerly suggesting, "Let's grab a couple of brewskys at Cosmos. I'm buying"

Miles hesitated. He was revved up, ready to drink away the pain in Miss Minnie's sorrowful eyes. He knew that no amount of alcohol would suffice. "Naw man, it's late. I'm whipped."

Early's head whipped back. Miles Sampson passing on a free beer?

Half hour later Miles opened the door to a sparse two bedroom apartment. The room was cold and empty. He sighed, too exhausted to care. Bubble wrapped artwork, courtesy of his mother, propped against stark white walls. Miles tossed his backpack on the floor and collapsed on the only seating in the room, a black vinyl Target loveseat. There was no point looking for food in the refrigerator. He had not shopped in over a month. He could recite the contents of the refrigerator by heart-a three week old giant bean burrito, too toxic to unwrap, pumpkin cheesecake sporting fuzzy green mold, two Coronas and bagged salad floating in green slime. He thought, maybe I should have accepted Early's invitation. At least my belly would be full and my mind too numb to think.

Fully clothed, Miles stretched out on the too short love seat with Gucci loafers intact. He studied ceiling shadows cast by a bulb flickering in a black Wal-Mart pole lamp. His tired eyes closed. He saw himself alone in an open field with ominous fireworks exploding against an ink black sky.

The rock 'n roll ring tone of his I-Phone startled him. He groaned. It was probably his producer probing about the package he submitted on the fire. "Do these people ever stop?" he groused. The ring tone would not let up. Without opening his eyes Miles unbuckled the front flap of his backpack and fished out the phone. He donned a British accent, which he employed when annoyed or in a playful mood.

"Miles Sampson here." No response. Miles muttered, "I'm in no mood for bs." He figured it was Early, bombed out of his mind, calling from Cosmo's Bar and Grill. His thumb moved toward the disconnect button.

"Miles," I whispered.

He did not recognize my tear strangled voice. "Who is this?"

"Your mother…"

Croaking sobs slapped him wide awake. He bolted upright. "What's wrong? You sound sick."

"Why didn't you tell me?" I pressed immediately.

"Oh shit", he said out loud. The secret was out. "Dad begged me not to tell you. Said he wanted to tell you himself."

"Your father's a wimp. Got a lotta nerve telling other people how to live."

His voice trembled. "It's not the kind of news you want to break to your wife." A deep sigh released the crippling secret Miles had harbored for months.

"I'm sorry they dragged you into this, son. You okay?"

"I'm hangin'… For a man who was so hard on me growing up, it's a huge disappointment. It's always been just the three of us…You know?"

"I know. What about Donovan? Does he….look like your father?" I stammered.

"He looks more like Dad than me."

A second dagger to my heart.

"You know the Sampson look. Broad nose, wide forehead and bushy eyebrows."

A palpable silence danced on the phone line and skipped three beats.

"You okay, Mom?"

"I wouldn't say okay, but I'll live. I won't give that bitch the satisfaction of killing me."

"Don't talk like that. Try to focus on forgiveness. I'm sending you my Wayne Dyer discs. *The Power of Intention.* "

The last thing I needed right now was self-help bullshit, I thought, but said instead, "Thank you baby. How did Donovan find you?"

"Social media. You can find anybody now. My face and bio are all over the station's website. I was on assignment in Mesquite. This dude steps up and says, we need to talk. I was a little leery, but he seemed nice enough, just a little spaced out."

"Spaced out how?"

"Saying my dad is his dad. I'm like, what the fuck you talkin' 'bout. When I calmed down we exchanged numbers. He "friended" me on Facebook. Sent a few messages back and forth. I called dad right away. Dad was a mess, useless."

"He's always useless in crisis---unless it's someone else's. Then he parades around like Superman. I'm sick of covering for his selfish ass."

"Mom, I know it sucks. Just breathe. And don't make any quick decisions."

I sighed hard enough to blow down an oak tree. "You're right. Get some sleep. I love you."

3

EARLY IN THE MORNING

AUBREY

"I hate a helpless woman. Get up and handle your business," I rallied myself.

At four a.m. my eyes unsealed. Muscles tense, body twisted in a pretzel, my age had doubled overnight. Cocooned in a sumptuous gray Michael Kors' down comforter I was an alien in my own guest bedroom. In the aftermath of Phillip's cluster bomb my mind was a fog, unable to see my way clear. "Walk by faith and not by sight", was my standby advice to others. Why was I struggling to apply that Bible verse to me? Crust crumbled into my lashes as I wiped sore, sticky eyes.

I creaked up and sat cross-legged in the middle of the bed. The mind lost for hours ambled back to me. I needed a plan, something greater than anger and feeling "woe down and toe down". I still wanted to fight somebody, anybody. A voice of clarity whispered in my ear, "Kill the bitterness before it strangles you". I galloped upstairs to the loft without washing my face. It was suddenly clear-a way to work out my confliction. At lightning speed my computer banged out raw, unfiltered words from my broken spirit.

———•(()•———

RULES FOR DATING A MARRIED MAN

Following are rules for the Outside Woman ("OW") and Ho-ing Husband ("HH") to abide by when little pee wee and itchy poo poo have a close encounter of the adulterous kind.

RULE NO. 1

No babies.

If you screw a married man, draw the line at having his baby. This is an invasion of the married woman's right to privacy. Outside Woman, you say "I jes' luv him." If you love him, do not add to his misery. The reason he is with you is that you offer freedom from responsibility. If he wanted to change diapers and start a college savings plan, he would be at home with his wife and kids.

Generally speaking, married men do not like fat bellies. As soon as your belly balloons, he will be back on the block trolling for the next Outside Woman. Wife will start looking better and better to him.

Think of yourself. If things do not work out with Ho-ing Husband, other men will not want to take care of your Outside Babies. In economic terms, you decrease your own marketability.

RULE NO. 2

Do not believe for one second anything that Ho-ing Husband says.

He is after the poon tang. A married man will lie, cheat, do whatever he needs to do to get you in bed. If he says, "I love you", he means that he loves what you can do for little pee wee. Little pee wee is no respecter of persons. He will screw anything that has an orifice. Never forget that you are a convenient watering hole in a desert of adult responsibilities.

RULE NO. 3

Planned Parenthood is your friend.

The two "P's" in Planned Parenthood stand for pussy protector. If you do not want to get pregnant, you do not have to. "OOPs" is not an excuse for anyone over the age of thirteen. If he truly loves you, he will divorce his wife and put a ring on your finger.

Do not fall for the okey doke, "I would marry you, if it weren't for the kids." If he was so into his kids, he would not waste time with you. Parenting is a full time position.

RULE NO. 4

Do not assume that Wife is stupid.

Wife knows when her husband is screwing around. She

is probably relieved that you have taken the needy bas-tard off her hands. There is only so much time in a day for kissing a man's ass. Between grocery shopping, work and taking care of kids, romance gets lost in the shuffle. That's why I admire husbands who set aside date nights with their wives and spend their money on babysit-ters instead of Outside Woman. It is a better long term investment.

RULE NO. 5

Do not buy the wedding dress until the ink is dry on his divorce papers.

Some men are wimps. They want to have their cake and eat it too. In all probability, he will not leave his wife and kids for you. You are a pleasant diversion. Once you get pregnant, you lose your allure. Waking up to Ho-ing Husband's garbage breath is an acquired taste. Only committed wives can handle it.

If Wife gets tired of his charade and kicks him to the curb, do not be surprised if he kicks you to the curb too. An Outside Woman is much more alluring when she is forbidden fruit. When she is available 24/7, she becomes a wife substitute. No self-respecting Ho-ing Husband wants another wife.

RULE NO. 6

Do not trip on whether he is screwing his Wife while he is screwing you.

Of course he is. Review Rule No. 2. Little pee wee is no respecter of persons.

RULE NO. 7

Do not assume that Wife will welcome your progeny into the fold.

Think of it like this. To Wife you are the devil. Would any sane person welcome Rosemary's baby into her home? That Outside Baby's head might start spinning any minute and spitting out pea soup. No matter how cute your Outside Baby is, to Wife he or she is the twin of Chucky.

I hear the uproar coming. Do not blame the child. The child is as blameless as Wife. True. Wife will feel a tug of sympathy for the child who is the product of her husband's ho-ing. But as the one whose privacy has been obliterated, Wife has the right to decide if or when she wants to deal with your baby. If Wife is a woman of true faith and extremely confident in her own skin, she may one day want to meet Junior. But do not count on it.

And if the answer is never, let it be.

Unfortunately, Wife must deal with legal consequences from Ho-ing Husband's and Outside Woman's trysts. Divorce and child support are common consequences. Bet nobody talked about the downside when they were screwing around without putting a sock on it.

RULE NO. 8

Do not call or show up at Wife's home or office uninvited.

Wife signed up for boot camp the second she found out about you. She has visions of planting the heel of her

*Giuseppe stiletto up every orifice that her husband vis-
ited. Never forget: Anger turns Wife into RoboCop on
methamphetamine. Watch your ass.*

RULE NO. 9

If and when you meet Wife, do not ask, "How you doin'?"

*That is a loaded question. You are asking to be jacked
up like a dog that shit on and chewed up his master's
Persian carpet? Apologize profusely, but do not demand
Wife's forgiveness. Forgiveness is between you and God.
Your apology will not take away the pain and humili-
ation that Wife suffered and will continue to suffer as
long as Outside Baby inhabits the earth wearing Ho-ing
Husband's face like a mask of deceit.*

RULE NO. 10

Do not approach Wife's children.

*Violate this rule and get ready for war. Like eagles, Wives
protect their nest.*

RULE NO. 11

Know who your baby's daddy is.

*Chances are, if you are messing with a married man,
you are screwing someone else to fill in the hours when
Sugar Daddy is doing home duty. The amount of time
you steal with a married man will be limited. You are not
his priority. If you were, he would have left his wife and
moved in with you.*

*Is this really fair to Junior? There is nothing worse than
Junior growing up being treated like a mutt. If all manner*

of sperm is swimming around in your coochie, you are playing Russian roulette. The gun will go off and leave a mess.

Word to the wise: in your child bearing years, be selective. Do not risk having a baby by everyone you screw.

So you did the nasty and broke Rule No. 1(No Babies) and Rule No. 3 (Planned Parenthood is Your Friend). Where do you go from here? This is where gold digging goes into overdrive. Outside Woman cannot wait for the District Attorney's office to open on Monday morning. Unless, of course, Ho-ing Husband has money. Then an out of court settlement looks real good. When Junior turns twelve get ready to explain that you used him as a bargaining chip.

And then there is the Outside Woman who "did it for love". Somebody has been listening to too much R. Kelley. Wife will inevitably speculate that your pregnancy was an intentional move to stake a claim on a man that you could not capture through legitimate means. That snake oil you bought did not come with a guarantee.

Once Junior drops, Outside Woman plants deep roots into someone else's marriage. Bravo! You succeeded at something very selfish. "If I can't have him, let me screw up everybody's party. Why should his wife be happy while I am a miserable, lonely _____(fill in the blank).

AUBREY

I needed nourishment before battling the enemy.

In my chef's kitchen, I splayed two Cornish hens resting breast side down in a white wine reduction. I had not eaten since breakfast of the day before. The hens, wild rice, and spinach salad, abandoned in the wake of hurricane Phillip, would make an excellent breakfast meal. I sliced a hen with a serrated Cutco knife and plopped half on a plate, nestled a scoop of rice beside the hen and slid the plate in the microwave. I tossed the salad, sprinkled a palm of dried cranberries and slivered almonds on top. The microwave chimed.

His voice was alcohol on an open wound. Phillip grinned awkwardly. "Something smells good in here."

I hated his face, his lips smiling as if nothing had happened. The red gash above his brow drew no sympathy. I was sure he expected me to say, "Sit down sweetie. Let me get the medicine kit and clean that up for you." But the Lord had yet to answer my prayer to release anger and bring forgiveness into my heart.

The unrighteous reverend did not have the decency to let me eat in peace. His big cajones suggested I feed him like a helpless chick bound to the nest, dependent on mommy. Not today.

"Help yourself." I pushed the plate across the golden crystal granite center island toward Phillip. "I lost my appetite." I sashayed past him.

"Aubrey, wait. Breeee…" He pleaded to my back.

In the exercise room I pounded the treadmill until I could not speak Phillip's name. On the stair climber baggy pajama bottoms twisted around my ankles. The reflection of a wild animal, ready to pounce, stared back in the mirror. I did not trust my own instincts. "Get control", my First Lady self murmured. But I was still on the prowl, willing to catch a case.

4

YOU'VE GOT A FRIEND

AUBREY

Hilton Long's mansion nestled at the Top of the World in Laguna Beach, California. Dizzying, sharp vertical turns brought me as close to Heaven as possible while tied to earth's gravity. The Top of the World was carved into the side of a steep foothill overlooking jewels of the Pacific. Although no one owns the ocean, a privileged few have placed a golden lock on the land surrounding it.

Drifting fog thickened with every rung I ascended in the metallic black Range Rover, a gift from Phillip presented shortly before he revealed the existence of his other "son". I wondered if the Rover was his way of mollifying me before the disaster about to unfold. The Rover was my dream SUV, impractical on every level, especially maintenance. Phillip said he wanted to spoil me for staying by his side for "richer or poorer", mostly poorer for the first fifteen years of marriage.

The gabled roof of Hilton's home was almost even with the sidewalk bordering his mini castle. I cut the wheels of the Rover sharply into the curb, killed the engine, rolled from the tan leather seat and stumbled out.

My legs were wobbly, energy zapped by physical and mental exertion. I clutched the door of the Rover for security, left full handprints. I took six steps down, crossed ten feet of hedge lined flagstone path and stood before an arched, rustic double door carved from knotty mahogany. Wrought iron embellishments added old world charm.

From the moment I called with a desperate plea, "I gotta get outta here," Hilton felt my pain. My friend of more than twenty-five years asked no questions, simply said, "I'll be here when you get here."

He was dressed like royalty. Black silk pajamas topped by a black brocade smoking jacket. On his feet were Christian Louboutin canvas slippers with lime green and yellow pineapple detail. Hilton's unlined chocolate skin was smooth and clear. His white teeth glistened as if coated with Vaseline. Every strand of jet black hair was tamed to his head. Not a week passed without a visit to his stylist's chair.

"I feel underdressed", I laughed nervously and folded into Hilton's slender, sinewy arms. At that moment it dawned on me. I was interrupting his morning beach jog. Since the death of his partner, David, Hilton ran daily to keep down stress.

"Sorry. I should have asked if you were busy or had company."

"Pa-lease. I haven't had company in two years. And you, of all people, know that. Get in here while I make some tea." Hilton slipped his arm around my waist and ushered me through the circular vestibule adorned with artifacts collected during extensive travels with David.

From the corner of my eye I glimpsed a framed wall- size poster of Hilton and David Grant, Hilton's deceased partner.

The poster unnerved me, as always. I adored David, but it had been two years since the memorial service. It was time for the shrine to come down, in my humble opinion.

Every corner of this magnificent house with a panoramic view of the Pacific held memories. On two walls of the Spanish tile guest bathroom were photos of Hilton and David on vacation in exotic places---Madrid, Costa Rica, Brazil, Bali, Monaco, Sorrento and Egypt. Hilton still slept on David's favorite six hundred thread count Egyptian cotton sheets. A glamorized oil painting of David hung above Hilton's king size bed. Absolute buzz kill.

I was the only company that could live with the ghost of David. I was the only one, friend or family, with standing to suggest that it was time to tear down the shrine and rejoin the living. But not today.

"Got anything stronger than tea?" I shamelessly asked.

"Ooowww," Hilton's heart shaped, perfect lips yelped. "Nothing like an a.m. party."

The party kicked off poolside on level one of the four-level mansion. Hilton popped twice baked potatoes and spinach quiche into an imposing oven with a red knob. The kitchen was an Architectural Digest advertisement for Wolf appliances. From leaded glass cabinets he retrieved etched crystal champagne flutes and poured teeth chilling Veuve Cliquot champagne, just the way I liked it. I murmured "Ummm", at the first sip.

"Want orange juice?" He asked.

"Don't mess up a good thing." I answered while wiping dew from a rattan couch. I flipped the cushions to the dry side. The fog drifted lazily from the ocean, coating the air with heavy dampness. It was refreshing, Holy water sprinkled on straying sheep. My shoulder length, press and curl reverted to its bushy, natural state.

The ocean, draped in blue violet ether, reached out to me. In my minds-eye calming water lapped in the distance. I remembered the sermon Phillip preached last Sunday. *"Trouble is just a pebble in the sand. This too shall pass."* Was he preaching to himself or to me?

Hilton crossed his arms and massaged wiry fingers up and down the brocade sleeves of his smoking jacket. "Aren't you freezing? Let me get you a jacket."

"Don't feel a thing." I glanced down at black velvet leggings, black silk turtleneck and ballet slippers tossed on before fleeing the house. I took a courtesy shower. Not one dab of makeup touched my face.

I rested my second glass of Veuve on the table inlaid with multi-colored glass tile. Was it time to let Hilton in on the secret that made me drive thirty-five minutes from North to South Orange County at blistering speed?

"Phillip has a baby by another woman."

"Whoa." Hilton's Juvedermed forehead stretched into a scowl. He fanned with an open hand. "When did all this happen?"

"When we were in Detroit. Six months ago Phillip's 'other' son, Donovan, approached Miles on assignment near Dallas."

"Whuuut?" Hilton's extended, curly eyelashes bucked in the breeze.

"Apparently, Donovan's been following my family for years. Knew all the details of Miles' journey, where he went to school, when he graduated, all about his news casting career. Knew the stations where Miles worked in West Palm Beach and Dallas. And get this. Donovan enrolled in seminary school...Like father, like son. "

"That mutha' fucka' is stalking you."

"Yep. Cyber stalking and who knows what else. Phillip

claims he didn't know about Donovan until he approached Miles. That is too hard to believe. Doesn't make sense. Why would Donovan wait twenty years to surface? I'm so pissed, I could spit."

"And who is this skank baby mama?"

"Delia Upchurch. That's the worst part. I don't remember her." She was in the choir at Tabernacle in Detroit. I called Aku, my girlfriend who still lives there, while I was driving down here. Aku remembers Miss Delia Upchurch very well. Described her down to what she wore. Said she was a sneaky freak. Quiet, mousey and grinning all the time. A 'tee hee hee kinda ho', whatever that means. Said she was a thirsty bi-iitch."

Hilton pursed his lips and shook his head at the end of a long sip.

"Will do any thang to get somebody else's man. She wanted it all, but couldn't get but a few sips."

Hilton high-fived me.

"That ho' wormed her away onto Pastor's aide committee. She was aiding him all right." I laughed for the first time since Phillip inflicted the raggedy wound.

Hilton smiled, reached over and curled my trembling hand in his. "You'll be aw-ight."

I nodded. Tears burning tired eyes, rolled down my cheeks. "My husband screwed a dumpy, flat assed whore... What's wrong with me?"

"Girl, don't even go there. You don't know how beautiful you are." Hilton tried to comfort me.

I cried even harder. "If you gon' cheat on me, do it with somebody memorable. Fine, brilliant, funny. Anything but dumpy."

Hilton's hand fluttered dismissively. "A man will fuck a shrimp, if he can find the hole."

Champagne spurted from my nose and mouth. Hilton's shoulder butted against mine. His slippered feet scissored the air. We roared. Howling laughter echoed through Laguna Canyon. Shoulder to shoulder, Hilton and I propped each other up until a feeble sun pierced low hanging clouds and the second bottle of Veuve Cliquot was drained.

5

ROUND MIDNIGHT

AUBREY

Round midnight I pulled into the driveway of my Hidden Hills home in Yorba Linda. The cocoa stucco finish was freshly painted. The stark white trim gleamed in darkness broken only by the glow of a looming yellow moon. A warm wind whistled through canyon brush draped in leering shadows.

I put the car in park and let the engine of the Range Rover purr. I breathed in through my nose, exhaled through closed lips to calm my racing heart. Motion sensor lights above the front door and garage illuminated. The soft glow of recessed lights in the kitchen shone through drawn Roman shades.

Hilton had done his best to talk me down. "The Delia episode happened twenty years ago," Hilton reminded me. In my mind I knew that Delia was not the end of it. My husband was a pussy chasing dog until God shut him down. He was a good dog. Knew how to find his way home.

What really ticked me off-his affairs were clumsy. Phillip acted like a child who wanted to get caught.

I could pinpoint his affairs with accuracy of a seasoned sleuth. The smell of his sweat, betrayal of funky phero- mones. Adultery bled into his system and seeped out over the course of his affairs. Then there were the foolish clues, cheap trinkets in a scavenger hunt. A receipt from the Holiday Inn in Southfield Michigan, torn into legible shreds and stuffed at the bottom of a basement trash can. Amateur. Phillip Sampson violated the first rule of creeping---always pay in cash.

When I confronted him, yelling and screaming, Phillip stuck to his implausible story. "I don't know nuthin' 'bout that receipt. Probably belongs to Jerome."

He blamed everything on his cousin Jerome, a long term guest in the maid's quarters of our Palmer Park home.

"Jerome's a grown man with needs. He may not feel comfortable fulfilling them around us," Phillip argued.

"This is not a pussy cave," I snorted, snaked my neck, then let it drop. Accepting Phillip's lie was easier than un- earthing the truth that would have killed our vulnerable, young marriage.

A few months after Miles was born Phillip was suddenly summoned to a church convention. Before I could explain my dilemma---getting a sitter for three days and pumping enough breast milk to last during my absence, Phillip in- sisted, "You wouldn't enjoy this trip. A bunch of old school preachers, selling sermons and yakking in sub-zero Chicago."

The day after Phillip's departure Miles, a happy child, who rarely cried, was burning up with fever. His face was fire engine red and his listless tongue hung out of his mouth. When he refused to nurse, I knew I was in trouble. Miles was a child who sucked on the tit till he passed out. His temperature read one hundred and five-life threaten- ing. Frantic, I dialed Dr. Blankenship, the rare neighborhood pediatrician. His message center blandly informed me, "Dr. Blankenship is on vacation for two weeks."

I grabbed the shovel from the side of the house. Dug, sweated, sweated and dug until I almost passed out. I raced inside the house, swaddled my screaming baby in blankets and skidded through the biggest storm of the year to Children's Hospital. Hail the size of golf balls pelted the windows of the Ford Explorer. I plowed down Woodward Avenue, pumping brakes in new fallen snow. Visibility was close to zero. I prayed that nothing would harm us as I found traction in the center of the road.

I snatched the wailing baby from the back seat. Bounced at the emergency room counter, pleaded frantically with the overwhelmed intake nurse, "My baby needs a doctor *now*."

The nurse peered over the top of dime store reading glasses and scanned the emergency room packed with misery. Children hacked with coughs that racked tiny bodies. A grizzled grown man moaned, head hung low, elbows balanced on his knees. "Ma'am, everybody in here needs a doctor."

"Sister Sampson, what's goin' on?" Dr. Frank Shepherd, a member of Phillip's congregation at Tabernacle Missionary Baptist Church, heard my cry. Dr. Shepherd whisked Miles into an exam room, bypassing all protocol.

On auto pilot I dialed the church office. Phillip's secretary, Gwen, answered the phone.

"I need to speak to Phillip. Do you have the number for the hotel in Chicago? It's an emergency."

"First Lady?"

"Yes." My breath stomped faster than a race horse's hooves.

"What hotel in Chicago?"

"The pastor's convention."

"That's not until next month. Pastor Phillip is on vacation. Said he'd be back on Monday."

I gulped for air, reeled, struggling to recover from the gut punch. I could have blown up his lie. Instead, I backed him up. Like I always did. "I'm sorry. I got confused. I had to rush Miles to the hospital."

"Is the baby all right?" Gwen asked.

"Yes. Thank God. Dr. Shepherd was on duty."

"Praise the Lord," Gwen chimed in.

The game of pretend kicked up a notch. "Phillip said he was meeting a classmate down in Ann Arbor. I forgot."

Haggard and tired, Reverend Phillip Sampson darkened our door round midnight on Monday. Although exhausted from a weekend of nursing a sick child, I made a point of being wide awake when he came dragging his tail behind him.

I smiled, kissed him on the lips and kept my eyes wide open. "Your breath smells like pussy." Phillip reared up. His eyes crowded his forehead. "Are you sick woman?"

"No. Your son is sick."

"Whadyou mean sick?"

"While you were fucking around Miles had a temperature of one hundred and five. I rushed him to emergency. He has bronchitis and strep throat. Thanks to Dr. Shepherd, he'll be fine. I found out about your lie when I called your office. Gwen said you were on *vacation*."

"I might have mistakenly said vacation instead of convention."

"The convention is next month. Stop lying. I am not stupid. Maybe a little stupid, following your buck wild ass across country to this cold ass place. Leaving my family and friends in California."

He reached out to touch me. I snatched my arm away. "Don't touch me."

"I'm sorry..."

"You haven't seen sorry yet...Either go to counseling and get your act together or kiss me and your baby goodbye."

Phillip stuttered, "Uh, ummm...I just needed some time."

"Time to do what? Make a fool outta' me?"

"Bree, you know I love you."

"Shut the fuck up!"

I dragged Phillip to one counseling session. Phillip bowed out before he could get comfortable in the seat. The Reverend was too righteous for anyone to judge him.

That's when I should have left him. I wouldn't be sitting outside my house like a stranger.

I pressed the button on the garage door opener. The wood paneled door screeched and sighed. The Range Rover idled. Far right, parked inside the four car garage, Phillip's sleek red Tesla Model S glistened like a candied apple.

I threw the gear shift in reverse. Squealing tires breached the peace of the sleepy cul de sac. The Rover accelerated up the hill, rounded two corners without braking and floated like a downhill skier to Yorba Linda Blvd. I copped a left, drifted into the far right lane and merged into the 91 freeway headed west. On instinct and without destination I followed the 55 freeway south to the 5 freeway. The freeway ended just north of Mexico.

⸺◉⸺

Aubrey

"He saw you in the driveway," Hilton cautioned when I took his call on the tenth attempt.

"So."

"Pastor is frantic. Threatening to call the cops."

"Call the cops. I'll have to tell them why I left. Pastor of the biggest Black church in Orange County commits adultery. The headline will look good in the Yorba Linda Star. BUSTED."

"You've got a right to be pissed, but there's more than your pride at stake. People look up to Pastor Sampson. So think carefully before you let this thing out. You can trust me with your life. Other people, especially church people, do not need to know. So where are you?"

"I don't want you to have to lie to your boss. It's best not to know. I'm safe. I got a room."

"You could've stayed with me."

"That's the first place he'd look."

"It's not just your safety. Pastor is scared to death that you're leaving him."

"He should be scared. If he was any kind of man, he would leave, so I can cry in my own house. I can't stand looking at him. "

"Aubrey, the church anniversary is coming up. Rehearsal is in a few days. Please don't let me down."

As Minister of Music at Trinity Baptist Hilton was in charge of the planned gala. A full choir, praise dancers, guest soloists and the top preachers in the National Baptist Convention were on program.

Hilton's flair for performance and extensive connections in the world of gospel and beyond brought prestige to the church. Still, Hilton had to prove himself. Phillip had methodically sought a Minister of Music, but no one lived up to Phillip's high standard. For two years I lobbied to bring Hilton on board. Phillip resisted. Not that he had a problem with the gay thing. "Half the choirs in America are conducted by a limp wrist," Phillip confided in me. "I don't want to have to fire your friend in case it doesn't work out."

Phillip took it slower than I liked, hiring Hilton to work on special events. The Christmas pageant, a mini play, sealed the deal. The audience was smitten by the majesty of the music and flawless performances by the children and the actors imported by Hilton for the special occasion. Who knew that Joseph could leap like Baryshnikov or that Mary could reach octaves as high as Mariah Carey. The coordination between message, music and dance gripped worshippers in the palm of Hilton's hand. Hilton's Julliard training lifted gospel to a new level. The Trinity choir sang traditional Christmas songs in perfect harmony, spiritual depth and great precision. Pastor Sampson got a crook in his neck from turning around to see if it was the same choir. An original composition by Hilton, an auria, set the sanctuary ablaze. It was a different type and quality of music that many had not experienced before. A male praise dancer evoked the balletic movement of Judith Jamison. A Hollywood set designer transformed the stage into Bethlehem during the birth of Jesus Christ.

At the end of the pageant, Hilton, wearing a royal blue suit, crisp white shirt and blue and beige striped tie, took a slow, deep bow to thunderous applause. That same night Pastor Sampson offered Hilton the position of Minister of Music. Come Sunday morning, service at Trinity Baptist Church became a happening.

"I smell liquor on 'em. They just left the club," Phillip groused when I commented on the radical uptick in attendance.

"Jesus didn't judge. Why should we?"

"Just sayin'. You come to church for the Word. Not entertainment".

The shadow of jealousy hung over Phillip, who shook it off as the membership roster swelled. Hilton's reputation for showmanship blazed through Orange County. It was hard for Phillip to accept that I loved another man, albeit a gay man, almost as much as I loved him.

"In what universe are you ministering? Mo' people, mo'money." That shut up Phillip every time.

"I can't make any promises about the church Anniversary," I belatedly answered Hilton. "For the last twenty-five years, I've lived for other people. I gotta take care of myself."

"I've never heard you talk like this. *Um skeeered.*"

"My so-called husband is the one who should be *skeeered.*"

6

HYPNOTIZED

PHILLIP

I loved Aubrey Seymour all my life and part of somebody else's. First time I saw her on the playground of Farragut Elementary School in Vallejo, California I was whupping upside the head of Robert Isley who was five inches taller and ten pounds heavier than me. My short, muscled arms tossed Robert across the asphalt, into the pole where Aubrey was on the brink of a tether ball win. The tether ball bounced off Robert's head, swung in the opposite direction, strangling him. Robert's freckled, red face turned purplish blue.

Aubrey scrunched her nose and snarled, "Watch where you goin'."

The fight chasing crowd egged me on, "Git him, git him." But Robert had had enough. I had proven my point. Don't tackle "Mad Dog" Sampson when he's about to score.

I elbowed away from the crowd to size up the new girl who dared admonish me. She was a twelve year old gazelle with skin as golden as the Oscar statuette. Her brown hair was sun streaked with lightning bolts of yellow and honey. She had no hips and endless legs that sprouted from beneath her chest. I remembered what she wore. A flared, yellow and peach flowered skirt, cinched at the waist with a white woven belt. Every time Aubrey moved the skirt twirled around her scruffy, tomboy knees.

"Did I mess up your game, country girl?" I teased. The rowdy crowd of fifth and sixth graders laughed and imitated Aubrey's strong, southern accent. She was a recent immigrant from Atlanta, Georgia, transported to the small Bay Area town against her will.

Years later Aubrey told the story of how her mother, Pearl, patiently explained that her Daddy, Winston, needed a decent job and California was the land of opportunity. That did not resonate with twelve year old Aubrey. Winston found work when he could as a day laborer, laying bricks, pouring cement and doing whatever he could to make a dollar. On Sundays, he was a strong tenor, singing in the choir at Ebenezer Baptist Church.

Vallejo was a long way from the only city she had known, Atlanta. Aubrey was not impressed by the rusty looking Golden Gate Bridge. The Pacific Ocean was an intimidating body of water that she swore to never, ever dip her toes into it. She missed her best friend Greta, a gaggle of cousins, streets filled with familiar faces and worn out buildings. A week into it, Aubrey concluded that California people were stuck up and unfriendly. Now she had to deal with bullies like me, alone.

"Naw, but I'm gon' mess up your game." She brushed past, backed me up by two feet.

"Woooo..." the crowd roared, urged me to put a hurting on Aubrey like I did to everyone else. I just stood there, mesmerized by the sass of lady Aubrey.

"Phillip's got a girlfriend, Phillip's got a girlfriend." Clarisse, an overdeveloped girl with acne blisters on her face, began the chant.

I, the school yard bully had met my match in a lanky southern belle, looking like she stepped out of a Tide commercial. She looked so clean. I thirsted to smell her up close. Her glistening white socks were spotless amid swirling red dirt. Aubrey loped across the school yard to join her class at the end of recess.

My class was positioned one line over from Aubrey's. She pretended not to notice me, jostling in line with a severe case of ADD.

After school I trailed Aubrey at a safe distance, making just enough noise to let her know I was there. Each time she turned to look, I did a cartwheel. Showing off.

Brenda Winningham, a girl from my class caught up with Aubrey. "Wait up. You wanna walk home with me?"

"Sure." Aubrey said.

Brenda turned to look back at me. "Don't pay him no mind. He's always clowning. Trying to get attention. He's older than us. Got held back. Missed too many days of school. His po' mama didn't know he was playing hookey."

If I had known Brenda was telling my story, I would've whupped her too.

My mother, Sylvia Sampson, worked as a maid in upscale white neighborhoods of Marin County where real housewives can afford weekly or daily maid service. Every weekday morning at six my mother shook me awake, which was no easy feat. I was a hard sleeper. Once I hit the floor, a scary energy unleashed. I never walked. I ran everywhere, including through the tiny rooms of our upstairs Waterfront flat. Built during World War II, the Spartan flat had no insulation. An echo chamber from its asbestos ceiling to the cold floor harboring original linoleum, the flat was my private jungle gym and roller skating rink.

The grumpy old man downstairs, Elijah Wilson, hated me for good reason. I slid down the metal railing above steep concrete steps instead of taking the stairs. I intentionally fastened a metal key chain loaded with unused keys to my belt, allowing them to scrape the railing as I slid down yelling, "Whoopee".

One morning Mr. Wilson decided to outwit his public enemy. Wilson parked his chair at the bottom of the railing. Ten minutes later I, his avowed nemesis, slammed the upstairs door on cue, saddled up on the railing and launched my rapid ascent. Seconds before dismount I glanced over my shoulder. Mr. Wilson stood on the landing, wielding a cane, poised to whack me on my ass or desecrate my manhood permanently. My arms flew up to Heaven. I flipped from the railing, crashed on hard ground frosted with ice. I rolled down the slippery straw slope and crashed into a chain link fence.

Wilson menacingly pointed the tip of his cane at me. "Next time."

A volcano of energy, I erupted in spurious fights with random victims. Seemed like the devil had a hold of me and would not let go. My reputation was so tarnished, when children spotted me, they ran the other way. Every night I sneaked out of bed and watched a thirty inch television while stretched out on a heavily soiled pink corduroy couch. I could mouth the lines with the actors on my favorite television shows. Well after midnight I lumbered into sleep, serenaded by TV voices.

"How do you know so much about him?" Aubrey questioned Brenda.

"He used to be my boyfriend before Mama made me cut that nigga loose."

Aubrey froze in her tracks, jarred by the boldness of Brenda's statement. She pivoted and took a long slow look at the man child named Phillip Sampson.

I figured Brenda was bustin' me out. For good reason. At least five times a day my poor mama reminded me that I was a bad child.

"You gon' get our lights cut off." Mama rousted me from the couch the next morning and plopped me on a straight back wooden bench in the breakfast nook. She sniffed a quart of milk before dribbling it over a bowl of Wheaties. "Eat," she commanded.

I scrunched up my face, twisted ample lips into a knot. "Not Wheaties, again."

My mother's chafed, unpolished lips kissed my crinkled forehead. She plodded downstairs from our rickety flat to catch her waiting car pool.

Miss Maxine's oxidized gray, Pontiac station wagon was crammed with six black women, domestic workers headed to San Rafael. Agnes Morehead dangled a lipstick stained Pall Mall from purple, nicotine coated lips while she interpreted a fellow passenger's dream. "That mean somebody gon' get pregnant. And it sho' as hell ain't me." Everybody laughed, except Agnes, choking and drawing smoke simultaneously.

"Agnes, what's the number for pregnancy?" Rita Wright asked, studying the Daily Tri-Fecta. "Maxy, tell that white woman you gotta leave early. I need to catch the last race at the Fairgrounds. I'm feelin' lucky." Rita's torso shimmied to emphasize the point.

The banter was always the same. Good kids, bad kids, playing the numbers, beating the odds at the racetrack, scoring one big hit to lift a sister from her knees.

Sylvia Sampson curled tighter into the door of the backseat. Her dreams were locked inside of her. If she lasted one

week without a call from Phillip's school about his bad conduct, a menacing glance and sour lips from Elijah Wilson or
a red shutoff notice from PG&E, she counted herself lucky.

I pulled back the tattered left sheer covering the window. From the second floor flat, I watched the station
wagon, back down the steeply sloped driveway, scrape the
broken asphalt alley and chug out of sight. The coast was
finally clear. I grabbed the mushy bowl of Wheaties, dashed
into the bathroom, dumped it in the toilet and flushed. In
the kitchen, barely wider than the sink, I rinsed the bowl
and dried it out. I pushed the knob on the television and
dialed up my favorite Road Runner cartoons. I did a three
hundred and sixty degree spin and dived backward on the
couch bearing my imprint. I loved cartoons almost as much
as I loved Baby Ruth candy bars and Hostess Cupcakes. Soon
as Hangover Nick opened the liquor store, I would buy my
favorite snacks with the money I snatched yesterday from
wimpy Jimmy Nichols. Until then, I would be content jacking
off in front of the rabbit eared television.

———— ⫸((◉))⫷ ————

Phillip

It was a long journey from the alley on Alabama Street to
the pulpit of Trinity Baptist Church. A long journey for a man
whose life began in the minus column. Minus money, minus
father and minus direction in life. Time sailed past like ships
parading the waterfront of Mare Island Naval Shipyard. As a
child I believed ships would carry me to exotic ports around

the world where I could be a man and be free. As fate would have it my destiny resided in the air rather than the sea. Rarely a week passed when I was not on an airplane headed for another state, another country. My ministry transported me to places far removed from Vallejo, California, places like Johannesberg, Calcutta, Rome, St. Lucia, Valencia and Akumal. My third trip to the Holy Land was planned for later this year. It would be Aubrey's first pilgrimage, if...

I tried not to think about it. Confliction had me in a noose. What's a man supposed to do when a woman puts it right in his face? Why couldn't Aubrey accept the fact that men and women are different. Having sex wasn't the same as making love. Bree kept jammin' me up. "What did you see in that cow?" I honestly could not answer. If I told the truth, it would give her more ammunition. Yeah, I was wilding. Doing things to Delia I wouldn't ask my wife to do. It had nothing to do with Delia being cute. She didn't look all that good. Was kinda plain in fact. But when I got that woman behind closed doors. Man!

I forced my mind to focus on less stressful thoughts. I returned from The National Baptist Convention as an overwhelming success. Bishop dubbed me "a rising "young" star, despite my biological age of forty-seven. Phenomenal success in of all places, Orange County, California. I was the buzz of the convention. In the span of ten years I shepherded the church from rented spaces to a new church home on a major intersection in Yorba Linda. Under my leadership the congregation grew from less than fifty active members to a membership roster exceeding five thousand. God willing and the devil don't rise, in two years the church would break ground on a larger, state of the art sanctuary.

When called to Trinity I considered the move a death sentence, exile to Siberia. What were my chances with a Black population less than two percent. I would draw a hand full of White folks who would soon tire of Chocolate City. Church Elders wagered on how long it would take the cocky young preacher's ministry to die a natural death? God had a different plan. With Aubrey by my side, fending off the naysayers, the church flourished against all odds and flurries of adversity.

I was on the right track. Nothing could stop me, except inconvenient fatherhood.

The engine of the 747 jet bound for John Wayne Airport hummed like a swarm of angry bees. *Oh Lord, don't let them fly into the engine, take down the plane.* I panicked before taking charge of racing thoughts. The drone crescendoed to a head pounding roar. I closed and opened my mouth wide to release pressure. The plane plummeted. Sudden weightlessness, nothing to hold onto. My arms reached for Heaven. *Have mercy Jesus.* A passenger ambling in the aisle stumbled backward into the lap of a snoozing passenger.

My fingers burned imprints into the skinny armrests. I willed myself to breathe. For a man of God, lack of faith in the outcome was blasphemy.

The flight attendant announced, "Please take your seats. Make sure your seat belts are fastened. We've encountered unexpected turbulence. As soon as it's safe to do so, we'll move through the cabin to pick up beverage containers and trash."

"Waaah." Seated immediately behind me a three month old baby squalled. Not the volume, but the piercing pitch of the baby's cry set already shattered nerves on tilt. My ears popped. I wanted out of this metal tube. There was no place to go. I closed my eyes to pray. Lord, I know I am not worthy. Can you make an exception for a wretch like me?

Fear of flying was a new sensation for me. Flying had

always been an adventure, an invitation to explore the world. This time felt different. Opaque gray clouds surrounded the aircraft. No land, no buildings were visible. Aloneness crawled under my skin.

Fatalistic thoughts intruded in jumbled prayers. A forgiving God would not take down the aircraft because of my sin. I called on the merciful God of the New Testament to fly with me.

The 737 shuddered, listed far right. The plane floated like a balsa wood model airplane through choppy air. Under my breath I hummed "Peace Be Still".

"Sir, please pull your seat back forward," a flight attendant's voice intruded into my tunnel of fear.

My eyes shot open to the pasty face of a sixty-something flight attendant. Her rumpled skin was the mask of too many youthful romps on Laguna Beach without sunscreen. I studied her face for fear. None was there. My hands and fingers remained curled around the metal armrests like monkey paws. I had accidentally pushed the recline button. I pushed it again to bring me up and out of my trance.

I glanced across at passengers seated in the center and window seats. They looked a little tight, but not at tight as me.

The jostling 737 broke through clouds shrouding coastal sky. A tangerine fireball sun saluted and dived into the ocean. A floating kite of red tail lights lined the 405 freeway. Almost home.

I imagined Aubrey waiting at baggage claim to pick me up. No chance of that. A week had passed since I had seen or heard from her. Twice daily I phoned Hilton.

"I swear on the Bible. I don't know where she is. Only that she is safe and needs time to think things out."

I repeated my idle threat to call the cops.

"Wouldn't do that if I were you Pastor. You know what she said, 'A strongly worded letter to the church's board of directors, the Orange County Register and the Tri-County Bulletin, would ruin you.'"

Aubrey held the trump card. For a man of control, I had lost control, forced to wait and pray that the woman I love will come home and to her senses soon.

A shuttle ride and dusty trek through long term parking Lot C were all that await my arrival. First, the pilot had to get the lumbering bird on the ground. The pilot's approach was too fast, I was certain. The plane would explode on the runway. For the first time in ten years I craved a drink to calm me. Liquor, the demon I could not control, was forsaken years earlier. My darling baby, Bombay Sapphire with a splash of tonic and a twist of lime, flirted with my mind. It called my name. "Phillip, you know you want me." I grabbed the wiry wrist of a passing flight attendant. "Miss, can I get a Bombay Sapphire?"

"I'm sorry sir. Beverage service ended. We're about to land."

On approach to John Wayne Airport the 737 shuddered again just to prove that we were not in charge.

My frightened eyes scoured the aisles. Did anyone hear me ask for alcohol? My face had been in the Register enough times to make me easily recognizable.

During the flight I had stoically endured the businessman in the aisle seat across from me knock back three Tanqueray's and tonic. Judging by the man's slurred speech, I surmised that his party started hours earlier in the airport bar. When the businessman struck up a conversation with a big bosomed bleached blond, I was relieved. Relieved that he had not passed judgment on me the way I passed judgment on him.

Every time the blond chortled, which she did often, the stench of heavy musk floated across the aisle and choked my throat. The businessman and the blonde would have to save their own souls tonight.

An overwhelming urge to see my wife seized me. I thirsted for Aubrey more than when our love was young and fresh. More than when desire made me drive from Cal State Hayward to the University of California at Berkeley just to kiss her goodnight. I had to hold onto what was slipping through my fingers--- mature love that I did not have the time or desire to cultivate again. What was I thinking? I was not thinking. Only Aubrey could bring peace in the midst of my storm. Without Aubrey I was nothing more than a naked little boy jerking off on the couch.

What if she leaves me? The thought grated louder than wheels spitting fire on the runway. Derisive cheers from re-lieved passengers jolted me back to earth.

"Please remain in your seats until we taxi to the gate and the plane comes to a complete stop." The shrill voice of the flight attendant was not easy to ignore. I ignored her anyway. I unfastened my seat belt, leaned into the aisle and glanced over my left shoulder. The flight attendant's evil eye lasered me.

"Patience, patience", I mouthed and crumpled into my seat.

Squealing brakes released. I sprang from my seat, re-leased the overhead bin, swiped my carry-on luggage. In the process I grazed the silver hair of a senior citizen. I jet-ted faster than the passenger's fish-eyed stare. I bogarted to the head of the first class cabin.

An irritated flight attendant nudged me aside to open the cabin door. "Someone's in a hurry," she scolded.

Absorbed in my mission, the flight attendant's rebuke rolled off my back.

The cabin door creaked open. My perennially stiff back and creaking knees were forgotten. I attacked the ramp like a Kenyan marathoner.

7

ONLY THE LONELY

PHILLIP

She was not at home, I realized, but refused to speak the words. I turned on the garage light to reveal empty space where her car should have been. I dropped my bag in the laundry room and jogged to the kitchen. No note. I clicked off harsh overhead lights and turned on soft, LED lights above kitchen cabinets. I robotically thumbed through mail stacked in a basket on the granite counter. The cleaning lady came yesterday, I remembered. So much wasted paper, I thought. Absolutely nothing important to me.

Motion sensors captured headlights in front of the house. I exhaled. "There she is." I squared my shoulders and waited in vain for the garage door to roll up. My moist fingertips rubbed against the grain of useless print advertising. I kept my eye on the door where she would enter with a bag full of groceries and none of my favorite sweets. She was a friendly hawk about my sugar intake. High cholesterol and diabetes loomed in my family closet before catching up with me when I turned forty. Once a week, Sundays only, Aubrey baked my favorite desserts. If I was especially conscientious during the week, she baked chunky chocolate chip cookies and topped them with Haagen Dazs vanilla ice cream.

During the three day convention, I passed on desserts served with every meal. Aubrey's protective eye followed me. Had I taken her love and protection for granted?

The outside light faded. There was no sign of Aubrey. I made a plan. Grab a bite to eat and wait a few more minutes. My cell phone chimed in my pant pocket. I grinned like a kid tasting his first ice cream. I checked caller I.D. My joy was short lived.

"Brother Hilton, what can I do for you?"

"Pastor Sampson, we missed you at rehearsal."

"My flight back was delayed."

"No worries. It should take about ten minutes to get you up to speed. Otherwise, everything is ready to roll for tomorrow evening."

"Have you heard from my wife?"

"Not since earlier in the week. She'll show up by tomorrow."

"Hope you're right."

"I know she confides in you. Whatever she said, please don't jump to conclusions."

"Pastor, I would never do or say anything to hurt either one of you. I love both of you."

I wondered how much. I could not imagine a man, gay or straight, hanging out with my wife and not wanting her. Aubrey was long and lean, but not skinny. She had just the right amount of ass. Enough to hold onto. Nothing extra hiking up her dress.

When I hired Hilton as Minister of Music I had concerns. Not about the physical thing, but about emotional intimacy. I was supposed to be her best friend and confidante.

Close friends at Cal, the bond between Aubrey and Hilton loosened when Aubrey followed me to Detroit and Hilton moved to New York to get his Master's Degree. Several times a year Hilton and Aubrey connected by phone. Hilton's calls had dueling impact on Aubrey. They filled her with glee, but also reminded Aubrey of her dream deferred---becoming a journalist. Hilton's career blossomed in New York. He played gigs at local venues, won a handful of awards and landed roles in off Broadway plays.

Aubrey's brief stint as a columnist with the Detroit Free Press was promising, but short lived. She had the drive, quick wit and burgeoning connections to turn her weekly column "Wheels of the Motor City" into the most read column in the Free Press. Local politicians, judges, celebrities and socialites soon clamored to be interviewed. Aubrey's columns were a combination of political commentary, news about the social scene and everyday people doing charitable work or community services. The intense, time sensitive work allowed Aubrey to penetrate the marrow of the City as a relative newcomer without an axe to grind. She was a young, pretty journalist garnering a lot of attention from powerful men who wanted to continue their conversations in private places.

Was I intimidated? Hell yeah. I seethed when men's roving eyes undressed my bride right in front of me. I prayed to avoid resorting to the untamed bully of my youth. It would not look good for an up and coming preacher to kick the Mayor's ass.

Was it sabotage when I begged my wife, "Let me slip it in, just this once, without the diaphragm. That thing irritates me."

Aubrey's unplanned pregnancy provided me with ammunition. "These articles you're writing conflict with your position as a minister's wife. People are talking. The minister's wife should not attend functions where alcohol is served."

"You chose to be a minister, not me," she countered. "Furthermore, behind closed doors you drink like a fish. That's hypocrisy."

Early contractions weighed heavily on Aubrey's wavering decision. By the end of the second trimester she was ordered by her ob/gyn to stay off swollen feet. It was impossible to write a community rag without hanging out in the community.

I won. Or did I? My wife was on lockdown, through no fault of my own selfish desires.

Aubrey's consolation prize was not too shabby—a healthy, happy baby boy who became the center of her life.

That guilty reflection brought me back to reality. I answered Hilton, "We love you too man." I could not bring myself to say "I love you" to a man. The less familiar "We" was the closest I could come.

"If she calls, tell her we need to talk. God bless." I hung up before Hilton could peep the depth of my misery.

I grabbed a plate from the cabinet, put it back and snatched a crystal wine goblet, rationalizing that it was too late to eat. One drink would take the edge off. I stood before the beveled glass of the wine cooler. My full body reflected in the looking glass. I backed away, gingerly rested the glass in the sink.

Three hours later I was curled on the couch in a fetal position. Law and Order episodes provided the conversation that I was missing. The armpits of my custom made shirt were sweaty despite the coolness of the evening. My wool cashmere slacks had ruched into horizontal pleats. I rose with the stiffness of a man unfolding from a box. The vigor from earlier in the day had evaporated. I shuffled to the bedroom, praying that I had slept through the sound of the garage door opening, Aubrey breezing down the hallway and performing her beauty ritual before going to sleep.

Our bedroom was empty, emptier than the day we moved into our dream home. Everything was wrong. In her right mind, Aubrey would not stay away this long without calling me. I groaned as splintering pain coursed through my back. I clutched the IPhone from my pocket. There were no new messages. No unanswered calls waiting to be returned.

I returned to the main menu. Two text messages were in the box. The first message, from earlier in the day, was from Hilton, a reminder of the rehearsal that I already missed. I scrolled down and there it was, a message from Aubrey delivered at 8:50 a.m., more than a week ago. "I know you're thinking about stopping at Von's for a cheese Danish or two. Don't do it. Your appointment with Dr. Lee is on Monday. Love you much."

Within a week she could not have stopped loving me.

I hit reply, cursed the iPhone for delivering messages late. Cursed it for refusing to cooperate with thick fingers. Misspellings jumped off the screen. I deleted two lines and started over. "Aubrey please come home. I am worried and sorry for disappointing you. I swear I will make it right. I love you."

I reminded myself to breathe as I waited for her reply. "Come on baby, don't do me like this," I muttered. I stared at the lifeless phone in the palm of my hand. The time was 12:30 a.m. The screen faded to black. I tickled the buttons, just in case. iPhone, my life line, was a corpse.

In the middle of the bedroom floor, standing on cold hardwood, my teeth chattered uncontrollably. It was a foreign sensation for a substantial man who weathered below zero wind chill factors in Detroit and had not donned an overcoat since moving back to the West Coast. Ice water shot through my veins, froze me in place. I had to wait. Wait on the Lord. Wait for Aubrey to come to her senses.

My arthritic right knee throbbed. My back, below the scapula, spasmed. Needles pressed on raw nerves. Muscles clenched into angry fists and made fun of me. I grimaced in pain. Maybe a hot bath with Epsom salt would help.

Time rocked on in a blur. I hoisted myself from lukewarm water, toweled off and reclined in my bed of misery. Mind racing, I thrashed against a nightmare so real that my heart thundered long after I opened my eyes and sat up.

Pain seized my low back and traveled down my leg.

"Dayumm", I cried out. "Dayumm", I repeated after the next spasm.

In bed, the space where Aubrey had slept for twenty-five years was empty. And so was I.

8

FREAKS COME OUT

"**C**over that up!" my index finger jabbed in the direction of Felicia Cunningham's heaving bosom. As featured vocalist of the Praise and Worship Team, Felicia had decided to let it all hang out. Not on my watch as Minister of Music of Trinity Baptist Church.

"This is the Church Anniversary, not a nightclub gig." I reminded Felicia.

Felicia's splayed fingers attempted to conceal bountiful breasts that rivaled Aretha's. Her eyes registered false modesty.

"Artrice, let Felicia borrow your shawl," I strongly suggested.

Artrice grumbled under her breath, "This go wit' my outfit."

My bloodhound ears picked up Artrice's complaint. "Lord, these people tryna' kill me."

I surveyed the choir, dressed in all black, except for me, the maestro himself. My eyes were trained on the soprano section. Artrice and her sweet singing cohorts loved calling me "Divo" behind my back. With way too much attitude Artrice tossed the shawl to Felicia.

I may be petite, but I will not be messed with. They know I've got Sister Sampson's ear and Sister Sampson is the pipeline to the Pastor. No boobs will bounce in the face of church elders and visiting dignitaries tonight.

"Take your places," I directed. "The program begins in exactly fifteen minutes. No C.P. time, people. "

I made a b-line to the Pastor's study. Through the glass door I spotted Bishop Terrell Henderson from Los Angeles and Apostle Ernest Henley from Pomona seated immediately in front of the Pastor's desk. *These Negroes tickle me, anointing themselves with clerical titles suggesting they are part of a religious hierarchy.*

Flanking the Bishop and the Apostle were their prim and proper wives, wearing floppy gold and silver church hats. Their old ass knees, that nobody wanted to look at, were draped in modesty panels.

Pastor Sampson paced behind his U-shaped mahogany desk. He wore a path in plush wool carpet. On his last lap Phillip glimpsed me percolating outside the door. Phillip hastily excused himself and popped into the atrium.

With trembling hands Phillip pulled me aside and whispered. "Is she here?"

"I left a million messages on her cell phone. She's not responding."

"How could she pull a stunt like this?" The question knotted Phillip's throat. Water dammed his eyes, on the verge of overflowing.

"I've alerted security to keep an eye on the parking lot. If...No, when she shows up, they'll whisk her right in. In the meantime, we will start the program as scheduled. Are you okay with that?"

Phillip's chin fell to his chest. He squared his jaw, exhaled frustration and lack of sleep. "We'll line up when you're ready."

Hilton

Bishop Terrell Henderson, adorned in a royal blue robe with intricate gold braiding and tassels, floated down the aisle. His sleeves, wide as angel wings, were cut above his wrists to reveal immaculate French cuffs on a wide collared shirt, enormous gold and diamond rings on two fingers and a gold Rolex watch. As head of the procession, he resembled a Catholic priest performing High Mass, minus the pointy head gear. His glistening African hair was tamed by years of disciplined brushing and light weight pomade. The Bishop exuded a blend of cultivated class and raw, mesmerizing beauty. Every movement of his lean, six foot three inch frame commanded attention. There was power in his presence and his adornment. The way he knotted his wide striped tie, old school bold with a perfect dimple was the envy of other preachers. At sixty-five years of age his skin remained as smooth as a Dove bar. He was perfect in every way, except one---marital infidelity. On this issue of imperfection the Bishop's church had taken a vow of silence.

In the long shadow of the Bishop, Apostle Ernest Henley humbled his way down the aisle past the standing room only crowd. His foot-to-foot off beat march threatened to tangle in the black robe drowning drooping shoulders. Although years younger than the Bishop, Henley's gray, tightly coiled beard gave him the appearance of the Bishop's father. Henley thinned out a crowd, if congregants had to listen to his lisping delivery for more than two minutes. I decided to get him out of the way early. Henley was on the program to deliver the opening prayer.

My upraised fist closed in instruction to choir and band. This was the final verse of "We've Come This Far By Faith". The band, driven by the lilting keyboard and bumping bass, slipped into a jazzy rendition of "Let The Praise Begin".

All eyes turned to the sanctuary's main entrance. In the towering archway Pastor Phillip teetered on the edge of collapse. Grape sized beads of sweat trickled down his furrowed brow, ignited by the fire raging inside his chest.

Phillip took one giant step forward and touched sanctuary carpet. His flowing white robe with gold embroidery, classic navy blue suit and razor lined hair cut could not hide the rummaging in his belly. I held my breath as his feet treaded peanut butter. Phillip clutched the six inch gold mariner's cross suspended by a forty-eight inch gold serpentine chain hanging from his neck.

I looked over my left shoulder with expectant eyes pleading to Phillip, "Come on, Pastor, walk."

A field of energy fluttered behind Phillip. He turned in slow motion. Stoic and stunning, his dutiful wife approached. Aubrey fixed her lips to smile with her teeth, but not her heart. Without making eye contact, Aubrey hooked Phillip's right arm and marched him down the aisle.

I exhaled, silently mouthed, *Thank You, God.*

Side by side Phillip and Aubrey sat in the pulpit decorated with lavish tropical flowers. The gold corset to Aubrey's dress matched the embroidery in the Pastor's robe. I gifted the ensembles to the king and queen on the church's anniversary. I had scoured the garment district in Los Angeles to find the right shade of white for the robe to compliment Aubrey's outfit.

"It has to set the right tone. Fashionable without being flashy, dignified without being dowdy. If I see another boxy, ill fitting suit on a First Lady, I will scream," I warned Aubrey as we strolled through South Coast Plaza shopping center searching for the perfect ensemble for Aubrey.

"Start screaming," Aubrey laughed.

We laughed our way through South Coast Plaza. Aubrey's outfit appeared out of nowhere. Actually it appeared in Escada's display window. Off one shoulder, winter white. Over the knee and body conscious. Sexy while revealing nothing more than a shoulder. A dress fit for a Ghetto Fabulous Queen, my nickname for Aubrey.

"Try it on." I rushed Aubrey to the dressing room before she could ask the price. In conspiracy, I slipped my platinum card to a sales associate named Greta. I detected a fake Swedish accent. Greta was one carrot stick away from starvation, dressed in high end black from head to toe, John Hardy earrings and bracelet.

Aubrey emerged from the dressing room, twirling like a princess in a fairy tale.

"This is gorgeous."

"They sewed you into that dress."

Aubrey examined her uplifted butt in the mirror. "You don't think it's too..."

"Not at all. This is a celebration, not a funeral." I turned to the sales associate. "She'll take it."

"Not so fast. Check the price tag first. We ain't printing money like you," Aubrey injected.

Greta turned in circles. Greta's pulled back, seal black ponytail whipped her face.

"I have strict instructions from the Pastor to buy what-ever you want," I lied.

"Pastor's as bad as you about spending money."

"That's why we balance each other out. I'm a shopaholic and you're scrooge."

The tug of war continued until Aubrey tortured the price out of Greta. Aubrey changed quickly and hastily exited the boutique, headed for Nordstrom. I pivoted and gave Greta a slow wink.

I caught up with Aubrey and pretended to be annoyed. She knew I could not stay mad at her for long, especially when she bribed me with lunch at Seasons 52 restaurant.

I was the one who convinced Aubrey to embrace her role as First Lady of the Church. "He's not resigning as Pastor and you're not resigning as his wife. You don't have to change. Being in church and being real are not incompatible. First Ladies are doing more than you ever thought about. Just be careful who you share the real with."

Aubrey wearing that dress should have been a celebra-tion in itself. Especially, after all I had gone through to make her accept it. After air kissing her cheeks in the parking lot, I had returned to Escada to pick up my package. Then I ar-ranged for Pastor to sneak the dress into Aubrey's closet. Each time she tried to return the dress to me, I would not accept it. "Quit blocking my blessing," I protested until Aubrey gave in.

The well planned Church Anniversary should have been all good. Aubrey had lost a few pounds during her self-im-posed exile, making the dress fit better than ever. But all was not well. Aubrey's expression was strained, like the face of a pouty runway model. Even when she forced a smile, I looked into the eyes of a lifeless doll.

I tried not to stare, but my gaze lingered on Phillip's

nervous grin, his awkward attempt to squeeze Aubrey's hand. Aubrey's hand fell limp, refusing to fully participate in the masquerade. Her body showed up, but her mind was in another place.

I knew her too well, absorbed her pain as if it was my own. All around us people basked in adoration for Pastor Phillip, their hero, the shepherd, the man with everything going for him.

In the finale of "Total Praise" Felicia Cunningham, tossed Artrice's black fringed shawl into the choir stand and holy danced across the stage. Bountiful breasts bobbed when she hit high "C". I threw up my hands in surrender and let The Holy Spirit, inhabiting the person of Felicia Cunningham, have its way.

Suh-ditty church sisters fanned incessantly to cool the fire. A hefty sister in a tight, tomato red dress seized up and shimmied. She spread floppy wings, tossed her head back and sprinted around the sanctuary. Flustered ushers, struggling to contain her joy, were repelled by Holy Ghost fire. The woman stomped, shouted and flipped her weave into sweaty ropes.

What began as a Baptist celebration ramped up into an apostolic revival. The denominational divide was crossed.

I signaled "softer" to the band and choir. The shouting sister crumpled in a crimson heap. An usher threw a modesty cloth over thick, dimpled thighs and legs shaped like baseball bats.

Bishop Henderson approached the pulpit, paused for the Holy Ghost fever to subside. "The hour has grown long, the Holy Spirit showed up and showed out."

In unison the church answered, "Amen."

"Ain't nothing like a Holy Ghost party!" the Bishop screeched. The nimble fingered organist underscored the point with a three key growl. The Spirit rocked on for another three minutes.

Bishop Henderson hugged himself and bounced. He caught himself thirty seconds into his praise party. "Y'all gon' get me kicked outta' here," he joked, took a deep breath. "It is my pleasure to announce that next door in the hospitality room there are trays of fried chicken, lemonade, German chocolate and red velvet cake like your mama used to make. I don't know 'bout you. I will worry about my diet tomorrow."

"And so I say in closing," Bishop Henderson looked into the eyes of Phillip, then Aubrey, "Love one another, protect your help mate. May the blessings of the Lord be upon you. The church should be the safest place on earth, but when you marry into the ministry...Watch out now. It's a jungle out there."

I wondered if the Bishop sensed trouble in paradise.

The organist's fingers trilled the keys. An awkward hush inhabited the sanctuary. All eyes were on Aubrey. I cued the choir for soft, background music.

Bishop Henderson continued, "Before we dismiss for the evening, if God has spoken to your heart, get out of your seat. Don't worry about what your neighbor will think. Give your life to Him. The doors of the church are open."

The choir hummed softly.

"Come to the cross. Claim your victory. He's waiting for you right now. That tingling up and down your spine is God reminding you of His Promise. Confess with your mouth, that Jesus is Lord. Believe in your heart that God raised him from the dead and you will be saved. Come on out of your seat."

With outstretched arms the associate ministers descended from the pulpit and spread out in front of the pews. The cross beckoned those who were out of church or looking for a church home.

Bishop Henderson's voice grew more insistent. "Surrender your life to Christ, He will wipe away your sin. Take your pain and turn it into a blessing. Leave it all here at the cross."

Onstage, Phillip exhaled audibly. His lips were smiling, but tight. Worry had taken its toll.

The woman in red strutted down the aisle to congregational applause. She was calm, weeping happy tears.

"Is there a man or another woman ready to put your hand in God's hand? Now is the time. You don't know the day or the hour when God will call your name," Bishop Henderson continued.

A young couple, the wife carrying a baby, strolled down the aisle to swelling applause.

Bishop Henderson leaned his elbows on the pulpit. He looked straight in the audience and warned, "God is watching. He knows who you are. Get out of your seat and be obedient."

At the rear of the sanctuary the spotlight shined on the head of a slight, twenty something young man. His auburn hair was twisted in neat, five inch locks. He wore a black silk shirt, black suit with a snug jacket and pegged trousers. His handcrafted shoes shined like onyx. Darting, untamed eyes leaped out of his chiseled face.

Phillip floated from his seat on the mock throne. He stood ramrod straight, fixated, as if a ghost had entered his domain. The young man cupped his face in his hands, tossed his head, yelped like a wounded dog. Down the center aisle he sprinted toward the cross. A student minister intercepted him, lovingly wrapped the stranger in his arms and inched the stranger's limp body toward the cross. With each step the young man wailed, "Abba, Abba". Buried in his sobs were indecipherable words between prayer and a chant.

With palpable trepidation Phillip stepped down from the pulpit. He inched closer to the young man, foaming at the mouth. "Look at me," Phillip whispered in a low voice intended only for the two of them. The young man refused to raise his bowed head. Sobs and moans interspersed with cries of intense pain. Phillip's right hand reached out, froze centimeters from the young man's face.

"Don't touch that demon Pastor," Associate Minister, John Bogan, cried out. Minister Bogan leaped four feet from the stage, landing between Phillip and the young man. Bogan nudged Phillip aside, raised his hand brandishing the Bible above the young man's head.

"Devil get thee behind me," Bogan demanded. He planted the Bible against the young man's forehead and pushed with power. "Pon de la ocias, me bashima eilo," Bogan spoke in tongue.

Arms outstretched, the young man floated backward and landed lighter than a feather on industrial carpet.

Minister Bogan peppered the supine young man with rapid fire scripture. The pupils of the young man's eyes rolled back in his head. Eyelids fluttered faster than a hummingbird's wings.

Like a buzzard guarding his catch, Minister Bogan circled him, whipped out a vial of Holy water and splashed until the vial was empty.

Pulpit ministers, including the Bishop, rushed from the stage to form a circle around the young man levitating in a different realm. The clergy converged in massive, simultaneous prayer reaching the tower of Babel.

At the center of the circle Minister John Bogan wrestled

with the invisible demon, leaping in multiple directions. Bogan slashed through electric currents shooting from the limbs of the young man's body. On the verge of exhaustion, Bogan continued to thrust and parry.

Other worldly sounds emanated from the young man's mouth. His guttural taunts to the saints of Heaven were punctuated by piercing cackling. He mocked the ministers, blasphemed the church. He cursed God.

A chill wind gusted through the sanctuary. Fearful congregants lapsed into an eerie pall. They prayed with one eye open. Unintelligible sounds from the demon possessed scorched their ears.

Speculative whispers sprinkled the crowd. "Demon possessed," "He called on the Father?", "Must be on drugs," "Work with him Jesus."

An African succubus ululated until her tongue glued to the roof of her mouth.

Fear gushed in random pockets. Worshipers had never seen first-hand this magnitude of spiritual warfare. A bold attempt at "deliverance" in a Baptist sanctuary played out before disbelieving eyes.

The young man's spastic movements slowed. His chest rose and fell with deep inhalations. John Bogan kneeled beside him. The intruder's head collapsed into Bogan's hands. "Come out, demon," Bogan demanded, jostling the head with locks resembling horns.

The young man's twisted, mangled hands curled into claws. "Heh, heh, heh " the demon voice laughed in Bogan's claret face. Bogan's designer suit and shirt were sweated out.

The young man's back arched, his body undulated. The demon inside him stared into Bogan's searing green eyes.

Bogan yanked the young man to his feet. Wild, red eyes

danced in the young man's leering face, rapidly transformed by lines, sagging jaws and bared teeth. He breathed fiery hot breath on Bogan.

In slow motion Phillip stumbled backward into the first pew. He turned to the frightened faces in the packed sanctuary. Most stood mesmerized. The faint of heart trickled out of the sanctuary.

Three ushers locked arms and fenced in the young man.

Minister Bogan and the ushers briskly shepherded the young man, arms flailing and reaching out to Phillip, from the sanctuary.

A chorus of "Hallelujah", "Thank you Jesus", rang out from the confused crowd. Was it salvation of a soul or an unsuccessful exorcism they had witnessed?

Phillip's chin rested on his chest. Sweat saturated Phillip's shirt through to his robe, clinging as if he had performed an ocean baptism. His face was ashen, walnut skin drained of blood. Under the weight of the stares and whispers his shoulders drooped like a defeated man.

Phillip swung around, searched the stage for invited dignitaries. The Mayor of Yorba Linda, four City Councilmen, Chief of Police, Congresswoman and state congressional representatives had exited stage right.

Phillip could not blame them. This was too much drama, even for a seasoned minister. Except for Hilton and the bewildered band and choir, humming the one hundredth verse of "Jesus, Keep Me Near the Cross," the stage was empty.

Aubrey Sampson had stepped, slipped into darkness without making a sound.

9

U GOT IT BAD

AUBREY

Two hours of intense therapy down the drain. It had taken two hours of therapy for Essie Sanchez to convince me to attend Trinity's tenth anniversary celebration. On a Saturday afternoon at her office on MacArthur near the Santa Ana airport Essie had found time to fit a new patient into her booked solid schedule of clients. The desperation and confusion in my voice, plus a phone call from her former client, Hilton, convinced Essie that this was indeed an emergency.

I had wrestled for days with seeing a therapist. In my head I heard Phillip's shrill voice insisting that therapists are for weak people. And weak was the last thing I wanted to feel at this time. Truth be told, I felt weak, insecure and extremely vulnerable.

I replayed Essie's assurances, "This time tomorrow you'll be glad you attended and your worst fears will be behind you." Strike one for the therapist. I felt like shit smeared across the sidewalk. My humiliation was now public and the demon had a face to go with the name, Donovan Upchurch.

"Remember the last twenty-five years. Your marriage is not the sum of Phillip's mistake. Yes, the mistake was huge, but there must have been some good or you wouldn't have stayed as long as you did," Essie reminded me.

I paused, touched the index finger to my lips before answering. "I can't stand looking at that nig..." I stopped short of dropping the "n" word. "I want him out of my face, out of my house. Poof! Disappear."

"And if he doesn't disappear."

"Maybe I will."

"Problems don't get resolved by ignoring them. Are you trying to hurt him by not showing up at the church's anniversary celebration?"

"I'd be lying, if I said I wasn't."

"There's more involved than you and Phillip. A whole congregation is depending on you. Let's get back to you. How did his confession make you feel?"

"Like nothing. I was...am nothing but an ornament to make him look good. The ink wasn't dry on our marriage certificate before he was screwing around." Burning tears welled in my eyes. I blinked them back and breathed deeply. "If he wanted to screw around, why did he hound me to get married? I went against my mother, my father and my friends to be with him. He was a broke, dope smoking ass."

"And you brought out the best in him. Helped achieve his potential," Essie added.

"Yes, I did."

"Did you ask why he cheated?"

"Sure."

"What was his answer?"

"She was available. *Available!* He had a baby with

somebody because she was available. That's not what he told that whore to get in her drawers."

"The penis disconnects from the brain easily."

I had to laugh.

"I doubt a baby was what he had in mind. Was she the only one?"

Ouch. Take my last ounce of pride, I thought. I let it all hang out. "Hell no." I exhaled. "I'm sorry. Don't know why I keep cursing."

"There's no censorship here."

"I am *sooo* angry. Years ago, I dragged Phillip to marriage counseling. He went one time and quit. I loved my husband, but he wasn't all that and a bag of chips. At times I was frustrated too, but I didn't compensate for his shortcomings... pun intended..."

Essie chuckled.

I continued, "By running the streets."

"So where do we go from here?"

My shoulders shrugged "I don't know...I will never look at Phillip the same way again. He lied when he was screwing his baby's mama. He lied again when it caught up with him."

"Why do you think he lied?"

"Claimed he did it to protect me. Another lie. He's protecting himself and dodging the truth. For a man so bold in the pulpit, Phillip can't face truth. Walking around like this will blow over in a few days. Hmmmph. I let him slide before, but no more!" My fingers dug into the padded arm of the floral couch.

Essie nodded in the royal blue threadbare chair she favored when interviewing clients. The room was quaint, surprisingly sedate for the office of a highly successful, Latina therapist. Essie herself was surprising, prettier in person than the woman I imagined when Hilton referred me to her.

The therapist's gravelly phone voice suggested an older, larger woman. Essie appeared to be in her early fifties, petite with glossy shoulder length raven hair. She was stylishly conservative in a Diane Von Furstenberg wrap print dress and Michael Kors wedge sandals. Her complexion was flawless, without visible pores or excess lines. She wore matte red MAC lipstick, an indicator of the fire within.

The quiet of the compact, intimate room simmered between us.

"Anything you want to ask me?" Essie added.

"Is it okay to share this with anyone else?"

"On a need to know basis only. I've had clients who shared with girlfriends only to regret it later. If you and Phillip stay together, and many couples do under similar circumstances, you will bear the burden of your friends' constant scrutiny. Looking for signs that the mirror has cracked. Your parents might be a different story."

"My father has Alzheimer's."

"I'm sorry to hear that."

"Thanks. It's like losing a friend who looks the same, but doesn't act the same."

My father and I had been close, at least on a superficial level. His illness forced me to question how well I really knew Daddy. I began wondering about missing pieces of his story, his relationship with his parents, his parent's relationship with each other. Were they a loving family or simply going through the motions as we sometimes do? Now I was left with empirical information only. What I yearned to know could not be filled in by Ancestry.Com or 23 and Me. Now it was too late to ask Daddy, who had always been sparing with information about his family. I would cling to the precious memories I had left.

The day I left for college was etched in my mind. I loaded

the final box filled with twin bed sheets and a Mickey Mouse comforter into a beat up powder blue Volkswagen Beetle. My father Winston Seymour stood stiffly with his hands jammed into the pockets of his khakis. I hugged my father. He hugged me loosely, never looking up until I cranked the overloaded Volkswagen. I looked out to see my father's tears rolling down his cheeks covered with a scratchy beard.

Daddy rarely expressed emotion. I could not remember him saying, "I love you" to me or anyone else, including my mother. I gleaned his feelings from ear hustling on conversations between him and his buddies. He stuck his chest out, voice dipped to a lower register when getting ready to brag. "My daughter gets straight A's in school." "Did you see my baby's picture in the Times Herald? She won the speech contest?"

Winston Seymour came to marriage and fatherhood with skimpy credentials. He rarely talked about his mother or father, who died before I was born. His brother and sister, residing in rural Georgia, provided few clues about how they were raised. Rudimentary facts---who died, got married, had a stroke or heart attack---were the sum total of what Winston or his siblings shared. Affection was not high on my father's priority list growing up.

While the Alzheimer's distanced him from his former self, Alzheimer's brought out the softer side of Winston. This was in contrast to what I had read about other Alzheimer's patients. Winston's painted on smile, at odds with his vacant eyes, came more frequently. He coped by being polite and clinging to things familiar, his home in Country Club Crest, Vallejo, California, my mother, his suddenly beloved wife, Pearl Seymour. Twenty-four, seven, for the past four years, Pearl took care of Winston. No caregiver, no housekeeper, none of the resources I strongly recommended and agreed to pay for. The only person allowed inside Pearl's dilemma was I. Once a month I was chief cook, bottle washer and maid. For me, the tasks were sometimes overwhelming. But I could not complain. My mother lived, or barely existed, in a state of perpetual exhaustion. She soldiered on like a good wife was supposed to do.

"Them heifers ain't comin' in my house," Mama snapped back when I hinted at the need for relief.

Like her mother, Allie Mae Washington, Mama exemplified a bull blocking a narrow country road. She would not be moved.

Mama was ecstatic when I left for college where she was certain that I would meet the right kind of young men. Men who were "marriage material". Not men like Phillip Sampson who took a job at C &H Sugar factory in Pinole, right out of high school.

A year before graduation from Cal I casually mentioned that I ran into Phillip at a café in Berkeley. Mama flipped. "If you wanted a thug, you coulda' saved money on tuition."

Mama tagged Phillip as the bad boy up the street harassing Mr. Wilson. She remembered Phillip playing hookey from school and bullying classmates, except me. "He's lucky I didn't snatch a knot in his lil' ass."

I spent the first ten years of marriage convincing Mama that Phillip was worthy of me. The first time Mama was re-introduced to Phillip, as a grown up, Mama could not stand him. She labeled Phillip "a fool living on pipe dreams." In Mama's cluttered kitchen Phillip spooled off "get rich quick schemes". Hyperactive, Phillip could not sit down, stood up when he ate and chewed with his mouth open. His mouth was always open.

Mama seized every available opportunity to remind me that Phillip Sampson was not the kind of man she wanted me to end up with. My small wedding to Phillip was a tense affair. When the minister asked, "Who gives this woman," Daddy continued to stand, right arm locked with my left arm, until Pearl tugged the tail of Winston's coat, "Sit down, man." Winston doddered backward onto the front pew and cried again.

In measured increments, Mama's attitude toward Phillip softened. First it was the birth of Miles, a blessed grandchild that Mama adored. By the time Phillip's money and prestige kicked in, Mama was one hundred percent in Phillip's corner. Still, there was no telling how Mama might react to news that Phillip turned out to be everything she said he was from the jump, "a low down dirty dog".

I decided to hold off revealing Phillip's latest and greatest transgression until I was ready for Mama's wagging index finger and barrage of, "I told you so."

"Do you journal?" Essie's voice snapped me into the present.

"Every now and then," sounded strange coming from a woman who quoted Maya Angelou, Isabel Allende, James Baldwin and Nadine Gordimer from memory. I was Editor-In-Chief of the Vallejo High School newspaper. I wrote prolific essays and dabbled in poetry. In the Vallejo High School Yearbook I described my greatest ambition: To become a novelist.

"Start journaling. Write down everything that comes to mind. Bad or good," Essie advised.

"You'll read it?"

"No. For your eyes only. And whatever you do, don't decide anything while steaming. Bring it down to a simmer before you make a move."

"Do I sound angry?" I laughed and trotted from the therapist's office with resolve to attend the church's anniversary. Nobody warned me that the anniversary would bring a close encounter with Rosemary's Baby.

10

THE NITTY GRITTY

AUBREY

Reverend Phillip Sampson swept through the family room so fast he missed the three piece set of Ralph Lauren luggage stacked in ascending size inside the vestibule.

"Bree," he called out in his dignified voice, the voice that commanded "All eyes on me."

No answer. Metal heel plates of wingtip shoes scraped against hardwood floors. He sailed to the back of the house. I loathed the sound of his shoes against floors that I shopped for, babied and polished until my reflection could be seen.

Phillip called out again. "Bree, you home?" He knew the answer. The Rover was happily home after an extended stay in parts unknown.

He stepped into the master bedroom where I stood with my arms folded. I pivoted to face him. My eyes were flat.

"Baby, where you been? I searched everywhere at church."

"Your progeny gave me acid reflux. "

"That thing at church. Crazy. I told him, never, never do that again."

"Far as I'm concerned, he's welcome. I won't be there."

"Aw, come on baby. Don't let one mistake ruin twenty-five years of marriage."

"One mistake too many. I was already pissed. Now I'm publicly humiliated."

Phillip took two steps back, assessing me from head to toe, the same way he assessed all women who interest him. Over the years I learned to ignore his tacky habit. I chalked it up to a man being a man.

"You lost weight. Your ass is shrinking. Are you eating?"

"Enough."

"Let me take you to dinner. Anywhere you want."

"No thanks." At first the sudden weight loss was alarming. Then I glimpsed myself naked in the mirror. My stomach was flat as a girl of twenty. I could move without fighting my jeans. My back was free of fat rolling like foothills. Not bad for a forty-five year old contemplating divorce. I was back at my pre-baby weight and loving it, except when I scrutinized my face. I did not recognize me, looking hard as a hooker on a rainy day.

I strolled to the kitchen. Phillip followed.

"What's with the suitcases? You've been gone for a week. That's punishment enough. Please. Don't run away again."

"I'm not leaving. You are."

"Where am I going?"

"Straight to hell for all I care. But I understand they have a special at Ayres Suites."

"Woman, have you lost your mind?"

"Yes. Thanks to you. Any decent man would have given me some space. This is *my* house too. I'm tired of living in hotel rooms. And tell your bastard son, keep far away from me."

The second I dropped it, I regretted the word "bastard". Donovan was a victim too, I reminded myself. A deranged victim, slithering around the sanctuary floor like a snake. Nevertheless, a victim. I needed to pray for him, but not today.

From the second Donovan entered the sanctuary, I knew who he was. His appearance had changed substantially from the wholesome, smiling young man in his Facebook profile picture. Under protest Miles' had surrendered his Facebook password.

"It's just gonna piss you off," Miles insisted. And it did, but I was determined to view the son that Phillip and Delia had created. I had to know whether he resembled Phillip or not. Maybe around the mouth there was some resemblance. Donovan was not the dead ringer that Miles had described. Or maybe he was. Maybe I was in denial.

"Foul language doesn't become you."

I didn't give a shit. "How long have you known about Donovan?"

"Two years ago he sent me a letter."

"*Two years*. Last week it was six months. Get your story straight."

"I thought it was a shakedown. Some nut trying to blackmail me for money."

"And you did not think to tell your wife?"

"You're right. I made it worse. I'll handle Donovan."

"Like you did today?"

"He doesn't want anything."

"*Yeah right*", I sniped. "And what about Miles? This goes against everything you taught him. Don't use women for play things. Don't get nobody pregnant, son." I imitated the righteous reverend's stern voice. "So the rules apply to everyone but you."

I pinched an exposed nerve, one that resonated beyond his immediate family. Phillip bit into his bottom lip. He used a gleaming white handkerchief, one that I had ironed, to stop the bleeding.

Reverend Sampson held himself out as an example to the young men in the church. He often reminded them that he was not perfect. His imperfections were what made the youth identify with him. Trinity Baptist Church's young adult ministry thrived while longer established ministries in Orange County faltered. A prime attraction of the church was the youthfulness of the congregation and the seeming openness of the Pastor whose favorite phrase was "Keepin' it real."

Reverend Sampson and his hip hop praise team attracted students from surrounding schools, Cal State Fullerton, U.C. Irvine and as far away as U.C. Riverside and Cal Poly Pomona. The youth at Trinity were encouraged to embrace new generation culture and to employ spiritual expressions of their own. Although students tended to be transitory worshipers, it did not discourage Phillip from counting them on the membership rolls. Phillip was a man on a mission, on track to claim his earthly crown, but for one major inconvenience: Donovan Upchurch.

"How long did the affair last?"

He hesitated too long. "It was just a couple of times…"

My deadly stare choked the lie in his throat.

"Okay, a few years," Phillip confessed.

"How many? Two, three?"

"A little more…"

"You fucked that whore the whole time we were in Detroit. Was she that hot?"

"No. Just available."

"*AVAILABLE*...Now there's a good excuse to ruin a marriage. I spent five years away from my family, had your baby while you used women like watering holes. AIDS was rampant. Did it occur to you to put a sock on your selfish dick?"

"Meanness...Not a good look."

He searched for signs of softness in my face. There was nothing but contempt. "I'll get my clothes."

"You're already packed. Shaving cream, toothbrush. Everything you need."

"How long does this exile last?"

"Until I can breathe."

Phillip reared up, puffed out his chest with authority. "You're not putting me out of my house. *I* pay the bills here."

Faster than a vampire's swoosh, I was in his face. "Get out or I call the cops. I'll get a restraining order faster than you can say "Amen". .. What's it gonna be, Pastor?"

The decision was easy.

I hunkered down in the kitchen, listening to the bumbling sounds of his slow exit. The engine of the Tesla purred in the driveway. No doubt, he was calling attorney Justin Flowers, renowned in Orange and Los Angeles Counties for his courtroom theatrics and over the top suits. Justin and Phillip shared a lot of mileage in the streets. I was not threatened by Justin, a criminal defense attorney who knew nothing about family law. No threat unless Phillip acted a fool and forced me to "catch a case".

Justin was an educated man, a graduate of Western State University School of Law. Justin combined street smarts with book smarts to establish himself as the "go to" man for criminal defendants in Los Angeles and Orange County. There was not a successful drug dealer or crooked politician within a one hundred mile radius without Justin's business card in his front pocket. Justin specialized in getting fat cats out of jail. Under present circumstances Justin would be useless to Phillip, who did not need a get out of jail card. He needed a get out of hell card. Justin did not specialize in salvation.

The Tesla backed out of the driveway. The garage door whined itself shut. Tesla was not welcome here anymore. I counted five minutes, making sure he did not circle back, making lame excuses, "I forgot this," "I need that." Maybe all he needed was that bimbo, baby's mama. I had to stop myself from thinking negative thoughts.

The silk Roman shade on the front window rustled as I peeked out. The street was empty, devoid of signs of life. The quiet neighborhood slumbered under the sliver of a moon with nary a star in the sky. No street lamps illuminated the path leading to my doorway. No headlights triggered motion activated sensors. I checked the lock on the massive wood door imported from Bali. I counted every click of the lock.

Searing silence was reminiscent of my first night in Yorba Linda. Moving here from Detroit was culture shock. In the darkest of night in Detroit there was movement. There was the sound of low riding Buicks crunching gray ice. The sound of muted voices jostling on street corners.

I savored the silence of Yorba Linda, listening to my own breathing, the breaking of my own heart.

At first the silence drove Phillip crazy. He had to be in motion, in pursuit of the action, to keep him alive. I introduced him to yoga and to walking without ear buds. I introduced him to the eucalyptus trees on Dominguez Ranch Rd., ancient cactus lining horse trails. In slow, mellifluous tones, Phillip eventually admitted that we were led to this quiet place to hear the voice of God.

And where was God now that I needed Him to right this wrong? It was easier to wait on the Lord when the elephant's foot was not crushing my neck. Where was he when my husband impregnated his whore and ran the streets with wolves like Justin Flowers.

I did not want to hear the voice that said: "It's your own fault. You knew who he was before you married him."

The voice was right. Did I think I was God, able to change a man's true nature? Phillip had sweet streaks that temporarily drowned out the wild child in him, especially when he needed me, which was seventy-five percent of the time.

Phillip Sampson got the call to fire up a sleepy pulpit after the retirement of Trinity Baptist Church's long term Pastor Isaiah Hawkins. The process leading to Phillip's selection was not smooth. Phillip deftly executed four trial sermons, paraded his cute young wife and handsome son before the congregation. Still, there was doubt as to the young buck's stability. Phillip came off as overly ambitious, too brash.

One night as I was seated at dinner between the retiring Pastor and his stodgy wife, First Lady Mimi Hawkins, I quietly injected details of Phillip's spiritual transformation into our casual conversation. I told them how Phillip was raised by a single mother, spent years searching for his purpose until God reeled him in. I recounted how we reconnected and married in college, how we had five hundred dollars between us on our wedding day. And that included cash wedding gifts. It was more money than we expected from friends who were students and parents with nothing to give but prayer and hope for a better future. "We were blessed with so much love-giddy young love- that five hundred dollars seemed like a million bucks."

First Lady Mimi Hawkins' heart melted as I recounted our

humble beginnings. Her gaze fell upon the retiring Pastor. Phillip's position as the new Pastor of Trinity Baptist Church was cinched. Pastor Hawkins and his wife saw me as the leavening force in Phillip's rise from hoodlum to man of God. As the spell was cast, Phillip fell uncharacteristically quiet. Phillip took a step back and watched me close the deal.

For me the slow mode of Yorba Linda gave our family a chance to bond. In Detroit Phillip was always distracted, too preoccupied to appreciate his own home. Runnin' like a wild ass banshee, as my mother would say. Yorba Linda allowed Phillip to recognize that he was blessed with a good, smart woman and an adorable son. When Miles was born, I recalled doubting whether Phillip had the right stuff to be a good father.

In Yorba Linda I witnessed a miracle, Phillip cheering on Miles from t-ball to triple A baseball, and onto the high school baseball team. Phillip boasting about Miles' oratorical skills as he won or placed highly in every speech contest. What at first seemed to him like exile to the suburbs, turned into a blessing. Phillip the proud father morphed into a family man. At least half of him did. From time to time Phillip strayed into the dark side where his divided spirit dwelled. Now that Phillip's family tree had sprouted one too many branches I had to decide if I could live with any part of him.

I sprawled on the family room couch. With no shades or curtains covering floor to ceiling windows, I gazed into the blackness of the night. The thought of calling Hilton breezed through my mind. I, who had traded places with someone else's life, was not in the mood to talk.

Get off this couch and stop beating yourself up, I thought, but my legs were water logged. I kicked him out. I should be joyful. Flashes of "What now?" stole my joy. Loneliness jumped on my back and took a slow ride.

A shaft of light shattered blackness hooding the patio. It gave me a reason to rise and peek outside. Debris, whipped by whistling Santa Ana winds, blew through the canyon, tripped motion sensor lights. A ball of needles from the neighbor's pine trees tip-toed across paver stones. Across the acre of evenly mowed lawn a lazy possum meandered, then froze. Flashlight eyes beamed at me. The possum's ratty teeth smiled.

A gritty gut growl reminded me that I had not eaten all day. I had fled the church before dinner was served. I ambled through the kitchen, dark except for the twilight glow beneath the lower cabinets. I opened both sides of towering Honduran mahogany cabinets, pulled out the snack shelf. It was empty, except for crumbling snicker doodle cookies and stale corn chips from a week ago. I nudged the retractable shelf. The cabinet closed lightly. Every sound in my empty home magnified itself.

I opened the refrigerator and verified what I expected. There was no fresh food in the house, only Styrofoam cartons from Phillip's carry-outs. Picked over WaBa Grill chicken bowl with white meat chicken and brown rice was Phillip's one concession to healthy eating. By day two Phillip spiced it up, pouncing on Flame Broiler's chicken and steak combo with lots of gooey brown teriyaki sauce. Day three, he got down to the real nitty gritty. Clumps of Chinese food from indeterminate source congealed in two separate cartons. Wimpy stalks of broccoli and medallions of carrots were mummified in gelatinous substances.

I decided to pass on the grub. How many times did I have to remind Phillip of Doctor Noble's order to lower his cholesterol? Phillip's relatively lean physique (minus the pooch around the middle) for a man of forty-seven, belied danger ticking inside. Phillip was one submarine sandwich away from completely clogged arteries. He did not get the message. Why was I stressing about the diet of a man that I just kicked out?

I poured half a glass of cranberry juice. A shot of vodka would be nice, I thought. A shadow moved behind me. I jumped. The glass bounced on the floor and shattered.

I whipped around. "Phillip?"

Caught my breath, exhaled loudly and tiptoed to the family room. No one was there. I would have heard Phillip's car pull in, the shameless yawn of the garage door that needed oil.

"Um trippin'," I spoke out loud. I returned to the kitchen, glanced up at the skylights. *Maybe it was a bird passing over. Birds don't fly at night. Do they?* Phillip could answer that Discovery Channel question. That was no excuse to ask him to come home.

I flicked on the overhead kitchen lights, pulled out the garbage can and paper towels to clean up my mess. Almost done, I needed a broom to sweep up shards of glass. I headed down the hall to the broom closet.

Big band music blared from the master bedroom. My heart seized in my chest. I snatched the broom from the closet with my left hand, grabbed a two gallon bottle of Clorox with my right. Hugging the wall, I inched down the hallway, checking over my shoulder with every light step.

The double doors of the bedroom gaped open. I inhaled from deep inside my diaphragm. I leaped into the entrance, pointed my broom like an AK 47. The room was clear. Tommy Dorsey and his big band boomed from speakers of the Bose radio. I sidestepped into the master bath. Empty. I used the broom to check behind the shower curtain for unwanted guests. I returned to the bedroom, squatted down, pulled up the bed skirt and checked beneath the four poster bed.

I clicked off the radio set to timed music. I caught my racing breath and squinted at the bleach, clutched in my hand.

"What was I doing? Bleaching him to death?" I laughed at myself.

When did Phillip start listening to big band music loud enough to scare the neighbors?

Still shaking, I returned my "weapons" to the closet. The mess in the kitchen would have to wait until day break.

I briefly contemplated taking a shower, but decided against it. All alone, no one would know if I was less than spring fresh.

Outside Santa Ana winds howled, blowing in a warm breeze that defied the winter season. I pulled back beige and white striped curtains, exposing cool white sheers. The sheers lifted in lazy languor to caress my face. I closed the window left open, apparently for hours. Grit from polluted air crunched beneath my feet.

I undressed quickly, left my clothes in a pile on the floor, intentionally defying my penchant for neatness. Naked before a beveled mirror, I assessed my body critically. Everything was substantially intact, if not on the exact plane or in the same proportions. Dimples on my rump winked at the mirror. My full rounded breasts were still good, although trending south with the tug of gravity. My waist had a decent indent, no muffin top. I remembered the good old days when my belly was wash board flat and my breasts stood at attention. My eyes fell to the trouble spot. Someone poured lumpy gravy into mash potato thighs. *I will never do another lunge*, I growled, pointing a finger gun at my image in the mirror and pulling the trigger.

Quit beating yourself up. I spoke to the universe for the twentieth time that day. The room felt stuffy. I headed to the window, then remembered poor air quality lurking outside. What was worse, stuffiness or sucking up bad air? To turn on the air conditioner in January was a sin. I tossed the duvet from the bed.

I slipped a nightie over my head and crawled between smooth cotton sheets. It felt glorious to be in my own bed again.

At the W Hotel in San Diego where I cooled out for a week, night time gaiety swirled around me. Singles mingled at the bar, sized each other up for a room key exchange. Not so single business travelers hit on hotties with freakishly uplifted silicone breasts and mini- skirts creeping up the yang-yang.

I could have played the game, feigned ten years younger than my forty-five years. My heart was not in it. I felt old, worn out and used up. My usually perky ass drooped like a pound cake with too much butter in it. My negative vibe repelled the horniest of geeks. A "Do Not Disturb" sign posted under my nose. I was powerless to remove it.

I clicked off the antique lamp with silk fringes next to my bed. A glimmer of guilt for not saying my prayers before hopping into bed quickly receded. A merciful God would forgive my tired butt one indiscretion. I tried to pray in bed, but the right words eluded me. For days it had been impossible to pray. My spirit was not clean. And so I listened intently to pregnant silence, waiting for God to speak to my heart. God was on extended sabbatical. I wondered if he cared about me.

I rolled to my right side, facing the center of bed, the place where Phillip's eyes met mine, where we embraced nightly for twenty-five years. He was gone, exiled by my choosing, but still gone.

I cried because the man I loved too much had thrown me into a deep well. At the bottom of the well, no light shined in either direction. My tortured mind shut down. My body surrendered, oblivious to the person pressed against the stucco wall outside my window. Only a closed window, gusts of debris choked air separated me from the face of evil.

11

DADDY'S HOME

PHILLIP

The red Tesla floated down the gently sloping hill and rounded the corner to the cul-de-sac. The car's precision engineered brakes stopped on a dime. I stopped in the middle of the street, flipped the gear into park and ejected from the driver's seat.

At a comfortable distance from the front yard of their custom designed home, neighbors Glen and Trudy Jarvis gawked.

A patrol car, lights whirling, radio squawking, blocked the driveway. I jogged toward two cops frisking a tall, clean cut, young African American man. My son. A pot bellied sheriff's deputy pressed my son's face against the roof of the patrol car.

"What the hell's going on?" I charged at the officer.

A towering, thirty-something, sheriff's deputy, pivoted, barred my advance with his baton.

"Back up. You're interfering with an officer," the black deputy warned.

"This is my house and that's my son!" My index finger grazed the officer's badge.

"I've been telling them that, Dad," Miles mumbled with his cheek pressed to the squad car.

The officer lowered his baton. "We got a call from your neighbor that a suspicious male was peeking in the windows of this house. We're just doing our job. Could we see some identification, sir?"

My mouth dropped to my chin. *Ain't this some shi....*

Glen Jarvis yelled from down the street, "He's okay officer. That's Pastor Sampson. Sorry about the mix up."

Steam sizzled from my ears. I was humiliated. A White man had to vouch for me. I reared up in the cop's perfect white grill, gleaming like fresh fallen snow against ebony skin. "I've lived in this neighborhood for two years. In Yorba Linda for ten. I can buy and sell you and that clown over there. Shame on you, brother. You see a Black man in a nice neighborhood and the profiling begins. Must be from out of town. Maybe L.A. or Compton. Give me your names and badge numbers."

"I'm Deputy Renard Broussard and that's Deputy Sherman Wilson."

"And tell your partner to get his friggin' hands off my son."

Broussard folded his arms, glowered down at me, a fire breathing dragon, at least six inches shorter than him.

I glared up at Broussard's midnight skin shining as if back lit by a strobe light. Six four, two hundred and thirty pounds of solid muscle gleamed in radiating sunlight.

"May I go now?" Miles lowered his hands, gingerly turned around. "I have no weapons in my hands. Nothing in my pocket. I come in peace." From his experience as a reporter and as a Black man living in America Miles knew that the level of provocation was low to shoot a Black man.

Still seething, I brushed past Broussard and hugged my son tighter than the day he was born. "The Mayor and City Council will hear about this."

"Would you prefer that we not respond?" Deputy Wilson lifted his belly from his belt buckle. Tiny spider veins colored Wilson's ruddy face.

"I prefer that you get the fuck away from my property and my family."

"Is that how a man of God talks?" Officer Wilson prodded.

"You son of a...", I stepped toward Wilson whose hand was firmly planted on his .38.

Miles grabbed me. "Dad, it's not worth it." Miles pushed me, spinning and kicking like a two year old, to the massive front door.

The officers eased into the patrol car and waited.

Miles nudged me inside. I tripped over the Turkish Bokhara runner in the entryway.

I grabbed my son, hugged him again, thinking about all the young, Black men who did not make it home. Finally, I exhaled my frustration. "Bree didn't tell me you were coming home."

"She didn't know. Where is mom? I rang the doorbell, bammed on the windows."

From room to room in the rambling house I strolled, yelling "Bree... "Aubrey, you home?" I opened the laundry room door leading to the garage. Aubrey's Range Rover was parked in the garage.

It suddenly struck me. The Tesla was parked in the middle of the street with the engine running. I hit the garage door opener, sprinted outside. On the window of my car was a yellow slip, "Citation to Appear in Court".

Miles loosened the latch of the floor to ceiling glass

NanaWall, pushed back the center panel and folded the glass doors into the far left and right sides of the walls. The lush outdoors merged with the open space of the modern interior. Fountains gurgled, limestone pathways meandered in multiple directions.

"You guys been busy," Miles marveled at the improvements that had taken place since he was home four months earlier. Between two maple trees we had installed an arch with rhododendron climbing white lattice. Midway the far left path a wooden bridge ran over a koi pond. His mother's footprints were all over the place, in every hedge defining spatial separation, in every rock rooted to blend with nature.

The sprawling five thousand square foot home in the Hidden Hills subdivision of Yorba Linda, California remained an anomaly to Miles. South of Yorba Linda Boulevard, in a house half the size and with little acreage, Miles grew from a boy to a young man. It was a house where we were happy, where we witnessed green fields and uncultivated rolling hills bow down to developer's thirst for the Benjamins.

This new home, surrounded by mature palm trees and giant bird of paradise yielded virtual privacy. Spring and summer brought tropical paradise. Lush, broad leaf foliage formed a shield around the lot.

Aubrey's childlike excitement at the first dahlia blooms, gladiola bursts, sweet scent of freesia, intrigued Miles. The miracle unfolded every year, nature's popsicles, showy splashes of lemon yellow, orange and fire engine red made Aubrey squeal with delight. She described it as touching the face of God.

"Have you ever seen leaves this green, blossoms snow white," she gushed every spring when fragrant gardenias strutted their stuff. She adored the perfumed, white blossoms weighing down branches. Tightly wrapped buds, straining to break loose, stole her heart.

Not understanding, but indulging her fervor, Miles listened as she praised, each spring, the blood red miniature roses shooting up overnight. Purple and pink petunias cascaded down clay pots painted the color of sea foam. Her prize possession was the pink and white peonies that the gardeners swore would not take root, let alone thrive.

Now that he was older Miles expressed appreciation for his mother's gardens, bordering the front, back and side terrace of the new home. She named the gardens-Garden of Peace, Dew Drop Retreat and Serenity Sanctuary. Benches strategically located in each garden allowed visitors to sit and meditate on nature's beauty.

"Gardens in full bloom manifest how faith, family and nature intertwine. They emanate from the same source. My grandfather was a farmer in Georgia," Aubrey explained to me and our son. "I watched him down on his knees, digging dirt and planting seeds. When flowers sprouted in spring, Big Daddy called it the wonder of God. It's like that for me. When I see beautiful flowers, something I touched, I am humbled to be a part of it."

Determined to be a part of her gardens forever, she left specific instructions for Miles. "When I die, scatter my ashes in the gardens. Phillip wants no part of it. Says cremation is a sin against God."

"You'd better outlive me. I'm not burning you up. I don't care if you're ninety-nine." I insisted to Aubrey.

I dawdled in the kitchen while Miles continued outdoors, in search of his mom. It was no surprise that Miles found her in the garden, planting for spring. I prayed that we would make it to spring. I was totally unhinged, Bree dug into an unyielding position.

In the far corner of our property, I saw Aubrey sitting on her haunches, squinting at blistering sun. Ear buds hung over a soil encrusted white, wife beater t-shirt tucked into frayed, cut off jeans. She wore a white bandana tied backward on her head. Basking in her element, she was oblivious to Miles calling, "Mom, mom. I'm home."

Miles jogged closer. A sago palm rooted in a thirty gallon pot was jammed against the plant menagerie.

Her head whipped around. She screamed, "My baby." In defiance of forty-five year old knees, Aubrey sprang to her feet. A rocking, exuberant embrace almost took Miles down.

"I *told* you not come." She chided while kissing him on each cheek. "I'm sooo glad you didn't listen."

"Had to make sure you're okay."

"Look what those arrogant bastards left me." I barged into the scene, waving a yellow parking ticket.

Aubrey bristled at the sight of me.

"They would have taken your son to jail, if I hadn't shown up."

"Whuuut?"

"The cops had Miles up against the car, ready to slap on the cuffs when I arrived. Your neighbors spotted him peeking inside the house, freaked out and called po-po. Guess that's the neighborly thing to do, if it's not your son. I know Sheriff Davis from the 'Keep the Peace' campaign. I will have those s.o.b.'s badges."

"Dad, just drop it. I'm okay. You've got enough to worry about."

The elephant trounced through the garden.

Aubrey cleared her throat. "Well, let's get you something

to eat. Looks like you've lost a few pounds. These girls don't cook nowadays." She peeled off gardening gloves, clutched her son around the waist and led him toward the house.

Wearing a 'What About Me' expression, I tagged along.

———— ((O)) ————

AUBREY

By six that evening twelve of Miles' high school and college friends clustered around the pool, sipping Coronas at the bar or draping lean bodies across white wicker patio furniture.

I loved the levity that Miles infused into every situation, including this home, filled with discord and tension.

The ten foot kitchen center island was spread with bountiful blessings-baby back ribs, salmon pasta salad, garden salad and strawberry lemonade made with fresh squeezed lemons from the orchard. The only shortcut taken was Bridgeford dinner rolls, dipped in butter, baked and served hot from the oven.

At the head of the island, between boisterous pronouncements, Phillip greased like there was no tomorrow, which might be the case as far as I was concerned. I was courteous, not once mentioning Phillip's high cholesterol in the hours since he slinked home. Miles' presence was Phillip's shield. Next to Phillip was a mountain of meatless bones sucked to the marrow and piled high on an oversized platter.

I smiled at our guests. "More hot bread, anyone?" I

moved the serving tray to the left, away from Phillip's hungry hands.

Phillip was a puppy, soliciting attention. His greasy finger creased perfectly spread cream cheese frosting on carrot cake. He knew I was watching. Phillip slathered frosting on his tongue. He burped gutturally, peeking at me, anticipating disapproval.

Polite indifference. That is how I worked it. Hostess incapable of being undone.

A six foot, statuesque Korean girl from Miles' high school, breezed toward the front door in six inch, clunky wedges.

"You aren't leaving, are you Sandy?" I asked.

"We've got to get dressed. We're meeting Miles and the guys at the club."

"There's a club in Yorba Linda?" I jested.

Sandy pressed the remains of a dinner roll between teeth perfected by years of expensive orthodontic work. She covered her mouth with long, big knuckled fingers and giggled. Everybody, including me, knew there were no clubs in Yorba Linda. Not in the Land of Gracious Living.

Miles and I walked Sandy and her two bubbly girlfriends to the circular driveway. "I'm glad you girls stopped by. Be careful out there. And send my son home at a decent hour," I joked.

Miles rolled his eyes to the perfect sky. My cue to shut up.

The girls giggled again. *When did I stop giggling?* I wondered. *There was a time when everything Phillip said made me laugh.* Just yesterday I was young and cellulite free like the diverse beauties parading through Miles' life. The road took a sharp turn without warning. Maybe the warning was there and I ignored it.

The guests, including Glen and Trudy Jarvis, trickled out

slowly. The Jarvis' had arrived earlier bearing a peace offering of freshly baked baklava and profuse apologies for mistaking Miles for a burglar. Once inside the home of neighbors they had been dying to get to know (get in our business) the Jarvis's made themselves right at home. Glen ate more ribs than anyone else, including Phillip, who overplayed his role as Lord of The Manor. I was tempted to push Phillip out the door with the Jarvis clan.

"Please don't make me stay at the hotel while our son is here," Phillip pleaded after Miles jumped in the shower.

I thrust the damp dish towel at Phillip. "Finish the dishes."

I opened the wine cooler and poured myself a generous glass of Patz Hall Chardonnay. Without missing a beat, I headed to the bedroom, closed the door and picked up *If Beale Street Could Talk* by James Baldwin. I loved all of Baldwin, having visited most of his work at least twice. With the movie based on the novel I wanted to re-read *Beale Street* to compare how closely the screenwriter followed the manuscript. I was in the thick of it, escaping into someone else's world when there was a knock.

Miles stuck his head in. "Mom, I'm going out for a couple of hours. I won't be too late." I appreciated his intention, but knew the probability of him coming home early was low. When he was home and out in the street I had a tough time sleeping. I knew it was crazy to worry about someone who had been on his own since eighteen. Miles has never given us any trouble. Well, almost never. He was not the one I worried about. It was those other people.

"You know not to drink and drive. If you need a ride, call me."

Miles stepped in, kissed me on the cheek. "If I'm not straight, I post up where I am. Worst case scenario, I catch a ride."

I cringed. I hated him catching rides with strangers, although while at Berkeley I was known as the hitchhike queen. "Okay, smartie. Be safe."

He took two steps, turned around and inquired, "You okay?"

"I'm fine. Can't vouch for your dad."

Miles laughed. "Try to be good."

"Doin' my best. Got your door key?"

"*Now mom*," he answered sarcastically. "Why do you think I got harassed by the cops? I left my keys in Dallas. Just leave the back door open." He blasted off before I could offer him the spare keys in the kitchen drawer.

AUBREY

Phillip was exiled to a remote guest bedroom at the opposite end of the house. His valiant, sustained attempts to worm his way into my bed failed. The minute Miles sped off in the Rover, the assault began. Surround sound blasted Al Green non-stop. At eleven forty-five p.m. I confiscated the universal remote.

"Enough already. I need some sleep," I screeched. Two clicks. The seventy inch Samsung L.E.D. flat screen faded to black. No Blue Ray. No nothing.

"Come on baby, just one dance. You love Al Green. " Tone deaf Phillip launched into an unrecognizable rendition of "Let's Stay Together". Singing was not Phillip's gift. Hilton served under my standing order to crank up the music anytime Phillip opened his mouth to sing.

"I love Al Green. If you love him, stop mutilating his music."

Phillip's eyes were red, his words slurred. "How can you be so mean?"

"Have you been drinking martinis?" I asked needlessly. Evidence was strewn on the kitchen counter. Tito's vodka. Green olives stuffed with blue cheese.

"Course not. Smell my breath." His mouth opened to expose a thick, pink tongue coated with a sticky white film.

"Go to bed, Phillip." I turned off lights blaring throughout the house. I slipped into the master bedroom and locked the door. Just in case Phillip pressed his luck again.

At one a.m. I drifted into a fitful sleep. Next to me in bed, *Vanity Fair* was open to an article about classic movies. *If Beale Street Could Talk* rested at my feet. My mind was a thousand piece jigsaw puzzle of the sky. Phillip with a snake-tongued woman, babies popping out of her hands and feet, populated my dreams.

The Bible says, "Be anxious for nothing". Was I anxious for trying to figure out the next move? My favorite scripture, Proverbs 3:5 reads, "Trust in the Lord with all your heart. Lean not unto your own understanding. In all things, acknowledge Him and He will direct your path."

I received it, but putting it into practice was another thing. I wanted Him to direct my path immediately. I waited, but not with faithful assurance that it would come to pass.

My brain ran faster than Ben Johnson on steroids. Where was Phillip the night our son was born? Was he with that woman on the most precious night of our lives ? After thirteen hours of my labor and a hot minute in the bonding room, Phillip was in the wind, unreachable by phone. I should have left his ass right then.

All the lies about working late. My enabling, being afraid to confront him. A woman can't corral a man. Let him run. The mustang gets tired, finds his way home.

Exhausted, I wrung out worry, hung it on a clothes line. Sleep was not deep, but a narrow exit from a hard night. Teeth clenched until my jaws locked in a grimace.

Down the hall floor boards squeaked. Did someone call my name? Maybe it was Miles, home early, contrary to my prediction. I slipped out of bed, tiptoed to the four lane hallway and called out, "Miles, is that you?" No answer. My eyes adjusted to darkness. I eased through the family room. Maybe Phillip was restless. Probably hungry. I whispered, "Phillip, are you up?"

The kitchen door gaped open. Hedges bordering the block wall rustled under the weight of a large animal. Too big for a rabbit or cat. I sprinted to the remote guest bedroom. Found Phillip snoring like a train. Alcohol reeked from his pores. I punched his shoulder.

In a fog, he responded, "What the fu...?" He reached up to pull me down. "I knew you'd come around."

"Negro, please. Somebody's in the house."

Phillip stumbled to his feet, bumbled to the hall closet and grabbed a baseball bat.

I grabbed the broom and trailed a safe distance behind, in case Phillip had to swing.

"What did you see?" he whispered.

"The back door was wide open. I heard footsteps, then noise outside."

"You left it open for Miles."

"I left it unlocked for Miles. The door was shut when I went to sleep."

"I'll check outside. You stay here," Phillip instructed.

"Are you kidding? That's the dumb girl in the movies."

I opened the drawer and grabbed a butcher's knife. The broom, I balanced against the granite countertop.

Barefoot, in his boxer shorts and v-neck under shirt Phillip led the way. Like a gun wielding cop, Phillip swung around the corner of the house and landed in Dew Drop Retreat. My night gown billowed in the wind. Someone or something had trampled hydrangea stalks and crushed them to the ground. The wrought iron gate at the end of the Retreat clanged open and shut.

"See. I wasn't imagining things."

"Could've been the wind."

"That opened a sliding glass door? C'mon now."

Phillip walked through the gate and looked out. The street was as still as the desert in summer. "Making sure it wasn't Miles. Sneaking back outside for one last... well, you know."

I flashed him the side eye. Phillip ran inside for a flashlight.

Inch by inch, we checked the perimeter of the property. Except for trampled shrubbery, there were no clues.

"Probably a hungry coyote..." Phillip speculated.

"Who opened the door and let himself inside." I finished his sentence.

We returned to the kitchen and flicked on the light. Shoe prints, wide athletic treads from a man's sneaker were imprinted on dark tile. Phillip reopened the door, flashed the light on sandy ground bordering landscaping. The same prints repeated outside.

A knowing glance passed between us. Reality of the complete invasion of our privacy sunk in. At one thirty in the morning we searched the five bedroom, four bathroom house, plus the attic. When the search ended, we plopped down, side by side, in the family room.

"Should we call the police?" I asked.

"So they can tell us we left the back door open and the fence blew open in the wind? Naw."

"What about the footprints?"

"One of Miles' friends or maybe Glen Jarvis forgot to take his shoes off in the house."

"Well I'm calling Miles. No way I'm leaving anything unlocked."

————)(◉)(————

AUBREY

Thirty minutes later Miles was back at the house. "Can we have a little less drama?" he quipped, trying to keep things light.

"There's been way too much drama for me. Frankly, I'm sick of it," I responded.

"And I suppose it's all my fault?" Phillip groused.

"You got that right, preacher."

"Hold up," Miles jumped in. "Everybody's tired and nervous. It's not a good time to argue."

"*Oh yes it is!*" Tears suppressed all day, saturated my cheeks. "This man," I jabbed my index finger at Phillip, "ruined everything. I was happy with what we had. But it wasn't enough for him. Now we've got freaks barging into the church, invading our home."

Miles' hands massaged my squared shoulders. He tried to lead me away. I shrugged him off. "I won't stand for this Phillip. You handle it or I will."

Miles lifted me up and carried me, screaming insults, to the master bedroom.

Phillip was smart enough not to enter the militarized zone.

Half hour later Miles joined his father in the family room. "She finally calmed down. Mom is really, really hurt dad."

"I know. I'd give anything to take it all back."

"It's too late for that. Right now you need to figure out how to deal with Donovan. Was he in the house tonight?"

"That's a stretch. We can't blame him for everything."

"It's not a stretch. After the way he performed at church. What kinda people are you dealing with?"

Phillip's head snapped back. His son speaking disrespectfully to him was a first. Miles was close with his father, but his bond with me was a rock that could not be chipped. While Phillip was out "doing God's business" Miles spent long, isolated hours with me.

Phillip refused to admit that at times he felt like the outsider, witnessing love in its purest form between mother and child. Phillip craved that kind of love---complete and unconditional without discussion about the baby, the mortgage, or the church building fund. He could never articulate his clawing need or admit to himself that he felt a twinge of jealousy. Phillip fathered from the sidelines, sulking in silence as my priority unconsciously shifted from loving wife to loving mother. The displaced look in Phillip's eyes, as newborn Miles nestled content between my engorged breasts, was invisible to me.

"I will protect my mother," Miles proclaimed, "no matter what. Maybe we need a restraining order."

"Slow down. We don't know it was Donovan. Let me talk to him first. The phone number he gave me is disconnected."

"I'll message him on Facebook."

"He friended you on Facebook?" Phillip asked.

"Yeah. He knew everything about me. My career, every city I worked in, who my friends are, all about mom and you. It's kind of weird. I friended him because he claimed to be a student aspiring to a journalism career. Then he rolled up on my job, saying that you are his father. It was like, like…."

Miles swallowed hard. Several beats later he continued. "I gave him an e-mail address to keep this somewhat under wraps. He keeps calling me 'Big Brother'. I'm not ready for all that. I've spent my whole life as an only child. I need a minute to get used to this."

"Son, I owe you an apology."

"Don't worry about me. Mom is crushed. I hate seeing her like this." Tears pooled in Miles' deep set eyes, the main feature he inherited from his father. Bushy eyebrows peaked above the bridge of his nose. Miles looked away and blinked back tears. He was determined to confront his father man-to-man, not as a whimpering child.

On opposite couches Phillip and Miles sat facing each other. They talked, argued and stood watch until dew rested on the roses in the Garden of Peace.

—◦《◎》◦—

Phillip

At dawn, taking out the trash, I stumbled over a gooey mass, the size of a grapefruit. I stooped to pick it up. Grossed out by the green and black coloring and slimy consistency, I jumped back. The mass appeared to pulse with life. It had no feet, arms or discernible animal features. Perhaps a cancerous tumor with veins and warts removed from a living thing. Why was it pulsing? And who would have left it here? Maybe it was coyote kill, the entrails of a vanquished animal.

I turned to call out for Miles or Bree, then reconsidered. They had gone through enough. I dropped the trash bag, hurried to the shed for a shovel and broom. The blob quivered like Jell-O as I broomed it onto the shovel. I felt the weight of it. Clammy hands trembled on the shovel handle. Yesterday's vodka was on the brink of betraying me. I plopped the remainder of the mass into the trash bag and dumped the entire bag in the garbage.

Shallow breaths came fast. My heart raced uncontrollably. *What the hell was that? Something ungodly. Miles and Bree must never see it.* I unreeled the hose, twisted the faucet to maximum pressure and sprayed until the shimmery green and tarry onyx stains lifted from the pavers.

<hr/>

Aubrey

"Where have you been?" Phillip snatched open the door of the Range Rover before I turned off the ignition.

My animal print flats alighted on the pavered driveway. I did a model's prance through the open garage door. Phillip dogged my heels.

"Miles and I were worried sick," Phillip fumed.

"Why? I left a note on the refrigerator."

Awkward silence. "You could have called. After last night...I didn't know what to think."

I left him stranded in a sea of confusion. I was not about to explain how an unscheduled visit to our financial planner's office had taken some of the weight off my shoulders. If I had to move, a distinct possibility, I might have to downsize, but would live well above the poverty line, thanks to solid investments.

In the kitchen Miles hovered over a plate of last night's salmon pasta salad. His elbows rested on the counter. Shoveling pasta into his mouth, Miles stood next to an empty seat. "Hey mom, you decided to join us."

"Yeah, when the devil gets busy, I get busier." I snatched a fork full of pasta from his plate. Miles pretended to fend me off with a fork.

"Watch yourself, I might not share my adobo with you," I warned.

"You made adobo?" he asked gleefully.

"Not yet, but I'm thinking about it."

"Do it before I go out, please."

There was no point begging him not to go out. He was a roadrunner. Just like his dad. There was nothing for him to do at home, except sit and watch me and his father fight.

"Speaking of going out, I want you to call your grandparents before you do another thing. Mama will be sad that you can't come up north this time. Tell her you'll make a point of seeing them soon. Daddy has gotten worse since the last time you saw him. Don't be surprised."

I dialed the phone before Miles became distracted by the steady stream of texts from his friends who circled in packs during his brief visits. I handed the phone to Miles on the second ring.

"Grandmama. Hey, it's Miles. No, I'm not calling from

Dallas. I'm in Yorba Linda for a couple of days. No, nothing's wrong."

I pantomimed in the background. No, I have not told them.

"I would love to, but I'm only here for a couple of days. You'll be at the top of my list for the next trip...Probably March or April. Let me speak to Granddaddy for a minute... Love you too."

"Granddaddy, how're you doing? This is Miles...Miles, your grandson." Long pause. Miles' eyes blinked back disappointment. I wrapped my arm around my son's shoulder. "Okay, it was good talking to you too. I love you." I heard a loud click on the other end of the phone.

"He didn't know who I was." There was a quiver in Miles' voice.

"Don't feel badly. Half the time he doesn't know me either. Even when I'm right in his face. Last month I took him for a doctor's visit. Doctor said the Alzheimer's is pretty advanced. The prognosis is not good."

"Can we do anything?"

"Just love him and be there as much as we can. I knew it was getting bad when he put raw chicken livers on his plate."

"What the heck?"

"I had fixed fish, potatoes and salad for dinner. Baked chicken was in the oven. I had the liver and gizzard in a bowl to make gravy. I look up and he's got raw chicken gizzards on his plate. Had to dump the whole plate."

"How's Grandmama coping."

"She's doing a great job, but it's taking a toll. When I'm there, all she does is sleep."

"Can she get help?"

"She refuses. Doesn't want anybody in *her* house. I've

contacted the Council on Aging, called a ton of caregivers and made arrangements more than once. You know how feisty she is. Told me, "I'm the HMIC around here. The Head Mother In Charge." I chuckled. "I know when to back off, but it still bothers me. On one hand, I can't stand to watch my parents go down. But I understand Mama's need for independence. That's what keeps her going."

"If it doesn't kill her," Miles concluded.

"Not to mention the constant worry about their safety. Last week my girlfriend sent me a link to a You Tube video called, "Voices From The Hood". Made me sick. These diddly bops grabbing crotches and bragging about selling dope in the Crest on video. Their lawyers will love it when the D.A. uses the video as evidence."

It seemed like centuries since I spent my formative years in Country Club Crest, marketed exclusively to African Americans starting in the late 1950's. "Living is best in Country Club Crest," was the sales pitch. And for families like mine that had never owned a home, the Crest was a dream come true. Without hesitation, my family piled boxes into a left leaning bronze Chrysler 300 and waved goodbye to the Waterfront where we lived in a shack masquerading as a house, on a lot owned and occupied by a Baptist Church and a second "broke down" rental, all bordered by a chain link fence that yinged and yanged with the wind. Loose window panes rattled inside rotted, mildewed frames calling out your name when wind from the Bay whistled. The back of our house abutted an alley, one block down the same alley where Phillip and his mother lived. Battered, broken cement resembled mosaic tiles. Telephone posts lifted black, sagging wires entangled with untamed trees threatening to collapse the fence. The flat tar paper roof had so many holes that we ran out of buckets, pot and pans when it rained.

There was no point complaining to the church that counted its tithes and offerings in coins and nary a Benjamin.

As older residents gave up the ghost, the homes in the Crest descended to their children and grandchildren, who had nothing invested in the dream.

The Crest developed like the soundtrack for an inner city musical. Songs of love and wooing gave way to hard rap and odes to sex. Gone were the days when a good girl could hang out at a garage party and come home intact. Gum cracking, ass wagging girls got sassier. Boys turned into macho men much too soon. The meek did not inherit the earth.

Good people, original inhabitants for decades, were sucked into a conspiracy of silence. "We have to live here," my mother said when I made a move toward a throng of boys goading thick neck pitbulls, or their knockoff cousins, to fight in the middle of the street.

"I should call animal protection," I threatened.

Mama laughed. "They ain't comin' out here for a dog fight. We cain't get people protection," Mama shut me down.

But Pearl Seymour did not have to live in the Crest. She chose to stay in familiar territory with familiar people. After years living in the only home she had ever owned, Pearl was planted like a rock. She watched friends and neighbors drop like flies from heart attack, diabetes and stroke. Not just old people, like Miss Blake, ousted by Adult Protective Services after her utilities got shut off. APS carted Miss Blake from her home in a dingy robe covering a filthy nightgown.

The big Demon of Death, mesothelioma, cancer caused by asbestos exposure during the Mare Island Naval Shipyard era, trolled like a pox through the neighborhood. Litigation dragged on for years, working men, wiped out by the hundreds, were replaced by unemployed youth in sagging jeans, grabbing crotches. Dope slanging youth served their diverse clientele in the streets of Mark Avenue and Gateway Drive while frustrated cops observed from a distance.

"It is what it is," Pearl declared, locking the screen and double barring the door against a threat that never pierced her armor. Pearl's tough talk and salty walk reached a truce with the young g's. They did not bother her and she did not bother them.

12

MAN IN THE MIRROR

PHILLIP

Three doors away from the Yardhouse Restaurant in the Irvine Spectrum I spotted Donovan, gazing at a store front display of giant Valentines. Donovan reminded me of my younger self--- compact in stature, body constantly in motion, hands jammed into pockets, shoulders weighted with insecurity. In less than ten steps my last chance to turn and run from this dreaded encounter would evaporate.

"Donovan," I called out in a voice so small that I alarmed myself.

Flashing a smile so broad that it must have rested on his lips before I called his name, Donovan spun around.

My right hand jutted out automatically. I conjured a self-conscious smile. Donovan's octopus arms enveloped me in a full body bear hug, not a man hug with one arm maintaining respectable space between us. I stumbled back on my heels. Too close, too soon.

"I'm not sure what to call you. Reverend Sampson, Pastor Phillip..." Donovan stammered.

"Phillip is fine." My stance widened. I folded my arms protectively in front of me. "I asked you to meet me because we have a lot to talk about."

"That's all I've ever wanted. To talk."

"Listen. I'm a public figure. A lot of people try to get to me. I know I should've responded to your letter. But it came out of nowhere."

"You don't remember my mother?"

"I'm not saying that. Look son..."

"There's a breakthrough," Donovan quipped.

My hands flew up, defensively. "If this is a shakedown, I'm outta of here."

Donovan backed up a step. "Is that what you think? If I wanted money, I would have contacted the D.A. years ago. Do you know how it feels growing up without a father?"

An audible moan escaped my lips. I melted into Donovan's deep set, moon size eyes, a reflection of my own. I recalled my life spent waiting for a man who looked just like me to drive up in a 1975 Fleetwood Cadillac with a guitar case riding shotgun. I remembered sitting on dusty gray carpet, massaging my mother's tired feet and listening intently to the story of how Sylvia Sampson met a travelling blues man.

"It was Friday night. I was too tired to go out, but my girlfriend Earline-she was in my carpool- wanted to see Bobby Blue Bland at the Veteran's Memorial Building. So I got up. Threw on some clothes. Me and Earline walked from Georgia Street-that's where we were living at the time-over to the concert. By the time we got there, the band was on fire. Most of the girls were looking at Bobby Blue Bland. So was I. But the bass player was looking at me. On break, Filmore Sweetwater told me I had the prettiest legs he had ever seen. And I did then, before they got varicose veins."

I rubbed my mama's feet a little harder to make her go on. "Long story short, we ended up together that night. And the next night. Earline borrowed her cousin's Plymouth Fury so we could follow the band to Oakland. Son, I'm not a loose woman, but I was in love with that man, Filmore Sweetwater. He looked a lot like you. 'Cept he had light skin and good hair or a damn good process. For months I waited for just one letter, a sign that the time we spent together meant something to him. I was a foolish girl then. Nine months later my blessing came. You. I ain't never regretted it."

I pressed my mama's foot with my thumb, drawing deep circles in her tight instep. I loved knowing the name of my father. I hated being the product of a two night stand. That's why I pledged never to abandon my children.

Confliction bubbled inside of me. Maybe Filmore Sweetwater went through the same thing. I doubted it since Filmore never showed up or gave my mama a red cent. Now I understood that it was not that simple. Being a father to Donovan risked losing the two most precious people in my world-Aubrey and Miles. It hurt too much to think about it.

Donovan's mouth said he wanted nothing. His needy eyes bore into my fragile soul.

I timidly touched Donovan's chicken wing arm. "Let's get something to eat. We can do Yardhouse or there's a Mexican restaurant called Javier's. If you've got a sweet tooth, the Cheese Cake Factory is over there."

We found a booth near the back of Yardhouse. Donovan talked incessantly about being a student at Wayne State University. "When I get my B.A., I plan to attend theology school, become a minister, just like you".

I floated between flattery and agitation, while scrutinizing the stranger who had barged into my life. The nose, flared like a shovel at the tip, was identical to mine. Except for Donovan's lighter complexion, I looked at a mirror image of my younger self.

Cautiously, I slid closer in the cavernous booth and patted Donovan on the back. "I'm sorry I ignored your letter. There's a lot on the line. A stain on my reputation is a taint on the church. I've worked hard to build the congregation."

Donovan nodded agreement. "I can appreciate that."

"My wife was devastated by the drama at the church. You should not have done that."

"You're right and I'm sorry. Nothing else got your attention."

"You got my attention last night."

Donovan's eyebrows shot up. "What're you talking about?"

"You broke into my house? Left slime on my patio."

"I swear it wasn't me. I'm not a thug." Donovan's hands rose in surrender.

"Had to get that out of the way. I don't know how. But I'll do my best to try to work this out. But nobody messes with my family. Understood?"

"Understood."

The conversation lasted more than two hours. Donovan revealed that he had followed my career since Delia broke down a few years earlier and told him that I was his father.

"You have brothers and sisters?"

"Three brothers, two sisters. Not counting Miles..."

Long pause. "Mama says she gets pregnant, if anybody looks at her."

I laughed, just a little, not wanting to appear disrespectful.

"What did Delia say about me?"

A wall suddenly went up. "She wants to maintain her privacy."

A request for privacy seemed strange coming from the woman who disrupted my entire life.

"I respect that. Next to God and family the church is my life. We don't need scandal. Did you say anything to the people at the church?"

"Of course not. Far as they know, I am a sinner searching for salvation."

I fidgeted in the booth, folded and unfolded my napkin, unsure where to go from here. "Let's get together again soon." I was dying to ask how long Donovan would be in town, but was afraid to alienate him. Instead I said, "Maybe I can give you some advice about the seminary."

At the Yardhouse exit Donovan and I exchanged a "man hug" and went our separate ways.

Only the security cameras of the mall saw what happened next.

Donovan danced in the direction of the retail stores, waited thirty seconds and circled back. He hugged the wall, peeked around the corner toward the parking structure. He studied my distinctive gait, how I overcompensated with my shoulders held high to make myself look taller. He watched my ghetto stroll, a remnant from back in the day, disappear into the parking structure.

Donovan sprinted to the end of the breezeway and dipped into the opening of a store front. His eyes were glued to the parking structure exit. Minutes later the hood of my candy apple red Tesla, Model S, appeared at the exit booth. He watched me bare perfect capped teeth and chat up the young, parking attendant with pigtails. The black out windows of the Tesla rolled up. I slapped on aviator shades and sailed from the lot. Donovan stepped out, aimed his cell phone camera at the back of the Tesla. A perfect photo of my license plate froze on his iPhone. Donovan scrolled down his contact list, attached the photo to a text message. Evidence of Donovan's first one-on-one meeting with Pastor Phillip Sampson launched into cyberspace.

13

MAKE THEM HEAR YOU

AUBREY

If it can happen to Maria Schriver, Tina Knowles and Elizabeth Edwards, it can happen to me, Aubrey Sampson. I do not know Maria Schriver or Tina Knowles, never met the late Elizabeth Edwards, but empathy runs deep enough to propel me to do what my mind has been telling me to do for years- write my way out of my confliction.

I cannot type fast enough to keep up with gurgling thoughts. Someone has to speak up for married women, sisters who submerge themselves in their husband's careers, then suffer in silence when what is done in the dark comes to light. Like Maria, I gave up a career in journalism to support Phillip's ambition. I took a job as the church's business manager, reviewing budgets and expense reports, performing tasks that could never take me higher. The church was Phillip's dream, not mine. I shut down my passion, subordinated my dreams to become a pastor's wife. Phillip was not to blame for my disappointment. The choice was mine. In retrospect, I chose poorly.

Many women never have a choice, not being rich or famous like Maria, Tina or Elizabeth. The pain and humiliation of a husband's betrayal run just as deep with poor and middle class women, who cannot fly off to Europe to lick their wounds.

If there was a blessing in this madness, I was determined to find it. At the lowest moment of my life, I rediscovered my voice. I did not care if no one wanted to hear what I had to say as long as I had the nerve to say it.

At twelve a.m. lights beamed from the upstairs loft. I heard the jangle of keys outside the front door, felt a rush of anxiety. I held steady, breathed. Miles bounded up the spiral staircase with cat like agility.

I looked up from my laptop, continued to stroke with the fervor of a woman possessed.

Miles breathed a heavy sigh of relief. "You okay, Mom?"

"Never better."

"What're you doing up this late?"

"Writing."

"About what?"

"I don't discuss work in progress."

"Oooh. Artiste. Where's Dad?"

"Probably in bed. I didn't expect you before sunrise."

"Can't hang like I used to." He lied. It was hard to party in the midst of family turmoil.

I swung my legs away from my desk to scrutinize my son. He looked beat. "I'm sorry you got dragged into this. Don't let our problems bring you down."

"Don't apologize."

"Somebody needs to."

"Dad apologized profusely. I didn't let him off the hook. Told him, straight up, you're a hypocrite. Talking the talk and not walking the walk."

"Amen to that."

Miles shook his head. "He's sad mom. Desperate not to lose you. Think about forgiving him. Get your spirit right."

He spoke truth. But I was a long way from forgiving. I was mired in Stage 1--- struggling not to fixate on the shit Phillip dumped on my doorstep and left me to clean up. *He's the one who needs to see a therapist*, I thought, then pushed it from my mind. Focus on my own healing, not Phillip's. My therapist gave me permission to be selfish for the first time in my life.

SISTERS IN SILENCE.COM
FEBRUARY 15

Rehab Anyone? No, No, No (Sorry Amy. R.I.P.)
Statistics are readily available on the number of single parent households in America, but few statistics address how many of these households result from Outside Woman having a baby with a married man. I suspect the number is staggering.

Ho-ing Husband may try to ignore Outside Woman's child out of existence or even worse, pretend that it is not his. What does that make Outside Woman? Ho, ho, ho.

Denial and confusion are Ho-ing Husband's typical response to the inconvenient truth of an Outside Baby. A Ho-ing Husband has good reason to be confused. Injecting an Outside Baby into an intact family unit is unsettling and dangerous.

Most men do not sleep with Outside Woman with the intent of creating an Outside Baby. They just want to have fun and go home where it is safe. Contrary to all the garbage Ho-ing Husband feeds Outside Woman to get into her pantyhose (My wife does not love me-She and I do not have sex-You are the only one who understands me), many married men are happy at home or content to maintain the status quo. Tyler Perry hipped us to the 80/20 Rule in "Why Did I Get Married?" Outside Woman, you are the 20%, which is one-fifth of 100% and a long way from keeping a man content after he gets his groove on.

AUBREY

Twelve hours into writing I was on a roll. As dawn filtered through the Hunter Douglas shades of the upstairs loft I hit the wall. Fuzzy brain pulled into the station like a heavy fog. I saved my work in a file titled "Saffronia", my pseudonym derived from a song by Nina Simone. The name had nothing to do with my text. I just liked the sassy sound of it.

My legs creaked. I had been in the same rigid position for hours without stretching. A recipe for blood clots. Next time I would remember to stretch every hour. I could not wait for the next soul baring session.

"Hallelujah!" I sang out loud. My depleted body sank into white wool carpet. I had a breakthrough, a cleansing of the mind that allowed me to write. But I was not yet home.

Writing opened the channels for spiritual healing, which led to mental healing and ultimately physical release.

My forehead pressed into the carpet. I envisioned the fiber imprint on my forehead- A QR Code of where I was going. I pushed back. My belly folded over my legs in child's pose. I chanted, "Thank you, thank you, thank you." My mind said, "Get up, go to bed." My drained body did not budge. I was in a space where I wanted to be, a space of safety.

Soothing sun settled over the foothills, washing the loft in lavender light filtered through sun censoring shades. The link between me and consciousness was broken. I floated into a dreamlike trance. All was heavenly, all was bright.

AUBREY

Phillip found me, stomach down, face turned to the side, stretched out on the floor. He whimpered, dropped to his knees and cried. "God no. No. Baby, please wake up." He shook me hard enough to pop my neck.

My sleep sealed eyes bugged at the violator of peace. I snatched my breath, rolled to my back. "What the hell?"

"I thought you were dead." Tears rolled down his cheeks.

"Not a chance." I crawled to my knees. "That's the best rest I've had in days. What time is it?"

"Eight o'clock. Why the floor?"

I hesitated before answering. "That's where God wanted me to be." My knees creaked as I rose up.

Phillip, kneeled on the floor, clutched my wrist. "Aubrey, will you ever forgive me?"

I placed my right hand on his forehead. "I forgive you Phillip. But I don't know what happens next."

"What does that mean?"

"I'm finding my way back to me. If we end up in the same space, so be it."

I left him hugging his knees. He called after me, "Where're you going?"

"To take a shower and see my therapist."

PHILLIP

I lingered longer than necessary in Aubrey's private space. My fingers glided across the mahogany desk she purchased ten years earlier after one of her rants, "I'm not using God's gifts. I am a writer."

"You are God's gift. His gift to me." I recalled my usual response to placate my restless wife. Was I selfish not to encourage her writing? Probably.

The desk, intended to unleash her creative juices, was relegated to a space for paying bills, scheduling meetings for church auxiliaries and booking my frequent flights, tasks easily delegated to the church secretary.

I flipped open her laptop. Maybe she left a file open. I rationalized that I was not snooping, just making sure she was not contemplating anything stupid. I hit the "on" button, heard the whirr of the machine. I panicked, almost slammed the screen, then reconsidered. I tiptoed to the edge of the landing. From on high I surveyed the sprawling living room from a new perspective. A towering fiddle leaf plant almost touched the vaulted ceiling. An antique Korean trunk hosted a menagerie of gold framed family photos. I smiled at the portrait of my dearly departed mother, Sylvia. A photo of Miles in his triple-A baseball uniform unleashed a tear. Two porcelain Lladro figurines and a Waterford crystal vase were strategically placed by my wife's artistic hands. Aubrey could take two broken tree branches and turn them into an awe inspiring creation.

In the space of twenty-five years we had evolved from a couple with nothing but love into a family with precious mementoes and collectibles. Where was I while my wife chronicled our lives in beautiful displays?

The sound of running water soothed my nervous ear. I tiptoed back to the sign-in screen that demanded a password. I typed in her name. *The password you entered is incorrect.* I tried Aubrey's birth date, then the name of her favorite actor, Idris Elba. Maybe I spelled it wrong. Her favorite artists, Jill Scott, Kem, Stevie Wonder, John Legend. No go. Miles' name and birth date were rejected. I tried the ATM password. No luck. *Why does she need a password? She was always transparent. That is, until now.*

———»«———

Aubrey

"Let's talk about what you mentioned on the phone. You saw Phillip's son. How did that go?" Essie asked after chit chatting about the unseasonably warm winter. Eighty-five degrees in February. Hydrangea in bloom weeks early. Yellowing leaves clinging to sturdy stalks. The seasons were in a state of flux, just like my life.

"Let's just say, my motherly instincts were not stirred." I laughed. "I can't see myself opening my heart to this other woman's child. And I feel selfish. It's not the Christian way."

"You're in the early stages of grief. Don't try to rush things."

My nose scrunched up in disbelief that Phillip's dilemma, which had become my dilemma, would ever be resolved.

"You're mourning the death of your relationship. That does not mean that it can't resurrect. If it comes back to life, and it can, it will be different."

"You ain't lying about that." My smile turned upside down in an instant. "I could kick myself for being so naïve."

"Would you prefer living in a fantasy?"

"No. I just gave up too much of me."

"Like what?"

"My swagger." We laughed.

I silently lamented the loss or better still, the relinquishing of my true personality. I molded myself into the image of a First Lady. I kept the confidence and dignity while suppressing the tendency to swear and tell it like it is. Many things I relegated to behind-closed-doors indulgences. Like sipping champagne and dancing hard until my skirt twirled around my waist. As a teen, the party did not start until I was in the house. My sparkle and spontaneity drew people to me. Energy siphoned from the room when I raced home to make curfew.

I was a bad girl in a good girl's dress. On the night of the debutante's ball, I escaped with a band of chocolate princesses in white ball gowns and elbow length gloves across the Bay Bridge to a party in Berkeley. In the car we ditched ball gowns for mini-skirts that left little to the imagination. On the steps of the function at the junction on Alcatraz we swigged cheap wine and sent clouds of reefer into the atmosphere.

What saved me during my teen years was the natural instinct to split moments before the cops arrived.

When my parents migrated from the Waterfront to the Crest in Vallejo I lost contact with Phillip. He moved across town and was assigned to a different high school. Occasionally I glimpsed him from afar on the football field when Vallejo High School played our cross town rival, Hogan High. I was a cheerleader for Vallejo High and Phillip a running back for Hogan. He was compact, fast, could elude a tackle with the shuffle of quick feet. Phillip had potential to be an all-star player, but he was his own worst enemy. Phillip would fight if you looked at him sideways. Sometimes he attacked his own teammates, if they failed to put the ball in his hands when he demanded. Phillip spent the better part of his high school football career brooding on the bench.

Fast forward, two years later, I attended a frat party at the plush home of a Black physician in the Berkeley Hills. The physician's son, Michael Brenner, a member of Kappa Alpha Psi Fraternity, drove a new Porsche and had the ladies of Cal in a swoon. Foolishly, Michael's parents left the keys to the crib while they vacationed in Aspen.

The last person I expected to see at the party was Phillip, who was far from Kappa material. The day after he graduated from Hogan High School Phillip took a factory job at C&H Sugar, located in the bowels of the Bay Bridge. The aloof location, and aged red brick façade of the factory reminded me of a prison.

I stumbled over the feet of a lone figure, slouched on a

stranger's couch, toking on a lighted joint dangling from his lips. His head nodded to Sly Stone's "Higher". A one inch arc of gray ash threatened to torch the doctor's white, peau de sois, French provincial living room couch.

I sailed to Phillip's rescue. "Whoa, brother man. Let's get you an ashtray." Phillip offered me a hit.

"I gave it up for Lent," I smiled and loosened the joint from Phillip's fingers. In a styrofoam cup bearing red wine sediment I crushed the joint.

Phillip squinted in horror. "That's good weed!"

"Thank you, Miss, for preventing me from burning down the house." I prompted, but didn't wait for his response before sashaying to another room.

Phillip, the misfit, dogged my heels. Finally, I relented and danced with him. "I remember you from grade school," Phillip reminded me unnecessarily.

I nodded. I knew who he was, the same aggressive, insecure boy, with added muscle and a cute beard. His eyes, still wild and thirsty, were bloodshot and droopy like a basset hound. Phillip looked as if he had slept in his clothes that were out of sync with the frat boy's preppy shirts and designer jeans.

"What brings you to this neck of the woods?" I asked.

"My cousin Jerome is a Kappa. My Aunt Bessie, Jerome's mom, is always bugging him to include me in 'civilized activities', since my mama passed away."

"Sorry to hear that." I remembered his mother Sylvia only slightly. On a hot summers' night, I would see her walk from her house in the alley down to the corner liquor store. When she returned with a little more bounce in her step she would smile and wave, if I was in the yard. "What hap...?"

"Life." He cut me off, reluctant to talk about his mother's death. "I didn't want to be at this sadditty piece of shit...Oh, 'scuse me. Then I saw you. Now I'm glad I'm here." Phillip's strong hands dipped into the small of my back and pulled me in.

For some strange reason, I did not resist.

My gaggle of girlfriends gave me nothing but grief for talking to a scrub.

I saw beyond his faults to the soul of a frightened young man in need. I agreed to meet him at a coffee shop on University the following week.

I drifted back to Essie. "Phillip was a hot mess when we hooked up. Still is."

"Yes. And you loved him enough to forsake all others, including your family. During this process what you have to decide is whether the love is still there."

I lapsed into silence. The million dollar question. The one I struggled with night and day.

"I don't expect an answer today. Your assignment for next week is to make a list of all the things you liked or loved about Phillip before the big disappointment. Our time is up. See you next week."

Aubrey

The second I climbed into the Rover I began composing my list. Topping the list of likes was Phillip's unabashed certainty that he would be somebody one day. I remembered how we sat in the coffee shop during our first date.

I found myself smiling at the vertically challenged, mildly

handsome man with nothing going for himself, except major attitude. He made bold, brash statements, "I'm gonna
be a millionaire," with nothing to back it up, except bravado
gleaned from Western movies he watched incessantly as a
boy. "I need a girl like you---pretty and smart, to balance out
my crazy ass. And tall, so I can have tall kids."

I laughed out loud, but did not discount his words. "How
will you make your dreams come true?" I baited him between sips of latte.

"I don't know yet, but I will improve myself until I am
worthy to be with you. Last week I signed up for classes at
Fairfield Junior College. I start school next semester. After I
saw those college boys sniffing you out..."

I giggled. "Nobody was sniffing me out."

"Yes they were. You're so modest. You wouldn't know a
hound if it bit you," Phillip declared.

My baby finger lifted the milk moustache above Phillip's
full upper lip. He clutched my hand before I could retract it.
He drew my fingers to his lips and kissed them lightly, one
by one.

The change in Phillip was drastic since our last encounter. He was clear-eyed, shirt was pressed, jeans were clean.
Phillip was gentlemanly beyond belief. He pulled out a chair
for me when I entered the coffee shop. I self-consciously
folded my lanky body into the wooden seat while glancing
around at scruffy students staring at Phillip's act of savoir
faire.

What did I like or love about him? I liked the way he
fumbled to unbutton my pants the first time we made love
on the leaves in Brione Park. Phillip was so unsexy that I
found him sexy in his hurried, bungling foreplay. Phillip
asked repeatedly, "Am I hurting you," as if his penis was the
first penis I had encountered. I let him cling to that fantasy.

Phillip was the opposite of the smooth, seasoned lover I was struggling to get out of my head and my life. Carlos was ten years my senior, master of many women and slave to none. I knew what I was getting into when I hooked up with the milk chocolate Dominican, tall, muscular with jet black hair coiled in smooth curls. Carlos' gleaming white teeth and sexy voice drove women to the point that they tolerated his infidelity. Females rolled up to his crib and rang the door bell before his semen was dry on sheets he shared with me. As much as he was capable of loving anyone, Carlos loved me, or so he claimed when I began to pull away. I refused to live my life in a procession of Carlos' women, women grinning at his unfunny jokes, women walking over me to get to him. He was too bold and unapologetic.

Compared to Carlos, Phillip was a breath of fresh air. Phillip was sweet where Carlos was smooth from years of rehearsing. My only complaint---Phillip approached sex the way he approached life, fast and furious. It took time to teach Phillip's hands to slow to the rhythm of my breathing and allow his exhalations to ride the ebb and flow of our passion.

"Open your eyes," I insisted in the throes of his runaway passion. "Breathe", I reminded Phillip, face twisted and on the brink of exploding. Phillip was not my best lover, but he was pure love, the kind that made me smile when our bodies intertwined.

I chose between the sensuous whispers of Carlos and the earnest dedication of Phillip, who promised me the world. A thin gold wedding band and Phillip's vow to be faithful won me over.

Headed north on the 55 freeway, bitter bile surged in my chest. Will this anger consume the rest of my life? I remembered Essie's warning--- life will never be the same. If not the same, will it be enough?

The loss of thought control was unnerving. Delia Upchurch and her hysterical son, Donovan, woke me up in the morning and refused to exit until sleep wrestled them down at night. They intruded between dreams, colored my days and stole my joy. Where was the faith that I ministered to others?

The Bible said to wait on the Lord and be of good courage. I waited and waited. So far, God was cruelly silent. In the meantime I did the only thing that brought me peace-writing because my sanity depended on it.

14

TEMPTATION'S 'BOUT TO GIT ME

SISTERS IN SILENCE.COM
FEBRUARY 21

*O*f course this blog will not change Ho-ing Husband's behavior. The hope is that it will cause HH to reflect and exercise some semblance of discretion when whipping out little pee wee. Quit producing Outside Babies. It messes up everybody's life.

Word to Ho-ing Husbands: If you wander in a foreign garden, do not linger long enough to plant your seed. Strange fruit will grow on your family tree, causing cross- pollination. Your original fruit will grow bitter. The first fruit of your vine will lose its sweetness and wither. Ancient African Proverb.

One tiny dick prick impacts many lives. Now Wife has to explain to her kids how papa was a rolling stone who gathered too much moss and only heaven knows what else. Wife must tell children about Outside Babies so they do not screw around with half-siblings. This information is relevant in small towns and big cities. Outside Baby syndrome is rampant everywhere.

Conceiving a baby is fun. Raising it is another matter. So let me speak to my brother who deserves as much blame as Outside Woman for the glut of Outside Babies. If you ask a man how his sperm got lost in O.P.P.T (Other People's PoonTang), nine times out of ten he will answer, "It just happened." Nothing just happens. At the root of fornication is specific intent. You intended to do what you did. What you did not intend was to get caught. And get caught you will when you defy the odds.

Quit pretending that you had a one night stand with a hoochie from the tittie bar. OW did not get pregnant performing a lap dance. Wife knows reckless, intentional behavior whether she acknowledges it or not.

Men who pretend that temptation just tracked them down and tackled them are delusional. OW did not jump on little pee wee and take a ride without permission.

Blinded by OW's beauty? Hogwash. Most of you bare back riding suckers have a bad case of spontaneous blindness. You marry someone who looks decent, presents well and will not embarrass you by picking her teeth at the company barbecue. Then you gravitate toward the lowest element while you are on the prowl. The dilemma comes when you slip and allow your mistress to become the mother of your child. For OW this may be a step up in the world. He is a responsible family man, takes care of his wife and children---that is exactly what she wants. And the means to her end are within reach, right between her legs. ATTACK OF THE VAGINA!

Let me remind you, Ho-ing Husband, that what looks good at night, may not look good in the morning. What looks good at twenty may not look great at forty. Take tattoos for instance. If tattoos are visible beneath her church dress, you may want to pass on that piece of fruit.

Let's try an experiment. Spend half the time and half the money that you spend on OW wooing your Wife. Miracles may happen. Your Popsicle might get licked.

Now and then ask yourself why you married your Wife. It had nothing to do with what a good mother she is, how organized she is, how well she cooks or washes your funky drawers. There was some butt slapping, sweat dripping, orgasm producing sex going on in the early stages. Wife had your butt shuddering, trembling and calling on Jesus. She did not suddenly change overnight. Did you start treating her like a Wife instead of the hot blooded, sensual being that she is?

Now you are out there telling some alien female how bored and misunderstood you are. Maybe you are boring, chugging along like the Ever Ready Bunny. Coordinate the signals between your brain and little pee wee. Every woman needs payoff, something more than simply going through the motions. If you have to ask, "Did you come?" you need help. Reason No. 1 that Wives stop responding to their husband's sexual advances: No payoff.

Outside Women are more responsive, you say. Sure they are. They put up with your selfish ass for fifteen minutes. Wives are relegated to full time duty.

OW's are masters at faking it. Some are paid to respond, although many OW work below minimum wage. Chinese carryout and a video are enough for them to drop their drawers. Too many OW are wooed into the ignoble ho-ing profession by visions of overflowing riches from dating married men. They are inundated with bad examples in this instant gratification world.

What messages are the sons of Ho-ing Husbands taking into their marriages? In some families men take pride in repeating their father's mistakes. Ouch!

I am usually hard on undisciplined ho's, those who fail to follow the "Don't Ask, Don't Tell," policy. The other night I saw one on television who almost made me weep. She was on TV bragging about sucking dick for a living. Her name was...OOPS. I would name names, but bitches love to sue you.

No one discounts the excitement factor in screwing someone other than your spouse. All that Wives ask is for a level playing field. If HH deserves excitement, Wife deserves excitement too. But excitement alone is not reason enough to bring life into the world. Excitement fades faster than red hair dye when babies get involved. Puke, piss and poo poo are instant mood killers.

15

BACKSTABBERS

PHILLIP

"Thanks for being discreet." I swiveled in the burgundy, leather executive chair rimmed in gold studs. Intertwined fingers rested beneath my chin as I contemplated the next move.

"Pastor you know I love you, almost as much as I love this church. We cain't let nobody mess up what's happening. This is just a glitch in a monumental move of the Spirit. *The devil is a liar.*" Associate minister John Bogan's voice raised to a fevered pitch. Bogan was on the verge of pulling a text.

I nodded agreement. The silence of conspiracy throbbed in my pastoral retreat.

"Tell me what to do. I'll handle this." Bogan's voice dropped to a whisper, "Nobody in the church needs to know." Bogan's deft fingers ran through gleaming auburn locks. A devoted soldier, he thirsted for instruction.

"Who was in the room when he claimed I was his father?" I asked.

"No one else. Just me and the kid. I made sure of that. I know trouble when I see it. Claimed he didn't want anything. Just to talk to his father. I took down his information. Told him you'd be in touch. He walked away very calm. Almost too calm. Like nothing had happened."

"What are church people saying?"

"There was talk. I wouldn't worry too much about it. The dude came off so crazy. Nobody will take his word against yours. Should you make a statement?"

"Noooo. Way too soon for that. Let's see how it plays out."

"Pastor, you know I've got your back. No weapon formed against you shall prosper." Bogan's lips smiled, but his sea green eyes were noncommittal. "Meanwhile, I'll tell security to keep his ass out."

I paced the length of the spacious retreat, situated on the opposite end of the building from my office. The retreat was sound proof, off limits to all but the privileged few- top donors, trusted board members and my closest brothers in the ministry. It was where I wrote my best sermons, disconnected from the world and figured things out. I needed to figure this one out. There was no telling when shit would hit the fan. I leaned heavily against the side panel of a floor to ceiling book case. My right elbow rested atop my left hand. Fisted fingers supported my heavy head. A wave of concern washed over me. Donovan had lied and confided in the one man who might lord the information over me.

Minister Bogan was a striver, an avowed sanctimonious, southern Baptist Christian who sorely tested my professed belief in inclusiveness. I warily embraced Bogan while others chafed against his ascent in a predominantly Black church. I fought to change the reality that 11 a.m. on Sunday is the most segregated hour in America. Inviting believers from other denominations-Jews, Catholics, Muslims- to worship at the church was a goal in my ministry. When Bogan's religiosity swept into the church like a sudden downpour in August, I saw it as a challenge and an opportunity. Tolerance and freedom of speech were lessons that nobody wanted to hear, except when it augmented their position. But when Bogan sang with the soul of a Black man his weird religion and political incorrectness were forgiven. His powerful tenor caused rafters in the sanctuary to tremble. "How Great Thou Art" was introduced to a new generation of Christians. His voice was a balm to the hearts of Bogan's critics.

Bogan held his head high like nobility. Some called him haughty. His chiseled Romanesque body had the ladies sniffing at his heels. Bogan held himself aloof, peacocking around in tailored suits, accenting well developed biceps and traps.

Bogan was sequestered inside his strict, Southern Baptist orthodoxy. No real woman lived up to Bogan's ideals, prompting speculation that Bogan was secretly playing for the "other team".

During breakfast at Snooze restaurant Hilton "outed" Bogan to Aubrey. "That wanna be nigga's as queer as the Sodomites he despises. You ever seen him with a woman? Probably using his Bible to jack off at night?" When Bogan, a self-proclaimed expert on "family values", rose to preach, Hilton went into self-imposed exile. At forty-seven mister family values never explained why he remained single.

An unabashed right wing Christian, Bogan was an enigma in the left leaning predominantly Black Baptist church. Bogan proudly declared, "A woman wearing pants is acting like a man." "Women do not belong in the pulpit." "Abortion is a crime and should be punished." The three Black Republicans stood up and cheered Bogan's first sermon, which stunned the otherwise Democratic congregation. Throughout his sermon everyone remained polite. Their ears were ringing. Tongues lay in wait to eviscerate the White man acting like he's "runnin' thangs".

I dubbed Bogan "The Second Coming of Elvis" with a Bible. If Bogan's name appeared on a Trinity Baptist Church concert program, outsiders trampled the congregation to witness his voice and compelling testimony.

"I grew up poor on a dirt farm in Alabama. Never saw a school room 'til the age of ten. My parents were traveling evangelists. They dragged me and five snotty nosed kids from town to town in the South, preachin' and singin' for our supper. I bless the Lord to be standin' here today. Man, we were poor, living off donations from the poor. Mama said I didn't speak a word 'til age four. When I did, I came out singin'. Hallelujah!"

Bogan packed out the church, brought in tithes by the tens of thousands. For some strange reason I tolerated his rants, hyper religiosity.

"He ain't nothin' but drama," Aubrey complained.

"Good theatre, baby. Look, if he's not singing here, he's singing somewhere else. There's less than two percent African Americans in Orange, County," I reasoned. "Our job is to spread God's Word, by any means necessary. We have to be open to all people, including those we disagree with politically...Besides, John Bogan will be outta' here in a hot minute, running like the wind to find his own element."

What I did not say was that in the Book of Bogan a man's adultery was not a stoning offense. I could not say that Bogan spoke directly with my putative son and had the goods on me. I could not tell Aubrey that as long as Bogan had my back, I had his.

16

FIRE

SISTERS IN SILENCE.COM
FEBRUARY 28

*T*o Wife an Outside Baby is the ultimate betrayal. It makes mockery of the institution of marriage. There is no point in reciting empty vows to be broken before the ink is dry on the marriage certificate. Too often marriage is just an institution to take women off the market while men continue to shop until they literally drop. Are men entitled to squeeze fresh fruit without buying it?

The answer is "No", according to the Bible. The Book of Proverbs issues dire warnings to Ho-ing Husbands. Do not squeeze other people's fruit.

"For the lips of an adulteress drip honey, and her speech is smoother than oil; but in the end she is bitter as gall, sharp as a doubled edged sword. Her feet go down to death; her steps lead straight to the grave." Proverbs 5:3-5.NIV Version.

"For by means of a whorish woman a man is brought to a piece of bread: and the adulteress will hunt for the precious life. Can a man take fire in his bosom, and his clothes not *be burned? Can one go upon hot coals, and his feet not be burned." Proverbs 6:26-28.King James Version. Translation: Keep rolling around in that whorish woman's bed, HH, and you are toast.*

"But a man who commits adultery lacks judgment; whoever does so destroys himself." Proverbs 6:32. NIV Version. Is Other People's Poon Tang worth destroying your soul? Really?

"For she hath cast down many wounded: yea, many strong men have been slain by her. Her house is on the way to hell, going down to the chamber of death." Proverbs 7:26-27. King James Version. This is way deep. Swear off of it now, brother man. You know you're skeerd. Run home while you still can.

"For a whore is a deep ditch; and a strange woman is a narrow pit." Proverbs 23:27. King James Version.

You need Jesus. Amen.

———=«(◐)»=———

AUBREY

On Sunday at 10 p.m. the call came. I was at my desk writing, at a fevered pitch. My eyes were tired, felt like someone poured salt in them. But I had to get it out, all out or risk an explosion inside my head. The shrill ring ruptured the stillness of night. Into the window of fear I crashed like a disoriented bird.

I snatched the land line from its base. "Mama, what happened?"

"How'd you know it was me?" Pearl Seymour questioned.

"Caller I.D. Doesn't matter. What's wrong?"

"They rushed yo' Daddy to emergency. I woulda' gone. Couldn't get my clothes on fast enough."

"They who?"

"The ambulance. I called 9-1-1 like you told me. I'm headed to Kaiser, soon as Sister Helen gets here. She's waiting for her granddaughter Kim to get home from work."

"Why did you call 9-1-1?"

"I was on the phone talking to Sister Helen. You know how Sister Helen likes to talk. We'd been on awhile. I looked around at the table. Winston had passed out. Head all up in his mashed potatoes."

"Why was he up this late?"

"Happened three hours ago."

"You still haven't gone to the hospital!"

"These folks wait for the ambulance to leave, then break into your house."

"Forget the house. Go see how Daddy is."

I imagined the run on conversation between Mama and the self-proclaimed evangelist. When Sister Helen called, Pearl settled in for a rant, ranging from Republican politics to why the devil is causing young women to wear micro mini- skirts.

"I don't sleep much anymore. Winston had been napping all day. Anyhow....I glanced over at Winston and he was slumped in his chair. He looked dead. But I wasn't claiming it. Lord, have mercy. I dropped the phone, ran over and shook him hard. His head kinda flopped to the other side of his plate. Potatoes all up his nose. I started screaming, ran back to the phone. I hollered hang up, hang up. Sister Helen kept yakking. I gotta get a cell phone."

"Did you call Kaiser? What's Daddy's condition now? " I asked.

"He's fine. Started breathing after I slapped him a few times. Paramedics gave him some oxygen, then wheeled him off. It was another one of those spells. This is the fifth time, Aubrey. This sickness of his..."

"It's Alzheimer's, Mama." I filled in the word that my mother had difficulty summoning. It was a part of Pearl's refusal to accept the seriousness of Winston's condition. Pearl insisted that Winston's refusal to perform certain tasks was symptomatic of general orneriness.

"This time I thought he was gone. Mouth wide open like a fish. All the blood drained from his face."

Footsteps on the spiral stairs signaled Phillip's return from dropping Miles at the airport.

"Hold on a second Mama." I covered the receiver. "My mother. They rushed Daddy to the hospital again."

"Anything I can do?" Phillip asked.

"Book me a flight."

<hr>

AUBREY

Gateway Drive, the main entrance to Country Club Crest, was alive, a bustling beehive. I rounded the corner in a tomato red, rented Ford Focus.

A Filipino girl with a table top ass and seal skin pig tails hanging down her back, leaned inside the driver's side window of an S 500. Her beautiful face was plastered with makeup. She pouted grinning scarlet lips. Baby hair edges were laid down with grease. Street merchants, aka dope dealers, waded into the street to hawk their wares. Wary faces said, I've got what you want, tell me what you need.

I swerved and stepped on the gas. The Focus failed to deliver the punch I needed. Lord, what have we come to, I thought. The Crest wasn't always like this.

"You've seen worse than this, Miss Yorba Linda," Mama snapped back when I groused about the maze of street hustlers blocking Mark Avenue.

"Another dig and I'm outta' here," I meant to think it, but said it out loud instead.

Mama could not get past the image of our family leaving Atlanta with a shoe box filled with fried chicken, a loaf of white bread and fifty dollars, including a dollar and seventy-five cents that I saved redeeming soda pop bottles at the corner store. The image was seared in my heart and soul, but it was not my final vision. I saw myself running into the Promised Land.

At the end of a four day journey on a Trailways bus, lurching to a halt every fifty miles to pick up and drop off passengers, the Seymours were exhausted, ripe as fruit in Mama's home-made travel bag and eternally grateful that God had delivered us to the land of milk, honey and mo' money.

But California was not as pictured in my mind's eye. The Golden Gate Bridge was rusty Orange. In Vallejo I saw few palms trees, no gated mansions or high rises. The sidewalks I walked on bore no tributes to the stars.

Pearl found our shack on the Waterfront. After weeks of living with an unwelcoming aunt and uncle, our shack did not look half bad. We got over looking through opaque plastic taped over windows to obscure the cracks and keep the riff raff from looking in at our shabby bed. We gave the roaches a three day notice, fumigated three times, before we moved in. Crunchy creatures did not care-kept going about their business. A perennial whiff of mold overwhelmed the power of Clorox bleach. No one complained, especially me. For the first time in my life I had my own bedroom and Pearl and Winston had privacy. We took in a stray caramel and white striped kitten, that I named Tinker Bell, to chase super sized mice that had no fear.

Winston found work washing dishes at a local Denney's. When Winston hired on at Mare Island as a pipefitter's helper, he strutted like a king. Pearl became the queen of domestics, cleaning houses in San Rafael until we moved to the Crest and she got licensed to keep foster kids. Banking fifty percent of every pay check, Pearl's savings mounted to what seemed at the time astronomical figures. In awe and admiration I watched my mother claw our way out of extreme poverty. With pride Mama showed me her passbook savings account, then crossed her lips with her index finger. "Shhhh, don't tell Winston," our in-house spendthrift.

Most of the time Daddy brought home his paycheck. When the devil got in him Daddy dug in his heels, did "what a man gotta do", and brought home a new car instead of the mortgage payment. That was a sign for me to hide in my room. An unholy war of words, him snorting, her hissing, raged for at least a month. When the coast was clear and fire shooting from Pearl's mouth subsided to a quiet groan, I risked taking a ride around the block in Daddy's new car. I sat up high in the seat of the Mark III, held my lips tight to keep from grinning too proudly at friends and neighbors who knew us. Daddy drove us over to the Food Basket, picked up greens and neck bones to bring home for Mama to cook. She rolled her eyes, clucked her tongue, but never failed to produce the best greens and corn bread I had ever eaten.

"I been in the same place too long," Mama complained while she cooked. I knew not to ask what she meant. The same house? The same marriage? Hers was not a conscious decision to stay, but a lack of resolve to do something different. Heavy footsteps metered out weariness trapped under her wings for decades.

Before she knew it Pearl, together with Winston, was one of the last pioneers of the Crest. Old friends dropped like flies. Heart attack, diabetes, and stroke rolled through the Crest like a plague. Generations of proud men standing on corners, waiting for their ride to the Yard, morphed into slinky eyed boys slouching beneath flickering street lamps.

Pearl's "hmmph" fast forwarded to life in the Crest thirty years later.

I rested my LV luggage on the cracked sidewalk to pick up discarded Twinkies packaging. A trail of Pay Day and Hot Cheetos wrappers clogged the gutter already filled with leaves. The neighborhood store, operated illegally from two houses away, was close enough to make the Seymour house a convenient dumping ground. Beneath an overgrown Juniper hedge tin soda pop cans burrowed in a blanket of damp leaves. I stifled my urge to instantly clean until I unpacked my luggage and changed my clothes.

It was an unwinnable war. Less than one month earlier I cleaned the same spot, as a final flourish to leaving Mark Avenue in better condition than I found it. In a contest of will between me and the neighborhood kids, the kids were winning. All I could do was bring up the rear in a race stacked heavily against me.

I ambled to the door, oversized Gucci purse on left shoulder, overstuffed luggage hanging from each hand. I did it again-overpacked for a brief visit to the Bay Area. Traveling to the Bay produced a mild form of schizophrenia. Umbrella, top coat and boots were essential in winter. I could never predict when we might be blessed with an unseasonably warm day. There was always the remote possibility that an event might arise, requiring a step up in outfits. Hope as I might, that event had yet to materialize. When would I admit, everyone I knew in Vallejo had moved, retreated into chemical abyss or died. Whatever happened I was ready for sunshine, rain, sleet or fog.

I took a deep, cleansing breathe and summoned a smile.

"Hey hon." Mama greeted me at the door. I sank into her soft, fleshy arms. Sarge that she was, Pearl Seymour stepped back, scanned me faster than the security machine at the airport. "Put on a couple of pounds," Pearl remarked without taking a breath. Again, I was that child, flunking Mama's approval. She abruptly changed the subject, "I didn't recognize the car."

"It's a rental, Mama. All I could get at the last minute." At least she said two words before calling me fat, I thought. As lean as I thought I was at forty-five, Mama's image of me was trapped in ancient history. In her mind's eye I was still that gangly girl, arms hanging to her knees, no hips, no butt and breasts longing for a Victoria's Secret push up bra. Everybody got to grow up, except me. No matter how many times I reminded her, "body shaming is politically incorrect", she did it freely, especially with me.

Despite years of regular exercise and fairly clean eating habits, never once did Mama commend my effort. I should have been beyond it, thankful that she got the insult out of the way right up front. Still, Mama's insult wrinkled my pride. Was she being intentionally cruel, hurling the same insult every time I arrived? This was Mama's way of bringing me down a notch.

I pretended not to notice. "How's Daddy?"

"Fine. He was awake, bugging the nurses about coming home. Sister Helen dropped me off a couple of hours ago."

"I'm going to check on him."

"Sit down a minute. Eat something. You look hungry."

Strange comment coming from a woman who labeled me "fat" two minutes ago. "I'll pick up something on my way back."

I blew through the galley size kitchen and rested my bags in a converted room that was once the garage. Shit was everywhere. Everything that came in the house that Pearl did not know what to do with, which was everything that came in the house, stayed in the house. Phone books, half empty food boxes from church giveaways, children's bikes (there were no children here), Idaho potatoes sprouting white tentacles six inches long, Goodwill purchases that would end up as Goodwill donations as soon as I had time, a mousetrap with bait still attached, and the capper-my daddy's shit streaked long johns. I'm home.

It seemed just yesterday that my daddy trolled, pausing at the end of the kitchen counter, eavesdropping on lame conversation with my latest boyfriend. Boys knew better than to attempt romantic maneuvers on the olive green quilted living room couch. I positioned myself a respectable two feet away from the hot pants pursuing me. Daddy's twisted sense of thug detection led him down a blind trail when it came to me. Daddy got hung up on appearances, which was the worst barometer of who would jump on my bones the second I entered their borrowed car. Winston should have been worried about the so-called nice boys who thought they could overpower my lean frame. I knew how to throw an elbow or crush nuts in the front seat of a Mustang.

Winston would clear his throat and run sink water to let

the male know that he was within ear shot. I pitied the fool who tried to mess with Winston Seymour's heart.

How could he forget his heart? I asked myself, cruising the aisles of Kaiser Permanente's parking structure, modeled after the Yellow Brick Road in Oz. "Let me park this damn car," I muttered out loud. Instantly, I begged forgiveness for cursing, a bad habit I had fallen into since Phillip's baby mama drama.

The sliding glass door of the new wing of the hospital greeted me with open arms. I broke into a trot, overcome with the sudden urge to see my daddy. I sprinted past a snow haired security guard, bearing an uncanny resemblance to Uncle Ben on the rice box. In the corridor I slowed down to breathe, to quell thunder rolling in my chest. An open door on the left side of the corridor drew my attention. An orderly, slinging a soppy mop, stepped out. His nose curled against the funk. The room was empty, sheets stripped and dresser cleared of personal belongings. Someone just died, I thought. A dam of tears broke. I back pedaled to the nurses' station, unattended seconds ago.

"May I help you Miss?" A pint size Filipino nurse with a bowl cut hairdo and heavy round black spectacles, approached the nurse's station.

"Winson Seymour. My father," I squeaked through trembling lips.

"He's the fourth room on the right."

Once again I let my heart get ahead of my mind. I sniffled and swiped the feather trim of my jacket across tired eyes. I should have been accustomed to the drill by now. Winston had survived numerous episodes of passing out, frantic 9-1-1 calls, sirens screaming down Fairgrounds drive, gurney sailing through the doors of the emergency room. I wondered how long his brain was deprived of oxygen this time. He was past the point of saying my name. In the recesses of his tangled mind, he knew I was a loved one.

The nurse added, "Mister Seymour has had a rough day. Please don't wake him up. Too many visitors for a man in his condition. That woman cursed me out when I wouldn't let her two little boys go in. We have rules here. No children allowed. "

"What woman?" I asked.

"His sister."

I was totally perplexed. Daddy's sisters were dead. Mama and Sister Helen left the hospital two and a half hours ago. We don't have close relatives in Vallejo with little boys. Maybe somebody from the church, I thought.

"I'll only stay a minute. Won't say a word."

I tiptoed down the corridor in peep toe booties. Everywhere I looked, human misery reached out. A bloated four hundred pound man covered in a web of attachments rattled and wheezed through every breath. Next room, a skeletal, pale woman with spotty tufts of gray, stringy hair stared into the great beyond. Purple veins traversed bony hands. Mucus drained from crimson rimmed eyes that cried, I'm alive.

The stench of vomit and human excrement overpowered industrial strength cleanser. I yearned to open a window. Let fresh air flow through the halls. I held my breath, tiptoed into Winston's clammy room ringed in gray shadows. The curtain was pulled close around Winston's bed. An uneven overlap allowed a sliver of light to seep in. Curled beneath a thin hospital blanket was a man who resembled my father. I gently stroked the hospital blanket and prayed. There were sharp bones where muscles dwelled four weeks ago. Winston rested quietly, too quietly for me, on his side with his knees drawn toward his belly. His left shoulder, protruding from the thin, blue hospital gown, resembled a chicken's wing. I removed my jacket and covered him, knowing Daddy does not like to be cold.

I pulled a blue plastic chair inside the curtain, sat down and closed my eyes. My prayer was rambling, unfocused. God's will be done. Please don't let my Daddy die.

Two hours later (I reneged on my promise to be brief) I was awakened by the sound of my father's voice. "What's this shit about?" My father's cursing increased exponentially with the progression of Alzheimer's. Winston Seymour tugged at the I.V. line attached to a needle digging in his arm. "What the hell is this?" He snatched tape that held down the needle.

I grabbed his arm. "Daddy don't pull that out. You're in the hospital. Everything is okay." I patted his hand. He recoiled as if my touch was the touch of a stranger. "Do you need anything? Water? More blankets?"

"I need to go home. Where's my wife? Where's Pearl?" he demanded.

"Mama's at home. She'll be back a little later."

Winston squinted at me. A look of non-recognition. "You work here?"

"No. I'm your daughter, Aubrey."

"Oh yeah?" It was a question, not an affirmation. "Where's my wife?"

"At home, resting. You don't want to wear her out, do you?"

"No, I don't. They got anything to eat in here?"

"Let me check. I'll be right back."

For the next half hour between sips of water and smacking on crackers Winston bombarded me with the same questions, "Where's Pearl? Where's my clothes?"

"I've answered a hundred times." My voice peterered out. "You need to relax."

Winston tossed back cover, landed cold feet on linoleum, attempting to escape. Gently, but firmly I pushed
his skeletal shoulders into propped up pillows. Wild, angry
flashing eyes cut into me. "What kinda shit is this?"
I wondered the same thing myself.

————⊷«(»)»⊶————

Aubrey

I left Kaiser in the same haste that I entered. The trot
was replaced by a power walk and lifted head. The hike to
the remote parking structure almost pushed me over the
edge. I jumped in the Focus and made a b-line for Chicken
Express. They had the best sauce of any fast food in Vallejo.
The eight piece family pack with Mexican rice, warm flour
tortillas and coleslaw talked to me in the car. I was tempted to rip open the steaming bag and suck on a wing while
driving.
Winston had finally fallen asleep when I stopped answering his incessant questions. No wonder my mother was
a wreck, fielding questions all day and all night.
A false veneer of peace descended on the Crest bathed
in indigo darkness. Behind closed blinds, inside my parents
home yellow light shined through curtains closed over plastic vertical blinds. Wooden clothes pins secured errant slats
of blinds. It was an written rule, no curtains or doors remained open after dusk.
With my free hand I knocked with a closed fist. The double dead bolted, heavy metal screen door rattled.

A lifetime later Mama asked from inside the door without a peephole, "Who is it?"

"It's me, Mama. Let me in."

Pearl freed one clothes pin, pulled back the errant slat and peeked out.

I made a goofy face. "You don't recognize me either?"

Two sliding door latches clicked. Next, she turned the dead bolt. The door squawked open. She unlatched the screen door. Wide-legged, in a leopard print caftan crowned by a flowered head scarf tied cock-eyed on a twisted wig, Pearl pushed open the screen.

The Chicken Express bag threatened to slip from my hand. "Hell to the no," escaped my lips.

"Yo' Daddy must be doin' better."

I warned, "Get the Ativan ready."

Pearl chuckled. "You see what I'm dealing with...I hate he's in the hospital, but I can use some rest...Phillip called about an hour ago. Call him back."

I rested the Chicken Express bag on the table, cluttered with stacks of bills, two pill boxes, brown speckled, over ripe pears in a chipped bowl, newspaper clippings and the same black and white, dust catching ceramic knick knacks I moved to another room on my last visit. I dropped my purse on a chair and fished out my cell phone.

"I turned my phone off in the hospital. Forgot to turn it back on." I located two paper plates and staked out a spot on the table.

"You're not gonna call your husband?"

"After I eat. He can wait." I answered.

Pearl's eyebrows shot up to her hairline. She had never heard that level of cynicism come from me. "And how is my son?" Phillip's generous checks to my mother promoted him to the status of "son".

"Your son-in-law is fine," I lied. I was chomping at the bit, in this case the chicken bone, to tell my mother about Phillip. With my father in the hospital it seemed like the wrong time. I was stalling. Halfway through the first half of a chicken breast, my cell phone rang.

"Told you to call him back," Pearl harangued. "Don't say I didn't give you the message."

I walked away from the table with the phone. Pearl stopped smacking to listen in.

"Hey, what's goin' on? Honey, when it rains it pours... Daddy is doing better. He's stable, but Alzheimer's is no joke." My voice broke. "He looks so frail..." I sniffed and pinched my nose to keep from crying. I paused to let Hilton get a word in.

"I'm taking it one minute at a time. I have no idea how long I'll be here. They'll probably discharge Daddy in the morning. Kaiser will kick you out on a ventilator." I laughed and then listened.

"Perfect. Call me back when you book the flight."

Pearl pretended to be engrossed in sucking on a drumstick when I returned to the table.

"Take the other wing," Pearl insisted.

I pushed my plate away. "I can't finish what I've got."

"Don't throw that meat away," Pearl warned.

I forked the other half of the chicken breast into the Styrofoam container and cleared as much stuff off the table as I could without a shovel.

Pearl's dinner table was a perfect venue for a treasure hunt. Every scrap of mail that had come into the house since my visit a month ago, including grocery store advertisements, was stacked on the smeared glass table. I played the waiting game until Pearl turned her back to stuff garbage in a paper bag. Pearl was two discount coupon mailers away from Hoarders. Stacked in various corners Pearl had magazines dating back to 2001. When I hit the door Pearl grew eyes in the back of her head. I touched the frayed Jet Magazine with long deceased Ruby Dee on the cover. Pearl warned, "Don't throw that out. I mo' read it. A lil' bit later."

"A lil' bit later" was Mama's way of getting nothing done. Each time Mama repeated it, scales grew on my back.

Our lives proceeded on parallel time clocks. I operated on compulsion to create order, put everything in its proper place. Now. Mama put off until tomorrow everything she should have done yesterday.

"What did the doctor say?" Mama asked.

"The doctor wasn't in. I'll wake up early, get to Kaiser before the doctor makes her rounds."

I dreaded seeing the doctor who had stamped an expiration date on Daddy's head. The sting of the last visit with my father's doctor was an open sore. The thirty something blue eyed, blonde with bone straight hair and no lips handed down the death sentence without blinking. Right in Winston's face, in total disregard of Pearl's sorrowful eyes or my scrunched up face. Winston grinned, oblivious to what she was saying. "Based on my observation, he has a year, no more than two to live."

Daddy looked like a child, expecting a lollipop for being good. After the numbness wore off, I was flabbergasted, furious. Don't they teach bedside manners in medical school? Pearl's mind played possum, migrated to a place beyond the sterile exam room.

Two days later, Mama asked, "Did the doctor say Winston has a year to live?"

I waved it off. "She doesn't know what she's talking about. Daddy might outlive us all. Dr. Grace should stick to writing prescriptions. And stay out of God's business."

Pearl nodded. She did not look convinced. My evasive response was easier to speak than the truth. Daddy was dying.

————)((•)) ————

AUBREY

Hilton lit up like fireworks when I joined him at Peju Winery in Napa Valley.

"I ordered for two. Drank your flight and mine," he slurred.

I double air kissed my favorite friend, dressed up in a cocoa suede jacket and wools slacks. His olive silk shirt matched contacts in flashing eyes. At church Hilton toned down the sartorial splendor. On his own time, he let it all hang out.

"You look fabulous as always," I reassured Hilton, who never heard a compliment he did not like.

"Not too shabby yourself. Those D & G jeans are fierce. And I'm stealing that fur vest. I don't care if it's not for boys."

"Did you wait long?"

"About an hour. No worries. I'm soaking up the atmosphere." Hilton batted extended, silky eyelashes at the sommelier one tasting table away. "Workin' on my flirt. I am sooo out of practice."

"I'm sorry. Had to make a run to Safeway for Mama. They've got chicken on sale for forty-nine cents a pound. She's making soup. Daddy's coming home tomorrow. "

"That's sweet. Forty years of marriage and still in love."

"I wouldn't say all that." I laughed, thinking about my parent's love-hate relationship. Can't do with each other and can't do without.

"Thanks for the excuse to get out. I've been house bound too long. Actually, since David died." Hilton took a long, slow swig of cabernet sauvignon and swallowed hard.

"That's about to change...soon as I emerge from my crisis. Or shall I say crisis'es... Is there such a word? " My cell phone chirped. The sound of sparrows singing with pointy beaks filled the air.

Hilton gasped and frowned. "You have *got* to change that ringtone. I'm looking around for Alfred Hitchcock."

I laughed. "It is pretty bad."

"Go ahead, answer."

I buried the phone deeper in my purse. "No thanks. I know who it is."

Two wineries later hunger lured us to the Rutherford Inn. Hilton broke his "no red meat rule" and ordered the ribs. "White folks cookin' up in here."

I stuck my fork in his plate. Meat fell from the bone. The remains of a miniature skillet of the house's special corn bread tempted my fingers

"I need to hire the chef." Hilton said.

"Yeah, and gain fifty pounds."

"This mess is sooo good." Hilton licked sauce from his fingers.

Mouth full, I nodded, finishing off a plate of seasonal vegetables.

"It's been too long since we did this," Hilton recalled. "Remember how we used to get fucked up, go out and close down a restaurant?"

"Yeah. I miss those times. All we worried about then was passing economics class. Now everything is heavy."

"Let's go dancing in the City."

"I wish. I promised Mama I'd come home early. She's nervous being alone in the house. She won't admit it, but daddy is her life."

AUBREY

Outside the fortress door I fumbled in darkness with multiple keys. I left the porch light on, but Mama in her nightly ritual turned it off. Nothing seemed to fit, just like my life. Wine did not improve my vision or patience.

On the tenth try I declared victory, stepped inside. With her arms crossed, mouth stern, Pearl posed like a statue.

"You been there all along? Why didn't you let me in?" I puzzled.

"I ain't standing by watchin' you wreck your marriage." Pearl's judgment jumped out before 'hello'.

The aftermath of red wine oozed from my lips. "It's already wrecked. Ask your 'son' who did the wrecking."

"I'm askin' you."

Soberly, I detailed the Delia and Donovan Upchurch fiasco. Pearl listened patiently as the story unfolded.

"Don't let no 'ho run you outta yo' house," Pearl advised. "Phillip ain't the first man to fall short. These ho's *keep* their legs open. Trying to take what somebody else has. You act like a lady now. Who were you with tonight?"

"A friend. A *very* gay friend. There's nothing sinister going on."

"You know I taught you better. Go brush your teeth. You smell like a damn wino."

She betta be glad she's my Mama.

17

JESUS IS ON THE MAIN LINE

AUBREY

E very fifteen minutes chirping birds, Phillip blowin' up my phone, were gettin' on my last nerve.

A stranger to cell phones, Pearl marched up and down the hallway demanding, "What the hell is goin' on?"

The house phone rang. Pearl raced to the white, clunky phone with oversize letters as if it was a slot machine spitting coins.

I waved her off, pantomimed, *I'm not here.*

Mama was relentless, grinning at Phillip's lame ass jokes, thrusting the phone in my hand like Jesus was on the main line.

In a high pitched, ultra polite voice I whispered, "Hello".

Phillip enumerated the list of church auxiliaries and activities falling apart without my expert guidance. "Don't forget, you're the business manager, my right hand and my wife."

I responded, "We'll see about that." The conversation fell flat. Mama's eyes shot a bullet down my throat. I flicked my hand, signaling her to give me privacy, to ease on down the hallway. She creaked up from where she had plopped down, dead center of my conversation. At seventy-five she intentionally moved with the speed of a ninety-five year old woman.

I did not need Phillip's affirmation of my work. He could do what he does best-preaching and public relations-because I was always there to back him up. I needed somebody to back me up for a change.

Days had passed since Donovan's performance at the church anniversary celebration. My history of daily presence at the church made sudden absence more glaring. Was I angry or afraid of what people were saying?

Phillip continued, "People are talking, asking questions."

"I'm not covering for you, Phillip. Right now, it's about healing me."

―――――――=»«(◐)»«=―――――――

AUBREY

I awakened to the sound of slanting rain whooshing down like a power hose. I welcomed rain to cleanse the earth and my soiled soul. Howling, whistling wind, mimicked sound effects in a haunted house, threatening to lift the fifties era bungalow from its foundation and deposit it in a foreign land. Somewhere nice, I hoped, but not Yorba Linda, California with its perfect weather and perfect pot hole free streets. Even with Pearl breathing down my back, I was glad to be in this place, keeping me on edge, a place with real people and raw truth.

I was not glad to pick up my father on the rainiest day of the year. Nurse's assistant, Lupita Gomez, wheeled Winston through the sliding glass door of Kaiser Permanente. Winston's toothy grin marveled at the pounding rain, peppering his face. Winston's ashy wrinkled fingers grasped at his first drop of liquid snow.

I pulled the Escort to the passenger loading zone, jumped out, opened the back door for Winston, then the front for my mother, holding onto her wig to keep it from blowing off. An oversize black and white umbrella wielded by Lupita inverted against gusts of whirling wind.

"Get in the car Winston," Mama hollered from the safety of the front seat and a closed window.

Two days in the hospital and Winston's bones had turned to mush. He moved like Gumby, bending and breaking at the wrong angles. I supported his shoulders, turned him around, trying in vain to back him into the car. His whole body was rigid, spine stiff as a board. Winston grinned, fascinated by the charcoal, angry sky. Rain gathered on his stubbly beard. Winston saluted the sky.

The rain rolled faster than gutters could swallow it. Winston padded in puddles of rising water. His socks were soaked all the way up to his bony ankles.

"Get-in-the-car, Daddy," I articulated as calmly as possible.

Mama muttered, "He's just showin' out."

Lupita, standing on top of the curb to keep dry, waded into the water. "Mister Winston. Time to go bye-bye," she cooed. She turned to me, "Allow me." Lupita flipped a waist length, wavy braid behind her shoulder, held Winston's right hand, braced his back with her left hand and guided him down.

A satisfied cheeky grin laced his face. Winston folded into the car.

A knowing glance passed between me and Mama. *Did you see that?*

I dived into the driver's seat. For a full minute I endured Winston fumbling with his seat belt. I finally crawled over the console, extended the belt and fastened him in. With his motor skills deteriorating by the day Pearl could not keep telling herself, he's just showin' out.

No time to commiserate. I counted my blessings. Winston was out of the hospital. Before day break I had accomplished major chores-mopping floors, cleaning toilets and shopping at Walmart before heading to Kaiser. All this after writing half the night.

I was a woman on a mission. Destination unclear. Phillip's long shadow loomed over every page, every sentence, every word. To speak truth, even if in anonymity, was the only way to heal.

18

STOP IN THE NAME OF LOVE

Sisters in Silence.com
March 3

Ho-ing Husband's unplanned parenthood actually frees you to be all that you can be. So Sisters In Silence I urge you to do one thing---stop. Stop suffering in silence. This does not mean announcing your predicament to the world. Your hairdresser and gossipy girlfriends are verboten unless you want your personal business posted on Facebook or tweeted in the middle of the night. I sympathize deeply with celebrities and public figures forced to confront HH on the front page of the National Enquirer.

Sisters In Silence, the first thing you need is prayer. Pray without ceasing that the Lord will guide you through this mess and lead you back to a place of peace. Spiritual guidance from a discreet, reliable advisor may help, if you can seek guidance without losing your religion and vamping like a moose on rampage. Personally, I do not have the control to prevent calling Ho-ing Husband an M.F. (I do not mean

Master of Finance) in front of my spiritual advisor. If you are like me, go to Plan B.

A good and trusted friend is invaluable in this situation. "Trusted" can be hard to come by with all the salacious tidbits that come with news of an Outside Baby. Friends will sympathize, but secretly thank the Lord that they are not in your shoes. Already, they are strategizing how to move you to the edge of the friendship circle just in case you become single and a threat to their marriage. It does not matter if their husbands look like dumb and dumber and drool tobacco.

Do not rely upon Ho-ing Husband to bring clarity to the situation. Like most men he will turn in circles with his thumb strategically planted, complaining "Woe is Me." Never mind that he is the source of the problem. He sees the Outside Baby primarily as a threat to his own security, glossing over the fact that you and your children have been blown out of the water by his unsavory deeds. He will probably expect your sympathy. Gag. Barf. Keep a straight face, but do not get sucked in. "Confidence in an unfaithful man in time of trouble is like a broken tooth, and a foot out of joint." Proverbs 25:19 (King James Version). Yes, he dumped a truckload of shit on your front porch and refused to clean it up. He expects Wife (aka mommy) to take care of it. That is what Wives do, unless Jodie has got his girl and gone. Read more about Jodie later.

Talk to a therapist. I know you say, "I do not need counseling. He does." Yes, he needs counseling and so do you. You have been through one of the most humiliating experiences a married woman can endure. An Outside Baby cuts Wife to the core, eviscerates her self-esteem, if she lets it. Not only did HH violate his marriage vows, he violated you. Thank the Lord you did not wind up with a not-so-cute social disease. If you did not dodge that bullet, consider a civil suit in addition to a divorce petition.

In HH's heart he knows that he needs counseling. He is not likely to get counseling unless mommy (Wife) sets it up for him. Do you really want to further enable his childlike behavior? Not. Tell him to get his own damn counselor. Do not waste your fifty-five minutes listening to more of his bullshit. At some point you may be able to have your kumbaya moment, but do not rush it. Selfishly pursue your own healing.

By seeking proper help you take the first step to no longer suffering in silence. The tendency of some brazen women will be to scream Ho-ing Husband's infidelity to the world. Think about the impact on your children and on you, if you end up staying with the lousy varmint, which is a possibility. Having said that, do not get caught up in what the neighbors, the church people or your friends think. A lot of nosey people are in the same predicament as you. If it slips out in a moment of rage (these moments will come frequently like hot flashes) while you are sucking on oysters at McCormick & Schmick's, chew first, then breathe. It could be worse. You could have taken a golf club to his SUV. Wooded him.

Wives have been known to lose their religion and fear of prison under Outside Baby stress. Wives have two unpleasant options. She can divorce HH and sever her roots, unless she has children, in which case her children will always be a branch on HH's family tree. The other option is to acknowledge Junior, which means that Wife will never be free of OW for the rest of her life. What a friggin' choice. Some Wives choose to ignore their husband's infidelity until there are baby boots on the ground nipping at her husband's heels. When someone else's child refers to her husband as "daddy", wife swears she is hearing things. Men have been known to totally lose their hearing.

S.I.S, scream, cuss, shout. Do whatever you need to do when HH drops the bomb on you. Do not let your Ho-ing Husband shut you down. You have a right to know where, what, when, and why. He will come at you with, "You haven't been a perfect wife." Of course not, but your response to his subterfuge, "Irrelevant and immaterial." Unless your imperfection has done irreparable injury to your family, do not let him change the subject.

He will pretend that he lied about his OW and his Outside Baby to PROTECT YOU!!! That kind of protection you do not need. The only person HH was protecting was his own sorry butt.

HH's next move is highly predictable. He will try to make you feel guilty about him screwing around. "We were having so many problems...You never had time for me...I needed someone to believe in me...It's hard being a man, blah, blah, blah..." That whimpering translates to---you did not kiss his ass constantly.

Get up close in HH's face and scream, "BULLSHIT". Disclaimer: Proceed at your own risk.

———)((()))(———

AUBREY

Bringing down the father of my son was not on my agenda. How could I write the truth without admitting that I too am a Sister in Silence?

Church folks are the worst folks in judging other people. We have no problem casting the first stone. I knew, if I validated the gossip, Phillip would be expelled from the pulpit, blacklisted and shunned. Was that what I really wanted? To hurt him as much as he hurt me. Maybe I was drunk on the fumes of Phillip's power, afraid to sink to the bottom of the murky ocean along with him.

Phillip did not stand a chance if fornication, adultery and procreation outside of marriage were pinned on his clerical collar. A baby's mama drama could be fatal.

I was worn out thinking about it. At the end of the day I collapsed into a fitful sleep-worn out Cinderella, not waiting for my prince to come. He had already shown up and turned into a frog .

Between dreams a hip hop blasting insomniac cranked up the volume on a car stereo. He rolled through the Crest, a demon cranked up on pharmaceuticals and blasting a gun that boomed like a cannon. My heart leaped from my chest. I found my breath, rolled to my knees and crawled to a crack in the blinds. The intersection of Gateway and Sage Street transformed into a speedway. Twenty-two's on a 1972 Chevy Impala squealed, brakes screamed as the speed freak "popped donuts". The back end of the Chevy twirled smoky circles beneath a flickering street lamp.

The thrill of pre-dawn entertainment was wasted on me. Sleep crusted in my eyes, squinting to see what was going on. It was a black and white movie, low riding BMW dancing on hydraulics, men moving in slow motion, soundtrack blasting the whole neighborhood. I dragged my tired ass to Mama's room and peeked in. Pearl had not missed a beat getting her snore on.

In minutes the street drama faded. I lay awake anticipating the sleep bandit's encore performance. Two hours later, on the edge of sleep, I heard the gritty sound of Winston's run-down house shoes shuffling toward the front door.

I called out, "Where you going, Daddy?"

"Get my paper before them bastards steal it," he answered gruffly. In forty years of subscribing to the Vallejo Times Herald, the newspaper had come up missing once. One loss was seared in his memory. .

"It's six o'clock. You don't read the paper this early. Please go back to bed," I said. Go back to bed and let me sleep, I thought.

"Whoosh," the wall heater flame ignited. Winston pushed the temperature gauge to the max, ninety degrees.

I could not let him fend for himself. Head spinning, I swung my feet to the floor and groaned. "Hold on, Daddy. I'm coming."

Winston was dressed for winter in Alaska. He wore a fleece lined pleather cap with ear flaps, upper and lower long johns pinned at the waist, a short sleeve yellow polo shirt, flannel button up shirt, bomber jacket several sizes too large, wool socks inside corduroy house shoes, everything from his closet, except his pants. The neighbors had learned to accept the bizarre fashion coming out of this house.

I dialed down the temperature on the wall heater, went to the window and watched Winston standing in the driveway, peering up and down the street, searching for who knows what.

"It's cold as hell out there," Winston shivered, unrolled the newspaper. He headed for the wall heater and stretched the paper wide to "warm it up". No point warning him about the fire hazard. This was his ritual and no one could break him out of it.

"At least it's not raining," I answered.

Before the cereal contamination plague, known only to Winston, Winston's breakfasts alternated between cereal and oatmeal. Now we could not pay him to touch his former favorite Raisin Bran Crunch.

I beat him to the stove to boil water. The giant box of instant oatmeal purchased six months earlier to keep Winston from turning on the stove remained unopened. Winston had developed a fear of the microwave. The water must be boiled, oatmeal stirred in and plopped into a graying Oakland Raiders bowl, a Christmas present from Miles ten Christmases ago.

The flame leaped outside the enamel sauce pan, stoking my greatest fear that Winston would burn down the house. "God, please take care of people with Alzheimer's and worn out spouses," I prayed every night.

I sat the bowl of steaming oats on the table, handed Winston the honey and milk. He swiped a bowl of sugar.

"You don't need sugar, if you use honey."

"Hunh?" He replied in the same way he answered every question.

"Do you want sugar or honey?" I foolishly asked.

"Whatever you want."

My bad for asking. I knew my father was incapable of making even the smallest decision. Mama was having major trouble coming to grips with Winston's condition. She kept giving Winston instruction that he could not follow. When he answered with the inevitable, "Hunh", Mama admonished him, "Quit being stubborn". It was Mama's way of refusing to accept how far the Alzheimer's had progressed.

Imagine the frustration of dealing with Alzheimer's twenty-four, seven. A few days of Winston's routine and I was ready to head for the hills of Yorba Linda. I begged Mama to take a break, hire a caregiver.

I offered to pay for the caregiver. Mama dug in her heels. "I'm all right."

She was not all right and I knew it. On the Alzheimer's

scale of one to eight, Daddy was easily a six. I did not need Daddy's doctor to tell me that.

I held my tongue, waited for the inevitable crisis that would force the hand of HMIC (Head Mother In Charge) to reduce the burden.

The oatmeal-crusted pot soaked in the sink. Daddy swallowed his morning meds and headed back to bed for the first of several naps. Ahhhh. A moment to breathe. Should I hit the gym or steal two more hours of sleep? I hyped myself up with the promise of a post workout Starbuck's and a crisp New York Times to read. Before I could meditate on being tired I hit the door.

Daddy was right. It was chilly, not bomber jacket chilly, but cool enough to throw a black and white L.A.M.B. hoodie over my head. Roving fog cooled out the Crest. Not a creature stirred. Night owls had crawled home to crash.

I basked in the chill of the Bay Area. According to the news, the East Coast was paralyzed by unrelenting snow and ice. Orange County registered ninety-three degrees in early March. Everything in moderation was good, including a touch of winter. Not the kind dished up in Detroit with months of muted skies and no sunshine to speak of. Make You Wanna Holler. The Beach Boys got it right. I am a California Girl.

———◉———

AUBREY

24 Hour Fitness was tucked in a strip mall between Sonoma Boulevard and Broadway, two doors from Raley's

grocery store. At 8 a.m. on a Tuesday morning the fitness center was packed. Bodies of all sizes and ages vied for spots on the treadmill. I reminded myself, you are not in Kansas anymore Aubrey. This is not the Yorba Linda 24 Hour Fitness Super Sport with two rows of treadmills, two dozen ellipticals and zero wait time. But it was all good, an incentive to hit it hard and quit within an hour. Winston would be awake by then and Pearl could pursue her sleep marathon.

Farther back and to the right of the check-in desk assorted muscle men lolled around weight equipment, preening and admiring their physiques in the mirror. A scattering of women worked out on the leg lift, chest press and ab crunch machines. Grunts and groans of diehards, pressed to fatigue, punctuated clink and clang of metal weights.

I plopped down on a stationary bike for two purposes: to warm up and stake out an available treadmill. A forty something sister in hip hugging spandex, sports bra and a yellow bandana knotted sideways on her head provided adult entertainment. In Yorba Linda she would have been arrested for her act. I caught her moves in the back mirror. Sister girl groped the stair stepper like a long lost boyfriend. Music from ear buds sent her jiggy with abandon. One ample thigh strangled a metal post. Her undulating torso humped an imaginary lover. Except for a strip club, I had never seen a woman in a close personal relationship with a pole. I wanted to ask what was in her water bottle. Could I get some of that?

I stole a glance around the gym. *Was anybody else experiencing this?* Gym Rats continued biking, lifting and jogging on the treadmill. The woman's coochie slid up and down the pole to climax. Her left leg lifted above her head, vertical to the floor. I laughed to myself. *That woman is flexible. Only God knows what she will do for an encore.*

A treadmill opened up. I sprang from the bike and pounced. At the far end of the room I lost view of Madame X's exhibition.

I switched my phone to Prince's station on Pandora. "Let's Get Saved" amped up and so did I. On the treadmill to my left a twenty-something sweat drenched Filipino banged out miles like the cops were after him. The pounding, jarring vibration from his gallop rocked the entire gym. I felt sorry for the Precor machine, trembling under his weight. Just when I thought the machine could take no more, he hit the "Stop" button. Praise the Lord, I wanted to say, but murmured instead, "Ummm. Good workout."

I caught the groove of "Raspberry Beret" and settled into my stride. Knees lifted slightly, elbows bent, my hands relaxed.

The vacant treadmill was not vacant for long. I was in the zone, staring straight ahead at the mirror.

"What you doin' over here, Trent? Who let you out the weight room?" Trent's meddling friend slapped his shoulder before Trent could press "Quick Start".

I glanced to my left, trying not to be obvious. As long as he didn't gallop, he was all right with me. Trent had the body of a basketball player-long and lean, with chiseled arms hanging to his knees. His biceps leapt without being flexed. OMG.

Black Adonis answered his buddy, "Getting some cardio."

"I bet you are," Skip sniped and sporty walked to the manly side of the gym.

I did not want to look like a wimp. I adjusted speed control from 3.2 to 3.6, kicked it up to a slow jog. My chest lifted. I pranced like a thoroughbred, running prettier than I had in twenty years.

I was feeling better than good, breaking a sweat and thanking creaky joints for working with me. A slower song,

"Beautiful" came on, threatening to slow my momentum. I glanced down, tapped my phone to fast forward. My finger-tip grazed the red, emergency "stop" button. The treadmill froze. I lurched forward, wobbled to the right, corrected to the left, feet scissored mid-air. I fell backward into a space without a safety net. Fighting hard to stick the landing, I latched onto the brick hard arm of Black Adonis, who had jumped from his treadmill to catch me.

"You okay?" He smiled with teeth as white as the tank top he wore. His smooth skin was the color of black sand with silver flecks. Soft, curly hair was cut close on the sides and lined with a straight edge razor.

I laughed, "Other than embarrassed, I'm fine."

He paused his treadmill, stepped within inches of my pounding chest. "I'm Trent Davis." Trent extended his hand. "I remember you. You were a cheerleader at Vallejo High School. My brother Cedro, they used to call him Pretty Boy, was in your class."

Trent held onto my hand longer than necessary. I looked deep into his cocoa eyes and remembered the young boy sitting near the front of the bleachers, staring up at me. He tagged along with his older brothers to Vallejo High School football games. When I kicked my leg, toe almost touching my head, his young eyes were lost beneath my flouncy red cheerleader skirt. He was always there on the front row watching me.

I wished I had used more cocoa butter on my hands that felt suddenly dry. "Of course I remember Pretty Boy. Wore his hair slicked back in a ponytail."

Trent laughed. "He still does. Got a lot less hair."

I laughed with him. "I'm surprised you recognize me."

"You look the same as you did in high school."

I liked him already. "You must live at the gym. You look incredible."

"I put in the time, usually before the gym rats get here. I meet my clients between five and seven a.m."

"Personal trainer?"

"Been doing it a few years. You must not live in Vallejo. I would've spotted you before now."

"My parents still live in the Crest. I'm down in Orange County now."

I felt a tap on the back, spun around to face Madame X's tight lips. "You working out *or working it*?"

"I was about to ask you the same thing," I shot back.

Trent intervened, "Settle down, Monique."

I pointed to the end of the row. "There's an open tread-mill. If you hurry, you can grab it."

Madame X, aka Monique, cracking gum open mouthed on the right side of her back teeth, cursed beneath Juicy Fruit breath and strutted off.

I hopped on the treadmill, hit the "Quick Start" button. "You can get lynched up in here." I had to add, "Is that your girlfriend?"

Trent flashed the fish-eye. "Why you wanna play me like that?"

"I'm sorry," I smiled.

"I'll forgive you, if you let me buy you a cup of coffee."

In my mind's eye I said, *"I can't because I'm married."* My suddenly thick tongue would not allow me, struggling to emerge from self-imposed exile for the past twenty-five years, to say that. "Sounds good. Meet you at the front desk in forty-five minutes."

Trent retreated to the familiar territory of the weight room, overflowing with testosterone, where the big boys peacocked unashamedly.

I wanted to turn around to see if Trent was watching my butt bounce to the rhythm of Prince. But I was too scared.

The first slip was a misstep. A second slip, and I would be labeled a hopeless klutz. I pounded the treadmill like it was 1999 and I was twenty-five again. Heat rose from the center of my body and went straight to my head, literally. I glimpsed myself in the floor to ceiling mirror. My press and curl swelled like shaving foam.

I remembered the Davis boys, high yellow (except for Trent, the youngest and the darkest of the brood), wavy hair, testosterone pumping in their veins. Every mama's nightmare.

More than their distinctive look, I remembered the Davis clan as some bad actors. Hoodlums, thugs, hyper-sexed neighborhood terrorists, magnets to the girls. "Dem damn Davis boys", as the neighbors called them, put fear of the fist into anyone who got in their way. If you fought one Davis, you fought the whole tribe.

Trent's mama, Cecilia Davis, was "Ma Barker", back in the day. Cecilia would "cuss" you out at the drop of a hat. Cecilia carried a hunting knife in her stockings at all times. She knew her way around a razor blade. Peace loving people in the Crest cheered when Cecilia moved her clan to Lofas, another predominantly Black Vallejo enclave.

There was always a crowd loitering outside the Davis house. They made the cops' job easy. Nine times out of ten, any fight, stabbing or the occasional shooting jumped off at the Davis crib.

Forty-five minutes on the treadmill reduced me to a hot mess. My snug t-shirt looked like a bucket of Gatorade had been poured over my head. I hit the cool down button on the machine and foolishly glanced in the mirror again. Without a scarf or towel large enough to take a shower I was stuck, a scarecrow's twin.

I'm sweaty, nervous as a coyote. I don't know this man. What was I thinking?

I contemplated ducking between metal rails and sneak-ing out. Too slow. Fine as a Mo Fo and barely breaking a sweat Trent leaned against the front desk. He looked per-fect. He had thrown on a warm up jacket that matched his navy blue wide white stripe pants.

"Can I get a rain check? I look like hell," I begged, pulling my hoodie over my head.

"I like a woman not afraid to sweat. We can go to the Starbuck's on Admiral Callaghan. Or, there's a Starbuck's in American Canyon. Let's do American Canyon."

I nodded. "Sure."

"My Jeep is out front."

I hesitated. Too much. What if he's married or has a cra-zy woman like Monique on his tail? "I'll meet you there."

"You know where it is?"

"Yeah. By Safeway."

Trent made me remember how good it feels just talking to a man other than my husband. Who made the rule that married women must cease "conversating" when they put on that ring? I was so out of practice. I did not know what to do with my hands, feeling heavy like shovels pushing wet sand.

In the past, if someone hit on me, I half-smiled, self-consciously snatched away my gaze. A sign hung around my neck, "Not Available". What was I afraid of? Myself? That I might enjoy spending a minute with a gorgeous man sitting across from me? I was enthralled by the way he looked at me, broken down, funky, moving past sad.

We talked for an hour over cold cups of coffee. Trent mentioned "Dem damn Davis boys" before I got the chance. I did the math. He was four years younger than me, en-tered Vallejo High School the year after I graduated. Trent shared a lot, maybe too much about his past. Two years in

California Youth Authority for a string of burglaries committed with his older brothers. "That shit taught me, don't go back there. I got out, got my GED, tried out for the Raiders. Got cut in training camp. I started doing drugs. Mama sent me to Oklahoma to stay with my grandparents. Best thing that could've happened. It was boring as hell. So slow, church seemed exciting. I hooked up with a church girl, got married and divorced within two years. Came back to Cali, got my AA from Fairfield Community College, B.S. from Cal State Hayward. I'm working on my Masters in kinesiology. I want to be a physical therapist. At the rate I'm going, I'll be too old to lift the patients."

I laughed. "How much longer do you have?"

"I'm a couple of units shy of getting my degree."

"So what's holding you back?"

"I'm pretty busy, counseling at Boys and Girls Club, working security, personal training...." Trent paused, took a breath. "I really have no excuse. Just need to do it."

"You're a success story."

"I can tell you're doing well?"

"How?"

"That rock on your finger." His eyes lingered on the blinding, S-quality, marble sized diamond, circled by a band of smaller diamonds. "Someone loves you... a lot."

"What if it's fake?"

"The love or the ring?" he asked.

"The ring."

"You're talking to an expert, remember?"

My laughter boomed out. I had opened up to a virtual stranger for no discernible reason. "Tell me about your security work."

"I work special events, mostly concerts---rappers, Ledisi, Laila Hathaway, anybody who needs beefed up security. I've gone on tour a couple of times. The lifestyle doesn't suit me. I don't drink, smoke or do dope. My only addiction is working out. I've confessed my sins, now tell me about Aubrey."

"Well. I have a degree in mass communications from Cal, and a Masters in journalism from Wayne State in Detroit. I spent a lot of time raising my son. I'm the business manager at my husband's church in Orange County." I listened to me, spouting a litany of jobs that failed to capture the essence of Aubrey. Maybe I did not have an essence. "I'm writing. I'm a writer. I know it sounds stupid at my age. You think it's too late?"

"Judging by the way you attacked that treadmill, definitely not. While you're here, maybe we could work out together."

I took a slow sip of cold coffee, buying time. "I never had a personal trainer. What's your hourly rate?"

"Did I ask for money?" Trent responded.

"No," I answered slowly, while asking myself, "*What do you want*?"

19

AINT' NO SENSE IN GOIN' HOME

SISTERS IN SILENCE.COM
MARCH 6

Did anybody see Wattstax? Wattstax is a seventies documentary filmed during a concert featuring some of the best talent in the country. Isaac Hayes, the Staple Singers, Rufus Thomas, Kim Weston singing Lift Every Voice and Sing and on and on. It was amazing seeing the young Jesse Jackson when his rhymes were still fresh. Of all the great performers on the show, my favorite was Johnny Taylor jammin' "Jodie's Got Your Girl And Gone". The song is about a woman who is creepin' while her man is out creepin' with another woman. Another popular song that came out during the same era was "Whose Making Love To Your Old Lady While You Were Out Making Love?"

In no way am I suggesting that emotionally abused women should take revenge in the form of an affair. I'm just laying out the options and helping you assess the risks. You run the same risk that HH runs when he is setting the world on fire. Fire burns. Just in case you get tired of babysitting or watching American

Idol while your dog is on the run, please review the Rules of Etiquette for Outside Woman. These rules apply to you as well.

Let me suggest something. Married men are not that much fun. Try something new and fresh. Single men have more time to dedicate to the deed (you know what I'm talking about) and to their bodies. Why creep with someone whose muffin top is bigger than yours?

The most important thing is that you keep perspective on what this is about. Remember the mess your husband made when he went buck wild? Do not repeat his mistakes. Do not search for a man to marry. You made that mistake already. I caution you the same way that I cautioned OW: Do not assume you are the only one that your boy toy is messing with. Proceed with extreme caution. There was a time when an affair could be conducted cavalierly. But with all the social diseases and disorders out there, you must prepare for a date in the way you prepare for war. Carry heavy armor.

Men love making love to married women for the following reasons.

***Number 1.** Married women have their priorities straight. Their purpose is clear---to have fun and go home. The sane ones do not get confused like HH about the mission. The last thing on a married woman's mind is having babies. That takes all the fun out of it. Married women operate under no illusion that a single man will drop everything he is doing to run away with her. Occasionally it happens, but this is not the norm.*

***Number 2.** Married women have an excess of pent up passion. In an affair they want everything they miss at home. Trust me, they are missing a lot.*

***Number 3.** Married women conduct their affairs with*

more grace than married men, who frequently act like school boys hankering to get caught. Remember, they are little boys with big feet. The only drama that a Married Woman seeks is in the bedroom.

Pay attention, SIS. This is usually the way it works. Your HH hooks up with someone who is available inside your circle of friends or at his workplace. I use the word "available" because she does not have to be a hottie, a smoke show, blindingly beautiful or brilliant. She need only be available. The standard is very low for Ho-ing Husbands.

SIS, the Outside Woman may not be someone who commands a lot of attention. She may be a sneaky freak, disguising herself in frumpy clothing, wearing a mask of innocence. Like a calf on its knees she gazes up at HH to make him feel important. This technique is particularly effective with men who stand less than six feet.

Sneaky freak will sit at Wife's feet to learn how real women look and act. OW will sometimes be your so-called best friend or the friend of your best friend. She wolves run in packs. Beware of women hanging around looking like ghouls. They are shallow. You can see right through them. Wife is shocked to find that HH fell into OW's pit so easily.

Outside Woman envies your life. She is desperate to get in it, to substitute herself for you. She will eat your food, drink your wine and devour your sock-it-to-me cake. Sisters In Silence, do not be afraid to warn OW that a half order of penis is not on the menu.

I hear the Carpenter's singing a swelling chorus of "Close To You." Think about this, OW. It is not too late to get out of the closet and out of Wife's life permanently. Unless of course, Junior has already dropped. Then we change the tune to "It's a Family Affair".

20

THOU SHALL NOT BE MOVED

AUBREY

Someone put a padlock on my hips from my lower back to the big toe of my right foot. From mid-back to lower scapula pain radiated, threading needles up and down my spine. At four a.m. Winston trolled the kitchen. I ignored him. Unless he sets off the fire alarm, I vowed, I shall not be moved. I inhaled deeply. A surgically aimed pain missile launched through my body. I felt old, ancient.

From my twin bed in the arctic add-on I pleaded with Winston, "Daddy please go back to bed. It's not morning yet."

Winston perched in the doorway, scrutinizing the stranger sleeping in the room he built with his own hands. "Hunh?"

"Turn off the lights and go to bed. It's four a.m."

Winston backed away from the door, scraping run down dress shoes over kitchen linoleum. Coarse sand paper grating cement.

My crusted eyes unsealed. Winston was fully dressed---hat

with ear muffs, dress coat and pee stained slacks over long johns. The sound of crinkling came next.

"Daddy, what are you doing?"

"Hunh?"

My volume intensified. *"What're you doing?"*

"What y'all got to eat in here?"

I groaned, rolled onto my left side, pushed myself up by the knuckles. Everything hurt. I ambled to the kitchen to see what was up. Winston was planted in front of the open refrigerator, gnawing on a hard French roll. He pulled the roll in and out of a foil bag each time he took a bite.

I gently led him by the arm to the table and sat him down. I retrieved a paper plate and lunch meat for his bread. That oughta hold him, I thought.

Two hours later the ritual repeated itself. Pearl did not budge from her bed. I knew Pearl heard everything that transpired in her house. Pearl was down for the count. Off duty. Virtually dead.

My eyes took two minutes to adjust. I mumbled in delirium, forced my feet to the floor and escorted my father back to bed. The bed was wet. He was wet. With zero cooperation I managed to change him and the bed. I made a mental note to speak to the doctor about a nighttime Ativan or Seroquel hit for Winston. Maybe one for my mother as well. How she coped with this shit, I could not imagine.

At seven a.m. Winston was on the prowl again, ready for his oatmeal. I had to laugh to keep from screaming. *This cannot be real.*

In my mother's bedroom a growl emitted from Pearl's chest each time she exhaled. Pearl's inhalations sang like a phlegm filled whistle.

Winston greeted me with childlike joviality. He did not

care who joined him in the kitchen as long as somebody rattled the pots and pans. I pulled out the sauce pan, singed to a crisp from repeatedly burned oatmeal. *If it's oatmeal you want, it's oatmeal you'll get.*

Winston's new found happiness contrasted starkly with his former cynical personality. My parents argued so often that I wondered for years, "Why did they get married?" But in his Alzheimer's addled mind, Pearl could do no wrong. She was his honey, the center of his life. She was the only person Winston called by name in his world that had shrunk to a pebble. Everyone and everything, except for Pearl and the bungalow they lived in, existed on the fringe. It was a cruel joke. My parents rarely expressed love for each other until Winston's mind bent under the limbo pole.

I drifted into my father's cataract shrouded eyes. His old self was somewhere in there. On lock down, no entry, no exit.

Winston was fed, filled up with meds and taken back to bed for a snooze. By then I was too geeked to sleep, without an excuse to ditch the gym as I had groggily plotted an hour earlier.

⸺ ⸨◉⸩ ⸺

Aubrey

I threw down my gym bag at the door of 24 Hour Fitness. "My ass is too tired and too sore to work out," I blabbered before saying good morning to Trent.

Trent scooped up the bag, opened the door and ushered me in. "No problem. We'll work around your ass."

This man is sick, I thought as he prodded me to the weight room.

Trent led me through a warm up. Neck and shoulder rolls, back and chest stretches, arm circles, torso stretches, alternating punches. We even did a little yoga. Then the nice guy from the day before turned into a drill master.

"Pick out your weights." Trent ordered.

I claimed the cute, five pound weights that fit easily in my hands. Without asking, he added ten pounds to each side of the bar.

"I don't want to bulk up," I whined.

"If you're gonna work out, might as well see results."

Forward bends, rows, clean and press, overhead press, then the dreaded lunges.

"I thought we were working around my ass."

"We are. Everything 'round yo' ass gon' be tight."

I did so many squats my ass quivered.

"Don't let your knees go over your toes. Hold up your chest," Trent instructed.

An hour later, my spaghetti arms were too tired to sock him.

My back was pressed against the weight bench. Above me a short man with a bald head, wearing a muscle shirt and shorts half way up his thighs, loomed.

"Hey Erroll. I'll be right with you," Trent said. Trent looked down at the shriveled version of me. "My eight thirty is here. That's a wrap for today."

The bar tilted uncontrollably to the right. I wanted to holler "timber". Trent mercifully lifted the bar from my hands. I took four deep breaths, rolled from the left side of the bench, wobbled toward the weight rack to steady myself.

"Grab a mat." Trent pointed me toward the cardio room. "Stretch for at least fifteen minutes. I'll check on you after I get Erroll started."

By evening my upper body joined my lower body in emitting distress signals. I felt pain in muscles I did not know I had. I collapsed on my parent's couch, clutching my new best friend---Ibupropen. Periodically I iced my knees, lower back and traps. I crawled to the bathroom, soaked so long that my skin blanched and turned into a prune. I was the survivor of a street fight, a fight that I lost.

The memory of Trent spotting me from behind, hairs on my arms rising in anticipation of his touch, lifted the pain.

I remembered how on the final set of bicep curls, my arms trembled like a scared puppy. Trent edged closer, braced my forearms with his. "I got you," he assured me. His breath cooled the back of my neck.

His arms brushed mine as he stepped in front. "Who said you couldn't do this?" Basketball size hands grazed mine as he took the weight.

I was oblivious to the prying eyes scrutinizing our every move. On the surface our dance was an innocent ballet, a fairy tale. On a deeper level, chemistry was stronger than perfume in a closed elevator. Everybody caught a whiff.

AUBREY

Trent designed a fitness routine personally tailored to me. The exercises alternated between cardio, strength training, kickboxing, stretching and toning. Anything to keep me constantly guessing, what is next. With fewer threats of mutiny from my body my confidence rose along with gnawing suspicion. What did he want? What did I want other than to see him every day?

"On the side kick, I want you to extend, rather than cave in." Trent's hand rested on my right hip. "From your head to the heel of your flexed foot is a straight line. It's not how high you kick, but how much power you generate."

I assumed a fighting stance, fisted left hand protecting my face, right fist loaded for the imaginary attacker coming at me. I whipped my right foot out at hip level. A crisp "whoosh" sliced the air.

"That's what um talkin' 'bout," Trent applauded, beaming. He squeezed my traps, almost allowed me to relax. "Now do it again," he commanded, stealing my momentary joy.

Three weeks into it I was reaping results from my personal boot camp. Muscles toned, booty lifted and I had more energy than before. There was calmness in encounters with my father. Either he had chilled out or I had. After days of uninterrupted deep snoozing Mama finally caught up on her rest. I knew this peaceful interlude would not last. My return to Orange County was imminent.

I met Trent on the Waterfront, minutes away from our first home in Vallejo. On the way to meet Trent I detoured to Alabama Street, drove down the crackled, poor man's flagstone alley where we used to live. It was hard to believe that people still lived there. Frayed plastic flying from fragile windows told me that they did.

The day was gray, drizzly, the sky a moving blanket of clouds. The Carquinez Straits, green and choppy, ruffled in a cold, easterly wind.

Trent's usual warm-up chatter about the kids at th

Boys and Girls Club, or last night's interesting security guard assignment, was gone. Beneath Ray Ban sunglasses, sweating heavy mist, his eyes sang a somber melody at midnight heard by one.

We hit the trail walking slower than normal. "When are you leaving?" was his first full sentence. The question, the perennial ghost in the air, loomed menacingly.

"Day after tomorrow." I shuddered. "Brrr. I should have worn Daddy's long johns." My joke fell flat.

"Take my sweat shirt," Trent offered.

"You'll freeze. This will warm me up." I took off sprinting. Fifty yards out, I turned around. Trent lolled behind, moving at a languid pace. His feet carried the weight of cement. I jogged back to him.

He stripped sunglasses from sad eyes. "What are we doing?"

"Working out." I bounced on my toes, boxer style.

Frustration fueled anger flashed in his eyes. The vein between his eyebrows throbbed. "You know exactly what I mean. We've been together every day for three weeks."

I stood flat footed and confessed, "I don't know what I'm doing."

"I didn't think so." Trent pivoted on the heels of pristine New Balance running shoes, flipped his hood over his head and walked briskly toward the parking lot.

I ran after him. "Trent, wait." I grabbed his arm. He paused. "Look, I didn't mean to...," I stammered, searching for the right words.

"Toy with a hood rat? Toss me out with the garbage? I know I'm not in your league..." He inhaled deeply, took his time letting air out. "Don't play with me."

Trent jumped into his Kelley green Jeep Cherokee, slammed the door and roared from the parking lot.

In mist turned to rain, I stood alone muttering, "What kinda shit is this?"

——⟫⟪⟫⟪——

Aubrey

"Bree, you miss me yet?" Phillip's phone call was an unwelcome intrusion.

On my end, there was stone silence.

"Guess I got my answer. I was calling to confirm your arrival time tomorrow."

"I sent you a text. Didn't you get it?"

"Let me check...Oh, there it is. Southwest, arriving 7:05 p.m., John Wayne Airport."

"Why're you trippin' on my arrival time? I drove my own car."

"Just excited to have you home. Look baby, I want you to know that everything is going to be all right. Donovan and I..."

The mention of Donovan's name sent me reeling. "You didn't let that devil in my house?"

"Of course not," Phillip answered. "He won't be a problem...We'll talk when you get home."

I ended the call abruptly, resumed packing feverishly. Should the shoes go in the suitcase or the carry-on? Soggy workout clothes. Should I wash them or wait until I get home. Wait. I've got enough to do to finish my parent's laundry. Don't want Mama to bless me out again for using too much water.

I thought about the discomfiting comfort of Orange County. The alternative was witnessing my father's daily disintegration, my mother's refusal to hire help, not to mention Mama's razor sharp tongue.

If I stayed, I would run to Trent's "not forever" arms. He would be a mistake, one that I was thirsty to make. My safe and sane world in the O.C. teetered on an earthquake fault. I could not stay in this masquerade of a marriage, thinking, analyzing my next move.

My soul cried out, "Just let me live." I needed to feel good, free of pressure from men. Phillip would swear that my sudden zest for independence was all about him. At first glance, it was. But it was far deeper than that. Phillip's adultery was my ticket to freedom, the wind beneath a billowing skirt. I was ready to show my ass for real, rejuvenated enough to wish Phillip, his hoochie mama and their offspring "good riddance".

That night I wrote the chapter I had wrestled with all week.

21

TENDERNESS

SISTERS IN SILENCE.COM
MARCH 17

I f your wife gets sick of your philandering and decides to try a little tenderness, be as gracious, HH, as she was while you were running the streets. Volunteer to babysit when wife hooks up her garter belt to go out with the girls. Do not make a scene, if she comes home at three a.m. reeking of cologne that does not smell like yours. If she says she is working late, accept her excuse rather than phoning her boss. Cryptic messages on her cell phone should not flip you out. When old girl starts dressing younger and has a bounce to her step, attribute the change to that new yoga class. No worries that the yoga instructor is a young man who specializes in downward facing dog. Keep a stiff upper lip when what goes around comes thundering around.

I anticipate a spate of complaints from men who truly believe that it is okay for them to mess around, but feel that ho-ing wives are despicable. My word. What will happen to the institution of marriage? The same thing that *happens when Ho-ing Husband cross pollinates the family tree. People get pissed, divorced, emotionally and some-times physically wounded. If a married woman gets preg-nant by an outside man, will husband forgive her and accept Outside Baby into the fold? Only in the Bible. And you ain't Mary, Mother of Jesus.*

———»«()»«———

Three hours before my scheduled departure from Oakland Airport my bags were packed and loaded into the trunk of the tomato red Ford Focus. I allowed extra time to return the Focus to Payless Rental Car, and board a shuttle to the terminal. If I timed it right, I could grab a burrito in the terminal and a glass of wine before departure. Trent's low carb diet and wine less workout regimen would be sab-otaged for this flight.

I liked what I saw in the mirror. More tone to my back, thighs and rear end. If I kept up the workouts Trent initiated, I could visualize long term results. More than anything, it felt good to feel good about myself. *I'll get back on target soon as I land in the O.C.*

A final foray through the house, I checked each room, closet and peeked beneath the beds. Winston had taken to stashing clothes and shoes-his, Pearl's and the stranger's visiting his house-in odd places.

Mama sat in an overstuffed armchair, blinking back tears. Her traditional, strong body looked fragile, ready to sink with the slightest puff of wind.

"I wish you could stay another day. Your Daddy enjoys having you here."

I leaned over and hugged my mother. "I'll be back in a

couple of weeks." I kissed her furrowed forehead. "I love you, Mama."

"I love you too."

Oblivious to my imminent departure Daddy lounged in a rattan chair with unraveling weave. The chair was parked next to the heater, jacked up to ninety degrees. It was a battle I could not win. Hopefully, the handy man would show up next week as promised to put a stopper on the thermostat.

I kissed his cheek. "Love you, Daddy."

With a vacant smile, Daddy answered, "Hunh?"

I smiled back at him. A sudden knock rattled the screen door.

"Who's there?" Pearl's caustic voice rang out.

I glided to the door.

Pearl warned, "Don't open it 'til you look out."

"It's still light outside, Mama," I reminded her.

"You don't know these people," Pearl reminded me, who moved away more than twenty years ago, making me an outsider.

I pushed back vinyl blinds and peeked out.

Trent's eyes were downcast to the Target welcome mat on the front porch.

I unlocked the door, unhooked the heavy metal security screen. "Hey. I didn't expect to see you."

"I came to say goodbye."

"Perfect timing. I'm on my way out."

"Who is it?" Pearl bogarted past me.

"Trent Davis, ma'am. You probably don't remember me."

Pearl answered, "Of course I do. You're one of them..."

Trent finished her sentence, "Davis boys. I used to hang out at Sister Gray's house up the street."

"That woman had a buncha kids," Mama said.

Trent laughed. "So did we."

Pearl assessed Trent from head to toe. "You grew up real nicely. Come on in." Pearl pushed open the screen.

I interrupted, "We don't have time." I knew Pearl would put Trent through the third degree. "Trent can walk me to the car. Love you, Mama." I kissed my mother again.

"Trent, you come back to see us, anytime."

"Yes, ma'am. I'll do that. Good seeing you."

Trent followed me to the sidewalk and cleared his throat. "I want to apologize for how I acted the other day. I was out of line."

"No, I should apologize. If I misled you, I'm sorry. I got caught up enjoying your company. I'll miss you."

"Me too. When are you coming back?"

"In a couple of weeks. I've got issues at home."

He nodded. "I hear you." Trent looked over his shoulder toward the house. "Your mother's hawking us."

I could feel Mama's eyes on me, but I refused to look.

Trent continued. "Don't worry about your parents. I've got their back."

"Thank you." I touched his hand. Heat rushed to the core of my being.

"What time did you say your plane leaves?" he asked, circling his thumb in the palm of my hand.

I eased my hand away, hugged him loosely and whispered, "Don't make it hard."

He whispered back, "You already did."

Aubrey

The toe of my Giuseppe Zanotti flats tapped a hole in concrete. The shuttle bus to Main St. parking, Lot C, took forever to arrive. From the second the plane touched down I was antsy to get on with it---tell my husband of twenty-five years, "Hit the road."

A group of baggage handlers hawked as I sailed past them in painted-on Helmut Lang jeans. My calves popped with each step. From the far end of the terminal my main baggage handler, Maurice, shouted out, "Hey pretty lady. Why didn't you text me, like you always do?"

I threw up one hand, hollered back, "I was in a rush. Brain dead. Catch you next time."

Maurice was unrelenting. He jogged twenty-five feet to the shuttle stop where I stood. "I like your new look." Maurice scrutinized my new hairdo, washed and wet set on rods. My intense workout routine was unkind to pressed hair, so I gave it up.

"You look fresh, like a new woman," Maurice complimented.

"I needed something different."

"Don't rush too much. Drive carefully."

"I will. Thanks."

Several feet away, Maurice turned and looked back at me as I boarded the shuttle. I felt guilty about the big tip he just missed. Next time, I would make it up to him.

I was in a rush, like never before. A first edition Johnny Mathis vinyl LP was stuffed in the outside pocket of my carry-on.

Pearl was so in love with Johnny Mathis she thought about naming me Johnnie, but Johnnie seemed too mas-culine for the doe eyed princess that God gifted Pearl after two miscarriages. When Pearl heard the song, "Aubrey Was

Her Name," my name was decided. I loved to listen as Pearl described me as the baby girl with curls the color of persimmon and lashes that curled up like a doll's. She said I was hyper alert for a newborn. My eyes followed every movement in the room.

An astute nurse observed, "This baby's been here before."

"Yes, twice", Pearl agreed, remembering two miscarriages. "This time she's gonna stay."

The night before my departure from Vallejo Pearl gingerly handed me an LP titled "Killing Me Softly with Her Song". A stunning profile of Johnny Mathis filled the cover. I nodded, received the LP like the family crest.

As a toddler I remembered Pearl squatting to my eye level, kissing my peachy cheek to introduce the song. "Little girl, this is our special song."

I remembered the LP playing over and over. The crackle and hiss of vinyl enchanting my ears. Our cramped apartment kitchen, infused with the scent of red beans and cake like cornbread, transformed into a magical ballroom. Enraptured by Johnny's airy tunes, Pearl twirled and embraced the air with flowing movements extending through her fingertips.

Pearl waltzed the linoleum floor with soulful inflections. Her movements were subtle, controlled and deliberate. I was spellbound, in a swoon. "Mama, you dance good," I exuded.

Pearl smiled to the soles of her feet. She bowed low, filed my compliment in the drawer of deferred dreams.

The transition was abrupt. Pearl and Winston got "saved" at a tiny Apostolic church in Vallejo. Johnny Mathis was tucked away in a trove of secular treasures. The "devil's music" was relegated to the bottom of a dusty closet, entombing the lightness of Pearl's joy.

The vinyl grooves were worn to mush. Scratches etched deeper than the hurt Pearl hid inside. Mama placed her music in my hands, brought her story into the light.

Prayers for peace and calm recited on the plane downloaded into the garbage bin. My stomach churned and muscles were tight. But my resolve was strong. I would not be persuaded by Phillip's lies. He had to leave, give me time to figure out my next move. My lawyer's warning replayed in my head, "It might be dicey getting Phillip to leave the house voluntarily." He ain't never lied. Phillip was hard-headed, extremely territorial and dependent on me to keep his life in order.

Phillip often beamed to the congregation, "My wife is the wind beneath my wings." Truth be told, I was the mule beneath his stubborn ass. I was sick of carrying him.

My conflicted mind circled back to Miles. What would he think, if his parents split after twenty-five years of marriage? All of Phillip's preaching about the importance of keeping family intact came down to this. I could not use Miles as an excuse. He was a grown man, old enough to handle a storm in his otherwise orderly life.

The shuttle lumbered to a screeching halt. The driver hoisted my bags from the luggage rack. My suddenly weary legs descended shuttle stairs. I passed a tip to the driver, stacked my bags and moved forward. I struggled to remember where I had parked. Facing future, my energy dwindled into a frozen mass.

A blue and orange Southwest Airlines 737 toddled into the sky. I wished I was on that plane, going anywhere but here.

⮞◉⮜

AUBREY

The house seemed distant like a leering stranger. The sandstone stucco paled to ashy gray beneath a blue black sky. No light shined from inside to welcome me home. Phillip had forgotten to turn on the porch light.

If he's in there sulking and drinking in the dark, I will turn around and leave.

My thumb pressed the garage door opener mounted on the sun visor. Nothing. He probably tried to fix something and blew out all the lights, I thought.

I put the Rover in park. Killed the engine. Maybe Phillip went out. Called a last minute church meeting. The story of our lives.

My pace quickened. I needed to get this over with, go on with my life. It would be just like Phillip to interrupt my flow, cause my courage to seep out.

I fished for the door key hiding in my bag. I felt the airline itinerary, bottled water, Extra peppermint gum. The motion sensor lights, lanterns standing watch near the front door, were off duty tonight.

"Why didn't I find my keys before I got out," I mumbled. I could not remember the last time I entered the house through the front door. In virtual darkness all the keys felt alike. The front door key is oddly shaped, I recalled, closing my eyes and feeling the smooth edge of a key in the shape of a yield sign. I burrowed into the hole like a boy virgin on his first time at bat. I jabbed and stabbed rigid resistance. Mercifully, the key sank in. I turned the key to the right, pressed the lever on the door handle and pushed. I stepped onto the runner padding the vestibule. A warm, sickly sweet odor assaulted my nostrils. The house smelled as if it had been closed since I left. I was anxious to open some windows, but first I had to find light.

I flipped the light switch to no avail. The power was

really out. I inched further into the vestibule, calling out, "Phillip, I'm home." No answer. The antique chinoserie writing desk was a convenient place to rest my bag. Withered leaves from a floral arrangement from three weeks earlier fell to the floor. "He can't even throw out dead flowers," I complained, as leaves crunched beneath my feet. I headed to the kitchen where candles were stored.

My fingertips traced the wall, glided over smooth Honduran mahogany cabinets. I took two steps beyond the wine cooler, pulled the handle of the retractable drawer and reached inside. The Tupperware container filled with candles and matches was missing. The smooth, empty melamine interior felt cold.

"What kinda shit is this?" I cursed unrelenting darkness. "Why would he take candles out of the drawer?"

I inched my way to the family room. I knew the layout of every rug, table and chair, unless Phillip rearranged the furniture after rearranging the drawers.

Blindly, I threaded the wide, extended hallway, culminating in an etched mirror and custom cabinets. Half way there my eyes adjusted to darkness. It suddenly dawned on me. My iPhone had a flashlight. Why hadn't I used it?

No point now. At the end of the hallway I saw a faint glimmer. Shadows danced in the mirror. I jumped, startled by my own reflection.

An amber glow filled the master bedroom doorway. I sucked in my breath. *I know he's not trying to get romantic.*

I turned a hard left. The bed was perfectly made with fluffy throw pillows in place. Phillip was not in the bed. I tiptoed inside. On the floor white Air Jordan's extended beyond the foot of the bed. Two steps closer. Phillip, with his arms folded across his chest, lay corpse still. A halo of burning candles surrounded his head.

I dropped to my knees, grabbed his shoulders and shook hard. Gooey slime greeted my touch. *"What the fuck?"* My scream echoed through the canyon, hands hit the floor, skidding in liquid velvet. Phillip's head floated on a pillow of blood.

22

FALLING IN LOVE WITH JESUS

AUBREY

The waiting room at Kaiser Permanente Hospital on La Palma, looked like the finale of a five day revival. Every seat was filled, every wall provided a back rest for those too antsy to sit down. Phillip's congregants hugged each other, fearing the worst, while holding loosely to their faith.

"Don't fall in love with the preacher. Fall in love with God," Phillip had warned them often. From his first day in the pulpit of Trinity Baptist Church that advice was ignored. They adored their scrappy pastor who spoke truth to power and strutted like he was ten feet tall.

Phillip's devoted followers were his own press corps, saying things like. "Pastor Phillip brings gospel thunder. He has a direct pipeline to the Lord." "Phillip Sampson is more than a gifted orator and teacher grounded in the Word. He can "hoop" in the old school mode when the Holy Spirit moves him." "He has papers, a Masters in Theology. He reads every theological text he gets his hands on."

Pastor Phillip's followers were not ready to let him go. When I asked for prayer, news spread through the tight knit church community like eczema, tying up phone lines, blowing up e-mails and texts. Phillip's face instantly appeared on hundreds of Facebook pages and Twitter feeds.

The false rumor quickly spread: The man sent by God is dead. At my urging Associate Minister, Ulysses Burns, calmest among the nervous associate ministers tripping over themselves, took charge and posted on my behalf. "Our spiritual leader is in emergency surgery. The outcome is beyond control of mortal man. And so we do what Christians do when faced with adversity. We take it to God."

In the emergency room lobby Minister Burns bowed his head. "We call upon you Almighty Father to be in this place, in the operating room, guiding the hands of the doctors, the nurses and everyone who comes in contact with our beloved Pastor. We need you right now, in the name of Jesus, to be with us in this dreadful moment that we, as a body of believers, must endure with abiding faith. Touch him Father. Heal him Father. Restore him to us so that he can continue to do the work that you have ordained." Burns petitioned.

Evangelist Hattie Lewis chanted, "Heal him, Deliver him, Heal him, Deliver him... Please Sir, have mercy."

From the opposite end of the waiting room, an ear splitting yelp erupted. Minister John Bogan, blushing the color of mercury, vied for center stage. He spoke in tongue, "Bala she, shana ne molo gume, dete mareh, me lo shi ma", followed by a string of nasally high pitched gurgles.

The startled receptionist bristled in her seat. She complained loudly to an amused Latino orderly, "That's way too much. What's the White guy doing?" She nodded toward John Bogan. Never in the hospital's history had this number of people assembled in a waiting room. "Too much." The receptionist hit the security alarm.

The crowd swayed en mass, answering call and response led by Bogan. "Deliverance, Lord Jesus. Protection, Our Savior."

Head usher from the church, Rebecca Johnson, glimpsed "rent-a-cop" rushing down the hallway. "May I have your attention? We all love Pastor Sampson, but we need to respect other patients and their families in the hospital. Let's take our vigil outside." Low slung and wide in stature, Rebecca politely snatched the startled Bogan from his perch atop a waiting room chair and pushed him outdoors to lead the exiled masses.

The receptionist, a retired senior citizen volunteer, nodded her appreciation to Rebecca with a wan smile. Rent a cop wiped sweat from his relieved brow. The last thing he wanted to do was evict a sad, anxious group of African Americans from the hospital.

John Bogan did not miss a beat. Minister Bogan clutched the frayed brown Bible beneath the arm of his Adidas track suit while raising his right hand to Heaven. "Pray without ceasing saints. Pray as if life depends on it. Because it does. Pray, brothers and sisters, pray."

"God has spoken to your prophet and servant. The Words he gave me were 'God's Will'. No matter what the circumstance. No matter what the doctor's say, it's His will that must be done. Hallelujah!" The minister's fervent prayer rose to a crescendo. Bogan's ruddy cheeks fluttered, his body spasmed as if struck by a bolt of spiritual lightning. Bogan planted the Bible to his chest, hugged himself into a Holy a Ghost pretzel and bounced on his own axis.

It was a balmy night. Temperatures hovered in the low seventies. A crescent moon hung beneath a single star in the sky. On the eastbound 91, a stream of red tail lights slogged late into Friday night.

A sudden gust of wind lifted the plume of Bogan's immaculate hair. "I rebuke you, Satan!" Bogan shouted, evoking images of Charlton Heston parting the red sea. A ribbon of electric light emitted from Bogan's fingertips toward the freeway.

A chorus of "OOOW AAAH" seeped from the mesmerized crowd. The Southern Baptist minister had frequently regaled them with his fire and brimstone bluster. But never before had they seen Bogan's display of magical power like tonight.

"When the storm of life is raging, I'm gonna pur-raise Him," Bogan screeched.

"If He strips all my earthly possessions, I'm gonna pur-raise Him."

"If He calls me home tonight, I'm gonna pur-raise Him." The crowd chimed in on the chorus.

"If He knocks me to my knees," Bogan led the call.

The crowd responded. "I'm gonna praise Him."

Bogan twirled three hundred and sixty degrees. In a cold sweat, Bogan Holy danced into the parking lot.

Inside the waiting room I swooned under the spell of the distant chant. Hilton summoned Associate Minister Burns. "Help me take her outside. She needs some air." Hilton and Burns hooked arms with me and escorted me to the hospital's interior courtyard. Away from the geeked up crowd, at a vacant table we sat down.

"I'll take it from here," Hilton told Burns.

"I'll be back with water and food," Burns offered. The women of the church had shown up with boxes of fried chicken and bags of refreshments from Von's and Ralph's.

"That's a good idea. When was the last time you ate Aubrey?" Hilton asked.

I was far from hungry, wrestling with indigestion from the burrito inhaled in the airport lounge. "No food please, just water."

Burns headed inside.

I looked up from the napkin folded into origami, "This is my fault. I wanted him to disappear."

"What are you talking about?" Hilton puzzled.

"I was going to ask Phillip to move out."

"You didn't say that to the cops?"

I did not know what I had said; did not remember calling 911 or opening the door for paramedics. The minutes between discovering Phillip on the floor and the ambulance arriving were a blur. Washing my hands. I remembered washing my hands while my husband lay on the floor dying.

"Don't go there. There's a deranged person out there who tried to kill your husband. This is not your fault," Hilton reassured me.

"What's wrong with me? I can't pray. I can't even cry."

"You're in shock. Traumatized. You need something to relax."

"I have to stay awake until Phillip is out of danger...Did anyone call Miles?"

"Miles is on his way. Don't you remember? You talked to him."

"I forgot."

Burns returned with two bottles of Arrowhead and a basket of food, just in case. Burns exited quickly to attend to the flock.

Hilton opened my hand and dropped a tiny yellow pill inside. "Ativan. It'll take the edge off."

I popped the pill and took a long, slow glug of water.

An hour later Hilton ushered me into the somber waiting room. The previous carnival atmosphere had taken on the tone of a wake. The crowd of fifty or more had dwindled to a skeleton crew of ten. Time was not on our side, but time was the sustainer of hope.

I slumped onto a well worn couch, closed my eyes and surrendered to Ativan's seduction.

A doctor, draped in green scrubs marched down the hall. Paper surgical booties rustled as they approached. I stirred, suddenly alert. I hunched Hilton, who had also taken a little something for his nerves. A whimper of despair escaped from his throat.

I stared into the non-committal face of the doctor. Bracing for bad news, I clutched Hilton's hand.

"Mrs. Sampson."

"Yes."

"I'm Dr. Sugarman. Your husband is out of surgery. He's in recovery."

I sighed in relief. "Oh Thank God."

"He's a long way from being out of the woods. The bullet penetrated the right side of his brain. Amazingly, it did not hit major arteries or veins. But it did a lot of damage. In cases of firearm related traumatic brain injury there is less than ten percent survival rate. We don't know how functional he'll be…if he survives… Don't get your hopes up."

"You've done what you can, doctor. And I thank you." I took the doctor's right hand into both of mine. Surprised by my intimacy, Dr. Sugarman's head pulled back. "The rest is in God's territory."

My voice crackled as I spoke. "God used your hands to answer our prayers. Thank you, Doctor, and your staff. You gave my husband a chance."

He patted me tepidly on the back, a gesture outside the realm of his austere surgeon's repertoire.

"Get some rest, Mrs. Sampson. Your husband has a long,

hard night ahead of him. Have them page me, if you have any problems." Dr. Sugarman turned and walked through the listing crowd, waiting anxiously to hear the verdict. The onlookers stepped back, allowing Dr. Sugarman to pass. He was a hero, at least for now.

A liter of pent up fear and tension drained out of me. I stepped inside the circle of the remaining church members. "The doctor and his staff did an awesome job. Phillip is in recovery."

Praise went up to Heaven. A deaconness exclaimed, "Hallelujah, thank you Jesus!"

In an isolated corner of the room Minister Burns lifted both hands to heaven. His purple lips trembled, talking to the Lord.

I brought them back in focus. "We thank the Lord for this victory. We are not yet in the Promised Land. The coming hours are critical. So what I'm asking you to do is to pray. I've asked Minister Burns to organize us into prayer groups. At all times someone will be praying for Pastor Phillip during the next twenty-four hours."

"I've got it covered, Sister Sampson. Whatever you need," Burns chimed in.

"I can't thank you enough for standing with me," my voice quivered, tears finally fell. I cleared my throat and willed strength into shaky legs. "Everyone, except those in the first prayer group should go home. Get some rest. We've got a long road ahead."

Glass doors to the emergency entrance slid open. Eyes wild, duffle bag slung over his shoulder, Miles ran into my arms. We held on to each other crying, rocking our blues until the world around us diminished to a footnote.

I wiped tears from my son's eyes. "Your father's in recovery."

"Can I see him," Miles begged.

"The nurse will let us know when we can go in."

"Who did this mom?"

I led Miles to the end of the corridor, away from prying eyes.

"We don't know yet, but I've got my suspicions."

Our eyes met in a knowing glance.

"That son of a bitch!" Miles cried too loud.

I grabbed his arm. "Hold on, son." I glanced back at ear hustling church members. Minister Burns hustled them off to their cars. It was like a wreck on the freeway, everybody putting on brakes to witness the macabre. We were hurting, desperate for answers, too consumed with fear to put on an act of being calm.

Shoulder to shoulder, Miles and I sat, his right arm holding me up, his left hand squeezing my hand. Minister Burns and Deacon Favre took up their posts, alternately praying and pacing.

The lights in the waiting room dimmed to twilight. A purple haze shined through the windows. The waiting room loomed large and lonely. For the moment, this was our home, a way station trapped between midnight and morn.

AUBREY

Nothing could have prepared us for what we saw. Miles' hand turned to ice when we entered Phillip's room.

I gasped. "Lord help us."

Phillip's head was the size of a basketball, perfectly round in circumference and deflated from nose to mouth stuffed with blue and white breathing tubes taped cheek to cheek. His closed eyes bulged like purple plums at the peak of ripeness. His walnut skin could not conceal massive bruising on every inch of his face and neck. His head was shaved, enveloped in a helmet of bandages. Vines of IV lines and monitor leads attached Phillip to machines beeping and keeping time with the erratic rhythm of his life.

I caressed the only part of Phillip that was familiar, his left hand wearing the ring I placed on his finger the day we married. I whispered near his ear swaddled in gauze. "Phillip, it's me. Aubrey. Miles is here."

Tears streaming down his cheeks, Miles inched closer. He placed his hand above my hand.

I spoke louder, "You hear me, Phillip Sampson. Everything will be all right." I wondered if Phillip, in a medically induced coma, heard anything.

I was at a loss for words and so I sang Phillip's favorite Fred Hammond song, "All Things Are Working For Me." My voice, less than stellar in good times, managed to carry the tune. Even if he did not hear me, I knew he felt all the love surrounding him. I kissed Phillip's forehead between his swollen brow and motioned for Miles to pull up a chair. From the front flap of my purse I retrieved a vial of Holy oil, slipped to me by Minister Burns. I saturated my index finger, made the sign of the cross on Phillip's forehead and palms. I chanted, "Please Lord, have mercy," until the drone of the respirator blended with the urgency of my voice.

"Mom, you want to stretch out on the bench?" Miles asked. "There's a blanket and a pillow."

"No. You take it. I'm sitting right here, next to his bed."

Throughout the night a parade of nurses checked

monitors, changed bags of fluid hanging beside Phillip's bed. Each time I lifted my head to ask, "What is that?" Eventually tired eyes outweighed my vigilance. I fell asleep, mouth open, neck crunched to the side.

Daylight seeped beneath the drawn curtain of the hospital window. I jerked awake, my face imprinted with the metal side rails of Phillip's bed.

Cocooned inside a blanket, Miles toughed it out on an unforgiving bench with his knees drawn up.

I slipped into the restroom and returned with a face cloth dampened with warm water. I patted the corners of Phillip's puffed up eyes, oozing yellow fluid. I dabbed crust from his purple lips, then I kissed him lightly to remind him that I was still his wife.

Even in his worst condition, Phillip was a vain man. Tenderly, I wiped each finger and massaged his hands. His left hand, attached to the IV was severely swollen. Fluid appeared to be collecting beneath his skin. I made a mental note to have the nurse check the swelling when she came in.

Miles' gritty yawn turned into a low growl. "Is Dad okay, Mom?"

"He looks better than he did last night," I lied. Phillip looked like a bus ran over him, backed up and took a second shot. Best case scenario, this would be a long, slow ordeal. I tried not to think about it, focusing instead on the fact that Phillip was still alive. "Soon as I see the doctor, we'll get out of here. Some questions I forgot to ask."

"Can we go home?"

"No. It's still a crime scene. Nothing you need to see. We'll go to a hotel. Hilton invited us to stay with him, but Laguna is too far. We need to be close to the hospital."

———— ◈ ————

Three days later Trent's road-kill splattered Jeep Cherokee pulled into my driveway. Returning from a shopping trip to Costco, Miles and I pulled up at the same time as Trent.

It had taken two days to gather the nerve to tell Trent, "I need you." Trent packed an overnight bag and hit the road. Miles was livid, insisting he could take care of me and his dad. I knew better. This was a job for a professional, someone not afraid to pull the trigger, if required. The only violence Miles had encountered was in a supervised karate class when he was ten.

In my phone call to Trent I admitted for the first time, I was afraid. Not just afraid for our physical well being, but determined not to let the bad guys take control of our lives. Police had questioned me twice since the shooting, but seemed to take a leisurely approach to pursuing Donovan, the prime suspect in my mind. The tone of their questions, the sweep of their eyes when my eyes failed to cry, led to my conclusion: The prime suspect is me. I could not deny Phillip's blood saturating my clothing. I was not thinking about how it would look when I fell to the floor to try and save him.

The more I implicated Donovan, the more they questioned my motives as an angry wife. "You were pissed when you learned about your husband's outside child, weren't you Mrs. Sampson."

The squad car doing surveillance around our home, they claimed was for our protection. I did not feel protected, I felt watched. Deputy Sherman Wilson parked boldly across the street at the end of the cul de sac. My son's tension would escalate every time Wilson tipped his finger and nodded his fat head to acknowledge his presence.

"You sure that's the same one Miles?"

"You don't forget a man who has you spread eagle over a police cruiser."

Head to toe, Miles surveyed Trent, leading with, "How do you know my Mom?"

Trent responded with a warm smile and a fist bump. The long road of resistance lay ahead of him.

"We work out at the same gym. In Vallejo. Let me introduce you to Laila and Ali." The hatch back on the Jeep squeaked and squirmed as Trent lifted it. The most regal boxers I had ever seen leaped out. The male was a broad chested brindle with a white mask and white socks on all feet. He had a long neck and cropped ears that stood at attention. Laila, the female boxer was fawn with a sweet face, soft round eyes and a black mask.

"No dogs allowed in the house," Miles asserted.

"Says who?" I countered.

"Says you. Remember. We can't have a dog, Miles. You've got asthma."

"Attempted murder trumps asthma," I answered. "Besides, you've pretty much outgrown your asthma."

Trent stepped in to referee. "During the day the dogs stay outside, keep the perimeter secure. At night, they sleep in the garage. If anything moves within a hundred yards, they'll let me know. "

"What about your gardens, Mom?"

"My dogs are well trained. You won't even know they're here, unless a stranger approaches. Then they go nuts, which is what you want them to do. I'll take the dogs around back. Wait here for a minute."

The second Trent was out of earshot Miles turned on me. "Are you letting this dude tell us where to go and what to do?"

"That's his job Miles."

"And how's he getting paid for his job?" Cynicism twisted Miles' lips.

My eyes rolled to the sky. "I'm the HMIC here."

"Whuuut?"

My index finger accentuated each syllable. "Head Mother In Charge. Don't question me, young man."

Miles snorted, bounded toward the front door. Trent rounded the corner and cut him off. "Hold up a second. Let me check out the house." I opened the garage door, tossed Trent my keys.

Three weeks in Vallejo, three nights in the Ayres Suites, our home felt like a hostile, foreign country. Light bounced off gleaming hardwood floors like ghosts. Behind each shade, every curtain loomed an unknown threat. The air inside felt unusually crisp. I approached the master bedroom with dread. Would there be a chalk outline on the floor?

The bedroom was clean. The floor glowed with no traces of blood. I touched the light switch. Trent followed closely behind, but did not interfere as I walked from room to room, opening closets, checking under beds and peeking out windows.

Finally, Trent asked, "What're you looking for?"

"Evil spirits. Something wicked has been in my house."

"You gonna let wicked win by being afraid?"

"You're right." I hurried to the kitchen and pulled a blue, yellow and white box of Morton salt from the cupboard. I opened the sliding glass doors. Laila and Ali ran up to greet me. They sniffed and vied for affection. Laila was the most aggressive, inserting herself between me and Ali. When it was Ali's turn to be petted he nudged my hand with his short snout whenever I stopped patting his head.

"I see they're spoiled rotten," I told Trent.

"Don't let that fool you. They have a strong protective instinct. Dogs know the good guys from the bad. They like you already."

I picked up the salt box, which I lay down while petting the dogs. I opened the metal spout and shook grains of salt around the foundation of the house. Trent watched in amazement as I went about my task. I rounded the corner of the house, shaking the salt box fervently and praying loudly.

"May I ask what you're doing?" Trent asked.

"Protecting this house from evil."

Trent laughed from his gut. "Oh my God. This is gettin' woo woo."

"You do your thing and I'll do mine. Mama told me what to do when the devil gets busy. I will fight them with every tool I have. With every weapon, man-made or spiritual. The difference between me and them–I come against evil in the name of Jesus."

"I didn't mean to laugh. I just didn't know you were so, ummn, spiritual."

"Lot of things you don't know about me."

My eyes focused on the foundation as I walked, shook salt and called upon the Holy Spirit.

Trent looked at me as if he was seeing me for the first time. We were on another plane, a different level from where we started out. Someone had violated our home, put a bullet in my husband's head. Everything had changed. I was at war.

I convened a meeting in the family room. We needed a strategy to cope in the coming days. For Miles' benefit, I emphasized, "Trent is in charge of security." Miles groused, but allowed his typically eloquent voice to fall silent.

I brought Trent up to speed on Phillip's condition. "My husband is on a ventilator in a medically induced coma. He was shot in the back of the head with a 9 millimeter Glock 19 semi-automatic pistol at close range."

"Somebody was serious," Trent observed.

"As of today, his condition is guarded, which is a good sign according to his doctor. He remains in intensive care. The next major milestone is to get Phillip breathing on his own." I paused to breathe in my new reality. "Trent, I appreciate you coming here on short notice. I know you have a life of your own. If at any point you need to leave, I understand."

"I'm here as long as you need me," Trent reassured.

"There're lots of security firms in this area," Miles interjected. "Speaking of which, are you licensed and bonded?"

"Let's lay this out right now," Trent clapped back.

"Everybody freeze," I demanded.

"Bam, bam, bam, bam, bam." A jarring knock at the door.

I gargled my heart.

Trent sprang to his feet, planted his hand on the .44 magnum stuffed in the waistband of his sweatpants

Chimes of the door bell sang.

"Stay put," Trent ordered, pouncing to the door.

Outside, Laila and Ali pounded paws, growled and slobbered against Nana doors. At blistering speed the boxers raced to alternate sides of the house. Wrought iron fences rattled against the dogs' full force assault.

Trent pressed his eye to the peephole. "Are you expecting two corny looking White people?"

I shook my head, "No."

I tiptoed to the library window, pulled back the curtain and peeked out at Glen and Trudy Jarvis, carrying paper bags from Trader Joes. "It's my neighbors," I announced and hurried to open the door.

"You guys didn't have to...," I said. Glen and Trudy's kindness caused tamped down tears to flow. From the hospital staff, church members, to people who heard about our trouble, the outpouring of love was overwhelming. It was their kindness that sustained me, fueled my desire to give a praise report.

"He's still in I.C.U., doing as well as can be expected," I answered, sticking to the facts, consciously declining to speculate about the assailant, except to police who received a full speculation report.

The awful secret, the one Phillip was desperate to hide, was now embedded in a police report, naming names: Donovan Upchurch and Phillip's baby mama, Delia Upchurch. The report recounted the scene at the church's anniversary celebration where Donovan showed his butt. Police classified Donovan as a "person of interest", a rung lower than a suspect.

In retrospect I wished I had been more receptive when Phillip tried to talk to me about Donovan. I was so pained that Donovan's name twisted my gut. I wondered if Donovan was lurking in Orange County or had he returned home to snowy Michigan that suited his icy blood? I loathed the fact that the demon possessed son of a bitch who squirmed around on the sanctuary floor still managed to elude police. I would always remember Donovan's dispassionate stare at the end of the deliverance service. Powerful, multi-denominational preachers beseeched the devil, "Get out," "Devil get thee behind me," until their voices went hoarse, clerical robes hung heavy with sweat. Minister's fell to their knees, exhausted. Donovan rose, smirked and strolled away.

The day after the shooting police questioned whether

blackmail was involved. "I honestly don't know," was my lame answer. "The night before I came home Phillip alluded to some kind of breakthrough. Said I didn't have to worry about Donovan anymore. I'm not sure what he meant."

That I had been so blind, knew so little, was my greatest regret. I deserved a label stamped on my forehead, "Dumb Ass, Stupid Bitch". I would never believe that Phillip had only known about Donovan for six months and never paid child support. Delia Upchurch would not have laid in the cut for twenty years, two years after eligibility for child support lapsed. Why wait so long to unleash her weapon of mass destruction? The question almost drove me crazy. I lassoed down my scrambling mind. *Do not to go there. You need your mind to survive.*

AUBREY

Like the seven priests bearing seven trumpets of rams' horns before the ark of the Lord Miles Davis blew his horn from sun up to sun down. Phillip's room was bathed in soft sounds, *Sketches of Spain, Poetics of Sound* loaded on a cell phone by Miles, who was named after Phillip's favorite musician. Before Miles was born Phillip announced, "If it's a boy, his name will be Miles." I could not argue with that.

To Phillip, Miles Davis was more than a musician, he was an icon. Phillip loved the way Miles Davis transformed the sound of the trumpet from a brassy wail, a la Louis Armstrong, to a trickle of raindrops falling from a leaf in the Amazon. In keeping with the pact struck with the tone deaf head nurse, I agreed to keep the music mellow and at low volume.

First, came her total ban on sound. "There's no music in ICU", Nurse Jenkins insisted. When I threatened to pump up Al Green, Bruno Mars and Parliament Funkadelic, negotiations began in earnest.

"If Phillip Sampson is here, there will be sound," I countered, then offered a compromise of quiet music to be contained within Phillip's space, unless other patients wanted to get in on the vibe.

I spied Nurse Jenkins unconsciously bobbing her silver mane to the bee bop sound. I saved the fierce *Amandla* and the lick splitting *Doo Bop* for Nurse Jenkins's day off.

On the seventh day my deejaying persistence paid off. We were listening to Miles Davis' magical version of *Time After Time*. I whispered in Phillip's gauze shrouded ear, "Remember the time we heard Miles play *Time After Time* at the Hollywood Bowl? It was the first time I totally understood what you were raving about."

Phillip squeezed my hand. He knew I was with him.

I pressed the red alert button for the nurse. Nurse Jenkins sailed in. Phillip relapsed into frozen mode. In her usual conservative tone, Nurse Jenkins cautioned, "Sometimes patients have reflexive movements."

"No. This was the real thing," I insisted. "Get the doctor."

Half an hour later the doctor on call dawdled into Phillip's room. The doctor examined Phillip, lying as listless as a turnip's head.

I pleaded, "Phillip, show them something. Do it for me, baby," to no avail.

The only good news was, Phillip's chief physician planned to bring Phillip out of the coma soon.

In the ICU waiting room I shared muted enthusiasm with Trent, the only person available. Miles had taken to visiting Phillip when Trent and I were not around.

Miles was having a hard time dealing with seeing his father, so strong and vibrant, lying in a hospital bed, wasting away. In one week Phillip had visibly shrunk. The liquid nutrition fed through an I.V. tube was not enough to keep Phillip, an avid beef eater, at normal weight. Despite my incessant massaging and oiling, Phillip's skin had turned ashy gray and lay flat against his bones, as if drained of water. The pallor of death made itself at home.

23

WHO LET THE DOGS OUT?

AUBREY

Vultures circled before the body was on the cooling board.

I barged in on a "special" meeting, called without my knowledge or formal notice, of the Board of Directors of Trinity Baptist Church. Deacon Favre, number one ear hustler in the church, gave me "heads up" in time to jump ghetto fabulous and boogie over to the church. I blew in dressed to kill in a white cashmere sweater that accentuated Phillip's rapper sized gold chain and cross hung around my neck. A matching pencil skirt hugged highly aerobicized hips and thighs. Dolce and Gabbana crème t-strap pumps with chunky gold heels added inches to my already towering height.

I knew that the "wanna be" pastors were licking their chops at the not yet vacant pulpit. Haters flagrantly fanned the flames of discord. The rumble in the jungle: Pastor Sampson was "all but dead". Since when did death have a qualitative bearing, measured in degrees of deadness?

I swept into the board room like a queen. Audible gasps rose from the treasonous throats of Board members, who foolishly assumed that I was too busy at the hospital to catch them at their game.

I swooped to the head of the table, stared down Deacon Dozier, head of the trustee Board.

"Warming up Pastor's seat, Deacon?"

Dozier's ebony cheeks flushed burgundy. The Deacon's chapped lips curled into a fake smile.

"No Ma'am. In Pastor's absence I chair the m-m-meeting." Dozier stuttered in his nervousness.

"Is this a board meeting or gathering of friends?"

Dozier creaked to his feet and yielded the seat.

I plopped down into the Chairman's chair. I plunked the studs of my gold clutch on the glass covered table for maximum impact.

Dozier cast a sideways glance at his cohort, Associate Minister John Bogan.

My white lacquered nails tapped glass covering the African mahogany conference table. Before speaking a word I searched the eyes of each of the twelve assembled board members. Several board members lowered their gaze from my intense stare.

Trent Davis stood, hands folded in front of him, at the conference room door in a charcoal lamb's wool sports coat, black slacks, a crisp white shirt and a red and gray diagonally striped tie. His freshly washed wavy hair gleamed beneath fluorescent lights. Yeah, I took the bodyguard shopping at South Coast Plaza. Gave them something to talk about.

A pregnant pause choked the board room. Brother McCroy's rasping wheeze and phlegm bottomed cough shattered awkward silence.

In a clear, steady voice I assumed control of the meeting.

"In keeping with Pastor's practice, let's begin with prayer. Deacon Dozier, will you do us the honor?"

Intentionally, I called upon the biggest lackey in the group, Deacon Henry Dozier, a mountain of a man with blue black skin, broad, shovel shaped nose and a belly shaped like a widening ski slope. Dozier's baritone voice frequently reminded everyone that he was a registered, card carrying Republican. I almost expected Dozier to end his prayer with, "In the name of Jesus and Ronald Reagan, the greatest Republican who ever lived."

"Thank you, Deacon Dozier. I invited myself to this meeting to remind you that in Pastor Phillip's absence I represent him in all matters, including church matters."

"Is that in the bylaws, Sister Sampson," Brother McCroy dared ask.

"That's God's law. A man is presumed alive, until pronounced dead. Now who called this meeting?"

Deacon Dozier answered, "We thought you were too busy to deal with church matters. Just t-t-t-tryin' to help."

"Thank you, but nooo." I let the "o" ring in their ears. "This church will follow the same protocol as before. Board meetings are called by the Pastor or his representative. Our By-Laws state that special meetings may be called by the head trustee upon fifteen days *written* notice to all board members, which notice will contain an explanation of the purpose of the meeting. Deacon Dozier, as head trustee, did you send out written notice to all board members?"

"No, I d-d-did not, First Lady," Dozier dourly responded.

"Somebody explain to me the purpose of this improperly convened meeting."

Papers shuffled on the table. Brother McCroy wheezed deeply enough to prompt an EMS call.

John Bogan breached the widening silence. "Perhaps I

can shed light on the subject. Several of us were concerned that the news about Pastor's condition was so disjointed that we should meet to dispel rumors. And to plan an agenda for upcoming church services, should an alternate agenda become necessary." Bogan's teeth glinted beneath his fake smile.

Bogan, a relative newcomer to the church, made a wild splash with his southern Baptist fiery evangelism that borrowed heavily from great Black Baptist preachers. Within weeks of Bogan joining the church Pastor Sampson added Bogan to the board as a show of diversity. Within months Bogan leeched his way into multiple ministries: teaching Bible Study, mentoring the youth, feeding the hungry, and singing songs so sweet women wanted to drop their drawers.

I stood aloof from Bogan's storm of Christianity.

"How did you gravitate toward Trinity?" I asked Bogan.

"Sons of the South have a lot to atone for. How better to do it than bringing my gifts to the largest Black church in Orange County. They say that eleven a.m. on Sunday is the most segregated hour."

"Why not work in the white church? Get their souls right?" I questioned.

Bogan flashed the grin he used to entice. "I go wherever God leads me."

I had to refocus on the improperly convened meeting and not let Bogan distract me.

"I don't see Pastor's doctors or nurses here." My eyes canvassed the board room. "Since I was not invited, there is no one present who can possibly speak to the Pastor's condition. So you..." I cast the fish eye at Dozier, "called a pointless, unauthorized meeting. Let me remind you that as Business Manager of this church, I approve use of this facility. Unauthorized, improperly called meetings will not take place here. Everybody clear on that?"

Board members nodded in unison.

"On the question of Pastor's condition, you will be relieved to hear that he is showing signs of improvement. Phillip is breathing on his own. That's a major victory."

A smattering of applause. "Praise the Lord" snapped simmering tension.

"Phillip is your Pastor, but he's also my husband. A man has a right to privacy. He's not ready to have church members trudging in and out of his hospital room. For the time being, visitors are restricted to immediate family. Please continue to pray as he has prayed for each of you."

Recently appointed trustee, Wanda Turner, spoke up, "It's good to see you back, Sister Sampson. We miss you."

I inhaled and exhaled slowly. "Thank you, Wanda. As some of you know, I am dealing with another family crisis." Board members visibly shifted in their seats. Eyes opened, ears perked up to their scalps.

I ignored the gorilla in the room. "My father has late stage Alzheimer's and I've spent a lot of time with him. Right now my father is stable. So I can devote more time to my husband's recovery and making sure that the church continues to run efficiently, as it has throughout my husband's tenure. I will continue to act as Business Manager. Nothing will change for the time being. Any questions?"

I called the name of each board member in the order they were seated, asking, "Any comments?" They bowed down like frightened dogs.

I imagined conversations in the choir stand and on cell phones with the speakers blasting. Facebook, Twitter and Instagram were alive with speculation and lies, the most vicious of which was the premature announcement of Phillip's demise.

It was clear that the conspiracy to replace Phillip was conceived early on, possibly the same night Phillip was shot. In the drumbeat of their prayers echoed the question, "Who is next in line." Factions formed to the left and to the right. Whatever Judas' plan, I vowed to snuff it out.

I closed out the meeting with a prayer by Associate Minister Burns, the only board member I trusted.

I lingered beneath the archway of Trinity Baptist Church, recalling in awe Associate Minister Burns' story. Burns was a founding member of the church and a true loyalist. When Trinity Baptist was between pastors, before Phillip's appointment, Burns labored to keep the prodigal membership intact. The church needed a new roof. The church treasury was bare. Burns dipped into his own pocket to keep rain from flooding the pews. Gardeners quit, the church could not afford replacements. Burns broke out his weed wacker and power mower to single-handedly landscape church property. A sixty something man of modest means, Burns attended seminary school while working full time as an administrator at Kaiser Permanente Hospital.

I pivoted, detoured to the darkened sanctuary. I climbed stairs to the pulpit and rested Phillip's weighty golden cross and chain on his chair, resembling a throne of hand carved walnut, red velvet upholstery and gold embroidery. Marking territory. I hoped Bogan or his lackey was watching. Deacon Dozier's head was so deeply imbedded in John Bogan's ass, I nicknamed Dozier "Black Crack".

Despite Phillip's admonition, Bogan insisted that women had no place in the pulpit. Bogan was down with freeing the slaves, but not the ones with slits instead of hoses between their thighs.

At home I recounted the meeting for Miles. He gave me the thumbs up sign, his first approval of me since his father was attacked. Miles' gesture warmed my heart more than he knew. At a time when we needed each other most, our relationship was stretched to the point of breaking. I loved Miles more than anyone in the world, but I was not about to allow another mortal man, including my son, to control my life.

The radical transformation in Miles' personality since the shooting had me going in circles. He was withdrawn, sullen, rarely left the house.

Essie explained during a counseling session. "He's afraid his father is dying. Donovan's sudden appearance was a shocker. Miles grew up an only child. Then you add Trent to the equation."

"Trent is not in the equation," I protested, too loudly. "I am not sleeping with Trent."

"What did Jimmy Carter say about lusting in your heart?"

"That's absurd." I waved Essie off.

"Your son doesn't want to lose his father and mother at the same time. This is a delicate time for Miles."

"You're right...but Miles is grown."

"So what?" Essie snapped back. "You're still his mama."

"The only thing I'm thinking about is bringing Phillip home."

"And then what?"

"I can't think that far. All I know is, I feel safe with Trent."

"How does Trent feel?"

"Pul-lease. Trent probably has a hundred women."

"Are these women wealthy, attractive and in need of protection?"

"Ask him. Maybe Trent should be on your couch."

Essie rested her chin on her fisted hand. "Hmmmn. Not a bad idea. But both of us can't be cougars."

I laughed. "Men do it all the time."

Essie wagged her finger. "Aubrey Seymour Sampson. You're grounded."

24

SUSPICION

AUBREY

Recently promoted Investigator Reynard Broussard swaggered into my home like he owned it. Miles alerted me to the fact that Broussard, along with his partner, was the same sheriff's deputy who accosted him outside of our home.

With broad flat line lips, nose tooted like he smelled shit, Broussard cut a wide path around Trent. Junior Investigator Amber Mitchell shuffled closely behind.

Towering like an oak tree, Broussard was tough to get a bead on. His broad weight lifter chest anchored arms of steel. His face shined like rinsed blackberries. He had perfect articulation and the regal bearing of a confident African prince, yet he refused to acknowledge that both he and I were black, which stood out in a population more than ninety-eight percent white. No head nod, fist bump or ebonic inflection in his speech. My best efforts to engage Broussard in conversation about the church or his family fell flat.

"Would you mind if we speak in private?" Broussard asked Trent.

Trent's icy stare could break bricks.

"Let's step into the library," I swiftly suggested to defuse the stare down. "Will Ms. Mitchell be joining us?"

"Of course. This will only take a few minutes."

Trent reminded me, "I'm right here, if you need me."

Broussard closed the library door behind us. Wearing yoga pants and running shoes, I sat behind my desk and swiveled in a mesh Aeron chair to face Broussard. I was very relaxed after a brisk walk down the horse trails with Trent, Ali and Laila. The air outside was clean from much needed rain. Our walk evolved into a slow jog. When Trent reminded me of the scheduled meeting with Broussard, dread rolled in.

"Aren't the police supposed to be on my side?" I had asked Trent.

Trent laughed. "You've been in Orange County too long."

I refused to let 5-0 steal my joy. I refocused on Broussard, hemming and hawing about nothing. I cut him off. "Is there anything new in the investigation?"

"There is still no sign of Donovan. We're in close contact with Detroit police. They questioned his mother. She swears she hasn't seen him in weeks."

My hands rose to heaven. "How long, Lord. Not long," I said, mimicking a famous MLK speech. Broussard did not get it.

"What do you know about Delia Upchurch?"

"Other than the fact that she slept with my husband? Nothing."

"Apparently that's her m.o. Miss Upchurch has six children by six different men, all married, or at least they were until Delia got a hold of them. Donovan is the oldest child.

What's strange in your case is that she waited so long to make a move. Once he turned eighteen it was too late for child support. Why Donovan would suddenly appear at this late date is a mystery. I suppose his DNA drew him to his father."

My hands and feet went cold. DNA. Did Phillip get the results that I demanded before I left for the Bay Area? Did the cops know something I didn't know?

"You found DNA evidence?" I asked.

"I used the term generically. Did Donovan and your husband do DNA testing?"

I shook my head. "Not to my knowledge." That was a true, but evasive answer. I remembered Hilton's advice to share nothing with po-po.

Until the subject came up in Essie's office DNA testing never occurred to me. What kind of fool was I, frozen like a deer in headlights? People demanded paternity tests every day on daytime television. If Phillip was trying to protect me, like he said, why didn't he do the paternity test before throwing shit in my face?

"Donovan looks more like a Sampson than I do." I recalled Miles' remark after I cornered him. Those words hurt the most, negated blind denial that a young man walked on this earth with my husband's face imprinted on his face.

In recurring nightmares I saw Phillip's curved penis deeply rooted in the v-jay jays of faceless women, his seed exploding into rainbow colored confetti and populating the earth.

Essie pointed out, "We see what we want to see. A resemblance to ancestors in their eyes or the way they hold their mouth. Either way, you need to know the truth."

I was afraid of the truth. What was done in the dark should have stayed in Phillip's locked closet. Every time I speculated on Phillip's motivation, or lack thereof, I wanted to throw up. Was he proud to have a second son? Was Donovan worth the train wreck in our marriage?

More than once I asked my husband, "Were Miles and I not enough?" Was it my fault that pregnancy was not a walk in the park as it was for some women like Delia Upchurch? Delia was what slavers called a "good breeder". Her stubby legs were the main thoroughfare for other people's husbands. Delia got plenty of traffic, but stayed stuck on the freeway. She did not know how to exit, crossed the bridge to nowhere every time.

"Let me ask a stupid question," My attention refocused on Broussard. "If you found DNA at the crime scene, could you check it for paternity?"

Broussard looked puzzled. "That's not what we're looking for. There were three distinct strands of DNA found at the scene. Two belong to you and your husband. The third strand may belong to the perpetrator. That's why we need to find Donovan. To test his DNA."

Broussard gave up on the DNA line of questioning. "Let me ask another question. What do you know about the man who is living here with you?"

"You mean Trent? Trent is my body guard. He's here because it's his job."

"Do you know that he spent time in jail?"

"Youth authority. And I also know that he's rehabilitated."

"How do you know that?" Broussard's left eyebrow raised in an accusatory arch.

"I just know."

"Where do you know him from?"

"We met in Vallejo."

Amber's pen, scribbling feverishly, made scrunching sounds in her notepad.

"That's rough territory. Not exactly Yorba Linda."

I pushed back in my chair. "What're you saying?"

"Mrs. Sampson," Broussard articulated in a bass tone. He refused to call me by my first name, despite repeated requests for him to do so. "You're a prominent woman, living in a beautiful neighborhood. Someone like Trent Davis might take advantage of this situation. Where was Mr. Davis when your husband was shot?"

"In Vallejo. I saw him. Right before I caught my flight."

"How do you know he didn't beat you to Orange County, shoot your husband and show up just in time to take care of the grieving widow?"

"I am not a widow! My husband is not dead. I resent you saying that," I huffed.

Broussard rested his elbows on the arms of the wing chair and interlocked his fingers. "I would be remiss, if I did not ask these questions. Anytime we have a case like this, which is rare in Orange County, we must consider family motivation as well. Right before the incident your husband informed you that he had a child with another woman. You must have been furious. You run into an old friend, who happens to be handsome, and is more than willing to help you out. There are witnesses at 24 Hour Fitness in Vallejo who observed you and Mr. Davis doing some very personal training. Monique Nickerson, for one, says that Mr. Davis was all over you. "

I glared at Broussard, inhaled long and deep and let it out. Thinking about Monique, the word T.H.O.T. (That Ho' Over There) formed in my mind. I suppressed the thought. *Am I hearing this? This wannabe Perry Mason is wasting time scrutinizing my relationship with Trent, that so far has failed to ignite, instead of finding Donovan.*

Broussard continued, "We also interviewed the woman

you sat next to on your flight home. She said you seemed distracted. Didn't say 'hello'. Never said a word."

"And..."

"A baggage handler named Maurice said you were in a big hurry. Not friendly like you usually are." Broussard waited for my response. I remained silent, as I should have done from the git go.

"You understand how this looks. Your husband betrays you. You move another man into your husband's house."

"Last time I checked my name was on the deed as well." I pushed up on the arms of the Aeron chair, stood over Broussard and his pale, frail partner.

"I've had enough, Mr. Broussard. I'm politely asking you and your sidekick to leave."

I addressed Amber. "Write that down, sweetheart."

I turned back to Broussard, uncrossing his legs, rising slowly.

I noticed old man non-elastic socks around Broussard's rusty ankles.

"Attempted murder is a heavy charge, Mrs. Sampson."

"Am I being charged?"

"No..."

"Then you've got a lot of nerve, insulting me in *my* home."

Hard pounding on the door. Trent called out, "Are you okay in there?"

"No I'm not," I answered.

Muscles pumped, Trent flung open the door.

"The officers are leaving," I announced.

"Perhaps we need to talk at the station...," Broussard threatened.

"That ain't happnin'," Trent puffed up.

"Not without my lawyer," I added, whizzing past

Broussard and landing in the vestibule. With a flourish of one hand, I pointed to the front door. "Goodbye."

Broussard eased toward the door, spoke over his shoulder. "You're making a huge mistake..."

"*Step, mutha fucka,*" I commanded so loud that the dogs, already on high alert, growled to get at the source of my irritation.

Trent slammed the door behind the unwanted guests. He pivoted, smiled in awe at me. "Day-ummmn. I didn't know you could go that hard."

"Me either." My insides roiled, mind churned, mapping the next move. Could they arrest me by mistake? Maybe it was a mistake getting Trent involved.

⸺⸺«()»⸺⸺

AUBREY

At exactly five p.m. the last person on earth I wanted to see, but needed to see, parked his gleaming black Bentley with luscious caramel leather interior in my driveway. Justin Flowers, renowned criminal defense attorney and Phillip's best friend, was as ostentatious in his personal life as he was in the courtroom. As always, Justin hugged me too close for comfort. The scent of Dolce and Gabanna's "The One" overpowered my nostrils and made my nose itch. He must have bathed in the bottle.

I braced myself for the onslaught. With Justin I was always on the witness stand, even sitting in my living room.

Justin pulled back and scrutinized me. "How are you doing?"

"Hanging in there."

"And my main man?"

"He's comes a long way. Breathing on his own. Responsive some of the time."

"I know you have this 'no visitors thing', but I really want to see him."

"I'll arrange that. At first, Phillip looked a mess. You know how vain Phillip is."

We laughed at the stone truth. Phillip carried his comb, tooth brush and breath mints to the gym.

"So what's this about being hassled by police."

I hooked arms with Justin, ushered him into the library. "Let me get you a drink."

Flipping through pages of Nelson Mandela's "Long Walk to Freedom", Justin did a double take when Trent cruised past the doorway and into the kitchen. He peeked out to see Trent pulling pots and pans from cabinets below the counter.

Carrying a tray with Grey Goose martinis, I returned to the library.

"Did you hire a cook?" Justin's eyebrows arched suspiciously.

"No. That's Trent, my bodyguard."

"I should've guessed. All buff and shit. A bodyguard who cooks," Justin's sharp chin jutted out. "What other talent does the brother have?"

I slapped Justin's shoulder. "You're worse than the cops. Let me introduce you."

Justin and Trent danced through the male ritual, circling the ring, assessing the opponent, jabbing lightly to see who would flinch.

"I see you got security cameras," Justin observed. "And watch dogs."

Laila and Ali sniffed at the glass doors.

"Trent thought it was a good idea."

"I agree."

Justin reverted to his twenty-one questions. I abruptly reminded him that he had a drink waiting in the library.

Behind closed doors Justin explained, "I wasn't being rude, just looking out for your best interest. They didn't have any short, fat bodyguards available?"

"Look who's talking. You rolled up to my birthday party with a twenty year old, wearing six inch stilettos and a two inch skirt. Did I say one word?"

Justin's signature laugh, a loud cackle, choked in his throat. "Woman, you play rough." Justin downed a third of his martini in a single gulp. "Now tell me what's happening with the cops."

A cloud settled above me as I recounted the night Phillip was attacked. I folded my hands in my lap, sighed deeply. "I told you how I found Phillip on the floor in the bedroom." I paused, hands started to tremble.

Justin patted my hand. "Take your time."

"I called 9-1-1 on my cell. Within minutes paramedics arrived. I was numb. Barely remember the ride in the ambulance."

"I was in the waiting room, trying to call Miles when two cops showed up. They pounded me with questions. What time did you get home? Have you and your husband argued recently? What was the purpose of your trip? Can anyone else confirm the time you got home? All this while my husband's on the operating table."

"You should have called me right then," Justin interrupted.

"I know. I just couldn't think. So I answered their questions, as best I could. More babbling than anything. Then they asked if I would come to the station for gunshot residue analysis. That's when it hit me. I was the suspect. I blew up. Said I wasn't going anywhere until my husband was out of danger. By then people from the church started flowing in. The cops kept badgering me, but I couldn't hear what they were saying. My mind shut down. All I could see was Phillip's head swimming in blood. I looked down at my clothes. His blood was all over me."

"Minister Burns started yelling at the cops, leave her alone. The woman's in shock. This can wait until later."

The next day I went to the police station gave them a statement and the clothes I wore that night. I talked with a cop named Broussard. Told them about Donovan and Delia. The whole nine yards."

Justin shook his head. "That was a mistake."

"What was I supposed to do? Lie? They're screwing around looking at me while Donovan gets away."

"Why're you so sure it was Donovan?"

"Who else wanted to kill Phillip?" I asked. His answer was too long coming. "Why're you looking at me like that?"

"I'm not looking at you. Let's get back to the subject."

"You knew about Donovan, didn't you?"

"Errr, uh," Justin stammered. "Phillip and I are friends. He confides in me."

"When did he confide in you? A week, six months before he confided in me?" In my mind the whole world, including Justin, was whispering about Phillip's secret son while I traipsed around playing the good wife.

"This ain't about Phillip. It's about you. What else did you tell the cops?"

"Nothing left to tell. Broussard came snooping around

this morning. Asking questions about Trent. That's when I kicked them out."

"Them?"

"Yeah. He had this rookie cop, Amber Mitchell, with him."

"They're checking all angles. Maybe your bodyguard has blood on his hands too."

I snapped. "I knew it was a mistake calling you."

"Hold up. Just playing Devil's advocate. Don't have any more conversations with the cops. You have no obligation to speak to them or let them in your house. Meanwhile, don't feed them any red meat." Justin nodded in the direction of the kitchen where Trent sauteed shrimp to serve over rice.

Justin handed me a business card. "This guy is the best defense attorney in Orange County. Call him and retain him just in case the cops circle back."

"You won't represent me?"

"No. It's a conflict. I know too much about Phillip and Donovan."

"You don't think I'd hurt Phillip?"

"Absolutely not. That's why I'm here. Whatever happened in the past, Phillip wants you and Miles protected."

<hr />

MILES

I sat in the same spot where I sat each day since my father was shot in the head-left side of the bed, near the site of my father's wound, wondering what the wound looks like, beneath the helmet like contraption where a portion of his skull was removed to allow for swelling of the brain.

I summoned images from photos of my father suited up in football gear, a formidable presence. Nothing could stop Phillip Sampson, not even a bullet to the brain. I almost convinced myself. All I had to do was wait. Wait until my father could keep his eyes open for more than a minute.

The light above my father's bed cast a harsh, diagonal shadow in the otherwise darkened room. How could my father sleep through leering lights and constant intrusions of doctors and nurses poking and prodding him? How could he sleep when I desperately needed to talk to him, slumbering deeper than Jesus through the storm in the angry sea.

I touched my father's gnarled fingers, always strong, quick to give instruction and quick to discipline me. Now those fingers were cold, rough and foreign.

"Dad, I need to talk to you. Please dad, I need you to hear me." Dad's fingers lay limp in my hand. "It's crazy around here. Mom's going through changes at home and at church. I know you're doing all you can. But you've got to get better and you've got to do it real soon. If anybody can make a miracle, it's you. The doctors keep telling us how lucky you are to be alive. They mean well, but they don't know you like I do. The man I know would not lie still for more than a minute."

My father had never shown weakness. That is, until the love of his life threatened to leave him. I recalled the look on Dad's face. A man about to lose his anchor. My father was the ringmaster, wore fancy suits, demanded all eyes to center on him. My mother was the organizer, the stabilizer, a fancy emblem on my father's hood.

I remembered the night, felt like years ago, but it was only weeks, when I sat in the family room arguing with my father.

My father's ego wrestled to maintain control. "Son, when you're a little older and married you'll understand that men have different needs than women. We can have sex with a woman and it doesn't mean a thing."

"It means something when a child is born," I countered. "When I turned thirteen, you gave me a box of Trojans and said, use them. They sold Trojans back in the day, didn't they?"

Dad was pissed, then begged my forgiveness. "I sinned against you, your mother and God."

I wondered if my father, drifting in and out of consciousness, was being punished for his sin. I prayed, "My Dad says you are a merciful God. Please forgive him."

I wrestled with forgiving my father who invited evil into our home. Forgiving Donovan for trying to kill my father exceeded my spiritual capacity.

Despite years of Sunday School and squirming in the pews during my father's sermons, I remained a babe in Christ. When I sought answers about religion, faith and the true meaning of God, my father's responses were frustrating, not satisfying in the least. "You'll understand these things, by and by...Just have faith, son...Faith is the answer, not a question."

In the stillness of the hospital room, praying prayers that I was taught as a child, I often wondered, is anyone listening? To hedge my bet I continued to pray, but had yet to find peace that surpassed understanding. I searched for that state of mature Christianity that says, "I know that I know that I know."

"I don't know shit," I finally confessed to an invisible God.

So-called Christians swooped down like vultures before my father was on the cooling board. A self-appointed stealth committee of church members circulated gossip as fast as they could hit the "send" key. They said that my father spawned a bastard baby with an "unsaved woman" whose demonic son returned to shoot the Pastor. After his infamous performance at the church Donovan certainly fit the description of the "demonic son". No amount of praying, sweating, calling out the devil or slapping the Bible on Donovan's forehead could wrench the beast from Donovan. It was deliverance gone astray, a three hundred and sixty degree turn from the polite, soft spoken young man who rolled up on me during a photo shoot at work. Donovan had seemed so compelling, so earnest that I felt sorry for him, growing up without a father figure.

The latest rumor- that my mother filed for divorce- was news to me. I envisioned Bible toting church members skimming through the files of Orange County Superior Court for a dissolution petition. Finding no record of a filing was no deterrent. A quickie Las Vegas or a Mexican divorce could not be ruled out, according to the naysayers.

Through it all my mother remained amazingly stoic. She resumed her presence at church and in the business office on a limited basis. On Sundays she hung my father's chain and cross over his chair to discourage "wanna be" Pastors from getting comfortable in the pastor's seat.

Although at odds over Trent's presence, I admired my mother's conviction and outward appearance of strength. Only I knew the toll my father's condition had taken on her. Her former sugary softness crystallized into taut, caramel surface, ready to crack at any moment. The harder they pushed, the harder she pushed back.

Military style work outs with Trent maintained my mother's sanity. Her skin was more radiant than ever. She had changed her hair to a natural style, toned down the makeup. She looked ten years younger, which was scary to me.

Church folks raised eyebrows. I overheard Deacon Dozier's wife speculating, "How dare she have "work done" while her husband is laid up in the hospital?"

I knew the secret of my mother's resilience. Her mind was sharpened by the blade of necessity. At heart she was a street fighter, fending off attackers from all directions.

The only sign of her true age was soft lines, etched by trauma, in the corners of her eyes. She was constantly on alert. Her smile was more controlled, less likely to flow from a stroll through her gardens. A stretch of chilly winter bled color from the vines. In garden nooks, where my mother once lingered in languid stretches, I found her strategizing, sometimes out loud.

Home was transformed into a command post, guarded by an armed sentry regarded by me as an intruder. My determined mother gave no thought to surrendering ground. She fortified her castle and dared the enemy to come and get her.

While quietly admiring my mother's steely conviction, I feared that the old Aubrey might never return. Her life revolved around home and family. Would she ever again squeal at the rainbow of towering gladioli? Could the purple and white beaks protruding from giant bird of paradise cause her to linger a little longer with a warm cup of coffee? She had not hummed her favorite song, "In The Garden", since my father was attacked. My mother's feet plodded dew on grass she once skated across like velvet carpet.

"Come back, Dad," I pleaded to my father. The world had flipped on its axis and was spinning out of control. I turned up the volume on my namesake, Miles Davis, hoping the sound of the trumpet would break down walls in my father's head.

Since the breathing tube was removed my father had not spoken. Could he sense my fear that he was running a losing race against death?

For me the periodic consciousness was a mixed bag-extreme elation that Dad was improving and deep foreboding that my father would never be the same. The pendulum had swung from the effervescent oratorical genius to a muted shell incapable of functioning on his own. My father could not persist in this condition, despite mom's insistence, "Phillip's remaining conscious for longer periods and he's more responsive. That is blessing enough."

Mom pleaded with me, "Get on with your life."

"Like you've gotten on with yours?" I carped at her suggestion. The gulf between us widened. I was convinced my mother wanted me out of the house so she could sleep with that man, Trent Davis. At night I lay awake, listening for footsteps down the hall, a squeaking mattress, any excuse to plant the plumber's flashlight, stashed in my nightstand, upside the invader's head. My father would expect nothing less.

My station manager, although kind and supportive, dropped not so subtle hints on a weekly basis. "We miss your energy at work". Translation: Return to Dallas or lose your job. Too long off the air and viewers would quickly forget my pleasant face with the high "Q" rating. There was a long line of fresh faces waiting in the wings to snatch my job.

In a weird way the crisis gave me an opportunity to reflect. I had grown weary of reporting. Every story on the "crime and punishment" beat involved death, loss and human misery. Experiencing my own misery made reporting local news less appealing than ever.

"Who did this to you?" I questioned when Dad's eyes

unglued momentarily. My father's chapped, dry lips pressed together to make a whimpering sound.

"You can do it, Dad. Tell me, who did this to you?"

A whistling wheeze preceded Dad's shallow cough that died in his throat. He coughed again. Phlegm rattled in my father's sunken chest. I was tempted to feed him water. The nurse had warned that water would choke him to death. My father's chest expanded as if taking his last breath. A rumbling wheeze accompanied a symphony of coughing and choking that ended in a sprinkling sneeze. I hit the red button for the nurse, then grabbed a wad of tissue to catch thick, yellow mucus trickling from my father's nose.

The nurse raced in with what appeared to be a mini turkey baster and suctioned my father's nose. "That was a good one," the nurse smiled to my irritation. She was condescending, giving a babyish response, demeaning my father's dignity. *How dare she diminish my Dad? This is a temporary condition, I thought.*

"When he gets choked up, we help him out. It gets a little messy, but it's good to have the mucus out. That means the cough reflexes are coming back."

Dad's heaving chest slowed its rapid rise and fall. His coloring brightened from the deep purple veil of oxygen deprivation. His eyes closed again. My father lapsed into a deep state of sleep resembling death.

I tiptoed to the rest room and ran water over a face cloth. I dabbed the warm, moistened cloth over my father's bloated face, patting gently around rheumy eyes. Maybe tomorrow. Maybe tomorrow he will talk, I prayed.

Trent

My elbows leaned against the granite counter in the kitchen watching my frisky dog, Laila, unsuccessfully vie for Miles' attention. Several times Laila approached as Miles, sporting a three week growth of beard, slouched in a lawn chair under a hazy sun. Laila's moist stubby snout pressed beneath Miles' forearm. Each time Miles ignored Laila's plea for affection. Laila was not to be deterred. She loved men and was determined to capture Miles, whether he liked it or not.

I spoke into the speaker of my cell phone. "Man, it's complicated. I know I'm risking my business, being away so long. But Aubrey really needs me. The crazy mother fucker who shot her husband is still out there."

On the other end of the phone Skip answered, "I ain't complaining. Your clients might be. I need the business. They say I'm a good trainer, but Trent's the bomb. Makes me feel like shit. " Skip laughed. "How's it feel, boppin' rich booty?"

"That ain't what's happnin', " I corrected him. "This is strictly business. For now."

"Tell me any ole' bullshit." Skip's laughter rang in my ear. "I ain't never known you to let a woman under your skin like this."

"Gotta bounce, man. We're due at the hospital." I lied to get rid of Skip. True, Skip was doing me a favor taking on my clients at the last minute. Not true, that I had to put up with Skip's nonsense. "Catch you later." I hit the "end" button.

On the patio Laila made another play for Miles. I was tempted to go outside and confine Laila in the temporary kennel I assembled in the back yard. I felt sorry for Laila, pining for Miles' affection and getting nothing but resistance.

Perhaps it was empathy more than sympathy that I felt. For the first time in my life I knew what it felt like to want somebody that I could not have. Maybe I could have her, but not in this moment.

Now was not the time to make a move. Aubrey was bombarded with problems: a semi-conscious husband, an assailant on the loose, a church board on the brink of insurrection, an angry son suspicious of my every move. Miles cock blocked from every angle, staying awake until not a creature was stirring. I joked with Aubrey that Miles had turned into a vampire-asleep during the day, up all night. If I woke up to pee, Miles' turned on his bedroom light as a warning: I am watching you.

There was too much on Aubrey's plate. I could not add to it. When I offered to leave, Aubrey begged me to stay. Was she keeping me in Yorba Linda to prove a point to the church, to Miles or to herself? I did not care as long as I could be with her.

Laila licked Miles' hand and put a bead on him with deep, puppy soft eyes. No response. Miles continued to nod out over Sports Illustrated. Laila edged closer, tossed his hand with her snub nose. The magazine dropped to his lap. His tentative hand caressed Laila's head. She sighed audibly, rested her chin on Miles' bare thigh. He cupped her ear. Laila whimpered satisfaction. Miles resumed reading. Laila slid down to pavers, planted her snout possessively on Miles' left foot and closed her eyes.

I smiled. At least Laila was satisfied.

25

TOSSIN' AND TURNIN'

AUBREY

The house rumbled as if seized by a powerful earthquake. In a pre-dawn stupor I rolled across the memory foam mattress and braced for impact on the hardwood floor with my left hand. Before splintering pain could reach my brain Trent stood over me with his gun drawn and a stiff woody beneath Under Armour shorts.

"I'm okay," I panted, pushing up from the floor. "Was that an earthquake?"

"No. Someone's at the door. Where's Miles?"

It took a second for the fog of sleep to lift. "In Palm Springs." I remembered that his buddies had dragged him, protesting all the way, out for a night of fun. I glanced at the crystal encased clock, registering 3:30 a.m. Only cops knocked on your door this time of morning. Something really bad was happening. They're here to arrest me. They don't use battering rams in Orange County. Do they?

"Stay here and lock the door."

"But, but...," Trent was gone before my sentence could

come together. Pounding erupted again, this time more focused.

My knees cracked like pork rinds, all dried out, as I stiffly stood. Ear to the door, I listened to deafening silence.

The dogs, locked inside their sleeping crates in the garage, howled to the brink of hoarseness. Why didn't Trent let them out? I could not take the suspense. I eased open the bedroom door and tiptoed down the hall.

Trent's eyes were glued to the peephole. His back was to me. I inched closer, tapped his shoulder. He swung the .44 to my chest. I gasped.

"Don't ever touch a man with a gun in his hand. I could've shot you. Why didn't you stay in the bedroom?"

"What's happening?"

Trent took a long deep breath. "It's my drunk ass brother, Wallace Jr. I'm sorry. I don't know how he found me."

"Well let him in before the neighbors call the cops."

"I don't let him in my own house. Definitely not yours. He's drunk."

The bamming resumed. Even in darkness, I sensed Trent's utter disgust. He took a deep, cleansing breath. His hand embraced the door knob.

"I'm going to touch you," I warned, standing close behind him. His body was rigid, on the brink of explosion. I touched his right shoulder, grazed his bicep, forearm, wrist and fingers. "Give me this." I eased the gun from his hand. "Don't ever approach a drunk man with a gun in your hand. You might be tempted to use it."

Trent flung open the door. Wallace Jr.'s back was to us. He staggered around to face us. A gold tooth glinted in the front of his mouth. He was tall like Trent, at least forty pounds heavier. Greasy, stringy, wavy hair hung to his shoulders. A gold hoop pierced his left ear. He had deep furrows in his forehead and heavy bags beneath hazel eyes.

Trent closed the door in my face and pounced out.

I skittered to the front window, snatched back the curtain.

"Nigga, what took you so long to open the damn door?" Wallace Jr. opened his arms to embrace Trent. Trent's fisted hands knocked his brother's arms away.

"What you doin' here?"

"That ain't no way to greet big brother." Wallace Jr. offered a fist bump.

Trent responded with the fish eye, jabbed his index finger in Wallace Jr.'s face. "Turn around and leave the same way you got here,"

"Man I'm tired. Hon-gry. And I gotta piss. Want me to pee on the lawn?" Big brother grabbed his crotch.

"Who told you where to find me?"

"Mama said you were hobknobbin' in Orange County. Got the address from her."

Trent turned and looked back at the house.

I jumped back from the window, looked down at my flimsy nightgown, taut nipples and bare feet.

I scampered to my room, pulled on tights and a baggy black sweatshirt. Back at the peephole I witnessed the argument between Trent and his brother escalate. Eye-to- eye. Nose-to-nose. Trent shoved Wallace Jr. in the chest. Wallace Jr. stumbled backward, landed in a freshly trimmed row of hedges. His legs flailed, lard ass winked at the ground.

I flung open the door. "This is ridiculous...Two middle age men tussling like little boys...Excuse me, fellows. You're about to get me thrown out of the neighborhood. Why don't we take this inside?"

"Not this trash." Trent stood his ground.

"You'll be a hit at the police station in shorts and a wife beater," I reminded Trent of his attire. "Come inside, boys."

Wallace Jr. rolled to one side, dropped to pavers and grunted to his feet. "Bout time somebody showed some class." He cut a wide path around Trent, begging for the slightest excuse to level his older brother.

"Wow." Wallace Jr. exclaimed, striding through massive doors. He surveyed art work, antique throw rugs on hard wood floors. "Skip wuzn't lyin'".

Trent's head dropped in resignation. That damn Skip had been running his mouth again.

"You let the snake in," Trent's balled up lips blew at me.

Wallace Jr. turned on his axis, spun in the center of the sprawling living room. His glassy eyes lit up like a kid entering Disneyland for the first time. "I didn't know niggas lived like this. Your old man a bank robber or somethin'?"

"Something like that. The men's room is the first door to your right down the hall. Towels are beneath the counter on the left. When you finish freshening up, I'll make you a sandwich."

Trent dogged his brother's footsteps down the hall. When Wallace Jr. entered the bathroom, Trent flanked left, stormed into his bedroom and slammed the door.

I pulled sourdough, Swiss cheese, turkey and Stefano's golden baked ham from the Sub Zero refrigerator. Wallace Jr. did not seem like a tuna fish and cucumber kind of man.

Trent's salty voice surprised me. "Where's my gun?" He had pulled khakis over his Under Armours.

"You want a sandwich?" I changed the subject.

"Nope," Trent muttered through tight lips. A long pause, then he finished what was on his mind. "He will steal you blind and slit your throat. Don't say I didn't warn you."

"I can't say anything with a slit throat." My lame joke fell flat. Trent was not laughing.

"Who you talkin' bout, Lil' Brother?" Wallace Jr. strutted in, extending a moist palm. "Um Wallace Davis, Jr., by the way."

"I know who you are. You were a senior when I was a freshman in high school."

"How'd I miss you? I thought I tapped all the pretty ass back then."

I searched for the compliment in his crude remark. Wallace Jr. spoke the truth about his checkered past. Back in the day Wallace Davis, Jr. was a fisher of women. He had three girls pregnant at the same time. Wallace Jr. openly bragged about "bustin' cherries", preying on innocent, naïve young shorties and swiftly bringing them to ruin. Before drugs and alcohol pitted his skin and rotted his teeth Wallace Jr. was a sight to behold. He had slicked back "pretty" hair that was fuller and longer than most females. An olive undertone to his "high yellow" skin gave him the appearance of a perennial tan. His hazel eyes, a trump card with the girls, twinkled like Christmas lights. He knew how to shoot the shit, tell lies. Girls ate it up. They stood in line to go to bed with him, fooling themselves into believing that they were special spending time with Wallace Jr. And they were special for about fifteen minutes. He had dozens of offspring in the same age group. People checked birth certificates before mating to avoid inbreeding.

Time and the revolving door of prison left Wallace Jr. with a waistline as thick as a pregnant panda's. His once sparkling eyes were a muddy, polluted river. The threat of violence he wielded over those unfortunate enough to enter his sphere had been neutralized by all the garbage that flowed through his veins. More a threat to himself than anyone else, I pitied him.

Wallace Jr. slid onto an off white kitchen bar stool and

launched a non-stop monologue about what a great stud he was, the women he knocked up and the skulls he split.

Trent openly laughed in his face. "Don't talk. Just eat your food and get the hell out," Trent warned.

Between shots of Remy Martin, Wallace Jr. leered like he wanted to eat me up. "Y'all got any tooth picks in Orange County?"

"They're somewhere in here," I answered, while he sucked rotten teeth and picked with his baby finger.

In silence Trent and I watched his brother mutilate his sandwich. To be polite I toyed with a slice of turkey, but was too grossed out to swallow. I suffered through the longest meal of my life. It was even longer for Trent, who seemed to shrink with every word that proceeded from his brother's foul mouth.

26

BORN AGAIN

AUBREY

P hillip lifted his head in the hospital bed and spoke, "Thirsty." The word was garbled, but I understood what he said.

I floated to his side and stared in disbelief at my husband who had not spoken an intelligible word in weeks.

"You're back." I stroked his shoulders, a rack of bones, covered with sagging flesh. "Do you know where you are?" I spoke softly.

Phillip surveyed dull hospital walls, touched the rails of the unfamiliar bed, patted his thin cotton gown, then grimaced at the I.V. stuck in his swollen arm. His head flopped to one side. Something was weighing him down. He struggled to raise his right arm. The arm froze. He fingered head bandages with his left hand, whispering, "Not home."

I cried out, "Thank you, Jesus. Thank you, Lord."

Nurse Chelsea Jenkins rushed in. "Oh my God. He's alert. I'll get the doctor."

I kissed Phillip's forehead, gently squeezed his hand. "You took a long nap."

His eyes asked, "How long?" A craggly voice, struggled to escape his scratched throat.

"Don't try to talk too much."

He nodded. Yellow, mucous filled eyes flittered.

I rushed to the restroom, moistened a face cloth with warm water. I dabbed his mouth and peeled away a string of white film that threatened to seal his lips. No matter how many times I removed it in the past, the pesky film, which reminded me of dead lips, returned within minutes.

Phillip's left thumb touched his lips, mimicking drinking.

"Not yet. Wait for the doctor," I responded.

A flurry of nurses, doctors and machines pushed me into the background. Phillip's weak eyes stayed steady on me. I was a mess, alternately crying and praising the Lord, not caring who watched my Holy Ghost party of one.

Trent

Alone, at the far end of the hospital corridor, I paced, fighting the urge to merge with the swarm of hospital staff converging on room 203. I held back. Whether the news was good or bad, I would only be in the way. A malignant shadow settled on my heart.

I remembered the first time I spotted Aubrey on a podium filled with cheerleaders. She was out of my league, a few years older, possessing a rare mixture of class and sass that intrigued me. She lived inside a window that I gazed into with longing, a window that was painted shut. All I wanted was to be close to her. Drama unfolding in room 203 could force me to face the fact: I could never have a girl like Aubrey.

Twenty-seven years later, the girl of my dreams literally dropped into my arms.

"He's awake. Phillip's awake. God is *so* good," Aubrey ran to tell me.

"All the time." My embrace was tentative, unsure. Her heart pounded against my chest. Her soft skin melted into me as my nose nestled the sweetness of her freshly washed hair. I stepped back. "I'm really happy for you. What did the doctor say?"

"A long road ahead. They'll do more testing in the morning. If all goes well, he'll be transferred to a rehabilitation facility. Phillip's so impatient. He wanted to get out of bed to pee."

For the first time in weeks we laughed without the threat of Phillip's death hanging over our heads.

"Did you call Miles?" I asked.

"I did. Miles cried. He's on his way." Her tears came quickly. She made no attempt to hide them. "Phillip is very weak. He's struggling to speak. You wanna meet him?"

"Not right now. He's got enough to deal with. Maybe tomorrow...or the next day."

Aubrey bounded to her husband's room like a young girl.

I waited five minutes, drifted in the direction of room 203 where Aubrey sat on the side of Phillip's bed, stroking his cheeks. The sunshine of her love illuminated Phillip's face.

I backed into the wall and eased away, wondering if Aubrey had any room left for me.

—— ·((()))· ——

PHILLIP

"Mr. Sampson."

"Pastor Sampson, is the proper way to address him," Justin Flowers corrected Investigator Renard Broussard.

"Attorney Flowers, I would appreciate it, if you did not interfere in my questioning."

"I'm not interfering. Just making sure you pay my client proper respect. How long will this take?"

Broussard shot Justin the fish eye and continued. "On the night you were shot, tell me what you remember." Renard Broussard had the bedside manner of a butcher slaughtering a hog. There was no foreplay, no attempt to gain the confidence of his subject. He just stuck it right in.

A confused look registered on my face. I garbled, "I know you."

"Yes. Before I made Investigator, I answered a call for a possible prowler at your home. Turns out, it was your son."

My chin dropped to my chest. I stared up in disbelief at Broussard, bold enough to show up in my hospital room. *Give me strength Lord, to clobber this clown.*

Broussard persisted, "Let me repeat my question again."

Justin interrupted. "Time out, dude. This man suffered traumatic brain injury. He's not ready to give long narrative. Ask a simple question requiring a one or two word answer."

"Pastor Sampson, do you know who shot you?"

I shook my head, no.

"Was it Donovan Upchurch?"

I answered, "No."

"How do you know that? If you don't know who shot you, how do you know it wasn't Donovan?"

My hands started to tremble. I opened my mouth. Nothing came out. I looked to Justin for help.

"He can't answer that."

"Can't or won't?"

"Whatever. Next question," Justin insisted.

"Did your wife shoot you, Pastor Sampson?"

My eyes knotted in anger. Lips trembled as I struggled to find words. Doctors had warned that I suffered a form of aphasia, difficulty speaking in complete sentences with a tendency to express myself in single words. A death sentence for a pulpit warrior. Recovery, if possible, was further down the road than the three days Broussard had given me.

"Nnnn...no," I finally managed.

"How do you know that?"

My teeth clenched to the point of grinding.

"Ask that question again, I'll shut you down," Justin warned.

"You people act like I'm the enemy," Broussard answered.

Justin snaked his neck. "You people? What hood you from, Brother?" Justin put a bead on Amber Mitchell, feverishly taking notes on her newly acquired iPad. "Let's step outside and chat?"

Justin nodded toward the corridor. Like a lamb Amber followed her shepherd.

Aubrey

At the far end of the corridor, out of hearing range, I watched the game of thrones between Justin and Broussard. They parried, jousted and crossed swords. Five minutes after re-entering room 203 Justin showed Broussard and Amber the door.

Back at the house Justin liquored up and stuffed his pooch belly with braised beef ribs and anything else I put in front of him. For more than two hours Justin, who loved to hear himself talk, debriefed me and Trent. "Broussard didn't get much information from Phillip. What he remembers is that he was searching for his keys, on his way to Von's to buy a bottle of champagne to welcome you home. The lights went out in the house. Then boom!"

Justin watched for my reaction. I stayed cool. "Could there be more than one assailant?"

"Everything's possible. Broussard's questions were somewhat illuminating. He asked if Donovan has straight or curly hair. That means they found hair fibers at the crime scene."

"That could be anybody's hair. The housekeeper's, window washer's. A lot of people flow through here," I answered.

"Yeah, but there's something they ain't telling us," Justin ventured.

"They ain't telling us shit," I added.

"Seeing my man like that was humbling. I can't believe how much weight he lost." Justin sniffed, blinked hard to keep from crying. It was the first time I had seen Justin cry over anything. His best friend confined to a hospital bed, barely able to speak, was tough to witness, even for a hard case like Justin.

Justin swirled Remy Martin in a snifter, sipped hard until it morphed into a slurp. "Gettin' kinda' low on the Remy, baby. You hittin' the bottle?"

"Maybe we had company," I laughed.

"You're a champagne lady. And my man doesn't drink." Justin nodded at Trent, fondling a glass of cranberry juice. "You've got to explain that to me one day. Maybe I should stop drinking, start working out. Can you do anything with this?" Justin pinched a muffin top hanging over his alligator belt.

Trent answered, "I can work with anybody."

Justin turned to Trent, threw air jabs. "Don't be shocked, if I join ya'll at the gym. Imagine how pretty I'll be, all buff and shit. I see what you did with Aubrey. Back lookin' tight, biceps defined. I was scared to say anything. She might accuse me of looking at her butt."

I slapped Justin's arm. "Shut up before I run you outta' here."

"Let's get back to my story...The questioning is going okay, then Broussard starts asking about your personal relationships."

Trent eased up from the barstool. "Would you like me to leave?"

"No. You've heard bits and pieces. Might as well know the rest," I answered quickly. Since Trent's arrival I had been reluctant to share intimate details of my relationship with Phillip. Trent never asked. Maybe he did not want to know. There were days when I wanted to let it all out, unburden to someone other than Miles and Essie. I was embarrassed for being a fool so many years. The shame of my humiliation spun me into a cocoon of silence.

"Broussard asked if you were talking divorce. Phillip answered "no". He asked if you were having an affair. Phillip almost cried. Then he shook his head 'no'." Justin's accusatory eyes danced between me and Trent. We refused to take the bait.

"He was a calculating bastard. Smart enough to shut off the power. Which suggests that he knew the layout of the house or had been here before."

"How do you know it was a 'he'? I asked.

"Either a 'he' or a broad with lots of muscle."

Justin refused to look at me. I felt some kinda' way about that.

Justin swiveled toward Trent "Is this your first time in Yorba Linda?"

Trent popped up. "That's it!"

"I'm just kidding, man."

"Before I catch a case, I'm outta here." Trent sailed away.

"Kinda sensitive...And what was the deal with the candles? Broussard kept asking about candles."

My mind went to a place I did not want to go. Flashback: Phillip's head, floating on a pillow of blood, surrounded by a semi-circle of candles. A ritual killing, the meaning of which I did not know. I struggled to erase the image from my mind, but in my dreams I saw and smelled snaking trails of smoke rise from the flames. The devil had Donovan tightly in his grip.

"Broussard made a big deal of the fact that I didn't mention the candles in my first interview. All I could think about at the time was the blood and the hole in my husband's head. I didn't move anything. The candles were there when the cops arrived." I exhaled. "The first time I spoke to cops, Phillip was in surgery."

"Don't beat yourself up, Aubrey. It's a miracle you've held up as well as you have." Justin pushed up from the barstool. "I gotta split and let you get some rest. Apologize to my man again. I didn't mean to run him away. Or maybe I did."

"Are you sure you can drive?"

Justin waved me off. "I have more drinks than this at lunch. "

I walked him to the door. "Thank you for coming. Phillip was so happy to see you, he cried."

Tears welled in Justin's blood shot eyes. "That's my main man."

I hugged Justin loosely. "Drive carefully." From the open door I watched Justin climb into his gleaming black, chromed out Bentley and glide away.

Funny how people you abhor become people you lean on in a crisis, I thought. If I've got to fight this war, it's good to have a snarling dog like Justin Flowers in my corner, if he is in my corner, which is yet to be determined.

I could not sleep at all that night. Vivid images of burning candles, Wallace Jr., bottom down, feet up, flailing in bushes like a beached whale, Trent in Under Armour with an over-size projectile in his fly, reeled in technicolor dreams.

27

HEAT WAVE

AUBREY

I t was the muggiest spring I could remember. Moisture lumbered in still air like lumpy gravy. At noon the thermometer hovered at one hundred degrees.

"Such dedication," Hilton quipped, nodding in the direction of Phillip and Trent, as he lifted a frosty glass of Cristal to his lips.

"Join them," I challenged Hilton. I propped my feet on the hassock and leaned back on the white wicker couch beneath a vine covered pergola.

Fifty yards away, Phillip's fingers laced through water as he lay on a floatie. A plastic cap covered Phillip's head. The bandages were gone, but his head bore deep surgical scars. After removing the bullet and the damaged tissue the doctors had performed a decompressive craniectomy to alleviate pressure on his brain. The hair was growing back, but the scars were wide and shiny, impossible to cover.

Trent stood outside the pool, wearing drenched

swimming trunks hugging him in all the right places. Trent demonstrated the motion he wanted Phillip to emulate.

"Relax your shoulders, pull through the water. As the scapula retracts, get the negative," Trent instructed. His back muscles rippled into powerful foothills.

"I'd love to join them, but I don't feel welcome. Trent seems like a nice enough guy. Maybe a little aloof." Hilton observed.

"What do you mean?"

"Like he's throwin' shade. Pretending I don't exist."

"That's hard to do with a man like you. He's a little shy."

Hilton topped off quiet bubbles in my champagne flute. I took a slow sip, let the bubbles fizz on my top lip, then closed the gaping hole in my bathing suit wrap.

"Whatever. It's a sin for a forty-something man to look that good," Hilton observed matter-of-factly.

"I hadn't noticed," I lied.

"Yeah right," Hilton replied cynically. "How long has it been? A month since he got here?"

"Two and a half. Feels like years, with all the shit that's been happening. Trent has been such a blessing. Phillip lasted less than a week in that depressing rehab facility. He looked at me and said, take me home. So we did. I couldn't have done it without Trent." I recalled how Phillip came home in a wheelchair. Trent became Phillip's legs and arms, hoisting and supporting Phillip whenever he moved. Recently Phillip had reached the stage where he could move slowly on a walker. I hired a second caregiver to relieve Trent and watch Phillip most nights. Phillip did not have the same confidence with Jorge that he had with Trent.

"I see all the equipment. Workout machines. Special bed. Lifts everywhere."

"It was a whirlwind getting him home. Everything had to

change, from the pottie to a special shower chair. We can't leave him alone. He requires twenty-four, seven attention."

"How is Trent adjusting?"

"Remarkably well. He's a couple of units away from a Masters degree in kinesiology. Wants to be a physical therapist. So this is right down his alley."

"How are you adjusting?"

"It's not what I had in mind. But I have to roll with God's plan. Four times a week we take Phillip to physical therapy. That was the doctor's condition for Phillip's early release. Between sessions Trent works with Phillip on rebuilding muscle strength. Phillip's muscles turned into Jell-O while he was laid up in the hospital. The slightest movement, like pushing up from a chair, requires extreme expenditure of energy. Not only did the muscles atrophy, they lost connection to the brain. Traumatic brain injury is no joke."

"You're the three musketeers. All for one and one for all."

I laughed. "The first week Phillip came home I hired Jorge. Phillip complained every time Jorge touched him. I was stressed. Thought I was losing my mind." Tears stung my eyes. I took another sip of champagne.

"That's when Trent took over. I kept Jorge, but it was clear who was in charge. Phillip took to Trent immediately. Said he has healing hands."

"I see." Hilton responded. "You getting healed?"

"Hmmph. Not in this universe." I could not confide, even to Hilton, that I was feeling a little left out now that Phillip was back home. Long, leisurely walks with Trent and the dogs diminished into tightly scheduled events. Trent lifting Phillip into bed, Phillip's arms wrapped around Trent's neck as he lifted him, left me feeling some kinda' way. Not jealous, just perplexed that the man who once held me in awe was now totally focused on being a superb caregiver to my husband. Trent had found his calling and "booty calling" was not a priority.

"We work in shifts, but it's still a challenge. Phillip sleeps in short bursts. Does a lot of kicking and jerking in his sleep. I think he's afraid he'll lapse back into the coma. I don't blame him. I hold him close and remind him of words from a sermon he preached. 'There is no fear in love. But perfect love drives out fear, because fear has to do with punishment.' That's 1 John 4:18. I tell him, God loves you, Phillip. He brought you back to us. Which is true. It's a miracle he survived."

"He survived because of your love. Having home cooked meals brought to rehab, a loved one rubbing his feet with oil. That's love. I would've told Phillip, skinny looks good on you."

I laughed. "You see he gained nine pounds since he got home. Phillip said hospital food tastes like iodine. How does iodine taste?"

"I don't know. I would've been munching on that iodine." Hilton chuckled. "God moves in mysterious ways."

"Mysterious ain't the word. It's downright freakish. Trent turned Miles from a hater to an appreciator. When he saw how much his father depends on Trent, he had to back off."

"How's Miles doing back at work?" Hilton inquired.

"Miserable. Calls every day, threatening to quit his job and move home to help. Just what I need-another child under foot."

Hilton shaded his eyes, peered toward the pool. Phillip faced Trent's back with his arms clasped around Trent's neck. Trent did a deep knee bend, lifted Phillip's knees and hoisted him up the stairs of the pool. Phillip latched onto the walker, his upper torso listed to the left as he moved with a pronounced limp. Trent steadied him, pushed his chest back. Phillip shuffled to the beat of a minuet-left foot led, right foot dragged two beats. Trent patiently waited while Phillip parked the walker in front of a pool chair. "Turn right, right, right. Stop there. Now sit," Trent instructed. "Reach back for the arms of the chair. One at a time." Trent's bent arm served as an anchor. Grunting in pain, Phillip lowered himself.

"That's it. That's it." Trent applauded.

"Last week he couldn't do that. Lower himself," I observed from afar. "Trent is definitely working miracles."

Hilton nestled into a seat next to me. "Maybe he's the second coming."

"I'd settle for the first," I cracked.

Hilton laughed so hard, champagne squirted from his nose and mouth.

At poolside Trent trained a questioning glance on the laughing duo. "They seem content with themselves," Trent commented to Phillip.

"It's all good," Phillip smiled.

Trent, dabbing his bronze face with a beach towel, remained mum. Concern dug trenches in his forehead. He had to stay outside of my relationship with Phillip. Our marriage, glued together by crisis, was a minefield waiting to explode.

Phillip and I tiptoed around the edges of unhappiness. I was overly attentive to Phillip's every need- monitoring his nutrition, combing his hair. Phillip literally cooed when I entered the room. It was sweet, but unnatural. Eventually we would have to deal with the topic that brought us to this place---the so-called son who rolled up on Miles like a stealth bomber, tracked down Phillip and, BOOM!

From across the compound I yelled out, "Anybody hungry?" In three inch wedge sandals, I towered above six feet. I could feel Trent's eyes sketching the outline of my body that he had sculpted. I pulled together front panels of the lime green, orange and yellow Pucci-esque bathing suit cover. Trent's eyes tore away, glanced at Phillip, watching him, watching me bend over to grab my empty champagne flute.

"Beautiful." Phillip commented.

"Yeah...It's a nice day," Trent deflected.

I floated toward the kitchen like an apparition in the desert, tempting a thirsty man.

Hilton barged into the frame. "Let me help."

Trent rose to his feet, swiped a towel over wash board abs. "Let me throw on some clothes. I'll be right back."

◦◦◦

AUBREY

"How long does the charade continue?" Essie cornered me.

I squirmed in the pancake cushion of Essie's flowered couch. "I'm doing the best I can with the cards I've been dealt."

"What happens when Phillip comes out of his coma?"

"He's not in a coma. He's home."

"His emotional coma."

"Look, I don't have answers. That's your job."

"No. I ask questions. You provide answers. What about Trent? He won't play third fiddle forever."

"I don't know what I'm doing from minute to minute."

"I'd hate to see you regress. When we started there was a problem between two people, you and your husband. Now a third element has been injected. Do you see where I'm going with this?"

"Yes." I rested my chin in the steeple of my hands. "I can't be angry with a man who can't take care of himself. "

"But you *are* angry," Essie pointed out.

"Yeah, I'm angry. While God is punishing Phillip, He's punishing me too."

Essie looked down at her watch. "Our time is up, but I want to pursue this notion of God's punishment. It implies that Phillip deserved to get shot in the head."

"That's not what I meant."

"I know, but we need to talk about it."

"Do I have a choice?"

"You always have choices. See you next week?"

"My schedule is so tight. I'll see what I can do."

"Try hard. This is a critical time."

"You telling me?"

Aubrey

Phillip's trembling arms pushed up from his throne to unsteady feet. Knees threatened to give way. He braced his back, squared his shoulders and shuffled to his second home, the pulpit of Trinity Baptist Church. For the first time in weeks he moved unaided by a walker or Trent's steady arms. An intricately carved walking stick, purchased in Jamaica, was his only support. Phillip led with his knees, dragging drooping shoulders and heavy feet.

Thunderous applause rose from the congregation. Even haters gave Phillip his props. Less than three months earlier this miracle man was given up for dead by many. Clinging to his faith, somehow he made it by the grace of God.

With his left hand on the walking stick Phillip steadied himself, raised his right hand to Heaven. Adoration radiated from the swaying crowd and washed over his crippled body.

His voice, previously strong and commanding, was a tremulous imitation of itself. "Before I bring the message this morning, I have to get my spirit right...Forgive me church for I have sinned. I sinned against God and I sinned against my family. I deeply wounded the person that I love most in this world, my wife Aubrey Sampson. My darling, Aubrey..." He choked up, sucked in the pain of revelation. Every slow, tortured breath emanated from his roiling belly. Pastor Phillip Sampson inhaled the air of forgiveness radiating from the crowd.

"Take your time, take your time," rang out from the Deacon's corner.

"Aubrey Seymour Sampson is the reason I am the man that I am today. Or I should say, the man that I could have been, but for my weakness. She married me when I was nothing, showed me life where there was darkness, lifted me up when I was destined to fail. I repaid her with betrayal and deceit." Phillip looked down at me, seated front row and center.

He watched me tamp down tears threatening to flow. I squared my shoulders, held my chin up.

"I beg her forgiveness and pray that she will remember the best of me. To my son Miles, who is not here today, I ask for time to heal the wounds that I alone inflicted. You see the teacher cannot teach when he lacks moral authority.

"And to you, my fellow Christians, I pray that you will continue to love Jesus, even if you find it difficult to love me.

"I want to talk about a man named Paul, formerly Saul of Tarses, a man whose faults were as great as the faults of the man who stands before you today. On the road to Damascus Saul was humbled by none other than King Jesus. Jesus shined a blinding light on Saul and brought him to his knees. Has anyone out there been brought to your knees?" Phillip raised his right hand as he surveyed a multitude of raised hands in the pews.

"I've been brought to my knees. One day God will bring you to your knees, if you live long enough. But you can get back up. Therein lies the victory.

"If God forgave Paul, a murderer and persecutor of Christians, I believe God can forgive a wretch like me.

"I see it in your eyes. Some of you are saying, "I ain't forgivin' that man. You want revenge. The big payback...You want me to feel as much pain as I inflicted on you. But you see, forgiveness is not for my sake, it's for yours. So you can free your spirit from the thirst for retaliation, a thirst that will consume and frustrate you. God cannot pour out your blessing until your spirit is clean enough to receive it."

"Amen", "That's right", "Teach", echoed through the sanctuary. Phillip's voice grew bolder, challenging its former majesty.

"Ahead of you lies difficult days. You think it can't get much worse, but it will. My crisis pales in comparison to the struggles that will be visited upon this church. How do I know? In my humbled walk through the valley of the shadow of death, my enforced exile, prolonged state of silence, the Lord revealed many things to me. Some of those things, I did not want to see.

"I must prepare you for what lies ahead. Today's scripture is taken from Acts, Chapter 20, Verses 29 and 30 which reads: "For I know this, that after my departing shall grievous wolves enter in among you, not sparing the flock. Also of your own selves shall men arise, speaking perverse things, to draw away disciples after them.

"That's taken from the King James translation. Some of the more recent translations don't pack the same punch. And so my subject this morning is, "Don't Be Afraid of the Big Bad Wolf".

Laughter spread through the pews. Three minutes into his message Phillip held them in the palm of his hand, again. A disquieting tension hovered in the rafters. Without specifically addressing the current problems at Trinity Baptist Church, Phillip documented the scriptural foundation for discord in the church.

"If the ministerial staff, the trustees and the deacons are in turmoil, take it to the foot of the altar and not to the street. The devil's purpose is to destroy God's work. It was the Lord who delivered this congregation. The Lord who built this sanctuary. The Lord who swelled our ranks. Who shall I fear? The Lord or the wolves in sheep's clothing? "

The Amen corner rose to its feet in thunderous applause.

In a detour from protocol Phillip summoned all ministers, trustees and deacons to the altar for special prayer. Enemies locked hands with enemies. Some kept one eye open as Phillip prayed, "Deliver us from evil, for thine is the kingdom, the power and the glory, forever, Amen."

Phillip, shrouded in purple and gold vestments, stumbled three steps back, collapsed onto his throne. His elbows propped against his knees. Phillip's gold chain and cross swung almost to the floor. Associate Minister Burns stood at his side, laying on hands of comfort. Phillip's first major exertion in months had drained him.

Tempted to run to him, I held back. I avoided appearing concerned, displaying quiet confidence in the first leg of Phillip's comeback.

The benediction concluded. Well wishing congregants clamored for a piece of their beloved Pastor. Trent stormed the stage and whisked the Pastor away. Phillip had given all that he had to give on this day.

The Range Rover backed up to the side exit door. Trent engaged the mechanical lift to deposit Phillip into the SUV. The Rover sped away.

The Rover slinked down Bastanchury Road. From the back seat I exulted, "You are back, baby." I happy slapped Phillip's left shoulder. "The church loves you. I don't care what anybody says. Haters had fifty shades of egg on their faces."

Quiet in the front passenger seat, Phillip dwelled in his thoughts.

I was confused. Surely, his stellar performance would bring him out of the cloud smothering him since resurrection.

"That was my final sermon," Phillip answered slowly, but clearly. His eyes were flat with resignation, mind in a place where he could not be reached.

"Don't let them scare you. Finish your rehab, get your strength back. You'll be running pews, jumping and shouting like before."

"It is finished." Phillip answered.

"Who told you that?" I challenged.

"The Holy Ghost," Phillip responded with unflinching conviction. I was stunned into silence.

God had brought Phillip out of the coma, but the man

who returned was different from the Phillip I knew. My wise-cracking, optimistic husband had turned serious to the point of morose. He obsessed over details. Everything had to be done today. His mind was closed like a steel gate. What did he mean by the Holy Ghost told him?

28

STAND BY ME

AUBREY

Essie was not fooled. "How do you feel taking care of the man who hurt you so badly?"

"I'm just thankful God spared him. But he's not the same man. It's like he had a brain transplant."

"It's not unusual for traumatic brain injury to cause personality change," Essie commented.

"Is it permanent?"

"No one knows. Talk to his doctor. The doctor can only speculate. Every patient is different. Your husband stared death in the face. He's probably worried. How's he getting along with Trent?"

"A true bromance. It's bizarre. The other night Phillip and Trent were studying the Bible together. Phillip counseling Trent about forgiveness. Go figure."

"And your relationship with Trent?"

"Strictly business. Since Phillip came home, whatever fire there was, got put on ice. I don't know if Trent's being super respectful or if I've lost my halo. Either way, it ain't what it used to be."

Aubrey

The master bathroom cabinet was a well-stocked pharmacy. From anti-seizure drugs to a rainbow of anti-depressants, Phillip had it all. The hard job for me was preventing him from taking more than was absolutely necessary. Down the line, I hoped my husband could lead a drug free life. Pre-brain trauma his only med was Simvastatin for cholesterol problems. Now there was a circus of drugs to contend with.

I separated bottles labeled Sertraline HCL 50 mg. (generic form of Zoloft) 1 tab daily, Alprazolam .25 mg 1 tab 3Xdaily for anxiety, Citalopram HBR 40 mg. 1 tab daily, Citalopram HBR 20 mg. 1 tab daily, Zolpidem Tartrate 10 mg., Mylan 1 tab at bedtime, Mirtazapine 15 mg. 1 tab at bedtime for sleep and depression (generic form of Remeron).

"I'm fighting the pusher man," I confided to Trent. "All these doctors and psychiatrists don't seem to have a clue how to coordinate prescriptions. One good thing, I've developed a close relationship with the pharmacist."

"He's lucky to have you as his advocate," Trent replied.

Every doctor had a different pill for what ailed Phillip. Phillip did not give a damn as long as relief was the end result. Unremitting headaches, hypersensitive nerve endings racked Phillip's debilitated body, at war with his whirring mind. He craved sleep while fearing sleep that could take him prisoner again.

The only peace he found was in the hands of Trent who kneaded Phillip's knotted muscles and accessed pressure points that provided temporary relief from pain. As Trent worked on Phillip's wounded body, I studied Trent's technique. One day I would be in charge of Phillip's massage and reflexology. Trent applauded my effort. My soft hands were no match for the strength and healing power in Trent's hands.

I laughed to keep from crying at the irony. The man I contemplated leaving was totally dependent on the hands of the man whose hands should be touching me.

I was a good wife. Good wives take care of wounded husbands. I wondered, who would take care of me?

⸺◈⸺

AUBREY

"How's Daddy doing?" I asked with my cell phone clamped between my ear and shoulder. Through a glass door I watched Trent, shadowing the physical therapist taking Phillip through stretching exercises.

Mama answered. "Goin' through a flasher phase. He thinks the caregiver has a crush on him. Starts taking off his clothes before the woman gets in the door."

I laughed, praising the Lord that Mama had finally agreed to hire a caregiver. When I was unable to travel to Vallejo as frequently as before the stress upon Mama reached break point.

Phillip needed me, my parents needed me. I was drawn and quartered by the people I loved.

"And Phillip. How's he doin'?" Mama asked.

"So so. He gets frustrated a lot. Can't do the things he used to do. Doesn't have the stamina. We had some good news though. He preached his first sermon last Sunday. Shorter than usual, but it went very well."

"He'll be up to speed in no time," Mama assured me.

I did not have the heart to tell her about the cloud hanging over Phillip. Mama saw Phillip a couple of days after the shooting while he was in the intensive care unit. Armed with vials of blessed oil and determined to help me in my crisis Mama journeyed to Southern California by train. Terrified of flying, Mama only boarded planes in cases of death in her immediate family. Cousins, aunts, uncles, nieces and nephews did not warrant dancing with the devil in the sky.

While Mama was away, Winston drove his temporary caregiver nuts with non-stop questions, "Where is Pearl? Where is my wife?" No matter how many times the caregiver answered, two minutes later the question recurred. Mama's stay in Yorba Linda was cut short by the urgency of Daddy's needs.

I intentionally left my mother in the dark or at least in the shadow of reality that Phillip's deck was now missing a few cards.

<hr/>

PHILLIP

A deck of cards rested on the wicker coffee table between two empty snifters leaking fumes of Remy Martin cognac. Justin Flowers leaned forward to cut the deck. My hand blocked him.

"Enough Black Jack," I declared.

"Your wife wants your mind to stay active."

"My wife isn't here. We need to talk."

"Okay." Justin popped up. "Let me get another shot. You want another one?"

"Naw. She'll smell it on me."

"You on a Breathalyzer?" Justin quipped and strode into the house through open Nano doors. Justin peeked around. The coast was clear. No sign of Aubrey or Trent who left an hour earlier to walk the dogs on the horse trail. Justin's earlier question to Phillip lingered in the air. "Why would anyone walk in eighty-five degree weather" Justin did not wait for Phillip's answer, formed his own conclusion.

Alone on the patio, I rested my elbows on chair arms and cupped my chin above intertwined fingers. I sighed at the beauty of spring, Aubrey's gardens revving up for a wild display. The sweet scent of freesia in the air made my head light. I closed my eyes and imagined what it would feel like to be invisible to the beauty of this world. I chased the sad thought away. I opened my eyes. A golden butterfly circled my head, landed on the lip of a fountain. I snapped the picture in my mind's eye.

Justin bounded out to the patio. Golden liquid swirled in a fresh snifter. "Okay bro. What's on your mind?"

"Justin, you know I've been blessed."

"That's right. And I've been blessed to know you man."

"I want to bless somebody else. Trent had some trouble with the law when he was a teenager. Got convicted with his brothers for a string of burglaries in Solano County. Spent three years in Youth Authority. Can you clean up his record?"

"No problem. A 1203.1 petition for dismissal should do the trick. That way, if anyone asks if he's ever committed a felony, he can answer 'no'. "

"He's thinking about becoming a physical therapist. He's good at it."

"There are exceptions for some jobs that require state licensing. I'll look into it and let you know. Why do you want to help him? I didn't want to say anything...but aren't you concerned about Trent and Aubrey? They spend a lot of time together."

"Her happiness brings me joy."

Justin shook his head. "I don't know 'bout you, man. You talkin' in parables and shit."

"The other matter I need handled is Donovan."

"They caught him?"

"No, but when they do, I want you to represent him."

Cognac dribbled down Justin's lower lip. "Fuck no! You're taking this Jesus thing too far. You can't be serious?"

"Promise me, no matter what happens, you'll represent him?"

"That's asking a lot. You want *me* to represent the man who shot you in the head?"

"What happened to innocent until proven guilty?"

"Not when you fuck with family. You're like a brother to me, Phillip."

"Promise...so I can rest."

"Is that what's keeping you up? Aubrey will kill me, if I represent that son of a bitch... I'll have to pray on it."

"This, I've got to hear." Aubrey's voice surprised us as she rounded the corner of the house. Sweat stained the mango colored bandana covering her brow. A cropped yellow t-shirt stuck to her chest. The image was not wasted on Justin, whose tongue hung from his mouth like the foam from the mouths of Laila and Ali. On another warm day in spring Trent and Aubrey had pushed the dogs up and down horse trails ringing Yorba Linda.

A triangle of sweat formed from the neck to mid-chest of Trent's sleeveless gray t-shirt. His hard muscles glistened under pulsating sun.

"What in the world has Justin Flowers praying?" Aubrey pressed.

"We're just b.s.-ing, baby. Would you get me some lemonade?" I asked. Aubrey plucked two empty snifters from the table. She rolled suspicious eyes between Justin and me. I braced for a lecture about the perils of drinking while taking meds. Aubrey fooled me, strolled to the kitchen.

"Gotta cool down the dogs." Trent tugged lightly on both leashes.

"Yep. The dogs are thirsty," Justin carped.

Aubrey

Winston slouched on the bedroom floor. His back rested against a chest of drawers. His knees were drawn to his bony chest. His only clothing was a poop packed Depends and white crew socks smeared with feces.

Mama's shrill cry for help catapulted me from the front door to the back bedroom. Still carrying brown paper sacks from Food For Less, I froze in the bedroom door, watching my father wallow in a sea of shit.

Pearl swirled in circles, swinging armloads of towels. Every step I made imbedded greenish, brown tracks in the cracks of the wood floor. Winston's starry eyes gazed up at me without the slightest recognition. I plopped groceries on the bed before realizing that it too was tainted by revenge of the poop patrol.

I squared my shoulders and took a deep breath. Mistake number two. The putrid smell almost knocked me to the floor. I turned to my hysterical mother. "Slow down. Throw me the towels and back away. Get 409 and ammonia from under the kitchen sink."

Mama's steely resolve melted to mush whenever Winston was in danger, which he wasn't. He was just flustered from falling and being unable to get up.

I was shocked by the rapid decline in my father's condition since the assault on Phillip. His gaze drifted even farther away, if that was possible.

"I'm your angel, your pride and joy," I wanted to scream, but knew the futility. Dr. Grace had warned us that this day would come. I had counted on Daddy to defy the odds. I blamed myself for staying away too long, long enough for Alzheimer's to chew chunks out of Winston's ebbing memory.

It was a humbling experience. The wrong day for the caregiver to take a day off. Winston Seymour required more clean up than a Gulf oil spill. I did a deep knee bend, clinched Daddy above the elbows, leveraged him to his feet and paraded him to the shower. Silently, I thanked Trent Davis for hundreds of lunges, military presses and squats he inflicted on me. Now I understood what Trent meant when he said, "I'm preparing you."

I dressed my father in clean long johns and escorted him to the guest bedroom where he could be warm, even though it was relatively warm outside. His blood flowed like ice water. Winston was cold all the time. One skill he retained was pushing the thermostat past ninety degrees.

I returned to Winston's bedroom, flung open the window and emptied a can of air freshener.

I collapsed on my father's clean sheets, reminding my-self, He won't give us more than we can bear. Somebody in Heaven had a twisted sense of humor.

"Why now Lord, are my father and my husband suffering at the same time?" The question haunted me from the moment I landed at Oakland International Airport. My sense of heaviness was more than the overstuffed luggage I hoisted onto the rental car shuttle rack. It was an inescapable feeling that life was running faster than me. I was losing the race badly. In our phone call two days earlier Pearl insisted, "Everything's okay with yo' Daddy. He's just hard headed." In my mother's voice, I heard unspoken despair. I bought a ticket to Oakland immediately.

I snapped out of my pity party. In the guest bedroom I hugged Daddy, sitting on the edge of the unfamiliar bed, looking lost. "Daddy, how're you doing?" His shrinking arm went limp.

"I-I don't know." Daddy stared through me like a stranger invading his personal space.

Quarter to midnight the floor boards remained silent. Daddy was literally too pooped to pace the floor. "Thank you Jesus", I said and crawled into bed.

AUBREY

At 4:35 a.m. Winston Seymour caught his second wind. The rude clatter of pots and pans jerked me wide awake. "Lawd have mercy", I muttered, stumbling to shaky feet. The after taste of vinegar and sea salt potato chips, crammed into my mouth minutes before I nodded off, came back to bite me. My healthy diet was history since arriving in Vallejo. Thankfully Trainer Trent, in Yorba Linda taking care of Phillip, was not around to dog me out.

My feet dragged into the kitchen. Every pot and pan was spread out on the linoleum floor like game pieces. Winston was caged in the middle, unable to move, without upsetting his display.

"Hold on, Daddy. Let me move these pots out of the way." There was no point asking why. Logic went on extended vacation and refused to return. I checked the clock to make sure I was not hallucinating.

"What y'all got to eat in here?"

"Flora doesn't get in until 6:30. That's two hours from now. Why don't you lie back down?"

"Who's Flora?"

"Your caregiver."

"I don't need no caregiver."

"Ooo-kay. Let's clean you up a bit and I'll make you some breakfast."

Daddy was dressed in four indelicately layered shirts, a fleece lined wool jacket, a plaid felt church hat, pants three sizes too large with a urine stain the size of a baseball front and center. He bore no resemblance to the man in the 1980's photo wearing pleated navy blue slacks that hung on his slender, model like frame. Where was the crisp, starched white shirt with nary a wrinkle or spot? I longed to see the cuffs turned back with gold cuff links inherited from his father, freshly cut hair, brushed into submission and slicked to his head with a swipe of Murray's pomade.

I thought, who is this unkempt man in my mama's kitchen with matted tufts of unruly, silver hair peeking from beneath a crumpled church hat? What happened to Mr. Debonaire, man about town? Was this where life was headed for us all?

No time to think. Ready or not, I had to move on my own. Mama slept, snoring hard Darth Vader breaths. I knew my mother heard every word spoken. She was too exhausted to scream her usual admonition, "Winston, quit cuttin' up in there."

—«(◉)»—

Aubrey

My Daddy died before the caregiver could draw her first paycheck.

He looked perfect in the casket, cherry wood veneer with gold handles. Wiggins-Knipp Funeral Home gussied him up so well that he resembled his old self. I placed a white boutonniere in the buttonhole of his black wool suit. His shirt was so white there seemed to be a light shining from inside his chest. From the slight smile curling at the corners of his full lips I knew he was in perfect peace. I was sad, but satisfied that Winston had found sweet release from the hellish week he had endured.

The morning he died Mama and I took turns sitting next to his bed. He was so weak Winston could not stand on his own legs. That did not keep him from trying. Winston refused to pee in the urinal, waging war against wetting the diapers hospice imposed on him. He ripped off each diaper, wriggled out of tightly tucked sheets and put his feet on the floor before Mama or I could restrain him. If we turned our back for a second, Daddy peed on everything in front or below him. He did not give a damn that he was forbidden to get out of the bed.

"What kinda shit is this?" Winston protested loudly, each time we tried to restrain him.

I asked the same question, over and over again. Why must we die like babies, pooping and peeing all over ourselves? I instructed Miles, cut me loose, let me run naked in a field, titties flopping to my navel until I meet my Maker on high.

The night before he passed away I slept in a chair at the foot of his bed. I was awakened by my father's conversation with people unseen and unheard, except by Winston and perhaps the specter of death.

"Daddy, who're you talking to?" I asked, bewildered.

His crooked index finger pointed to the open closet. "Those people over there. They want me to go home with them," he said in the clearest voice I had heard in days. His speech had deteriorated into guttural gurgling and incoherent phrases. The hospice literature warned that my father's voice might develop an unnatural, gravelly tone, the rattle of death. Despite the warning, I freaked out when the lights were dim and I was awakened by the "demon" voice.

Four days before the "people" came for Winston, he stopped eating and drinking completely. I longed for him to ask "What y'all got to eat in there?" We cajoled, then tried to force feed him food, water and medicine. Winston developed the fine art of appearing to swallow while holding food and pills beneath his tongue. Two days into his act Winston clenched his teeth and sealed his lips. "It's over." His distant eyes foretold the ending of his story.

The hospice worker cautioned, "Don't worry too much

about the meds." Translation: They can't do him any good at this stage. That was, except for the liquid morphine and Ativan, liberally dispensed to ease Winston's transition.

He created a distance between his earthly family and his final home. Winston pulled a curtain beyond which Mama and I could not pass. It was nothing new for me, the stranger in his home, giving orders, forcing him to take a bath. For Pearl, to whom he had clung every minute of every day for fifty years, letting go was devastating. Winston was all she had.

Footsteps, the "people" coming for Winston, echoed through the 1950's bungalow. I raced from Winston's room to the front door. Who had penetrated multiple locks and latches? No earthly being. A heavy, controlling presence invaded the atmosphere. A band of angels lifted Winston's spirit from the pain, worn out body and whisked him out the front door.

"He's gone," Pearl surrendered. Even before she said it, I knew there was nothing more to be done. Winston's lifeless eyes and laughing mouth lay open to glory.

Huddled together, Mama and I cried until a peace that defied our helpless situation settled over us. I looked at Winston, younger and more handsome than minutes before. I smiled, closed my Daddy's eyes and kissed him goodbye. Mama tied a flowered head scarf beneath his chin and over his head to close his mouth.

I dialed the mortician's phone number and gave the dreaded news. On the living room couch, Mama rocked back and forth. I joined her. Together we swayed, listening in timeless quietude for the sound of Daddy wriggling beneath tucked sheets, planting shaky feet on the urine drenched floor. That sound we would hear no more.

AUBREY

Pastor Bentley, my father's minister, arrived before the undertaker. We prayed, but my mind was not in it. Respectful stillness settled into the walls. Even our tears were muffled in what became a holy place. I untied and removed the scarf, used warm water to wash my father's care free face.

Commotion at the door. The undertaker's men, dressed in suits, gently shooed me away. "We'll take care of him now."

They rolled in a metal gurney, lay Winston in a black plastic bag and zipped him up.

"He can't breathe," I freaked. My hands patted my head in desperation. "Let him out!"

Pastor Bentley tried reasoning with me. "This is God's will. You've got to let him go."

Mama held me around the waist with both arms. "Sh, sh, sh, now baby. They'll take care of him now."

Outside the house a respectful crowd of neighbors gathered. A war wounded veteran in a wheelchair saluted Winston, a veteran of the Korean War, as the morticians rolled Winston toward the hearse.

I hollered, "Don't take him. Daddy, don't go." Pastor Bentley and Mama were dragged along by my supernatural strength.

Otis Biggs, the neighborhood dope dealer, jogged down the block to lend Mama and the Pastor support. I rushed the hearse. Otis grabbed both of my arms and held me back. "Okay, little Winston. It's gonna be okay." My flailing arms broke free. Mama and Pastor Bentley backed away. Otis clamped me, a whirling dervish, to his chest.

The black hearse, carrying Daddy's body, pulled away from the curb and blended with the sunset down Sage.

I cried myself breathless. One shoe was on the browned out lawn, my other shoe was in the gutter. Mama tried to lead me into the house. I collapsed on the concrete step leading to the door. I don't know how long I sat there or how long the gawkers buzzed around, observing. People came and went like a dolley shot in a Spike Lee movie.

When the spell of grief was broken I raced through the living room filled with people and landed in the room where, minutes earlier, my father's body lay.

Hospice meds beckoned from the dresser. My trembling hand lifted a bottle of liquid Ativan, opened it, clasped the dropper in my free hand and filled the dropper to twice the prescribed dose.

If it takes three milliliters to die, it must take twice as much to live, I reasoned. I closed the bottle, slipped the Ativan and the dropper into a drawer. I waded back into the sea of Mama's visitors, waiting to console the consoler, First Lady of the church, crumbling to pieces when my father died. I stayed busy to keep from crying.

That night I wrote Daddy's obituary, selected photographs for the program and family video, ordered flowers, conferred with Pastor Bentley about funeral arrangements and smiled when I felt like hiding beneath my father's bed. For the first time in life I was a fatherless child, feeling betrayed by God and Ativan.

Mama took the easy way out. She slipped into the twilight zone and stayed there.

PHILLIP

Next morning at seven a.m. Trent backed the Range Rover into the driveway. I was positioned in the passenger seat, wheelchair and walker already stored in the hatch back.

Trent ejected from the driver's seat. "Gotta grab the last two bags. Be right back." From the corner of my eye I spotted the patrol car parked in the far end of the cul-de-sac.

Trent bounded inside the house, returned with the bags as fast as his legs could carry him.

"You see that?" Trent nodded in the direction of the patrol car.

"That's the s.o.b. who roughed up my son. Sherman Wilson...fat bastard. Looks like he got a new partner." Riding shotgun, a young deputy slept with his mouth wide open, oblivious to the movement of his surveillance subjects.

"Shall we say good morning?" Trent asked.

"No. We've got a long trip ahead."

"I'll text Jorge to let the dogs out. Check the cameras and keep the house locked down."

"Good thinking. It's a shame when you have to keep an eye out for the people we pay to protect and serve."

Aubrey

I checked her face for signs of life. Fireworks exploding before her eyes would not have moved her. Mama's dilated pupils stared straight ahead as Pastor Bentley preached a humor filled eulogy.

Pastor Bentley told it like it was, not sugar coating Daddy's life in death, as pastors tend to do. Bentley recalled Winston's good deeds and his quirks. "Deacon Seymour would listen politely as I corrected him on an issue of church protocol. Then he would turn to me with a straight face and say, 'Son, I've been doing this since you were in diapers. It worked then, and it works now. Then he proceeded to do whatever he intended to do in the first place." Mourners howled. The pastor had captured the essence of Winston's stubbornness.

The eulogy ended. The mood turned somber. Myron Mosely, funeral director, gave instructions. "You may file past for final viewing and proceed immediately from the sanctuary. The family has requested a moment alone with their loved one." The organist piped up "Goin' Up Yonder." My skin crawled as the finality of it all sank in.

Friends and family paused to clasp my limp hands. Unfamiliar cheeks pressed close. In a fog, I returned their embrace, breathing deeply to keep from fainting. *Ativan don't fail me now.*

Miles gathered Phillip's walker, helped him to his feet and positioned him next to me as we stood over the coffin. Mama lightly kissed Daddy's face. Her fingers glided over his cold, hard hand. I could not bring my lips to the cold, refrigerated corpse masquerading as my father. From the moment I saw Daddy's lifeless body at the wake, I acknowledged, "Daddy is gone". His spirit was on the other side, just as he wanted.

It seemed like a long time ago, but it was only days since Daddy had begged, "Gimme' my coat and hat. Let's get the hell up outta here." Daddy had done just that.

Miles escorted Phillip back to the front pew. When Mama and I lingered too long. Miles laid hands on our shoulders. "Mom, Grandmama. It's time to let go." He led us reluctantly, back to the front pew.

Director Mosely cranked Daddy lower and lower into the casket. Reality smacked. This was the last time I would see my father's face on earth.

Myron Mosely folded white fabric over Daddy's face. An ominous rumbling thundered down the center aisle. A hefty four foot eight inch woman, carrying a child under each arm like footballs, planted herself before the casket and ordered Mosely to, "Wait."

The woman wore a knee length flowered wrap skirt, flip flops on elephant feet and a sleeveless aqua polyester blouse on a chilly day. Her ankles and legs were tree trunks capable of composting dirt. Overstuffed, golden brown sausage arms protruded from the too tight blouse. Black wavy hair cascaded down her back to her thick waist crowning wide, unruly hips. She turned and sneered at Mama with a snub nose punctuated by nostrils flared like a pig's snout.

Myron Mosely's eyes bucked, his dignified demeanor evaporated. "Ma'am, the time for public viewing is over."

The woman protested loudly, "I'm not the public. I'm his wife!" Loud whispers from the lookey loos standing at the back of the sanctuary muffled her words.

"Get that 'ho outta here," Mama shrieked, springing to her feet and back to life. Eyes blazing hotter than Satan's, Mama's balled fists punched air.

I caught Myron Mosley's eye, sliced my hand across my neck. Cut...

Myron gently nudged three hundred pounds of human flesh away from the casket. The wide load, planted like a tree by the water, wailed and cackled in a tribal tongue. Myron's flustered assistants pried the screaming five year olds from the woman's arms.

Myron spun the woman around. He gained no ground pushing her off the line of scrimmage. Less than a foot away my mother and I reeled in shock. Those who had left the sanctuary sneaked back in to witness disarray.

"Aw-igh, aw-igh. He loved me the most," the heifer squealed at the top of her voice.

"Don't make me go off up in here." Mama tossed her wide-brimmed black hat to the floor.

I hunched Miles. "Get Trent. Quick."

Miles bounded to the foyer.

In seconds Trent freed Myron Mosely from his struggle. Trent bound up big foot's flailing arms and hoisted her, screaming and cursing, to the curb.

As a preacher's wife I witnessed more than my share of funeral drama. This was the funkiest funeral I had ever seen.

It all started to come together. This was the woman with two kids who acted up at Kaiser when Daddy was sick, the same woman who called my mother's house repeatedly in the middle of the night and hung up. His other life, the one he led when he left the house every day for hours, finally caught up with my father. Regrettably, it happened when Mama was on her knees with grief and Daddy was in a box.

I was too pissed to talk. I used my only weapon, the pen, to work it out.

29

EYES JUST LIKE MINE

Sisters in Silence.com
April 1

The worst Outside Baby's Mama Drama plays out at funerals. Funerals bring out anger, jealousy and gold digging tendencies. The body of the deceased might as well not be there. At a recent funeral the vulchers circled the open casket, gossiping about the decedent's Outside Babies.

"Don't he look good? Just like he sleepin'. " Vulcher 1 hunches his cousin standing next to him and whispers loudly, "That's his illegitimate daughter over there."

Who made the rule that when a man dies, his previously unknown Outside Babies are listed on the obituary and are welcomed to attend the final rites for their biological father. I am making up my own rule. Unless openly acknowledged during the decedent's lifetime, Outside Babies should not stand over the dead, cold body of a man that they hardly knew.

A church elder explained this bizarre ritual to me as being a matter of respect. Respect for whom? If the funeral is for the living and Wife is among the living, Wife may not enjoy seeing Outside Babies during the lowest moment in her life.

I was particularly puzzled by a display of photographs of children that close friends and family had never seen during the decedent's life. Since husband never introduced me to his Outside Babies, I really did not want to find out about them at his funeral. It was too late to share the joy of fatherhood, too late to share in his pride for his Outside Babies' accomplishments. Disturbed by the timing of the revelations, I resented having too much information foisted on me. Layered on top of my grief, was a feeling that I had been snookered by my deceased friend and his wife.

I was not surprised by the revelations of infidelity that had borne bitter fruit. My friend was a notorious Ho-ing Husband. He oozed that doggish scent of deceit that lingers on Ho-ing Husband's even after they bathe and spray on tons of cheap cologne. You know those eyes that slit into laser lines every time an attractive (or not so attractive) woman strolls by. All she needs is tits, ass and a toothy grin, the "tee hee hee" kind that exposes too much gum. You can hear him humming under his breath in anticipation of sin.

My deceased friend had it all, including an incredibly beautiful wife, who suffered in silence until the moment of her husband's death. It took a long time for her to cry and even longer to admit that she was relieved the bastard was dead. And then remembrance of his filth spewed out of her mouth like a broken sewer pipe. Too much shit to hold.

Aubrey

"Miles get off okay?" Mama asked.

"Yeah. He texted me after Lyft dropped him off at the airport. He wanted to stay here with you, but he's lost too much time off work."

"No point everybody's life being upside down."

I had planned to wait, but could not hold back. "When were you going to tell me about my little brothers?"

"In my coffin. Her name is Moriah by the way. I don't acknowledge her or her critters."

"Well, it's out there now."

"Do I give a shit? I been knowin' 'bout that big footed 'ho for years. I gave Winston a choice. He could move in with big foot or stay here. Long as they didn't mess with me, I was all right. Yo' daddy thought he had the magic dick, but his shit was weak. Hmmph. I was tired of dealing with it. Now there's some young stuff out there..."

I clamped hands to my ears and hummed, "I don't want to hear this."

"Listen. You might learn something."

"You think those kids are his? Daddy was kinda old."

"Ummm hmmm. His equipment worked 'til recently. Then God put a stop to that nonsense. Yo' daddy dealt with some of the lowest trash in Vallejo." Mama teetered on the brink of breaking the tough facade. She sucked in courage, rocked on. "Aubrey, don't let anything surprise you about a man. He'll screw a goat, if it stands still."

I laughed despite the dirt still loose on my father's grave. A sense of betrayal eased in. My smile faded. For years I had seen what I wanted to see, ignoring Mama's innuendoes about Daddy's "other women." I could not picture it.

Mama gave me the 4-1-1 on what she had been dealing

with. "Winston's Guamanian sweetie met him at church. She's a regular, non-tithing member of Unity Temple. They say she was living on dirt where she came from. To somebody that broke, Deacon Seymour was a real catch. She lives in a rundown shack owned by the church, pays five hundred dollars a month in rent, subsidized, of course, by Deacon Seymour's social security check...Not anymore. That check's coming to me," Pearl boasted.

"I thought you left Unity for religious reasons. "

"When the church condones maintaining a 'ho right under your wife's nose, there's something wrong with that church."

"Amen to that," I responded. Stronger and longer than I had in years, I embraced my mother, then headed to the back bedroom.

I stripped off confining repast attire, slipped into running tights and Nike cross training shoes.

Phillip and Trent, engrossed in a Laker's game, were oblivious to my impending departure.

Pearl's caustic voice ripped the air, "Where you goin' this time a night?"

"To the gym. I need to work out."

Phillip begrudgingly pulled his attention away from the game. "Do that in the morning, baby. We've got a game going on here. You shouldn't be out this late by yourself."

"It's nine o'clock. 24 Hour Fitness is open late. I can't sit here another minute."

Phillip pleaded, "LeBron is on fire. It's the third quarter. Wait 'til the game is over."

"I don't need a chaperone," I insisted.

"Apparently, you haven't been to the gym at night." Trent threw in his two cents. Trent reluctantly rose to his feet. "Okay. I'll go with you. I'll catch the end of the game at the gym."

"Thanks man," Phillip offered. "If it's not too much trouble, bring back some ice."

All afternoon and into the night Phillip drank lukewarm Coca Cola and imprinted his butt cheeks into Pearl's sagging brown velvet couch. The twenty year old refrigerator refused to make ice, growled in protest every fifteen minutes.

"Mama, it's time to let it go. I'm buying you a refrigerator tomorrow," I insisted.

As always, Mama resisted. "That's what's wrong with people. Want to throw out everything old. Ain't no refrigerator comin' in this house."

Are we talking about you or the refrigerator, I wondered, but let it go.

Trent emerged from the bathroom dressed like a sports fitness model. His stretch t-shirt clung to his bulging biceps and rippling back. Adidas sweats accented his tight ass and cinched at his ankles. His sneakers were blinding white, as if they had never seen the outside of the Nike Kyrie 4 box.

I reconsidered my outfit, consisting of over washed, ill fitting tights, a wrinkled, faded tank top and a scarf tied around my head. It was my house cleaning, "do not fuck with me, I'm here to work out," foul mood matching attire. Perfect. "Let's roll."

<hr />

AUBREY

The fifteen minute drive to the gym was a journey between distant strangers. I could not remember the last time

Trent and I really talked. I did a brain scan to pinpoint the moment. It was Phillip's return from the hospital when Trent locked into an overly respectful distance. Air that once sizzled whenever Trent came within arms-reach turned cold as a January night in Detroit.

I understood Trent's predicament. We each had roles to play: I, the dispassionate First Lady, and he the paid protector of all that was virtuous and Godly.

A smattering of cars populated the 24 Hour Fitness parking lot. At the end of a row, near the back of the lot, midway between Raley's grocery store and the fitness center I parked the Rover.

I hoisted my gym bag from the back seat.

Trent slouched in his seat, unnaturally still.

Hurt eyes, that needed healing, turned to him. "I can't believe Daddy had a second family."

"At least you had a daddy. That's more than some of us can say. Winston wasn't perfect. But he stayed with his family to the end. " He tried to console me.

My rising anger steamed up car windows. "To show up at a funeral like that…Takes some nerve. Do I embrace his babies? Go to their birthday parties? What kinda shit is this?"

Trent's long fingers stroked my cheek until the tension in my lips eased. My hand reached out and covered his. I drew his middle fingertip to my open mouth. Wet lips swallowed the first, then the second joint.

He moaned. Something about Jesus.

I turned my back to him, eased my butt across the console and burrowed into his lap.

Trent squeezed me close, nibbled my left ear.

I turned my head, desperately searching for his lips. In iridescent moonlight, I studied him up close. *God, he is beautiful*. Emotions flowed like molten lava, cooled only by our kiss that tasted of cool mint.

Trent reclined the passenger seat to a prone position.

He flipped me over, climbed on top, swam into my angry ocean and dropped anchor. The turbulence of the waves stunned me. I surrendered years of unrequited desire. Our bodies shuddered and spasmed until the glacier between us melted into liquid sunshine.

———◉———

Aubrey

We had drifted from the safety of the shore. Returning was not an option.

I smiled into Trent's soft, vulnerable eyes. My fingers played in his close cropped curls. "You made me happy," I sighed.

"I'm happy too." His hard, sweat slick thighs intertwined with mine. Then he trampled blissful silence. "You're never leaving him, are you?"

Buzz kill.

"Can we talk about this later?" I asked.

Trent pushed back. "I won't sneak around behind your husband's back."

"Give me a minute to think."

"I'll drive you back to Orange County, then I'm out."

"Phillip needs you." Translation: I need you. I was afraid to say it.

"That's why this is wacked. That man depends on me. Here I am, fucking his wife."

"Nobody twisted your arm."

"Jorge is looking for more work. He'll be happy to take my spot."

"I don't want Jorge."

"No appetite for a bald guy with a big belly?"

"I resent that. Hand me my tights," I demanded. Trent did not budge. "That's the meanest thing that has ever come out of your mouth." I thought, typical male. Give 'em a piece, they get funky.

My tights were in the back seat. I pushed away from him, suddenly conscious of the tight space we inhabited. My bare ass was in the air. Swollen nipples chafed against leather seats.

I strapped on my sports bra, wriggled into my tights, wrestled the tank top over porcupine hair. Fear set in. I can't go home looking like this, I thought. I rummaged between the door and the front passenger seat, found my scarf and tied down sweat drenched, nappy hair. How did the scarf get down there? I smiled at the image of my most acrobatic feat of the night.

"I'm not the first married woman you slept with."

"That was different. I was different."

My muscles tightened. My mind screamed, please don't go there. I could not handle it. Not tonight. The night of my father's funeral, the night I learned my father was leading a double life.

I played it off, pretended I missed what he just said. I just wanted to feel good, to do what men do under stress. Mindless sex.

I leaned forward to kiss his neck.

Trent backed away. "Don't touch me."

"Whuuut?"

"Drop me off at my house," he snapped.

"I can't go home alone. They'll be suspicious."

"Did you hear what I said?" Trent barked.

"Whoa". I should have bought him dinner, chocolates or something.

———— «◉» ————

Aubrey

The house was dark. Flickering shadows from the Jimmy Kimmel show danced across the wall. My key turning inside the lock sounded a fog horn inside my guilty mind.

Phillip's head bobbed up from the sagging couch. "How was your workout?"

"Excellent," I responded, a bit too cheerily. "Mama gone to bed?"

"She passed out right after you left. I see you forgot the ice."

I looked down at my empty hands. "Yeah."

"By the way, Miles called. Said he couldn't reach your cell phone."

"Uh. I had on my ear buds. Tuned everything out."

"He got home fine. He felt badly about leaving Pearl alone."

"I'm trying to get her to go home with us. But you know how she is."

"Where's Trent?"

"I dropped him at his house. Said he had some things to handle."

"Booty call." Phillip laughed. "I don't blame him. The

man's been locked behind the Orange Curtain for months."

"I'll join you in a minute. Let me jump in the shower."

It took more than a minute to erase the lingering scent of passion and even longer to shake Trent's sensuous whispers from my head. He was in my hair, my mouth, oozing from my pores. Trent permeated my body, bound up for years.

Even before Phillip was shot, my husband's diabetes wreaked havoc on our love life. I hypnotized myself into believing that I was okay with it. In sickness and in health, that's what the preacher said. But in the parking lot between Raley's grocery store and 24 Hour Fitness, I surrendered to animal instincts. Let it all hang out.

Now Trent was threatening to leave because he wanted more. In a perfect world, I wanted more too. But love was not always kind. Love would kick your butt and rock your world. I could not go there again, ceding control of my heart to another man.

30

BEWILDERED

I maneuvered around Phillip, avoiding him while my guilt stirred. On the long ride home to the O.C. I played possum in the back seat of the Rover. Trent drove like a man intent on reaching Orange County before dark. Phillip, who was months, maybe years from driving a vehicle, rode shotgun. Phillip seized the opportunity to drop words of wisdom and Biblical insight on Trent, his captive audience.

"Forgiveness is the foundation for freedom. Whenever you're feeling animosity toward anyone, including your oldest brother, think about forgiveness. When we get home read Psalm 32. The first verse says 'Blessed is he whose transgression is forgiven, whose sin is covered.' Unforgiveness is a sin, you know."

Trent nodded agreement.

From my bed of leather, I briefly raised up. "Lighten up, Phillip. I thought you weren't preaching anymore."

"Naw. This is good," Trent rebuffed me.

Phillip rocked on. "You see how that works. Forgiving others and asking forgiveness for your own sin."

"Ummm Hmmm." Trent agreed. The road dropped, a miniature roller coaster.

The un-Godly scent of cattle grazing in the Tejon Ranch invaded the vehicle. The stench penetrated to my gut. I wanted to puke. I pulled a hoodie over my nose, clogged my nostrils. I held my breath until nature forced me to breathe poop scented air.

"In many ways being in a coma was my path to freedom."

Trent withheld his "Amen" to Phillip's nonsense.

"Hear me out now. When you can't talk or control your thoughts, you are totally at the mercy of the Holy Spirit. The Lord humbled me. I had a lot of time to beg forgiveness, which He mercifully granted."

"What if you do something unforgiveable?" Trent asked.

Telepathically I pleaded with Trent, don't go there.

"There is no such thing as unforgiveable. Psalm 32, Verse 5 says, "I will confess my transgressions unto the Lord; and thou forgavest the iniquity of my sin."

By the time we reached Bakersfield, I was ready to scream, "Shut the F up!"

I threw off the hoodie, opened my eyes. Trent's jock strap was wedged in the track beneath Phillip's seat. I sucked in my breath, tugged on the jock strap until my fingers went numb. Elastic expanded in my hand, then snapped back, laughing "Tee hee, hee." I wrapped the elastic waist band around my hand, twirled the ding dong shaped crotch into a mound. With waning strength I pulled and prayed, *Lord if you just let me out of this mess...*The elastic fabric ripped, sounding like a stealth fart.

Phillip's head spun around. "You say something, Bree?"

"No. I was just getting a bottle of water." I stuffed the

jock strap in my purse, exhaled audibly. Trent's squinting eye stared me down in the rearview mirror. My scowl met his. Trent looked away.

Like old war buddies Phillip and Trent yakked for the next two hundred miles. I pretended to sleep. Tiny tears squeezed from the corners of my eyes, knowing, he was going away.

Trent told Phillip, "Thank you for helping me embrace my passion."

How about thanking me? I thought.

Trent continued, "Physical rehabilitation. That's the exact focus I needed."

"The Bible talks about 'laying on hands'. That's your spiritual gift. Develop it. The Lord put you in this situation for a reason...When do classes start?"

"Next week."

"Have you told Aubrey you're leaving?"

"I mentioned it. I'm not sure she was listening."

"She's got a lot on her mind. Aubrey won't admit it, but that scene at her father's funeral was devastating. Now, Pearl's a tough cookie. She can handle it. Aubrey's another story. Straight up daddy's girl. She ignored Winston's faults... Wish she could do the same with me."

Silence endured long enough to crack an egg and fry it.

Phillip continued, "I had a strange dream last night."

Thud. Trent's tension leaped into the back seat.

"I was in a huge, all white room with lots of doors and no windows. If my mother was alive, she could tell me what it means. That woman could interpret dreams, like Joseph, in the Bible."

"What do you think it means?" Trent asked.

"Maybe something to do with the church. I've been struggling with a succession plan. Trying to stay one step ahead of tyranny."

"They're plotting against you?"

"Hell yeah. Some so-called Christians even prayed against my recovery. I'm trying to decide what the church really needs. They'll vote on it, of course. Flaws and all, my opinion still carries the most weight. Minister Burns is an honorable man. Not a dynamic leader."

Trent asked. "What about John Bogan?"

"Aubrey can't *stand* him. Says he's a chauvinist. On the plus side, he brings diversity to the church, which is not a bad thing, especially in Orange County. If we elected him, half the congregation would leave...He ain't taking over my pulpit." Phillip laughed.

Phillip continued. "I'm gonna let the Lord lead me. Wait to make an endorsement."

Trent thumped the steering wheel of the Rover like a drum.

I meditated on his fingers. Long, sensitive fingers. Strumming my butt like a banjo. Hmmmn.

31

END OF THE ROAD

AUBREY

The antique German clock gonged three times, defiling the peace and quiet that had eluded me for months. Not a wisp of air stirred in the room. Walls closed in like the lid to the casket that held my father for eternity. According to the Bible, his spirit rose on the day of his death. That is what I would focus on to stay sane. I willed my mind not to think about death, dying. Even for the staunchest Christian, death was the ultimate mystery. I conceded, I would not solve that mystery tonight.

Phillip's latest sleep medication must be working, I thought. The sound of open mouthed snoring, fitful gasping, body jerking and muscles twitching were absent. I cautiously rolled to my left side, mindful that an unfortunate side effect of the Mirtazapine, restless leg syndrome, could suddenly erupt and take out my shins. I gladly traded this relatively minor side effect for the trembling and paranoia that prior prescriptions had caused. After weeks of doctor's experimenting it appeared that Phillip's medications had finally leveled out.

When I had broached the subject, "We might both be more comfortable, if I move into another bedroom," Phillip grew visibly distraught, insisted that I sleep with him. We had slept together for twenty-five years.

Now I was awake, thinking too much. Thinking first thing tomorrow morning, Trent will pack his bags and leave me.

My eyelids were clinched dry, shoulders shrugged to my ears. I willed my body to relax. The right eye responded with a pulsing twitch. If I was lucky, Phillip might sleep through the night without needing water, medication or a potty break.

Between Technicolor dreams, I floated above my worries. There was nothing I could do to make him stay. Trent had a right to live his life instead of mine.

In the space between sleep and consciousness Phillip's preacher perfect voice called out, "Wake up, Bree."

I bolted upright. An instant chill invaded the room. Why was I so cold, shaking uncontrollably? In a single motion my feet and fear landed on hardwood. I fumbled for the lamp switch.

Sixty watts of liquid light framed Phillip's rigid face. His mouth gaped open like a yawn frozen in flight. His eyes were closed.

I backed toward the door muttering, "No...God no. Not now." A terrified, wounded animal, I howled until my cries blended with yelping of the caged boxers.

Trent busted through the door, pulled me away from Phillip's side of the bed.

"Call 9-1-1."

9-1-1 could not help him. No one could help him now.

32

GOIN' UP YONDER

Aubrey

I loved the Lord with all my heart. Sometimes He has a lousy sense of timing. How could the two most important men in my life be taken within a fortnight? I knew I had sinned. But the God I loved was not a vengeful God. What else would He take? I was afraid to ask through gnashing teeth.

The entrance to the memorial park resembled the gates to Heaven. A long line of black stretch Cadillac limousines led a procession of hundreds of vehicles beneath an archway draped in cascading rhododendron. It was the longest funeral procession I had ever seen. People traveled from as far away as London, New York, Detroit and Florida to pay respects to Phillip. The archway opened to rolling hills covered in velvet lawns. There were no standing monuments, only in ground plaques. As I walked through the cemetery, taking care not to step on plaques, I paused to read tributes to mere mortals elevated to the status of kings and queens.

In the crook of his arm, Miles held my left arm. His

fingers intertwined with mine, gently guiding me forward. Miles' young face carried the burden of fear that I would come undone. But I was through with mourning, through with crying, a stone hearted, virtual dishrag.

"Come on, Mom. They're waiting for us," Miles nudged me forward. I heard the words proceeding from his mouth. There was a disconnect between my brain and feet. Miles whisked me along, seated me in the front row, within arms' reach of the gleaming, navy blue box with heavy gold handles and fancy gold edging. The "Cadillac of Caskets", was how the mortician described it.

"Wake up Bree," echoed in my head. If I awakened from the unending nightmare, I would scream without ceasing and fly over the cuckoo's nest. My intellectual self struggled to maintain the dignity of the occasion. Phillip would have loved the elaborate ceremony. Towering gladioli, white orchids, pink princess lilies and roses on stands. Beautiful flowers do not belong at sad occasions like this, I felt. Gospel music, abundant praise, resolutions from churches near and far, fond remembrances, were too numerous to squeeze into one service. A river of tears fell for Phillip, who loved me even when we both fell short of God's glory.

My mind was absent from the body, still curled beneath the sheets of the guest bedroom where I hibernated for a solid week. Three hours before the funeral Miles dragged me out of bed. Mama pushed me, protesting, into the shower. Water pelted my face. Mama turned me around. I felt warm water cascading down my back, reminding me how it once felt to be clean.

Hilton plopped me down in front of the vanity to repair my scary face. My eyes were swollen with the weariness of a thousand years.

"No self-respecting diva faces the world like this," Hilton

warned while dabbing concealer over dark circles and bags that drooped lower than my spirit.

"How could I lose so much? Is God punishing me?" I begged Hilton for an answer. My father's death was a setback, the impact subtle compared to what I was feeling. I reasoned, Daddy was older and sick with Alzheimer's. His expiration date was predicted almost to the month by his physician.

Never did I expect to lose Phillip, even when he was in a coma. Mr. Magic, the ever ready preacher, could not go down like this. God played a cruel joke, snatching Phillip from the jaws of death, then leaving him to die in his sleep from a heart attack. Angry jaws welded to my sunken cheeks.

I sat with a Joker's smile and parched lips, dressed in all black, choking back the scream curdling in my throat. My husband of twenty-five years was imprisoned in a box, ready to be lowered into the ground and dirt shoveled over him. The climax would be witnessed by a ghostly crew of grave diggers, relegated to the shadows until the decedent's friends and family retreated to their limousines and cars.

The door of the limousine was open. I lingered at the gravesite long after there was nothing left to do. Ashes had been sprinkled, many prayers prayed. What remained was for me to walk away from this lonely place and go in search of my peace.

Miles squeezed my arm. "Mom, people will be arriving at the house. Don't you think we should leave?"

"Go on, son. I need a minute."

Miles turned to Jorge, official substitute for Trent, who left the house days earlier.

"Jorge, I'll leave a limo for the two of you. Give her five, ten minutes at most. Then bring her home."

"Yes sir." Jorge's bald, shiny head nodded. He wiped his gleaming scalp with a white handkerchief. His round belly peeked from beneath a plaid J.C Penney's sport coat. I waved as the limo carrying Miles, my mother and Phillip's cousin Jerome pulled away.

On the opposite side of the circular drive I spotted Trent's Jeep. Laila and Ali's heads stuck out the back window.

"Wait here," I instructed Jorge. "I'll be right back."

I plodded through recently laid, sopping wet sod. Trent's face was turned away. My nails tapped the passenger side window. Through dark sunglasses, I could still see his pain.

"I thought you left."

"We posted up at a motel for a few days."

"Why didn't you join us for the service?"

"I didn't want to get in the way... Laila and Ali wanted to say goodbye."

I moved to the back window and hugged Ali's big head first. Laila whined, nuzzled me with her jealous snout, lapped my face with her wet tongue.

"Did their master want to say goodbye, too?"

"I said goodbye once." Trent swallowed the lump in his throat. "Your husband... Phillip was a good man. Take care of yourself...and eat something."

Since Phillip's death the smell of food sickened me. I didn't mind losing a few pounds, but not like this. "It would help, if I had somebody to cook for me."

No response.

My tears bubbled up. "You picked a helluva time to leave, Trent." Quivering lips could not say the three words that might make him stay. Too much was happening at once. Daddy was gone. Phillip was gone. The one who made me feel like a woman again, was about to be in the wind. "You didn't have to take my dogs."

Trent laughed. A single tear rolled from beneath his sunglasses. "They'll miss you too."

"Call me some time," I pleaded.

Trent shook his head. "Not a good idea…" He looked down at his lap. "Your ride is waiting."

Jorge leaned against the hood of the limo. The limo driver stood outside the car, lifting his black, chauffeur's cap and wiping sweat trickling from his brow. Jorge waved me toward the limo. I backed away from the Jeep, tossed a tepid wave, turned and walked. The heels of my Prada pumps sank into the ground. I had an eerie feeling of desecrating bodies with each step.

Shoulders held back, I swallowed my tears, and pranced. Trent's final view of me would not be that of an old, broken down woman.

In the distance a bowlegged woman in a black wool, winter suit, wide- brimmed felt hat and carrying a single red rose approached Phillip's casket. I did not remember seeing this woman during the funeral or at the interment service. The woman carried an old lady's square black pocket book. She had the gait of a younger person, although not too graceful. Her heels rolled outward every time her feet pounded the ground. She would not win any modeling contests.

I breezed past the limousine. Jorge shouted, "Mrs. Sampson, where you going now?" He threw up his hands, muttered expletives in Spanish.

I did not stop to answer. I wanted a closer look at the out-of-season woman. The woman leaned in, placed a red rose in the center of Phillip's casket on top of the elaborate white spray.

Oh, hell no. Ain't no bitch showing up at my husband's funeral, disrespecting me.

A few steps closer I saw the hairiest legs I had seen since visiting Aunt Lucy in Lithonia, Georgia. Aunt Lucy swore that milk bottle, hairy legs turned a man on. But this woman's bowed legs were bony and tight with well developed calves.

I called out, "Scuse me, Miss...The service is over. Do you know my husband?"

The woman turned to face me with squinty, blood shot eyes, drawn lips and a pronounced Adam's apple. Donovan Upchurch. He tucked his pocket book in his armpit, ran like a cheetah with fire torching his balls.

I kicked off my pumps, tossed my purse and sprinted in hot pursuit.

Without three inch heels, straight wool skirt and a hat weighing him down Donovan was younger and definitely faster. Donovan in drag ran like a man with an inverted umbrella holding him down.

A blast of adrenaline propelled me within seconds behind him. I ran for life that, because of Donovan, was about to be lowered in the ground. I ran like Flo Jo, arms churning, knees lifting, for the pain and sorrow Donovan visited upon my family.

His skinny ankles wobbled as he tried to pick up steam. I kicked into second gear, opened my arms, took a flying dive for the man who had turned my life upside down.

With both hands I held his left foot to the ground. He flipped me over, my back pummeled the ground. Oblivious to pain, I held on. Donovan raised his right foot. The skinny heel of Donovan's pump aimed at my face. I closed my eyes, bracing for impact.

Ali leaped into the air, pinning Donovan to the ground. Snarling, Ali's teeth were at his throat. Laila, tossing her head from side to side, gnawed on Donovan's exposed ankle. Donovan's scream could wake the dead.

I released my hold.

Above my head Trent called off the dogs. He planted his

knee in Donovan's chest, pounding Donovan's face, smashing his ears. Yelping cries emitted from Donovan's mouth. Trent's forked fingers struck Donovan's neck, paralyzing the sound.

Jorge, tardy to the beat down party, tried to pull Trent off. "Don't kill him, man. Don't kill him. " Jorge flipped Donovan on his face, crunched his knee in Donovan's spine and secured Donovan's hands with his tie.

Trent circled Jorge, sitting astride Donovan. Jorge threw up a protective hand, "Enough. He ain't goin' nowhere. I got him."

Trent lifted me from the ground, took me in his arms. "You okay?"

My heart beat faster than Sheila E's drums. I had not been in a street fight since sixth grade when I arrived in Vallejo. Typical testing of the new girl in town.

Trent pulled my head to his chest. "Did he hurt you?"

Still winded, I could not talk.

"I was pulling off. The dogs were going *crazy* in the back. Rocking the Jeep. I jumped out, saw what was going on."

"I'll be sore as hell tomorrow. But I'm fine. Thank you." I kissed his cheek as he held me one last time.

I dragged my discombobulated behind to Phillip's casket, slapped Donovan's red rose to the ground and crushed it beneath my feet. I touched the casket. "We've got him, baby. We've got him now."

I could breathe again. Or so I thought.

33

I FOUGHT THE LAW

Aubrey

"What do you mean, they won't charge him with first degree murder? He killed my husband."

I hovered over the desk of Renard Broussard, ignoring his repeated requests to "Have a seat, Mrs. Sampson."

"According to the coroner, a heart attack killed your husband."

"A heart attack precipitated by a bullet to the head!"

"The investigation is not complete. Charges can be added later. We're still gathering evidence."

"What more do you need? He had the murder weapon in his purse. Could've shot me."

Broussard corrected me. "Attempted murder weapon."

"Oh I see. You need a video of him holding the gun to my husband's head."

I bit my trembling lower lip, blinked back hot stinging tears. *I did not come for sympathy. I came for justice. Can't let him see me cry.*

"I know this is emotional for you, Mrs. Sampson. But listen. The worst thing the D.A. can do is over charge a case. They'll have a hard time proving attempted murder."

I slumped into the well worn, burgundy fabric covering the metal frame office chair. Until now I had avoided contact with hard surfaces in Broussard's office that smelled like two day old Fritos.

My chin rested on a balled fist. I looked up and locked eyes with Broussard. "I'm tired, drained by all the bullshit. That psychopath should be off the streets for good."

"We both know that, but his mental health will not be an issue unless his attorney raises it."

"How does he do that?"

"The insanity defense. It will be awhile before we know their strategy. As expected he pled 'not guilty' at the arraignment. His new attorney, who by the way subbed in today, will take his sweet time bringing this to trial."

"Public Defender not good enough for Donovan?" I casually inquired.

"Donovan hired a high profile lawyer."

"Johnny Cochran's twin?"

"A Johnny Cochran wanna be. Justin Flowers."

I gagged on my own spit.

34

MY CONFESSIONS

SISTERS IN SILENCE.COM
APRIL 10

I *cannot write another word until I get my spirit right, tell the truth. Sisters in Silence, you and I are one. I wrote the beginning installments of this blog from the perspective of a dispassionate third party observer of men behaving badly, doing damage to someone else's life. Truth is, I had a Ho-ing Husband until he up and died on me. There were times when I was angry enough to hurt him, hammer his short ass into the ground. But I never expected him to be taken out by the hands of someone else. He seemed so strong, invincible.*

I want my husband's killer to walk the plank. That's right. I have not reached the level of forgiveness that Martin Luther King, Jr. preached about, that Jesus talked about in Mark 11:25-26. "And whenever you stand praying, if you have anything against anyone, forgive him, that your Father in heaven may also forgive you your trespasses.

But if you do not forgive, neither will your Father in heaven forgive your trespasses."

I spend a lot of time on my knees asking the Lord to elevate me to a level of forgiveness so I can go on. Help me Holy Ghost. Revenge thinking is not healthy, so says my pounding heart.

Why now, you ask, am I in the business of confessing? I must keep it real or you will peep my deception faster than I can spell it. I have a lot of shit to work out with my therapist.

I listen to the late Wayne Dwyer's tapes non-stop. I resisted Wayne at the inception of my crisis. It took a minute to settle down, get my head in the right space to listen. I'm harboring too many unhealthy thoughts. I drive down the street, repeating, "Not a match. Not a match." Listen to Wayne's audiotape, "The Power of Intention". You'll know what I'm talking about.

If my husband had not given up the ghost, would my rage against peripatetic little pee wee see the light of day? Probably not. I would have gone on living the masquerade I lived the last twenty-five years, lacking the audacity to leave or reclaim my life. I was chained to the big house, the luxury cars and the safety of a marriage that others envied. It looked good from the outside. Year after year, day after day I sanctioned the facade until the plastic mask melted into my skin and became the only face I knew.

Some will suggest that I write from a place of pain. Damn right I do. Ironically, that pain allows me to focus on the end game. Appreciate life, love more clearly and don't let yesterday's blues define who I am.

Love came to me in the strangest way while I was healing. A man, the polar opposite of my husband, invaded my space. I did not banish him, which would have been my natural tendency, had I been operating in a state of sanity. When I found out my husband had a baby by another woman I lost my mind, at least the former mind conditioned to walk in lock step with my husband's beliefs. For twenty-five years I walked around with blinders. I took my vow to forsake all others seriously. That is what my naïve ass did.

Enter Jodie. Names have been changed to protect the not-so-innocent. He was no Prince Charming on a white horse. The man drove a dented, ten year old Jeep Wrangler and did not have the proverbial pot to piss in. But he had a killer body, velvet eyes and arms strong enough to carry me.

Unfortunately, my fairy tale did not have a happy ending. I lost my husband, who despite his multiple faults, was a good man and my Jodie, lover of my loins, in the same week.

God is punishing me. I deserve every bit of it. I broke the Lord's commandment, "Thou shall not commit adultery". I only broke it once, but when I broke it, I shattered it. Downright enjoyed it! Here's a new rule dedicated to yours truly.

Rule No. 12: DO NOT FOOL AROUND AND FALL IN LOVE.

My excuse: Leveling the playing field. The truth is, I fooled around and fell in love, which makes me no better than my Ho-ing Husband.

To hell with the Rules. My life is screwed. I can't tell anyone what to do.

Writing is my salvation. It is the only time I am not boohooing like a crazed you know what. Half the time I don't know whether I am crying about my husband or the beautiful man who walked away from me. In my lover's defense, I pushed him away when he sorta, kinda confessed that he loved me. His timing was lousy. I was married and confused about love and lust, whether they can co-exist peacefully?

How do I write about these things while still in mourning? If I don't get this off my chest, my head will shatter like a ripe watermelon dropped on concrete. I can't tell it all in

one sitting. But I have to tell enough to buy myself some
sleep. I have no one to talk to but you. I am sick and tired of
yakking to police.

━━━◅«(◉)»▻━━━

Aubrey

The hush over Phillip's illegitimate child had officially
lifted. Relatives, friends and strangers felt free to openly
discuss the subject with me. Two weeks after the funeral
Trudy Jarvis stopped by with a plate full of oatmeal raisin
cookies. Trudy claimed the cookies were homemade. They
bore an uncanny resemblance and taste to Bristol Farms
cookies. Did not matter. Of late, I was an equal opportunity
destroyer of cookies and anything sweet.

Trent's admonishment to "eat something", did not go
unheeded. I ate everything that was not on somebody else's
plate. Once my fork found its way to sweet potato fries on
Hilton's combo platter at Wood Ranch BBQ & Grill. Hilton
politely called it nervous eating. I called it "searching for satisfaction" in the only place I could find it-at the dinner table.
Who cared if my thighs were half an inch thicker or if my
waist was at war with my belts?

"I've been abandoned by three men," I groused.

"Death is not the same as abandonment," Hilton reminded me.

"Either way, it sucks."

I wanted to be alone. With my cookies, I thought, but
was thankful that Hilton had the patience to tolerate me.

Trudy droned on. "It's not fair that you have to live with consequences of his sin. How dare that boy...what's his name? Donovan? Disrespect your beautiful family?"

Trudy's chapped, pink lips quivered. Deep wrinkles around her mouth caved in. Trudy's searing blue eyes burned righteous indignation.

I thought about lighting her ass up. She was not my BFF just because she brought cookies. Who did she think she was, getting in my business, turned into the world's business since the article on Donovan's arrest appeared in the Orange County Register. The light blinked on. Trudy Jarvis was a sister suffering in silence. I could not imagine dull, yellow toothed Glen Jarvis pushing up on another woman, his face, white as a sheet, sniffing poontang.

Trudy meant well with her clunky "sin" comment, her awkward attempts to comfort me.

I found myself still covering for Phillip, struggling to elevate his legacy above the drama that brought him down. Word got back to me that a church member suggested that I was pressing for a first degree murder charge against Donovan to avoid splitting Phillip's estate with his "other" son. The naysayer leap-frogged over death and destruction of a family unit, reduced our lives to dollars and cents. It all came down to money for someone on the outside looking in.

As Trudy blabbered on, my eyes glazed over. Trudy was not what men referred to as a "looker", standing less than five feet tall with mousey brown hair that had a stubborn curl reminiscent of Little Orphan Annie. A devoted member of Fanatics Gym, Trudy could not claim one pound lost from her pear shaped frame.

What bound her to Glen? Trudy was sharp as a Cutco knife. She held tight rein over multiple successful pesticide related enterprises, inherited by Glen from his father, who inherited the original business from his father, an immigrant from Israel. Theirs was the All American story. Bugs that make you filthy rich.

"These cookies are delicious." I glanced at my watch. "Girl, I've got ten minutes to make my hair appointment in Orange."

"I'll get out of your way." Trudy turned to leave. I grabbed her arm. "Hey, if you ever need to talk about anything, let me know. I'm still having trouble talking about Phillip."

She hugged me goodbye. "Honey, you've been through a lot. These things take time."

I grabbed my keys and purse, followed Trudy out and jumped in my car. On the freeway, I agonized, where do I go now? The bogus excuse of a hair appointment meant that I had to spend at least two hours out of the house. What I really wanted to do was take my cookies to bed and cry. No conversatin', no questions. Just me and my mind.

It was too early for a movie where darkness would protect me like a shroud. I had watched everything Cinema City, Edwards Regal and the new theater in Yorba Linda Town Center had to offer, including G-rated animated features.

I drove the 55 freeway to the 22 freeway west. Before I knew it, I was in Long Beach, near the airport. I popped into the Westin for coffee and a doughnut. Just what I needed. More carbs. I could not wait to get back home, behind closed doors, where I could pretend to be in witness protection. There was no other way to justify the self-imposed solitude, long stretches of listening to the ticking clock, unheard when there was music, laughter, voices in my home.

⟩⟨⟩⟨⟩

Aubrey

My trip to the grocery store ended badly. A bubble eyed ten-year old with freckles and flaming red hair pointed his grimy finger at me and exclaimed loudly, "Look, mom. There's the lady in the newspaper."

I recalled my hideous photograph in the Orange County Register after Donovan was captured. My mouth was agape, makeup smudged, hair dusty like a wildebeest.

I ditched my over loaded basket in the check-out line and fled. So much for my plan to start eating healthy again.

Time was frozen tighter than a malfunctioning computer. I could not reboot, shut down, move the cursor or process words into sentences that made sense. People tried to console me. "Sometimes you have to go through something," which was not consoling. How long would "going through" last?

Abiding loneliness lingered from the rising of the sun to the reigning of the moon. Darkness swooned in slow motion. I missed Phillip, even though he created my confliction. How dare he get a pass?

Phillip's sudden silence created a wider gulf than the absence of his sounds-calling me, "Bree", rummaging through the refrigerator for forbidden food. Phillip loved the way I fussed when he acted like a child, filching sweets that foiled his low-cholesterol diet, casting a guilty glance, making sure he got caught. In the end I was more his mother than his lover. I saw it coming, waited too late to turn it around.

The moments I needed to hold onto- a rendezvous on a verdant hillside, a tryst in Brione Park, the first time we made love on a prickly bed of autumn leaves-receded into a mirage. Phillip left on a lilting breeze, never looked back or accounted for the pain he caused.

Some say that the spirit lingers on the earth for forty days. Not so with Phillip. He could not stand the heat. Got the hell out. Poof.

35

QUEEN OF SORROW

AUBREY

"If Jesus is coming back, this is the perfect day for His descent," I spoke out loud to myself, took a seat on a wicker patio chair. Wearing a long cotton, Little House on the Prairie flannel nightgown with petite flowers, I waited expectantly for the Rapture. My rambling prayer was audible when Hilton found me.

"Honey, if the Rapture's coming, you'd better get dressed." Hilton shook his head. "How long have you been out here?"

"You see that sky? Slate gray, empty of clouds. Can you feel the thick, milky yellow mist, floating around. I know it's a sign."

"Of June gloom, Aubrey. If God saw you looking like this, He would definitely leave you behind. Up, up." Hilton shooed me into the house.

Hilton's furrowed brow said it all. Extreme emergency, is how Hilton explained my condition to Essie.

An hour later Hilton's Porsche Carrera wove a path

through bumper-to- bumper traffic, headed south on the 55 freeway toward Newport Beach.

He ignored my plea, "All we have to do is wait."

Hilton pursed his lips. "Ummm hmmm."

I rolled down the passenger side deep tinted window, stuck my hand into a dewy mist. I sucked in my breath, exhaled loudly. Like an imbecile I grinned at distant lightning, scorching the sky. "What did I tell you?"

Two miles before the John Wayne Airport exit traffic cleared. Hilton cast me a furtive glance and stepped on the gas. He turned right on MacArthur Blvd., sailed into a parking space in front of Essie's office.

Hilton cautioned, "Be careful what you say to the therapist or the men in white coats will carry you out."

I ignored Hilton's advice. "I gave myself away. A whore in a grocery store parking lot," I confessed to Essie.

"We'll come back to that. How is your infidelity related to Phillip's death?"

"He knew."

"You told him?"

"No. Phillip was psychic after he came back."

"Back from where?"

"The dead."

Essie's face contorted. She took a deep breath, deciding whether to "5150" me (send me to a psych ward) or hold a rosary over my twisted head.

I explained myself. "When Phillip came out of the coma he was a different man. It was like living with a psychic. He knew my thoughts before I could think them."

"You blame yourself for Phillip's death?"

Finally, she asked the question keeping me up all night. I sat silent.

Essie interrupted my guilty thoughts. "You're not God.

You don't have that much power. Listen to me, Aubrey. Severe trauma, burying your father and waking up next to a dead man, has temporarily set you back. I'm going to write a couple of prescriptions to help you get through this..."

"I don't want poison in my system."

"You're in over your head. You've lost the two most important men in your life. It's clear you're not sleeping. You shouldn't be by yourself. What about your mother?"

"We were gettin' on each other's nerves. She went home."

"Hilton says you refuse to let him help. Why is that?"

"Nobody wants to be around a downer."

"That's what friends are for. To watch over you when you're depressed. Yes, you're depressed. You have a couple of options..."

———«()»———

Aubrey

The Porsche crept west on MacArthur at twenty miles per hour. Hilton turned to me, "Now that you've been released into my custody..."

I laughed so hard, snot sprayed from my nose. I cackled until tears pooled beneath my chin. Finally, I blew out repressed anxiety. "Wheeew. I'm a hot mess. How do you put up with me?"

"You're my best friend." Hilton sniffed back tears.

"If we both cry, who's driving the car?" I joked, dialing back heaviness a notch.

Hilton reached over, squeezed my hand and held on. "I'll never forget when David died. You slept next to me in my bed. I was a funky mess. That's love."

On the drive to Hilton's home in Laguna Beach we demolished a box of Kleenex. The Porsche floated over the hill, crossed San Miguel. The ocean rose in a panoramic snapshot. My tears fell slower, softer as Sade wailed "Queen of Sorrow".

<hr>

AUBREY

Trudy Jarvis pounced the driveway, carrying a wicker basket crammed with four weeks worth of yellowing L.A. Times and bundles of mail. Phillip was the last man in America subscribing to the print newspaper that I had forgotten to cancel. During my vacation-luxury rehabilitation at Hilton's, I lost track of the outside world. I climbed out of Hilton's Porsche.

"You're back and looking great. I noticed the newspapers accumulating. I figured you were on vacation. Good for you!" Trudy's shrill voice dropped to a whisper. "Didn't want the wrong people to know you weren't home."

"That was sweet of you, Trudy." As I reached for the basket, I silently thanked God for sending his angels, like Trudy and Hilton, to see me through.

Spending time at Hilton's turned out to be the right medicine at the right time. By day, I basked in seventy-five to eighty degree sunshine. By night I was fanned by refreshing ocean breezes. My bedroom had a one hundred eighty de-gree view of the ocean. Before the visit I was not an ocean person, hated the sand and was respectfully leery of the moving body of water without end.

Flowing dance of the Pacific rocked me to sleep at night. I embraced the ocean, taking long slow walks until my legs screamed against resistance from wet sand. At the edge of the ocean, in the midst of my deepest pain, I scolded God, "Why have you deserted me?" God refused to speak to my angry heart.

Days later inside a cove on the beach in Corona Del Mar the answer came. "I didn't desert you. You deserted me."

My eyes scanned the coast in search of the man behind the resonant voice. No one was in sight. I walked deeper into the spray of heavy ocean mist. There were no strollers, no joggers. Not even yesterday's romping cocker spaniel blaz-ing a path for his master. I was utterly alone, hearing voic-es. Again. My humanness cried panic. Run to the nearest emergency room and check yourself in. An unnatural peace pervaded the atmosphere, resided in my spirit. Calmness washed me from head to toe. Arms raised, head bowed, I submitted to the will of God.

I raced into forty-five degree surf. I was not the one in control. He was in the waves, cradling my listless body, rock-ing me until all resistance was gone. I floated on wave after wave until being delivered safely back to shore.

In the vestibule of Hilton's home, I dripped water on im-ported Spanish tile.

"What the hell happened?" Hilton asked, simultaneous-ly running for towels to wrap his ocean phobic friend. "You decided to take a dip at the last minute?"

I paused before answering. "I got baptized."

I walked out of wet sandals, went directly to my room.

For the first time in months I picked up the Word flung haplessly at my unfaithful husband. I prayed without consciousness of time, eschewing oratory spouted by stiff-necked people in public places. My soul opened to an unfiltered conversation with God.

The richness of my renewed relationship with the Source allowed me to finally heal. From that day forward God spoke to me in a quiet voice. It was time to go home.

Trudy's laser focused scrutiny of Hilton snapped me back to the real world. From top to bottom Trudy checked out Hilton's blistering white Ralph Lauren polo shirt, blue seersucker slacks and Gucci loafers.

"I'll let you two get on about your business," Trudy said.

"I'm so sorry. Trudy, this is my good friend Hilton Long."

Hilton's manicured hand floated out to meet Trudy's.

"I assumed you two met at the repast. I was so out of it. A terrible hostess."

Hilton's angel wing, coal black eyelashes messed with Trudy's mind. I watched Trudy actively calculate the probability that I was screwing a gay man.

36

PRISONER OF LOVE

AUBREY

I came loaded for bear, prepared to loathe him. But his childlike appearance, hair matted and twisted into horns, saucer sized bouncing eyes inside a head too small, twiggy limbs jutting out of an orange jump suit two sizes too large, reminded me of a fragile doll.

Judge Cleveland Kennedy called case number OC193292. Donovan rose to his feet. Minus the high heels, he was shorter than I remembered. Peacocking defense attorney Justin Flowers turned toward a camera that captured the moment for the Orange County Register. Justin's bloated head tilted toward his good side. His pitiful client stared, bewildered. A space cadet. Time had done a number on Donovan's once peachy complexion and smooth skin. Being small prey living in a cage surrounded by hungry hunters did not suit delicate Donovan. His skin was ashy, two shades lighter than when he entered the sunless pit of Theo Lacey Jail in Orange, California.

Months of underground existence in Toronto Canada

had taken a toll as well. According to Broussard, Donovan breezed across the porous Canadian border virtually undetected.

Photo op completed, Justin dwarfed his diminutive client. Donovan almost disappeared behind Justin's blue pinstriped suit, stretching a tad too tight across Justin's spreading rear. The side vents of Justin's suit gasped for air.

Justin leaned his ear toward Donovan.

Judge Kennedy cleared his throat. "Are you ready to proceed, Mr. Flowers?"

"Uh, yes, Your Honor. I was just answering my client's last minute question."

"You've had two months for that. Proceed."

Donovan stepped out of Justin's shadow. His head turned in my direction. The corners of his mouth curled up and blossomed into a radiant smile. He raised manacled hands, pumped puny fists.

Something stirred behind me. Two rows back sat the one who incubated the demon seed, Delia Upchurch, the face I could not bring into focus until now. Her hair was shorter, hard pressed and glued into rows of individual curls sturdy enough to withstand gale winds. Glittering swap meet earrings hung to her shoulders, which was not a feat given the fact that Delia had no neck.

I did a double take. Maybe that's not Delia. Then that silly "tee hee hee" grin spread across Delia's doughy face. A dead give away. From the recesses of suppressed memories I recalled how Delia used to melt, almost break into a swoon, any time a man paid her a compliment.

"You look nice today, Delia," Phillip would say.

"Tee hee hee." The tricky slut grinned, exuding an air of innocence like someone a tad bit slow. I never paid Delia much attention, assuming Pastor Phillip, always charming, was being polite. Devious intent, percolating in both of their minds, went undetected.

Now it all made sense. Delia Upchurch was low hanging fruit, begging to be squeezed.

Delia waved fire engine red, pointy witch shaped fingernails at her son. Delia pretended not to notice me noticing her. She probably had observed me arrive earlier, sit on a hard wood bench outside Dept. 45 of the Central Justice Center. She saw me ditch two hungry reporters, hounding me for useless comment. I was sure she saw me, head held high, enter the courtroom and take a seat two rows behind the district attorney, while Delia lurked in the shadows, observing the competition, like twenty some years ago.

From start to finish the preliminary hearing lasted all of thirty minutes. Judge Cleveland Kennedy read the charges, headlined by attempted murder and aggravated assault. The D.A. decided not to call me as a witness. They had enough evidence, including the attempted murder weapon, to ensure that Donovan would be held over for trial.

In a kittenish, Michael Jackson, voice, Donovan pleaded not guilty. I almost laughed at the sharp contrast with the growling, insistent voice, bellowing through Trinity Baptist Church, "Abba, Abba."

The hearing adjourned. My meat was stuck in the seat, unable to rise. Mind in a blur--- confront, not confront, speak, not speak, kick ass, not kick ass. I gathered my Chloe bag from the empty seat beside me.

In the center aisle, just above my head, Justin Flowers, carrying an alligator briefcase, stared down.

I threw shade darker than an eclipse.

Justin persisted, "I'm glad you made it. We need to talk."

"Phillip sends his regrets," I shot back.

"Aubrey, I left a thousand messages."

I only remembered hitting the delete button five hundred times. I stood, acknowledging the burly bailiff's displeasure at our conversation while the next case was called. I brushed past Justin, caught a glimpse of Delia from the corner of my eye and hit the corridor.

"Wait up Aubrey," Justin called after me.

I turned on my heels. "Talk," I commanded. My steely eyes warned that he was on a short clock.

"Phillip begged me to represent his son."

"Phillip regulating from the grave?"

"Before he died. Remember the day we were sitting on the patio. You and your boyfriend came back from walking the dogs. Phillip made me promise to represent Donovan, if he was caught. Paid the retainer. By the way, where is Black Adonis?"

"None ya'." Translation, None of your damned business.

"I tried to talk Phillip out of it."

"*Bullshit.* You never saw a dollar you didn't like. "

"Just listen for a minute." Justin toyed with the white cuff of his Pepto-Bismol pink shirt. The flashy lawyer had hundreds of shirts with French cuffs, folded and stacked on shelves in a barn sized closet. The first time Phillip corralled me into attending a dinner party at Justin's gawdy, Hancock Park house I endured the tour of his closet, a man cave complete with floor to ceiling mirrors, a sit down dresser equipped with a telephone, big screen Samsung television, jewelry chest and a rack of two hundred hand tailored suits organized by color. Justin caressed white marble countertops as he quipped to Phillip, primarily for my benefit, "A man could get laid up in here." Phillip had the good sense not to laugh.

I let the snake slither in, remaining silent as Phillip and Justin conferred over Justin's "guilty-as sin" clients in need of character witnesses before appearing in court. In Phillip's study the client would miraculously experience a religious epiphany, make a large donation, pay enough visits to the church to establish him on the membership rolls. The congregation never knew the high octane level of criminality nesting among them. The men, and they were usually men, wore expensive tailored suits, heavy gold and diamond jewelry and bathed in the best cologne. White collar criminals trafficking in drugs, illegal gambling and using fronts like waste disposal and water treatment businesses, became regular tithers. Phillip was incentivized by their generous tithes to render spirited testimonials on behalf of Justin's clients.

When tithes exceeded six figures, the Holy Spirit fell especially hard on Pastor Phillip. Phillip converted Justin's Russian Mafia, racketeering client, Rusty Antonovich, into a scripture quoting, homeless ministry deacon. So thorough was the client's conversion, Rusty relinquished his life as a gangster (or played it on the down low) and became a full time evangelist.

To his credit Pastor Phillip was an equal opportunity defender. He accepted jail calls in the middle of the night from men without a dime to make a call. Paying a poor man's legal fees or making bail balanced the scales of injustice in Phillip's mind.

This time he had gone too far, protecting the man who sent him to an early grave, made me a widow and Miles a fatherless child. "How much did he pay you, Justin?"

"Judge not, lest ye be judged," Justin Flowers quoted the Bible.

"Holiness doesn't suit you."

"As a defense attorney my job is not to judge a man's guilt or innocence. My job is to give him the best defense available under the law. Have you considered the possibility that Donovan did not shoot his father?"

Spiders ran up and down my spine when Justin referred to Phillip as Donovan's father.

"Who shot him then? The one-armed man from the Fugitive?"

"Please don't rush to judgment."

"Okay, Johnny."

Justin nodded to the far end of the hallway. "Delia wants to meet you."

Delia Upchurch cowered at the east end of the corridor looking meek in a skirt too short to hide the extra flesh mooning her knee caps. For a forty-something woman Delia was still somewhat attractive, except for the plastic curls. Delia's navy blue suit and white blouse were sufficiently conservative for the occasion. She should have left the wide ankle strap, fringed stilettos, in the closet. Every step she took mimicked the Budweiser stallions in full trot.

"I've already had the displeasure."

"For God's sake, Aubrey. She wants to apologize."

For what? Fucking my husband or sending her ballistic son to put a bullet in his head? I thought, but remembered my eight week Bible study on the subject of forgiveness. I could not jeopardize my soul by turning my back on T.H.O.T.

"I understand how you feel," Justin persisted.

"To be at peace with the Lord. That's what I have to do."

Justin looked puzzled by my words.

"It's the Christian thing to do. Tell her to trot on over here."

Justin took my arm. "Can't you just..." He released my arm, thought twice about asking me to move. Justin plucked Delia from the wall.

It was ironic how Delia's presence within inches of me

felt insignificant. My mind had elevated her to the status of boogey woman, caped nemesis out for vengeance. Reality revealed her as an insecure, fragile insect waiting to be stepped on. I could not do it. I was "washed in the blood". For the first time I truly understood what that meant.

Her timid voice squeaked, "Aubrey".

"Mrs. Sampson." I had to get that in.

"I apologize for the pain I caused your family."

"Okay."

"My son didn't do what he's accused of doing."

"The jury determines that. Not me."

"I just want you to understand..."

"That's probably beyond me. Understanding any of this. But I will say that I forgive you and I will pray for you. As best I can."

Delia burst into choking tears. The corridor froze. Had it been anyone else, I would have reached out and hugged her. I did not want the demon spirit rubbing off on me.

I caught my breath, reached into my bag and thrust into Justin's manicured hand a copy of a neatly folded letter, which I had memorized. I sailed away from the overpowering scent of Justin's liberally splashed Dolce and Gabana cologne, "The One".

I walked lighter than my grandmother's freshly baked biscuits. My clear mind counted down seconds until Justin's eyes got past the meaningless series of numbers and fancy terms: "Locus, allele sizes". By the time I reached the elevator, Justin would reach the bold letters that read, "CHILD: DONOVAN UPCHURCH, TEST DATE March 15th. When I punched the button for the first floor, the next column would read: "ALLEGED FATHER: PHILLIP SAMPSON, TEST DATE March 15th.

The elevator door closed with yawing resolve. By now

Justin had reached the grand finale, the stunning, final paragraph that read:

"*Interpretation:*

Combined Paternity Index: 0

Probability of Paternity: 0

The alleged father is excluded as the biological father of the tested child. This conclusion is based on the non-matching alleles observed by loci listed above with PI equal to 0. The alleged father lacks the genetic markers that must be contributed to the child by the biological father. The probability of paternity is 0%."

By now Justin's muddy eyes would bulge like Step N' Fetchit's.

I could have sworn that Delia's scream echoed down the elevator shaft. That shrill sound was my glee kicking the enemy's ass.

The open air parking lot of the Central Justice Center glowed like the streets of Heaven. Flags unfurled and saluted the flawless sky. Gemstones burst before my smiling eyes. I dropped a twenty dollar bill in the bucket of a homeless man. He stepped toward me. I shot him the fish eye.

37

DANCE LIKE DAVID DANCED

Aubrey

I flashed back to the moments before God delivered my healing. For many days I had prayed for a word from God. God had been silent since I returned home from Hilton's. Maybe my house was cursed, I was starting to think.

On the way home from Body Pump at 24 Hour Fitness I decided to stop for breakfast at McDonald's on Yorba Linda Boulevard and Lakeview. I was lethargic, out of shape after a month long hiatus from the gym. My mind was ready, but my sluggish body would not cooperate.

It was all I could do to keep from ordering a breakfast combo with eggs, hash browns and pancakes. My left hand clutched a cup of hot coffee. In the crook of my right arm I balanced a bag containing dry oatmeal, all the fixings on the side, one cream and one sugar.

A chipper, gentleman with copper hair and the palest skin I had had ever seen held open the door. "Good Morning," he chirped like a leprechaun. I was startled by the unexpected friendliness of the stranger who pressed a business sized card into my already full hand and said, "God bless you."

The card contained a Bible verse. "But those who wait on the Lord shall renew their strength. They shall mount with wings as eagles. They shall run and not get weary. They shall walk and not grow faint. Isaiah 40:31". I knew that verse like the back of my hand. On that Saturday morning the message resonated loud and clear. I had waited anxiously, not faithfully, for prayers to be answered.

I cruised down Yorba Linda Boulevard, marveling at beauty that I had not noticed in a long time. My blessings had been taken for granted. Lush foliage lined the boulevard. Pink and purple blossoms swayed like poms poms on myrtle trees. Despite external and internal turmoil raging, at this moment in this corner of God's earth, all was well and so was I.

The Rover crested verdant hills that greeted me every morning. The hills looked different, fresher. Now I could tackle the stack of mail avoided for days.

Bills marked "Urgent" in red lettering, an envelope from Publisher's Clearinghouse, a seven figure check from New York Life insurance Company. That was a blessing, I smiled.

From the bottom of the pile a yellowed, battered envelope from DNA Testing of America addressed to Phillip Sampson surfaced. My heart leaped. I held my threaded breath. The numerals in the address were missing a digit. A handwritten notation read, "Return to sender. Not at this address." The letter was postmarked March 16th, three months earlier, the day before Phillip was shot. Apparently the letter bounced around the neighborhood and the post office before landing at the correct address.

My hands shook uncontrollably. I ripped the envelope, read and re-read the letter that lifted a boulder from my heart. I shouted and praised around the ten foot kitchen center island. Under the grip of His grace no walls contained me. My back arched, head whipped in circles. The Spirit fell fresh, I danced like David danced. I tried to catch myself, to regain my bearing. The Holy Ghost would not release me. A molten hot frenzy ensued, self-consciousness retreated.

In a cold sweat I emerged twisted like a pretzel in the middle of Persian carpet, teeth chattered, I shivered uncontrollably. The top layer of clothing was ripped from my body. I glanced through the archway into the kitchen. The McDonald's bag sat unopened on the counter top. I unfurled my body and rose to my feet. I caressed the brown paper cup of coffee that had grown cold to the touch.

How many minutes elapsed? I wondered. I hugged myself and murmured repeatedly, "Thank you Lord."

Keeping secret information more precious than enriched uranium in the hands of a terrorist was a feat. Only with Miles, I shared the truth about Donovan's paternity. Crying intermittently, we talked about what the news means.

"Dad died for nothing."

"Don't say that, son. God makes no mistakes."

Miles fell silent on the other end.

"Do you think Donovan knew the truth all along?"

"Why would he submit to DNA?" Miles reasoned.

Thankfully, someone was thinking straight. My ability to reason was long gone.

"From the way he acted when he rolled up on me, I'm sure he believed Dad was his father. That's what his mother told him all along."

A long shadow fell over Delia's motives. Why did she wait twenty years to rear her ugly head? Pun intended.

JUSTIN

"You sandbagged me," I snorted at Delia, hugging the passenger side door of the Bentley. I breathed so hard my nose spray penetrated opaque Mary Kay foundation layered over Delia's high yellow skin.

"I don't know what you're talking about?" Delia purred innocently.

I snatched the crumpled letter from my pants pocket and thrust it at her heaving chest. It was all I could do to prevent confronting Delia in the courthouse corridor, packed with witnesses to the impending debacle, including a dozen members from Pastor Phillip's church.

I could not believe I had been played by a hoochie who swore that Phillip was her only lover at the time Donovan was conceived.

In Delia's adoring eyes she elevated Phillip to near deity status. Hook, line and sinker I bought Delia's story about one-on-one Bible study with the Pastor. When she confided, "He taught me how to love" I snidely replied, "*I know that's right.*" The second Phillip walked through her door that bitch had her thighs high, I speculated.

I studied Delia's expression as she finished the letter and blinked back non-existent tears. The Bentley swerved to the curb on Civic Center Drive in Santa Ana.

My diamond heavy index finger jabbed in Delia's frightened face. "You knew the truth all along."

She squeezed a tear from one eye. "Not till the letter came."

"You hid the DNA results from your son?"

"Not intentionally. Donovan was on the run. It was too dangerous to call him." She pleaded, "I wanted to tell him. I knew it would break his heart."

"You knew he would know you were fucking the whole city. Do you have any idea who that boy's father is?"

Long pause. Eternal hesitation. "I, uh...," she stammered, unable to form a sentence.

I cautioned, "Make it good now, baby. Your son is on trial for attempted murder. He could spend a long time in prison. Frankly, I don't think he can handle it... Why'd you lie to me?"

"Phillip's the only man I ever loved."

"That don't make him yo' baby's daddy."

"Donovan looks just like Phillip. Acts like him."

"Tell that shit to the DNA lab."

Delia sniffled. "All I want is what's best for my son."

"Jail ain't it, lady."

"Donovan wanted to be somebody."

"And Phillip was his best opportunity. Or shall I say, your best opportunity." I clutched the steering wheel as if it was Delia's missing neck. My head shook in disgust. "You don't shop for a baby's daddy like a watermelon. Tap it here. Tap it there!"

Delia rested her forehead in her hands and cried, in earnest this time.

"Do you know what you did to my best friend? His family? Not to mention your own son."

Delia whimpered, "God forgive me."

"Get out of my car, woman." I flung open my door, ejected from the butter soft leather seat and bounced in black and white spectators to the passenger door. I yanked her door open.

Delia's head reared back. Her body was tense. Saucer-sized eyes beamed up at me.

"You can't leave me here. I don't know where I am." Near the intersection of Civic Center and Bristol three Latino mothers pushed babies in strollers. Clumps of Latino children meandered on their way home from school, munching Hot Cheetos, churros and slurping red soda pop.

"You're from Detroit. You're used to tougher neighborhoods than this." I peeled two twenty dollar bills from a stuffed gold money clip and tossed them at her. "Call Uber."

"Drop me at the hotel. Please. "

"Get outta my ride. You stink."

Delia's stiletto heels sank into hard pavement. She lifted herself up and out of the plushest car she had ever had the privilege of riding in. For three days I had treated her like a queen, working closely with Delia to develop her son's case. Hours of talking over lunch and dinner at the best restaurants in Orange County had Delia convinced that I was interested in more than her son's defense. Maybe I was a little curious about what Phillip saw in her. Just a little.

She plopped against the blue stucco façade of a bail bond/lawyer's office and watched me scroll through Apps from inside the comfort of the Bentley. She watched me fidget with my phone that would not connect fast enough with Uber.

I saw regret in her face. Her silly son had submitted to a DNA test after repeated warnings from his mother.

"That's insulting. Making you take a test... His evil wife put him up to this." Delia had reasoned with Donovan.

"He's my father, why shouldn't I take the test?" Donovan insisted.

Donovan did not fully understand his mother's struggle. Her history of betrayal-kicked to the curb by Phillip , broken engagements, no marriage, six children by different men-was enough to make anyone paranoid.

A hopeless romantic was how Delia characterized herself during our long conversations. I was sure Delia's neighbors used different, less flattering terminology. Still, Donovan adored his needy mother, did everything within his power to fill gaps in her soul. Fueled by Delia's graphic fantasies that one day he would be a great man, just like his father, Pastor Phillip Sampson, Donovan worked hard at odd jobs-fast food, janitorial and tutoring-while in school at Wayne State University. He dreamed of earning a degree from Claremont School of Theology, becoming an associate pastor at Trinity Baptist Church and taking his rightful place as heir to his father's throne. But it was hard to dream inside a jail cell.

"You can't come to Detroit. Popo's all over my ass. And I can't come to you. I raised you to be stronger than this," Delia snapped when Donovan begged to come home.

Always fatherless, now motherless, Donovan hid in the shadows of the streets of Toronto. Delia's fantasies of Donovan's greatness wore heavily on her once obedient son. His appetite for being a hunted man, without a future, quickly soured.

Donovan hopped an Amtrak train, winged his way to the City of Angels and prepared to turn himself in. Police interrogation did not sound as bad as enduring a cold Toronto winter, alone.

At Roscoe's Chicken and Waffles on Manchester in Inglewood Donovan celebrated his last supper of freedom. His disposable cell phone brought devastating news. "Your father is dead."

A plate brimming with fried chicken and waffles, drenched in maple syrup, floated in front of him. Donovan stabbed his fork into the sizzling hot fried chicken breast. Air seeped out in an audible hiss.

Donovan decided to make a move, the wrong move. He returned to Orange County.

38

NOW OR NEVER

JUSTIN

Fifteen minutes into the Uber vigil the waning sun sought refuge behind an ominous cloud with the face of a wizard spewing fire from pouting lips. Three men in a 1998 Buick Regal with a rusted out grill, peeling white vinyl roof, and faded burgundy paint, sidled up to the Bentley. The hopped up low-riders, blasted "Cisco Kid" by War on a custom sound system.

"Cuanto se cuesta?"

I waved them off. "Naw man, she's done for the day."

The driver waved goodbye with his middle finger. The Buick peeled off in a cloud of gray smoke.

"Get yo' ass in the car," I shouted out the window at Delia Upchurch, quaking in her polyester jacket and balancing on stilettos not intended for surfing concrete. Delia's aching feet teetered to the door of the Bentley. She shivered against the radical drop in temperature. Delia waited in vain for me, the previously valiant attorney to open the door. She got the message, peeped in to make sure it was safe to enter and slid into the Bentley. Too soon she breathed a sigh of relief. I burned rubber, passenger door flapping in the wind, Delia's pony feet flying.

"Where're we going?"

"To see your son."

"Don't make me tell him today," she begged.

I was not hearing it. The Bentley sailed around the corner, heading north on Bristol. At Memory Lane, I made a U-turn.

I parked in the farthest lot from the jail.

"Why didn't you park closer. My feet hurt."

"Figured you could use the time to get your story together."

"You're such a bastard."

"Don't confuse me with your kids."

I trotted toward Theo Lacy Jail. Delia limped at a distance behind me. Under my breath I cursed Phillip for entangling me in this mess. Donovan was not my first messy client. I specialized in messy clients. I reminded myself, don't judge.

At the check-in desk I signed my name, produced my driver's license and instructed Delia to do the same.

"I need a large booth for privacy. And oh yes, I need to pass papers."

"Buzz us when you're ready, Mr. Flowers." The buff, khaki clad sheriff's deputy answered.

Delia scanned the premises. It was not too late to run. I could hear her heart beat like a metronome. Her mind raced in all directions at once. She could whip off devil high heels, hit the main drag and catch a cab with the forty dollars I forgot to collect. What could she say to soften the lie perpetuated since the day Donovan was born? She always knew there was a chance the child she carried was the seed of her trifling fiancée, Larry Evans. Larry was too

Amanda G.

ordinary, a worker on the assembly line at Ford Motor Company, not sophisticated enough to motivate her "special son". And then there was Bruce, a simple case of hit and run, who sneaked into her britches on a Friday night when Larry was out gambling and the preacher had to stay home with his wife. Bruce left Delia with something to remember him by-an itchy case of crawling crabs. Delia resolved never to sleep on the sheets of a man too nasty to turn the lights on.

"You've been assigned to Q-9," Deputy Leland dryly informed them.

Delia followed Justin robotically, through a courtyard with pretty trees sprouting bright pink flowers, resembling orchids.

"What kind of trees are these?" she asked.

I was not in a chatty mood. Single file we proceeded up stairs with mustard colored railings. We entered tube like, stark corridors with frigid white walls and exposed metal pipes. One corridor connected to another by spearmint green accented doors and frames. Delia hobbled to keep up.

At Q-9 we entered a rectangular space lined with booths. On the visitor side two Latino women slouched on metal stools in front of metal counters. On the other side of milky glass, men in orange jail scrubs put on brave faces. Behind the men was a wide, white railing. Twenty feet below a central office imbedded in mottled concrete flooring was shrouded in dark, opaque glass.

I ushered Delia to a wide corner cubicle reserved for attorneys. A single metal bench, without back or side support protruded from the wall. Delia plopped onto the bench. She winced as a cold splinter shot from her well padded tail bone to her stiff neck. Anyone without hemorrhoids coming in, would certainly have them going out. On either side of impenetrable plexi-glass was a black phone attached to a metal snakelike cord for communication.

"Can I have a moment alone with my son?" she asked.

"Knock yourself out. Holler when you're finished." I backed into the corridor, and conveniently perched in a booth next to the wall.

"Honey." I heard Delia purr when Donovan was deposited into his seat by a Deputy. "I've got some good news and some bad news. First, the good news. Your father is not dead."

I eased to the edge of the partition and peeked into the cubicle to see Donovan's eyes light up like a child's on Christmas morning.

"Whaddayou mean? I was at his funeral," Donovan mouthed.

Delia continued. "Now the bad news...Phillip was not your father."

Donovan's eyelashes fluttered faster than a hummingbird's wings. His eyeballs rolled under the lids, revealing ghostly white orbs. Backward, he floated into free fall, landed like a felled tree in a deserted forest. He made no sound.

I pounded the call button. "Emergency. Q-9. Man down. My client fainted."

39

GUESS WHO I SAW TODAY?

SISTERS IN SILENCE
APRIL 17

Guess who I saw today? My nemesis. She almost made me believe my trifling husband's lie that he was hittin' that shit just because it was "available". Don't you just love the way men lie without blinking or attempting to remember if today's tall tale jives with the one he told last week.

The amazing thing is that I sit here writing about this episode as a free, unbound woman when the Outside Woman who injected my life with a double dose of misery was within fist's reach. For months I wondered how I would react, if I laid eyes on her. Would socialized civility prevail or would the animal in me leap out, maul her like a tiger, beat her down and stomp until I could not breathe? Mind you, it is not just ghetto girls, like me, who exact revenge when scorned. Remember Jean Harris, proper head mistress of East Coast girl's boarding school. Jean planted lead in the Scarsdale Diet doctor who did not know how to control little pee wee. And she was not even married to him.

I stand totally opposed to gun violence. But...the sharp tip of an umbrella, a hobo bag loaded down with apples for lunch, the six inch heel of a stiletto that you are sick of wearing (Do not use your good shoes because there will be blood), all appear to be spontaneous, yet functional weapons of choice. You will be proud to know that neither potential weapon was used by yours truly.

You will be even prouder to learn that the words conveyed to my nemesis were, "I will pray for you."

Admittedly, my first prayer for the Outside Woman was twisted. "Lord, clean up this doggish bitch so she can do no further harm. Sew her rancid pussy into a seamless slit. Find her a different hairdresser so that the planet will not run out of oil. Keep her out of my sight, Dear Lord, just in case I lose my religion. While I am down on my knees, I pray for her sick son who had the misfortune of spending nine months inside a filthy vessel. Amen."

The Lord will not bless that prayer. I continue to work on it.

40

OOPS I DID IT AGAIN

AUBREY

I knew the rule, "Thou shall not get pregnant?" How did I, preacher to Outside Woman, protector of Sisters In Silence screw up this badly?

"You don't have cancer, AIDS, malaria or any other imagined illness. You are pregnant, My Dear. That explains the tiredness, and desire to eat every five minutes. It will level out."

At age forty-five I sat on my spreading ass, stupefied, mouth gaping wide open. I, who wrote the rule, "Thou shall not get pregnant. I, who was looking forward to menopause, being a grandmother and nobody asking, "What's for dinner?" had literally screwed up. Dick had become such a distant memory to me that I forgot about protection.

I muttered, "How did this happen?"

Doctor Stamper's bellicose laughter roared through the exam rooms and into the waiting room. "Same as always, except in one reported case...You're almost three months... Might not feel like it now, but this is a blessing. "

In addition to being my gynecologist Dr. Stamper was a good friend of the family. I met him walking through Stater Bros. grocery store on a Sunday afternoon. Yorba Linda is a small town where another Black face brings a head nod unless the brother or sister is in hiding, which is sometimes the case.

"I thought I knew all the Black folks in Yorba Linda," Dr. Stamper chuckled.

"We just moved here from Detroit." I removed my frosty hand from shrink wrapped chicken breasts and extended it. "Hi. I'm Aubrey Sampson. My husband Phillip is the new Pastor at Trinity Baptist Church."

"Someone told me Trinity has a new Pastor. I'll have to check him out. See if he really knows how to preach. " Dr. Stamper's warm personality claimed me as a friend and patient. Six months later, Phillip welcomed Dr. Stamper into the congregation.

It took a minute to find the blessing in pregnancy. Within two days of Dr. Stamper's diagnosis I got real, told the pizza delivery man to lose my address. "No matter how much I beg, do not deliver here," I snatched the pizza with extra cheese and pepperoni and passed a ten dollar tip.

I worked hard on internalizing forgiveness. First, I had to forgive myself for getting into this mess. Then I had to truly forgive Delia and her son. The latter would take some time, no matter how many times I cried while watching the movie "Emanuel". Maintaining a stale life, sleeping with anger long after its expiration date had lost its appeal.

When my time of trial and tribulation came, I blew it. I tossed the Word at Phillip's head and guarded my heart with vengeance. I forgot that "Everyone should be quick to listen, slow to speak and slow to become angry, for man's anger does not bring about the righteous life that God desires." James 1:19-20.

I had to change. My child could not flourish in a womb filled with negativity.

My stomach mimicked a lumpy money belt. By month four my belly was a football on a tee. This was outside the range of my pregnancy experience. With Miles I hardly showed until my sixth month. Of course, that was more than two decades ago.

By month six I surrendered to the invasion of the body snatcher. If I rested on my right side, the baby demanded a better view from the left.

Every morning I awakened and asked, "What do we want to eat?" "Did you say, pecan waffles?" By the time I grabbed my tapestry shawl and headed toward the pan-cake house, I had talked myself down. White egg omelette, no cheese, two slices of turkey breast. Filling, but boring as hell. Pecan waffles would have to wait until Sunday, my cheat day. It was only Tuesday. Could I make it until Sunday? I didn't count on it. After my appointment on Thursday, the dreaded weigh-in with Dr. Stamper, all bets were off.

Things could be worse, I thought. The cloak of gloom had been replaced by waves of anticipation. Anticipation of the next scrumptious (or not so scrumptious- the bar hung low at this point) meal. Anticipation of how and when to break the news to Trent or create a false narrative that I would be babysitting my grandchild for the next eighteen years.

41

I CAN'T STOP LOVING YOU

TRENT

"Nigga, where you been?" Skip yelled across the Kaiser Permanente Hospital parking lot while jogging to the hospital side entrance. Skip leaned in for a chest bump. "I been textin' and callin' yo' ass for weeks."

"Handling my business," I replied.

"What the hell you doin' here?"

"Mama's in the hospital again."

"What's wrong?"

"What's not wrong?" I was in no mood to recite my mother's litany of ailments, headlined by pneumonia, diabetes and refusal to do anything to help herself. Weeks spent in the hospital or rehab were the only times her ailing body rested from booze, drugs and flirtation with the devil.

Cecilia Davis was lucky to be breathing inside her battered seventy-two year old shell. Before I could cross the Carquinez Bridge and pay the five dollar ransom to enter Vallejo, I got a call from my brother Cedro. "Mama's in the hospital. She's real sick. They don't know if she gon' make it this time." The twilight zone of one tragedy blurred into another for me.

"How long you been back, man?" Skip asked, shifting foot to foot in the latest Michael Jordan's.

"A few weeks. I've been meaning to call. Just got wrapped up."

"And you ain't been to the gym? Come on wit' it."

"I work out at school. Almost finished my degree. Runnin' back and forth to the hospital. Lotta shit on my plate." My lips twisted into a frown. I surveyed the chaos of the Kaiser parking lot. Two-thirds of the nearby parking spaces were reserved for handicapped. Entering the newly built parking structure was like falling through the looking glass. You never knew where you might end up, especially on a weekend. "They built this huge new parking lot, now it's harder than ever to park. I'm up there in Never Never Land."

Skip laughed. His overlapping teeth had butter residue along the gum lines. "Gotta pick up my dad's prescription from the pharmacy. You got a minute to yak?"

"Uh, yeah. I'll text you in a few. Gotta check on Mama first."

———— ◈ ————

TRENT

Cecilia's raven hair lay flat against moist, pale skin, virtually colorless from pneumonia that had racked her frail body for months.

"How you doin', baby?" Cecilia's gravelly voice startled me. Open mouthed breathing, lapses into dark, far away spaces were what I was accustomed to witnessing.

I took her blue veined hand, tried to ignore clotted blood and scars pre- and post hospital.

She had coal black eyes and lashes sweeping to her brows. For a second I was reminded of Cecilia's beauty before the dope and procession of ghostly men threw darts at her life.

"I'm doing good, Mama. Real good...You need anything?"

Cecilia shook her head. Dry, cracked lips smiled. Rotted teeth, decimated by crack, peeked out. "You were always my good son."

Gingerly, I raised her bruised hand to my lips. Sudden movement might cause pain or dislodge the IV from the usable vein the nurses struggled to find. Cecilia's wrists were tiny and limp like a sleeping toddler's.

"You should rest."

"Don't leave. I want to talk."

I did not want to talk. I was in exile in my home town, avoiding familiar places and faces. I needed to be by myself to sort out the madness. My brothers caused few distractions. They were elated that Mama's baby was back to take the weight that none of them would carry. I was the only one who could handle Cecilia's mood swings and detox rants.

Between midnight and dawn was my favorite time to visit. The corridors were empty, doctors off duty, nurses huddled in offices over bowls of pancit and lumpia. Long after visiting hours they turned a blind eye as long as neither patient nor visitor asked for anything.

Cecilia's arms were vanilla twigs. Flesh hung like melting icicles from her triceps. Gone were the tight, wiry biceps flexed over the years to launch sweeping backhands against misbehaving sons. Back in the day Cecilia's foul mouth and clenched fists were enough to strike fear into anyone, including men who used her like a watering hole. There was always another one, and another one.

In her presence I reverted to a three year old, cowering in the shadows, hugging sharp corners. I balled myself into a knot, covered my ears against grunting, bed springs crying, my mama groaning into the ear of a stranger, "I get paid for my 'work'." The John's transient pleasure jeckyled into a string of cursing. I waited until a rush of unfamiliar footsteps rumbled down the hall. Doors slammed behind the stranger. The smell of smoke from Cecilia's post "date" Kool cigarette permeated the air.

By age four I learned to follow my mama's instruction, "Stay outside and play, while mama works."

Age six. Wallace Jr. escorted Mama's date outside with the barrel of a sawed off shotgun. He returned to the house, pointed the shotgun at me, *"Don't ever leave Mama alone with them suckas, you hear?"* With one hand Wallace Jr. lifted me by the neck and squeezed until I blacked out.

"You want ice chips?" I whispered in muted light of the hospital room.

"Unh unh." Cecilia rolled her head against a stark white pillow that dwarfed her skeletal face. She was eerily beautiful despite self-inflicted damage. Her crimpy hair was knotted into a rope slung over her sunken right breast. She had frame filling eyes of a starving child.

A coughing spasm shook her frail body until it seized into a knot. Two minutes later the spasm released into a faint wheeze. Cecilia grimaced, cleared her throat and swallowed hard.

I looked away, battling tears. If one tear fell, the

floodgates would open. I would drown in sadness bottled up for forty one years.

"I should'a done better," Cecilia confessed. She waited for the answer trapped inside my three year old mind. Her heavy eyelids drooped. Cecilia lapsed into the safety zone of sleep.

I, the strong, indestructible man rose, ambled to the corridor and agreed imperceptibly, "Yes. You should have." Still, I could not stop loving her.

———— ((•)) ————

Aubrey

Except for dust and cobwebs, making themselves at home, the spot where my Daddy's bed had been was empty. Less than forty-eight hours after Daddy breathed his last breath hospice had whisked the hospital bed and the heavy green oxygen tank from the premises. It was a jolt, a harsh reminder that Daddy was not coming back. Daddy's doorless closet bulged with Value Center retreads, urine stained khakis and dingy, stretched out, baggy-in- the- knee long johns. Day and night, summer and winter, Daddy wore long johns during the last four years of his life. Five trench coats in assorted colors and sizes, run over house shoes, made of pleather and fake fur and dusty dress shoes, crowded the closet.

"Mama, it's time to let these things go." I softly reminded her. She had kept his room intact since the day he hastened behind fleeting footsteps of angels.

"I keep expecting him to come down the hall grinning without his partial in and say, "Where's my wife at?"

Mama's melancholy seemed ironic, coming from the woman who complained about Daddy for the last fifty years. Complaining was Mama's way of deflecting Daddy's indiscretions, his inability to be all that she expected him to be. Only after his diagnosis, did she accept reality. Daddy did not have it in him. He was a simple man brought up to believe that a man was defined by the length of his penis. When his penis malfunctioned, Daddy shrank along with it.

Despite the tragedy of the Alzheimer's diagnosis, it was a new beginning for Mama and Daddy. In sickness Daddy became the husband Mama wanted-adoring and always smiling at his honey.

Daddy's shrinking world became Mama's world, coaxing tenderness out of Mama that I had rarely seen. I watched Mama hold Daddy's hand as he stumbled into McDonald's on Broadway. I cried, believing the love between my parents had died. It had only been in hiding.

Time had done nothing to dull Mama's pain or pull her out of the malaise of a chilly, overcast spring.

The lot fell to me to pack up Daddy's room, donate his clothes and dismantle Daddy's hoarder's paradise. I gathered empty weapon cases (his gun collection was confiscated for his own safety). Assorted rounds of ammunition rolled out of odd places-inside soiled socks, empty Murray's pomade cans. A Mason jar filled with dead batteries was stuffed in the cabinet beneath his bathroom sink. The bigger surprise beneath the sink was a mammoth ball of used scraps of soap, which he saved just in case another Depression hit. "Poverty is no excuse to stink," Daddy used to say.

Then there was the coin collection, virtually worthless,

mostly pennies, rolled into stacks, which he refused to cash in because he did not trust the banks. Stacks of pennies adorned the mildew covered window sill, jangled in a chest of drawers and trickled from the broken seams of his jeans. In his final year Daddy weighted down his pockets with change that ripped frayed fabric. Each time I confiscated his stash, assuring Daddy that his money would be safe in his drawers, Daddy's cataract covered eyes burned as if I was a traitor in a grand conspiracy to keep him broke. I relented, gave him back his coins and his dignity.

Cleaning provided an excuse to live in baggy sweats and extra large t-shirt.

"That shit ain't fit to wear to the dump. Fix yourself up," Pearl ordered.

"For what? Cleaning toilets?" I snorted.

"The girl cleaned the toilet yesterday."

"The girl's name is Sabrina. Sabrina is not a cleaning lady. She needed quick money to buy a dime bag. You can afford a real cleaning lady."

The day long sniping contest continued. Day three of my visit was always the worst. Two days of love and commiseration followed by a day of open warfare was our routine.

"Sit down. You'll wear yourself out. I'll do the dishes... In a little bit."

Aaargh. The hated phrase, in a little bit. I seized rubber gloves, a bristle brush, Comet and two rags from beneath the kitchen sink and toddled down the hallway. Almost eight months pregnant, I was not moving swiftly.

When did my mother develop such a high tolerance for dirt? Mama spent her whole life working, cleaning other people's floors, wiping other people's asses. Suddenly, she just quit cleaning her own house. I wondered if it had anything to do with Winston and his mistress. *Mama got tired of cleaning up Daddy's shit.*

"Boom, boom, boom, boom, boom." The locked screen door rattled under the weight of heavy fists.

"Who's there?" Mama screamed without moving from her seat on the couch.

"It's Trent, Mrs. Seymour."

I twirled in three directions at once. "Oh shit." In a tailspin, I dropped cleaning supplies.

Mama pursed accusing lips and rolled her eyes at me chasing my tail. I dipped into the bathroom, closed the door. The swollen door stuck at the top. I slammed it harder, instantly regretting resounding reverberation.

Mama unlatched the chain, turned two locks and let Trent in. "Trent, I didn't realize it was Monday."

"Yes, ma'am. Monday, 6 p.m. Same as always. Am I interrupting anything?"

"Nooo. Just sitting here watching the news."

"I'll set the garbage cans on the curb. Be right back."

"I ain't goin' nowhere."

I counted to twenty and peeped out. Mama sat alone on the couch, looking smug.

I whispered, "What's he doing here?"

"Emptying trash."

"Don't play with me."

"Every Monday Trent stops by to take out garbage cans and see if I need anything."

"Why didn't you warn me?" I whispered.

"I told you to get dressed."

Before I could scream, Trent's size thirteen sneakers landed on the porch. I dipped back into the bathroom.

Trent opened the screen door and stepped inside. "You talking to somebody, Mrs. Seymour?"

"Just the TV. The news is so ugly. Fools killing folks left and right. Have a seat."

I pressed my back against the door and slithered to the floor. Trapped. Suddenly, I had to pee something fierce. The bathroom was just a few feet from where they were sitting. He would hear my pee gurgling out in a torrent. Pregnancy pee was no joke. Pressure ground against my bladder, threatening to break like a levee. Trick, trick, trickle from the faucet. An awful reminder. I needed to go in a hurry. I released tension in my jaws, breathed in through my nose, out through my mouth. I tried helplessly to meditate on something else.

"Before I get too comfortable, you need anything from the store?"

"Not today. She...uh, I ran over to Safeway this morning. They had chicken, thirty-nine cents a pound. Can I get you something to drink?"

Oh no she didn't, I thought.

"No thanks. I can't stay too long. My last final exam is in the morning and I'm whipped." Trent stretched his wing span across the wide arms of the chair he sat in during every visit.

"You've got your hands full with school and everything goin' on with your mother. How's she doin', by the way?"

"Little better. Last week the doctor's were telling us to make final arrangements. This week, she's back being feisty."

"Doctors know what they know. King Jesus knows the rest. So you keep prayin' and askin' Him for help."

"Yes, ma'am." Trent leaned back and stared at the television screen. A police siren wailed through the streets of Fairfield. Confused neighbors huddled on the periphery of a local park. Beneath a tarp lay a thirteen year old girl, naked and dead.

Trent's voice emerged from a distant place. "I'm supposed to be helping you. Here you are lifting me up."

"We lift up each other. And if stopping by is too much
while your mother is sick, I understand."

"I promised to check on you. And that's what I'll do, if
you don't mind."

"Mind? You're my only company. Since Winston left."

"What about...?" He hesitated, not wanting her to know
that Aubrey was his first thought in the morning and his last
wish at night.

"Aubrey? She's tied up with that trial in Orange County.
I'll be glad when it's over. Won't change a thang. Phillip still
gon' be dead."

"You got that right." Trent pushed up from the chair, covered with a clean sheet. "I'm heading out." He bent down,
kissed Pearl's cheek. "Call me, if you need anything. Lock
the door behind me."

"Tell your mother I'm praying for her."

As the door closed, I rolled to my knees, crawled and
used the tub to push myself up. Flash dancing on my toes, I
snatched down the elastic band of the sweats and plopped
down on the toilet. Sweet release.

A full five minutes later I yanked open the door. Pearl
loomed in my face, arms crossed. Her raised eyebrows
scratched the scalp beneath the floral, polyester scarf she
wore.

"When you gon' tell him?" Mama's hand dropped to her
right hip.

"Tell him what?"

"That *you* are car-ry-ing his ba-by." Mama articulated
each syllable.

My chin fell to my swollen chest. I could not look my
mother in the eye.

Before I could fix my mouth to lie, Pearl injected, "And don't give me no shit about it being Phillip's. That man could barely feed himself. You *know* I knew better the first time you told that lie."

I covered my face, boo hoo'd like a baby. Mama pulled me into her arms and led me to the couch. A guttural moan released from my throat. Mama grabbed the remote from the coffee table and hit the power button.

"You ain't the first woman made a mistake."

"I feel so stupid."

"Every woman gets heat in her pants, now and then."

"Daddy fooled around for years. You didn't panic."

"If you only knew. When I first found out, I was ready to kick some ass. Then I thought about it. Yo' daddy was past the point where I coveted what he had. Get my drift?"

I blushed. Too much information.

"Long as she didn't mess with me, that elephant legged heiffer was doin' me a favor. Winston's shit was like riding cooked spaghetti for years."

"Mama, please...," I begged.

"You betta' listen." Mama's finger wagged in my face.

"When the ding dong don't work, men get real nasty. My mama warned me. Now I'm warning you. What really hurt..." Pearl paused before continuing. Tears welled in her steel magnolia eyes. "What hurt is that you, my only child, took yo' daddy's side."

"That's not true. I never said..."

"You didn't have to say. You acted like the sun rose and set on Winston's ass."

"You should've told me what was happening."

"Did you tell me what was happening with Phillip?"

Ouch. I was stunned into silence.

"Some shit we just don't talk about." Mama rocked on.

"I did what I had to do. Then his 'ho got bold. Started calling my house all times of night."

"Did Daddy know she was calling?"

"Sure, he did. That silly old bastard was proud that a younger woman wanted him." Mama looked to Heaven for forgiveness "Shouldn't speak ill of the dead. Winston said I was imagining things. I told him to kick rock.

"At times I thought my head would split wide open. I just kept on prayin'."

I reached over and held my mother's hands. "I'm sorry, Mama. I should've been a better daughter and a better friend. Daddy always said you were mean to him. That's all I ever saw. You complaining."

Pearl's tears fell freely. Snot trickled to the top of Pearl's trembling lips. "I didn't mean to harm you."

"I'm okay." I rubbed my mother's back. "We should have talked sooner."

I grabbed the box of Dollar Store tissues from the coffee table and handed them to my mother.

"I was humiliated. All the neighbors knew. Vallejo ain't big as a minute. But I held my head up. Kept on steppin'."

Mama blew into the rough tissue until her pug nose turned red. She sighed out fifty years of frustration. "Funny thing is---much dirt as he did, I still miss him. Sometimes I wake up and forget he's dead. I go in the kitchen, turn on the water for his oatmeal. That man loved him some oatmeal." Mama laughed. "Halfway down the hallway I realize, Winston's not here. I'm all by myself."

I huddled close to my mother, the same way I did when I was a little girl. My arm circled Mama's shoulders that felt surprisingly fragile. The strongest woman in the world was human and afraid. Just like me.

TRENT

One block away on Gateway Drive I crouched low in the cushioned seat of the Jeep Cherokee. As darkness encroached, I hoped the driver of the rented Ford Fusion parked in Mrs. Seymour's driveway would come out to check the car.

I knew, without asking and forcing Mrs. Seymour to lie again, whose car it was. Aubrey's signature scent of freesia permeated the living room where I sat and chatted while my heart pleaded, "Come out and face me."

I could not blame Aubrey for refusing to appear after my angry fingers texted, "Leave me alone", in response to her countless text messages, begging me to talk to her. The beauty of technology, conveying words that my lips could never say, was now the bane of my existence.

My hard-on strained against the zipper of baggy jeans. Fingers strangled the leather wrapped steering wheel. I cursed myself for still wanting her, not being in control of this shit. Minutes later I drove away in a raging debate between mind and soul. The scent of her, the image of Aubrey's endless, dewey thighs wrapped around my neck had ruined my "fuck 'em and duck 'em" attitude. Now what?

AUBREY

A clunky garbage truck farted exhaust fumes on Mark Avenue. I was wrenched from the well of a deep sleep. The squeaky garbage truck lift broke silence savored after a night of rambling people ranting obscenities. A controversy that started at twilight flared up throughout the night. I never heard so many "mutha fuckas" spew from a young woman's mouth.

I peeked out the window. Across the street, two doors down was the center of the action. A bony teenager screamed to the point of lung injury, tossed shoulder grazing hoop earrings to square off against a middle age man. Her words were staccato gunfire from her mouth. Her arms flailed, feet stomped like a Korean soldier's stiff knee march. Mutual verbal aggression sprayed through amber light of a blinking street lamp.

Mama was not phased. "Don't turn on lights, stay out the window," Mama yelled from her bedroom. "They'll get tired in a minute."

The grizzled man's hand rested above a bulge in his waist band. I recoiled. The bow legged skinny girl with weave down to her knees might be shot. The girl dived into the front seat of a revving Dodge Charger. The Charger roared off. At the corner of Sage and Griffin Drive the Charger's 22's spun out of control, jumped the curb, reared up and fish tailed out of sight.

Mama's minute lasted all night. Half hour later, just when I assumed embers had cooled, Boney Girl threw gasoline on the fire. The Charger cruised the block, idled in front of Old Dude's crib. Boney Girl and her posse of two tossed Old English 800 bottles from the Charger. Centimeters from Old Dude's vintage Cadillac shattered glass glittered like diamonds.

Old Dude stormed out the crib. The sash to his house coat lifted in the wind. His weapon, longer than Dick Tracey's, glinted against the charcoal sky.

I slid from my bed, crawled to the living room and climbed on the couch.

I rested on my left side. The baby was not happy. A tiny foot stretched into my bladder. I had to pee. Again.

"Damn," I cursed and dropped to the floor. "My knees are getting a workout."

Minutes later I returned to the theater of madness roiling outside my mother's door. Po-po was on the scene. Old Dude was nowhere in sight. Boney Girl, feet stomping pavement, twisted and turned in handcuffs. Her tanked up posse had disappeared like vampires at sunrise. Finally, I got some rest.

——————⫸((◉))⫷——————

AUBREY

He was on his knees checking the faulty connection between the treadmill plug and the socket on the newly painted wall. The soles of my black flats squeaked on gleaming refurbished oak floors. His gaze rose upward to shapely legs, lifted to thighs he knew intimately, froze at my belly, jutting out like a bullet.

I wore a below the knee, fitted black dress, cut low to reveal breasts swollen to the size of ripe cantaloupes. My hair was faded on the sides, longer on top in a crown of natural curls. My lips were moist with MAC's Oh Baby lip gloss. Eyelashes blinked slowly as I murmured a long delayed, "Hello".

Trent took to one knee, rose slowly. A screwdriver twirled in his hands. "Is that all you have to say?"

"I am soooo fucking fat."

He could not resist laughing.

"I know you don't want me. I'm here because you ignored a thousand texts and a hundred e-mails. You threw shade on my snail mail. Came back, "Return to sender. Not at this address."

"It was ninety-six texts, not a thousand. I blocked your e-mails. Didn't get your letter. What'd it say?"

"You gon' make it hard?"

"Yep." He answered as a matter-of- fact.

I gulped my pride. "I said I'm sorry. I miss you and I love you. I knew it then, but couldn't say it. I was confused." I nervously twisted a curl. "A hot mess."

We laughed together.

"I moved to a bigger house, on the Waterfront. To be closer to my business, give the dogs space to run."

"Congratulations. I like your new place." I surveyed the brand new exercise equipment, mirrored walls and three offices flanking the central workout room. I wanted to tell him that I sat in the car for half an hour building courage to enter the Georgia Street building bearing the huge sign "Physical Therapy and Rehabilitation".

"Mama said you're doing well. I'm not trying to get in the way."

"In the way of what?"

"Your dream. Here I am with this big belly." My arms flopped in exasperation.

"You are my dream," Trent confessed.

"Why didn't you come back?"

"You had to come to me."

His eyes fell to my belly. "Congratulations to you too."

"Thanks. It's a girl. I've already named her. Ella Joy. Do you like it?"

"Yeah. I like it...What's her last name?"

"That depends on you. After she's born, if you like, I'll do a DNA test..."

"I don't need a DNA test. Do you?"

"I haven't slept with anyone else. Phillip was diabetic. We hadn't had intercourse in two years."

The words rolled out unexpectedly. Sexual intimacy ended with Phillip long before the bullet pierced his head. Diabetes rolled up like a cop and arrested him. BAM! I never complained or told anyone about my lack of satisfaction between the sheets. Until today.

"I don't need money, so if you don't want to be her father...," I blabbered.

Trent lowered the screwdriver to the treadmill, took three steps toward me and pulled me to him. His nose nestled in my freesia scented neck, kissing it, nibbling my ear, cradling my head.

I melted into his body. Home again.

We were lovers thirsting for water. My dress crept up beneath his hungry fingertips.

The door creaked open. A man cleared his throat.

My lip gloss had transferred to Trent's lips. He smoothed my dress into place, released me from his grip.

"Uh Skip, you know Aubrey."

I smiled, nodded, then turned toward Skip.

"Whoa," Skip exclaimed at the sight of my belly. "Somebody's been busy."

Trent's chest rose. "Yeah. I'm gonna be a father. Can you finish up here? Aubrey and I need to talk."

"Sure thing. Will you be back to accept delivery of the elliptical?"

Trent shot him the fish eye.

"No problem. I can handle thangs. You know me, man," Skip grinned.

"That's the problem."

———)(()(———

AUBREY

At 10 p.m. I phoned Pearl. "Mama don't wait up. I'm with Trent."

"I figured that. You been gone since this morning. Everything all right ?"

"Better than all right."

———)(()(———

AUBREY

As the sun lazily rose on the Bay there were zero degrees of separation between me and Trent. His cool breath fell soft against the nape of my neck. His right arm draped possessively across my belly. My eyes were open. I lay still and silent for fear of breaking the shadow of love enveloping us.

At six a.m. Ella Joy kicked his arm away.

I laughed, "She's hungry. Like clockwork. I can live off love, but this baby ain't goin' for it."

Trent gently caressed my belly. The baby's foot kicked his hand. "Wow. I've never felt anything like that. It's a miracle. I'll make breakfast," he offered.

"No. Go back to sleep. I gotta get home anyway."

He fondled my ripe breasts. "I can't let you go."

"Your grand opening is two days away. My flight is tomorrow. We both have work to do."

"I just wanna do you."

"Don't start no stuff."

"It's your fault. Rolling up with all this hanging out." I turned to face him. He took my engorged nipple in his mouth. I moaned, half-heartedly protested, "Aw baby, don't do this."

An hour later we landed in the shower. He eased behind me and cupped both breasts.

"Back away from the booty," I demanded.

"You are the hottest pregnant woman I've ever known."

"How many pregnant women have you *known*? No. Don't answer that." I pushed open the shower door, stepped out, dripping wet on the area rug. "Somebody has to exercise common sense."

Big pee wee stuck out like a flag pole. "See what you do to me? Get me excited, then run."

"We've been here almost twenty-four hours. This is overkill."

Trent reluctantly stepped out of the shower and caressed my slick skin. "I'm happy. You happy?"

"Delirious." I kissed him lightly, avoiding full body contact.

"What if I kidnap you?"

"The D.A. will send the sheriff, if I don't appear. Besides,

I have to the get the house on the market. I'll call every day... unless you're still blocking my calls."

"That was your fault," he reminded me.

Laila and Ali yelped and scratched the garage door, summoning their master who was an hour late for their walk.

"Okay. Okay. I thought Ali was having a seizure, jumping around and whining, when he saw you yesterday"

"That's my dawg." I pecked his cheek, sprouting fuzz softer than a peach. "I'll be gone when you get back."

Trent grabbed his crotch. "You gon' miss this."

"Get outta here." I slapped his arm.

He squatted down, kissed my belly button. "Take care of our baby."

I dressed quickly and rambled through the house built in the late 1950's. It was quaint, had character with lots of light and a side yard for flower and vegetable gardens. I envisioned playing up the Berkeley vibe. Oversized pillows, flowered curtains that Trent would hate. But that was the price he would pay for refusing to move with me to a new home in the Bay Area. He wanted to stay close to his new business. He also wanted to earn his share of the down payment, which I understood. All night we struggled to map out our future. Between a hefty life insurance policy and Phillip's pension I was set for life.

Trent wanted no part of it, which I respected, coming from a man fighting to be his own boss. "For the first time in my life, all things are working together for good. I won't jinx that. Put your money away for the baby. Let me take care of you."

It sounded good. *Does he know how much a pair of Manolo's cost?*

It would take time to work this out.

One thing we agreed on immediately. Orange County

was out. There was nothing there for me, except bad memories.

My decision to sell my dream house in Yorba Linda came at the oddest moment. Climax number two, as his cool tongue searched for treasure south of the border. Was that any way to make a business decision?

Since I had broken all the rules, I contemplated naming the next chapter, "Pregnant Woman's Night Out".

42

IT'S GONNA TAKE A MIRACLE

Sisters In Silence.com
November 28

When little pee wee died, my husband's swag died with it. Two years before baby boy dropped the bomb HH turned over on his side of the bed and pulled the cover up to his chin. No more arm reaching across my body. No fanning the flame burning at my core. No more hunching up behind me in the midnight hour and groaning, "Baby gimme some."

The sudden shift was drastic. At first, I took it as a personal affront. Maybe I needed to do more sit-ups, change my hairstyle. One day it dawned, the problem was the diabetes and the meds he was taking to combat the disease.

My husband acted selfishly. He blamed his erectile dysfunction on me. "If you would help me out a little bit"; translation, suck my _____. Ain't nothing wrong with me." He deluded himself. I suggested counseling. He rolled his evil eyes at me.

What about the pump? He acted as if I asked him to commit hari kari. I had never seen him so edgy.

The meanness that comes out in a man when "ding dong the dick is dead" is astounding. They say shit to bring you to your knees. Don't fall for it sister, not the way I did.

I went on reconnaissance to the mall and found a slut shop. I hastily purchased a lacy bra with peek a boo nipples and matching panties with a slit in the crotch. Spent long money on a room at the Ritz, smuggled in a bottle of Cristal, then rode my husband till I was feeling it. I licked, purred and teased him like a hooker on speed.

The big payoff? Little pee wee wilted.

"Oh, honey, it's okay," I lied, then dreamed about a plump grape shriveled into a raisin. It would take more than Victoria's Secret to make that snake dance.

That's when I started doing Keegles religiously. I am not a ho-in' kind of woman, but I got to stay ready. If the opportunity presents itself again in this lifetime, I will send big pee wee screaming for mercy.

Ain't it a joy being a woman? Wrinkles may come, titties crawl to our knees. But a woman's equipment keeps on ticking until one hundred and three. The hole outlasts the pole. Peace.

43

HAVING MY BABY

DISTRICT ATTORNEY RHONDA MADISON

Judge Kennedy glanced above the rim of his bifocals at the litigants going at it in center ring. I gloated in victory over defense attorney Justin Flowers. Justin's raised arms revealed sweat rings in his three thousand dollar tailored suit. Except for the bedraggled defendant, bailiff, court reporter, Delia Upchurch and Investigator Renard Broussard seated in the last row of the galley, the courtroom was empty. The masses missed Wonder Woman, breaking bad without the cape.

"If you two are this animated at an evidentiary hearing, I dread your tone when we get to trial." Judge Kennedy lasered his attention on Justin Flowers, blowing like a locomotive. "Counselor, I've already ruled. The evidence will be allowed. Unless you have other matters to discuss, this hearing is adjourned."

Justin's nostrils flared into the shape of a shovel. He hated to lose, especially to a hard ass, white girl like me, unable to disguise the smirk on my face.

The sting of Judge Kennedy's unexpected ruling against Justin's motion to suppress evidence, sent Justin reeling. He had argued forcefully, "What do rag dolls, gris gris, and ropes tied into knots have to do with attempted murder?"

My flour white cheeks blushed pink as Judge Kennedy pounded his gavel.

In an intentionally seductive, whiskey voice I schmoozed, "Thank you, Your Honor."

"Will you entertain a motion for reconsideration?" Justin pleaded.

"Let it go, Mr. Flowers. There was ample evidence at the crime scene of witchcraft, as well as evidence seized from the defendant's locker. I don't know where Ms. Madison is going with all this, but she has a right to offer it into evidence."

"Even if the only purpose is to inflame the jury?" Justin persisted. "There's no such thing as a witchcraft expert."

"The time you're wasting could be better spent with your client, Mr. Flowers." Judge Kennedy rose from the bench and exited, stage right, to his chambers.

The raven haired Latina bailiff clasped twitching fingers beneath a broad belt holstering her .38. She stuck out her bountiful bosom. The buttons on the khaki sheriff's deputy shirt threatened to pop. Her hazel eyes warned Justin, "Sal si puedes." Get out while you can.

I took my sweet time gathering notes I never referred to while arguing against Justin's motion. I savored the victory that would allow me to present damaging evidence from Donovan's past. A childhood spent under the domination of a single mother who spent more time in church than with her family. Church boy crossed over to the dark side, full of vengeance fueled by rejection from his presumed father. A man of God made to pay for his sin with a bullet to the back of his head. Everything was laid out-motivation, opportunity, a gaggle of witnesses from the church anxious to testify about Donovan's command performance- falling out, foaming at the mouth, body stretched rigid, fingers curled into devil claws.

Donovan's fate was cinched by the "smoking" gun found in his purse on the day of his arrest. The gun matched the one used to shoot Phillip. Donovan's mug shot with fire engine red lipstick smeared to his chin would make a great teaser for the jury. I could not wait to see Justin Flowers try to dance his way out of this. I snickered, remembering Justin's argument, "More provocative than probative." It took all the strength in my steam roller body, not to shout, "Hell yeah."

Without "provocative" Donovan was an everyday, run of the mill criminal. Man dressed in a woman's clothing, practitioner of witchcraft, attempted to murder a man of God. This case was perfect, a law and order politician's gift.

I tucked the accordion file folder under my armpit. I thundered out, leaving Justin sweating like a pig at the trough.

I sailed through the corridors of Central Court in Santa Ana, California, dreaming of the day I would be top dog. Orange County District Attorney Rhonda Madison.

I sailed like a cruise ship surrounded by a fleet of dinghies. Big boned, towering almost six feet, I flowed smoother than the average "big girl". I was on a mission: convict Donovan Upchurch and use his conviction as my election calling card.

Nothing could stop me...except a key witness. Aubrey Sampson was AWOL three days before trial.

Fifteen years as Assistant District Attorney, I was famous (well semi-famous) for an unbroken string of high profile convictions- rapists, child molesters, mass murderers and a few rare white collar criminals unable to buy their way out. A win in this case would be the exclamation point for my crime fighting career.

My opening statement was already written. Donovan Upchurch is the Anti-Christ, threatening the sanctity of everything Orange County stands for- safe, clean streets where Christians raise their children without fear. Donovan will be portrayed as the flim flam man who conned his way into a rich preacher's life with a lie about paternity.

I was still ticked that my missing witness revealed the DNA test to Justin Flowers before telling me. Whose side is she on? I would be less ticked, if the dead preacher's wife would just phone home.

I blew past the receptionist, the law clerks and slammed my office door. I snatched the phone and dialed the cell phone number procured by my investigator.

—————⟫(⟨())⟫⟨—————

AUBREY

"Where the hell are you?"

"Visiting my mother in Vallejo," I answered, surprised that Rhonda Madison had accessed my new number.

"Is that a-hole Justin Flowers bugging you again? He can't intimidate my witness."

"No...it's not Justin. I needed time to think."

Rhonda's heart sank to the fallen arches of her size ten feet. She sniffed her witness going South. Rhonda's shoulders slumped. She loped the expanse of her well appointed office. Photos of Rhonda and an eclectic mix of celebrities and conservative politicians covered the walls. Rhonda hobnobbing with then Governor Arnold Schwarzenneger and Maria Shriver at a charity event. Rhonda, seated next to General Colin Powell, at a lecture. Rhonda chatting up Congressman Darryl Issa at a pricey fundraiser. And her favorite photo, Rhonda smiling cheek to cheek with boxer Mike Tyson after his one man show at The Grove in Anaheim.

Rhonda sucked up her anger, knowing that her normal aggressiveness would alienate me. She took a seat. "Is everything okay, Mrs. Sampson? You don't sound like the same woman from a few months ago." Rhonda squeezed the head rest of the non-County issued executive chair, leaned back and took two deep cleansing breaths.

"I know you're not happy that we didn't file this as a murder case. But we're three days from trial. A lot of the evidence I'm presenting is coming in through you. You were the first witness to the crime scene. Only you can identify the keys to your home discovered in Donovan's locker."

Rhonda's list grew longer.

My mind drifted to the incidents where someone, now presumed to be Donovan, crept around our house, searching for who knows what. Why didn't he attack me when he had the chance, I wondered? The missing door key was no big deal to me. Miles was notorious for misplacing keys, usually discovered weeks or even a year later in odd places like the freezer.

"I need you in the game, Mrs. Sampson."

"My priorities have changed."

"Whuuut!" Rhonda snapped, abandoning her plan to go easy. "Your husband deserves justice. We've *got* this punk. Don't let him get away."

"You don't understand..."

"No. I don't. "

"I'm pregnant."

Long pause. Rhonda's breathing rattled on the other end of the phone. "How pregnant are you?"

"Almost eight months."

I could hear Rhonda's mind calculate. Who was the baby's daddy? Seconds ticked like a schizophrenic time bomb. BA DOOMP, BA DOOMP, BA DUUMP. To blow or not to blow? Eight months. Around the time Reverend Sampson died. We're safe.

"That's great. You'll be an even more sympathetic witness. Imagine a child forced to grow up without a father. Even though it's not a capital case, everyone who reads the newspaper or listens to the news knows that your husband was shot in the back of his head. It's a miracle Reverend Sampson lasted as long as he did. I don't care how many times the judge admonishes me, I'll put the evilness of this crime right in their faces."

I lacked the energy or the courage to reveal to Rhonda that Phillip was not my baby's daddy. It wasn't her business. "Leave my children out of this."

Rhonda's natural instinct was to ask why, but she decided to stick to advice she received when entering the law business. "If you don't know the answer to a question, do not ask it."

"Okay, if you insist."

"I'll call you when I get home," I offered.

"And when is that?"

"Tomorrow."

"Do you need a ride from the airport?"

This woman is relentless, I thought. A perfect D.A.

RENARD

My right hand steered the Dodge Charger south on Lakeview Avenue near the old Kaiser Building. My left hand toyed with light fuzz on my usually clean shaven head.

I felt Amber Kelley staring at my face and head that she barely recognized without the stingy brim of my well worn fedora. Self-consciously, I rubbed sunscreen into my bald head, beading with sweat in eighty degree weather.

Amber averted her eyes away from my protruding lower lip.

I rammed the Charger onto the westbound 91 freeway and slammed on the brakes. The Charger fishtailed centimeters from a Prius' humpty trunk.

Amber exhaled nervously. "Why're you so uptight? The perp is behind bars, seconds from trial and a quick conviction. D.A.'s got evidence up the yang yang,"

"That's the problem. Too much evidence."

"Who gives a shit? Long as his ass is off the street."

My golden eyes stabbed her hollow chest. "Don't talk ghetto. It doesn't suit you."

Amber's freckled, chicken wing arms shrank into her seat. Another clutzy effort to blend in was rebuffed.

"Now close your lips and listen. I lived in New Orleans until I was twenty years old. Seen more than my fair share of gris gris. Everything in Donovan's locker was laid out too neatly. Gris gris is not a neat pile of shit. It's messy. Why would he put it in a locker? It would be in a place to do harm. And the key to the locker was conveniently stashed in the same purse with the gun. What's still bugging the hell out of me is why Donovan would submit to DNA, if he was just a con man trying to make a dime."

Amber nodded, too intimidated to speak.

"I've never seen a case this neatly tied up. Pun intended." I alluded to the knotted rope also found in the locker. "Donovan's mother was in court today, brandishing her Bible. There's more to Delia Upchurch than the Holy Roller vessel."

The Charger skipped across three lanes without signaling.

Amber gasped, stiff armed the dash board. "Where're we going?"

A chorus of blaring horns crescendoed at the exit for the 55 freeway south. My determined eyes focused straight ahead.

"To shine a little light on Delia Upchurch. What's better than one perp off the street?"

Amber's turquoise eyes flitted in confusion.

"You chew on that." I gunned the Charger's V8 engine, ripping the commuter lane of the 55 freeway.

Amber closed her eyes and clutched the door handle as if I was trying to kill us. Maybe I was.

44

MUSCLES

AMBER

The man's muscled arm slithered across Delia's exposed back and massaged her neck. She leaned her head full of frozen curls on his shoulder. He leaned in, whispered in her ear, consoling her. Delia folded her arms on the bar. She lowered her forehead and sobbed. The man massaged her neck with a gentle hand.

In a remote corner of the bar of the Doubletree Hotel Investigaor Renard Broussard and I nursed glasses of tonic water with twists of lime.

"Can you believe she's picking up men?" I mumbled into my cocktail napkin.

Broussard shook his head. "Unh unh. She knows this guy. We need to get a picture of him."

"How're we gonna do that? Ask him for his mug shot?" I wisecracked.

Across the room Delia Upchurch slid off the barstool and jogged out.

"She's probably going to the lady's room. We've got five minutes." Broussard checked his watch.

"Women don't pee that fast," I corrected him.

"Whatever. Get out your cell phone. I'll sit across from you. Pretend to take my picture. Snap him instead."

Broussard moved to the other side of the table, with his back to the bar, fedora intact. His lips stretched wide into an unnatural smile. From the side of his mouth he spoke, "Am I blocking the shot".

"No, but the neon beer sign might make it blurry," I explained, searching for a better angle.

"Just shoot!" Broussard demanded through clenched teeth.

Like a flash, Delia was all up on us. "Would you like me to get both of you?"

"Uh, we don't want to be a bother," I stumbled.

"No bother." Delia tossed her fake Louis Vuitton on the table. I joined Investigator Broussard, who stood reluctantly.

Delia focused on the screen of the iPhone. She squinted at Broussard. "You look familiar."

"Just that kind of face, I guess." Broussard mouthed.

Delia inched closer to her subjects. "You guys from around here?"

I jumped in. "We're from Kansas. On our honeymoon."

Delia motioned with her hand. "It might be better if you stand over there. There's too much neon glare."

We moved out of the line of vision for Delia's date. Broussard's smile turned into a grimace.

The camera clicked. "That's a good one," Delia oozed. "One more. This time, kiss your bride."

Broussard clutched my bony hip to his thigh. He leaned down and pecked my eager lips.

Delia lowered the camera phone, squinted hard at Broussard.

"Are you from around here?" Broussard inquired.

"Detroit. Out visiting relatives."

"Would you like a picture of you and your friend? We'll e-mail it to you," Broussard offered.

"Oh no. He's camera shy. It was nice meeting you." Delia skittered away.

My freckled face wrinkled into a frown. "Any more bright ideas?"

"Just wait. Dude slapped cash on the table. She's not sitting down. They're leaving. Time for you to pee. Leave your purse."

I was baffled. "I don't have to pee."

"See if they get on the elevator together."

I scampered out behind Delia and mystery man.

Broussard rushed to the bar. He sat on the barstool abandoned by Delia. Her empty tumbler was easy to identify by the magenta lipstick on the rim. He took a bar napkin and lifted the glass of Delia's companion.

The bartender startled him. "Sir, I'll move that out of your way."

"Please don't", Broussard quickly replied.

"Look. I don't know what's going on here. Are you house security?" the bartender asked.

Broussard flipped open his badge. He sank the tumbler into my purse. From my wallet Broussard fished out a twenty dollar bill and slapped it on the counter. "Thanks for the drinks. Have a good night." Broussard tossed the strap of my purse over his shoulder and marched out.

⸺◈⸺

AUBREY

My hand clutched the plastic glass of ice long after flight attendants made their final foray through the cabin. At 9:30 a.m. my plane touched down at Long Beach Airport. I had intentionally avoided flying into John Wayne Airport in Orange County. It was better to avoid running into folks I had not seen since Phillip's death. I was in no mood to explain my swollen belly or why I avoided the church. It was another world, another lifetime.

I recoiled like a snail beneath a boot threatening to crush its back each time church members reached out. Were they concerned about my welfare or looking for the inside scoop? Donovan's failed paternity test was not yet public knowledge. As far as the church was concerned Donovan was on trial for trying to kill his father.

With the exception of Hilton, hovering like a hen, church members were not my real friends, just people who knew me as Phillip's appendage. I had no one to blame but myself.

Every woman I perceived as a threat. It was a sad fact I was forced to face after Phillip's death. I had allowed Phillip to circumscribe my circle of friends. Because of his weakness for women, his incessant tendency to flirt, it was safer not to let anyone in. My cloak of protection was to ignore Phillip's indiscretions that gained ground like a runaway horse. Eventually, I was overtaken, trampled and crushed.

As a young girl and into my early twenties I had many close friends, women and men. After marriage my life centered on Phillip and Miles. I lived on a remote island surrounded by church people. There was not a soul I confided in, except for Hilton, considered by Phillip to be safe. Non-gay men were out of the question and women, I kept at bay. I was not consciously unhappy, just lonely and displaced.

Phillip filled up all the space, sucked up every minute of my day. I was his girl Friday, taking care of Phillip's business while he built his empire.

My life divided into three distinct periods, pre-, during, and post Phillip Sampson eras. After confirming in writing that the Pastor's pick for his replacement was Associate Minister Burns, I quietly backed away. I did not need to hear gossip raging before Phillip was lowered into his grave.

At the funeral trustee Wanda Turner tittered, "The Bishop delivered a helluva eulogy. I don't know if Burns is up to the task." A Deaconess lamented, "Pastor Phillip used to walk pews, do the splits, jump up and not miss a beat in the sermon. Takes a helluva show man to top that. Minister Burns ain't got it."

John Bogan swooped in to fill the void. Bogan mounted an all out assault against Burns. He went so far as to question the authenticity of Burns' Masters Degree from the Claremont School of Theology. When Bogan was questioned about his credentials everything went vague.

On several occasions John Bogan heavily lobbied me to endorse him. I tried to let him down tactfully.

Bogan got up in my face. "If I were Black, you wouldn't raise this resistance,"

"My resistance, if that's what you want to call it, has nothing to do with race. It's your philosophy. You are misogynistic, homophobic...," I answered before he cut me me off.

"I believe in Scripture, as it is written. It's time for the church to get back to its roots. The Holy Bible. God didn't give permission to pick and choose between the Word. He said take all of it, follow all of it."

"John, I don't doubt your sincerity. But fire and brimstone is not the way to grow a ministry. Phillip believed in inclusiveness. He welcomed all of God's children."

"That's where Phillip and I differed. He allowed Sodom and Gomorrah into the temple. It's blasphemy. Men acting like women in the choir stand."

Bogan touched a nerve. I knew he was referring to Hilton, but refused to go there. "The church decides who replaces Phillip. It's not my decision."

"They respect you. Maybe even more than your husband. One word will move them my way. Stay on as business manager. Name the position you want."

I laughed. "I don't need a position, John. I need peace. Bye." I backed away in total disbelief. How dare he bargain with me? Why would I suddenly endorse John Bogan and destroy the ministry Phillip and I spent years building?

It was Phillip's energy, his frenzy that brought converts racing down the aisles to join church. Saving souls was the public plea. Mo' members, mo' money was the unspoken reality.

When did the spiritual motivation end and the lust for power and money begin? Perhaps it was always there. In the beginning we had nothing but a dedicated group of friends, chomping on chips and talking about the Lord in the living room of our Palmer Woods apartment in Detroit. The spirit was real, raw. In the middle of a sermon the Holy Spirit would fall fresh, casting Phillip to the floor, crawling on all fours. That was the man I fell deeper in love with, the one with a direct pipeline to God. As our treasury grew, the gulf widened in Phillip's relationship with God. Phillip could still put on a show. I knew it was not real and so did he. We were in too deep. Neither one of us knew how to let go.

RENARD

I trounced around my office. A bull ready to charge.

Amber steered clear, kept her eyes glued to her notepad. I was searching for a fall guy and she was the closest target.

"Nothing back from forensics?" I asked.

"Nothing I didn't reveal ten minutes ago. We searched California and Michigan databases. The only thing that came up was a 2006 charge, no conviction, against Delia for welfare fraud. With that many babies, I'm not surprised."

"And her companion?"

"Still looking. It's like he parachuted into California from Mars. Maybe he's clean. He walked Delia to the elevator, gave her a hug and hailed a cab. A man looking that good..."

"Oh. You like that?"

Amber answered in her Valley girl accent. "Well, yeah. I mean, men don't dress like that in California. Tailored suit. Shoes shining like glass. He was totally buff. I was rooting for Delia to get a taste." Amber's blond lashes fluttered to the sky.

"What did you just say about California men?" I asked.

"Uh, I said, they don't dress like that."

"That's it. He's not from California. When do we get federal fingerprint results?"

"Whenever. You know the feds don't move that fast. Unless you have priority."

"How do we get priority?"

Amber's bony shoulders kissed her ears. "Judge's order? We don't have enough to ask Judge Kennedy for that. He'll say we're on a fishing expedition. Which we are. Wait a minute...One of my law school buddies got a gig with the Justice Department. I'll see what I can do."

"You come up with the goods, I will kiss your pink ass."

Amber twirled a No. 2 Staples pencil in her mouth. "That's sexual harassment, you know."

I mimicked Amber's Valley girl speak. "What Eh-ver. I respectfully withdraw the offer."

Three beats before Amber responded. "Not so fast."

<hr />

AMBER

And think about it I did. That night, during a rare relaxing bath, a bar of Dove soap substituted for Renard Broussard's stiff man pole. In my mind we had done the nasty a thousand times. His dark chocolate hands knew every inch of my pale body. His full lips left hickeys on my narrow butt, the place he promised to kiss. Sweat and steam streamed down my freckled face. A seeping sigh evolved into a shudder. I quaked to a climax, sank below the suds.

What the hell was I thinking? He was blacker than midnight, ten years older and my superior. I surfaced, gazed down at my freckled chest and pert titties with nipples like fresh raspberries.

I prayed out loud, "Father, forgive me. I am about to sin."

<hr />

DELIA

Donovan clawed at matted hair to free it from his itching scalp. Knowing what awaited him there, he avoided the jail shower.

"I gotta get outta here. I've been sweatin' in this fucking cage for months."

"It's almost over son. The Prophet says, there's no way you'll be convicted."

"Fuck the Prophet!" Donovan roared.

I cupped my ears against blasphemous words. Four diamond rings, blinging on my right hand, refracted in my son's wild eyes.

Donovan pressed ten fingers against impenetrable security glass. He willed the glass to disappear, gritted his teeth. "I can't hear myself." With ragged fingernails Donovan dug into ashy skin. "Fuckin' ants crawling all over me," he cried. His head swirled in circles.

My balled fist pounded security glass separating us. I screamed, "Stop it! Stop it right now. Don't you dare pass out again."

Donovan's breathing slowed. He settled his narrow rear end into the metal seat.

"Now that's better," I said in a soothing voice. "Listen to me. The Prophet's never been wrong. Has he?"

Donovan nodded in agreement.

"The reason you're here is because you didn't listen. You shouldn't have gone to that damn funeral. I told you not to take the DNA test. Every time you go against me, you fuck up...Look at me, baby."

Donovan's blood shot, puppy eyes met mine.

"The case against you is circumstantial. If you go to trial acting like a nut, these Orange County White folks will convict you in a second. Pull yourself together, get a hair-cut..." Donovan's hair sprouted like weeds, protruding in poufy patches.

Stinging tears fell from my eyes. I sobbed, "This is killing me too. I'm your mother. Haven't I always taken care of you?"

Donovan nodded.

"Trust me. And trust the Prophet. He sees you walking out of here. A free man. He sees you in a green field with children all around you. My grandchildren. All you have to do is hold on."

45

LOVE ME NOW

AMBER

I n the background "American Gangster" blared on BET. I remembered how the night began innocently. Renard, as I planned to call him from now on, answered my plea to help set up a new sixty-five inch Samsung LED television purchased from Costco.

"It's in the back of my Tahoe. I can't get it out. It'll cost a fortune to get someone to hook it up," I pleaded.

The scent of beef burgundy simmering sumptuously on my stove greeted him. A bottle of Cabernet Sauvignon from Rutherford Winery in Napa Valley, two goblets and a corkscrew beckoned from the countertop.

"Would you open that bottle for me," I purred when Broussard entered wearing relaxed jeans and a t-shirt. I had never seen him without a uniform or a frumpy suit.

"No problem, but I've got another engagement this evening. So let's get started. Where's the TV?"

I pointed him to the garage where the dolly stood ready.

Back in the kitchen he found the table set, food on fancy China and wine in goblets.

"Like I said, I've got a banquet. Where do you want this hooked up?"

"In the bedroom." I pointed to a door at the end of a narrow hall. "At least have a glass of wine. This is Rutherford's signature cabernet."

"You know I can't drink. I'm driving."

"I'll bet that old banquet won't have beef burgundy like my mama used to make. Take two bites and tell me it's not the best beef burgundy you've ever tasted."

Two plates and three drinks later Renard's butt tooted in the air as he plugged in the final cable.

He stood back, clicked the universal remote. The picture was so clear, he looked hypnotized.

"Damn. I have to get one of these." He surfed the sports channels, the History Channel, HBO, then landed on BET. "Oh, no. This is my favorite movie. Denzel is the man." Renard mimicked Denzel's sporty walk.

I roared. "I like it when you take off the Superman suit."

Renard stiffened, caught himself acting human. He handed me the remote. "I have to get going. Enjoy your TV."

"I'd enjoy it more with you."

"Thanks for dinner and the wine. You're a pretty girl, but this is outside of protocol."

"I'm not a girl. Why're you afraid of me?"

"Afraid?"

I leaped into his arms. I climbed him like a tree that fell into my bed without bending a branch.

I clung so tight to Renard Broussard, I almost disappeared. My gripping thighs wrapped around his waist. A white sash around a mountain of a man. For months his powerful black ass had me wondering, how would it feel?

Now I knew. The answer raised questions that would not let me sleep.

In the afterglow I was trapped beneath him, afraid to move lest the spell be broken and Renard would resort to his stodgy, former being.

I wished I could ease from beneath his log like arm, reach the remote and turn off the TV, spawning five minutes of commercials for every ten minutes of viewing. I lifted his arm, gently placed it on his thigh. I rolled to my left and sat on the side of the bed. Commercial number seven kicked off. I played a game of counting commercials while Renard slept off wine. I would have to teach my big man how to drink.

I rose, grabbed a kimono from the doorknob. Commercial number eight. Exterior shot of an imposing church edifice. Voice over: "Join us for worship service every Sunday at 8 and 11 a.m., Trinity Baptist Church in Yorba Linda". Close up of a young Black woman's smiling face. "We are a church where young people can come as they are." Close up of elderly Black man. "We are a church that honors its elders and our Christian faith." Cut to an attractive White man in his mid-forties, wearing a three button tapered jacket, crisp white shirt and a skinny tie. "We are a diverse congregation where the true Word of God is preached."

"That's him! That's him!" I shrieked, stumbling backward over Renard's boat like sneakers.

Renard, ripped from a deep sleep, catapulted to his feet in seconds. His Smith and Wesson forty-five jostled from hand to hand. "What the hell...?"

"The man from the restaurant. Delia's date."

"What're you talking about?"

"He's on television. Church commercial." I crossed my index finger over his lips. "Shhh. Just watch."

Renard rested his wobbly legs and spinning head on my bed. The church commercial faded into commercial number nine.

"I'm telling you. The man we saw in the bar at the Doubletree with Delia was in the commercial. I swear it was him."

"What was the name of the church?"

"I think it was Trinity. That's where Phillip Sampson was pastor."

"The guy with Delia was white. Why would he be on a black church commercial?"

"I don't know."

Renard stretched his wings spanning the width of my white, wrought iron girlie bed. After round two of our love-making, Renard had said that the pink sheets and purple flowered Laura Ashley comforter reminded him of a teen-ager's room.

"Maybe you had too much to drink." Renard speculated.

"Oh pul-ease. You had too much. That was just a taste." I jetted from the room.

Renard called after me. "Where're you going?"

"To my computer. Check the church's website."

I Googled Trinity Church in Yorba Linda, California. And there he was, Associate Minister John Bogan, clutching a Bible. I swung around on the barstool. "Are you thinking what I'm thinking?"

Renard answered, "Yes."

"Let's run a background check immediately."

"Giving orders now? That's why I keep my business and personal life separate," Renard groused.

I laughed, turned back to my computer without answering him. Images of lively worship services bounced off the screen. The home page still listed Phillip Sampson as Pastor.

I clicked the tab labeled "Associate Ministers". The magic name, photograph and bio popped up. "John Bogan, associate minister, Bible Study teacher, gifted vocalist and charismatic preacher joined the Trinity Baptist Church family three years ago. Raised in the State of Alabama, Mr. Bogan hails from the Southern Baptist tradition."

"That's it! Send his prints to Alabama. See if we get a match," Renard directed.

I gazed at the computer. It was two o'clock in the morning, Pacific Standard Time. "It's Saturday night, 4 a.m. in Alabama. I won't reach anyone, except the desk clerk."

"Do it anyway," Renard barked. He looked down at his nakedness. Suddenly ashamed. "Get dressed. I'm jumping in the shower."

My head snapped back. *Is this the same gentle giant I snuggled with minutes ago?*

AMBER

He spotted us the second we appeared in the archway of the sanctuary. In the middle of his impassioned prayer with his eyes half open, during the altar call, his eyes recognized us, the couple he had encountered at the bar of the Doubletree Hotel. We sheepishly entered the sanctuary.

A dutiful usher offered us a church bulletin. Renard declined. I smiled and accepted, as if offered a bouquet of roses. We stuck out like coyotes. Renard towered above my five foot, petite frame. I trailed Renard to the back pew, sat uncomfortably close to him. Renard angled his shoulder away from me.

John Bogan did not miss a beat. "If you love the Lord, give him a rousing hand clap of praise." Worshipers at the altar trickled back to their seats.

Minister Burns replaced John Bogan at the podium. "Now is the time in our service where we welcome first time visitors. Will all first time visitors please stand."

I looked to my left. Broussard's wide eyed glare warned, "Don't you dare stand up."

A white gloved hand fell on my right shoulder. I jumped, looked up into the face of a beaming usher. "Are you first time visitors? Please stand and let us welcome you properly."

I popped to my feet, grabbed Renard's listless hand. He rose slower than unleavened bread.

From the pulpit, Minister Burns entreated, "Please give us your name and your church home, if you have a church."

I piped up, "We are Mr. and Mrs. Broussard. Honeymooning from Kansas. Had to take time for Jesus. We just love the Lord."

My testimony was greeted with energetic applause. Renard squeezed all the blood from my hand.

"Ouch," I mumbled as we took our seats. My bony elbow nudged him.

"What the hell are you doing?" Renard badgered.

"Blending in. If we didn't stand up we would have drawn more attention."

"I told you to stay in the car," he snapped.

"You're ashamed of my pink ass." My words came out louder than intended.

"Now look what you've done," he accused.

"Stood up for myself," I snapped back.

Renard gestured toward the pulpit. "He's gone."

46

GIVING UP

AUBREY

B ulbs would not bloom until I was long gone from this house. Gladiola were my gift to the next family. I could get over leaving the house, but leaving my gardens would be traumatic.

I remembered the day we moved into our dream home. I turned to Phillip and said, "I am never leaving this house." I was wrong about that and many other things.

A six inch, solid gold cross on a serpentine chain dangled from my neck, almost kissing the ground. I tucked the cross that Phillip wore every day of his ministerial life inside the neck of my baggy t-shirt. Sod saturated hands left the imprint of my fingers in dirt. With the first rain my imprint would wash away.

I lifted my eyes to the Chino foothills preening beneath a canopy of floating charcoal clouds headed my way. I welcomed the rain that would sprinkle my bulbs. Planting was slower, less result oriented than in the past. I should not be on my knees pressing against the child dancing inside my belly. I had to speak to my gardens one last time, let the fleeting flowers and seedlings set to blossom in the spring know how much I would miss them.

A blue and orange ERA "FOR SALE" sign stood sentry in the front yard. The house would sell quickly according to the realtor. Once the house hit the Multiple Listing Service a flurry of inquiries poured in from agents with qualified buyers.

"I warned you to wait until I'm gone," I told Jeff, the realtor.

"And give you time to change your mind?" Jeff scoffed.

"I know I've got to leave. Too many memories. But don't sell my house to anyone who doesn't like flowers." The realtor laughed while remembering how hard it was to talk me out of putting a "gardening clause" in the listing agreement.

My heart lived in every flower. I talked to the leaves, encouraged them to let the sun shine through in moderation. I turned rich soil with gloved hands, careful not to mangle scrambling worms. I would be lying if I said I would miss the worms too.

Stiffly, I rose to admire my work, unfurling one vertebra at a time. My knees creaked. I pressed my palms against the small of my back and stretched. My arms opened wide in eternal gratefulness.

God was good to me even when I groveled in anger. What was intended to cause paralyzing pain became the source of spiritual resurrection, freed me to quit playing church and move on.

Around the corner of the house I heard rustling feet. I held my breath, teetered off balance.

"You scared the mess outta me." I patted my heart, pounding out of my chest.

"Well I wouldn't have, if you had answered your phone," Hilton replied. He blew an air kiss, came in for a hug.

"That phone is getting on my last nerve. If it ain't Rhonda Madison, it's Renard Broussard, you remember him. The Black cop who tried to blame me for shooting Phillip. That Nee-grow is blowing up my cell. Says he needs to talk to me. Something about the church. The last thing I want to think about is the church. On Thursday, I blow into court, testify and blow out."

"I hear you. Speaking of the church... I resigned."

I clutched Hilton's arm, leaving dirt prints on Hilton's ecru Armani sports jacket. "I am so sorry. Let's go inside. See if I can clean that off."

"No worries. I'm headed home. Got a date tonight."

I moved in for a congratulatory kiss. Hilton's first date in two years. Hilton wisely backed up.

"I am such a klutz. My balance is off," I admitted.

"Anything but the suedes," he warned, referring to the blemish free off white suede shoes on his feet. "I'm rocking these tonight."

I led him to the family room entrance, kicked off my shoes and dropped gardening gloves.

I poured Hilton a glass of Argentinean Malbec, retrieved a water bottle for me and sat down at the counter. My hand caressed the Golden Crystal granite that had taken months to locate. Seven extra wide, perfectly matched, book end slabs. Every now and then I felt a twinge of regret for selling this house that I spent so much time personalizing. But I was in acceptance. The house and everything it represented was in the past. As soon as the trial was behind me, new life could begin.

"Where do I begin?" Hilton sighed.

"With the date. Tell me all about him."

"You actually met him at The Winery in Tustin. Tillman Franklin. Dark skin, bald headed brother, a financial advisor.

We've been out a few times. The "No Nooky" rule is still in effect. Want to make sure he wants me and not David's money."

"Protect. Protect. That's our motto. Where're you guys going tonight?"

"He said it's a surprise. He'd better surprise me and take me to his house. I don't need no man on the down low, tipping out on his wife."

"I know that's right," I concurred. "So what's happening with the church? You didn't leave because of me."

"With you and Pastor gone I felt like a stranger. Plus, Minister Burns, or should I say Pastor Burns, deserves to pick his own staff. He's been nothing but gracious. But, honey, I don't want that job. And that's what it felt like. A job. Let me tell you the latest. Burns and Bogan had a *huge* blowout. Bogan is on a crusade against "faggots in the Lord's house"."

"I was afraid of that." I sympathized.

"I had to get out."

"I don't blame you. Bogan lobbied me from the moment Phillip died. I cringed at the thought of him in charge. So where are you fellowshipping now?"

"Bouncing around. Saddleback, Friendship, COR, Second Baptist...Basically, I'm a bedside Baptist waiting for the Lord to lead me. Ain't that many choices in Orange County. Will your boo mind, if I follow you to Northern Cali? I've got my eye on a vineyard right next door to Francis Ford Coppola's." Hilton laughed.

"Trent knows you're a part of this package. And Ella's godfather."

"Speaking of which, I found the most darling baby dresses at Bloomingdale's. I ordered five."

"Don't you dare buy another baby gift. Mama says it's bad luck. And Trent is Mr. austerity."

"How's that working for you?"

"Not at all. But I'm adjusting."

"Guess it's on me to keep the economy strong. I won't deliver my packages until the baby is out. And how did Mr. Trent react to the news?"

"He was so happy, he almost cried. I didn't think I would ever be this happy again. Especially so soon after Phillip's death. It's like my heart opened up and let me breathe. This man, this man..." Water welled in my eyes. "He is so different. Can you imagine me approaching Trent with a big belly. That was too deep."

"I should've been a fly on the wall. What did you wear?"

"The black, over the knee Donna Karan you made me buy. I was glad I had it with me. Everything else was Little House on the Prairie."

"Fleek and sleek."

"Yay yuh! I got my hair trimmed and nails done. Slathered on perfume, even though it was morning. I had to compensate for this extra forty pounds."

"You look good. You're carrying it all in one spot."

"Trent calls my belly the Bullet," I laughed. "I am blessed that he still wants me. Bullet and all. Listen to this. Trent gave me a massage that was to die for. Did some kinda reflexology between my toes. My Lord!"

Hilton fanned with his hand. "Don't get me excited. I might have to break down and give Tillman some."

I cackled until tears squeezed out. My sinuses stung. My cell phone sang a jazzy tune. Caller I.D.: Renard Broussard marked Urgent.

"Renard Broussard will not give up. I cannot imagine what he wants. The trial starts next week. I won't have to see him after that." I balanced the iPhone in the palm of my hand. "I should turn this sucker off, but Trent might call," I giggled. "I'm like a teenager tied to a cell phone."

Hilton's well defined arms pushed up from the barstool. "I'm getting out in case this love thing is contagious."

I squeezed his forearm. "Thanks for checking on me." I kissed his smooth cheek.

Hilton's latest toy, a black Maserati SUV circled the driveway, swooped over the hill and merged with weeping clouds.

In the doorway I paused for a moment of reflection, inhaling the freshness of coming rain, the lightness of wind caressing white roses, swaying in the wind's embrace. My eyes lifted to the sky. Tepid sun separated low hanging mountains of clouds. A drop of cool rain anointed my forehead.

I scurried inside, locked the door against the mounting storm.

In the distance thunder mimicked Disneyland fireworks. There was no escaping to the gardens, no company to distract me from the dreaded chore-washing clothes and packing them for the Salvation Army. In the laundry room I stripped down to the granny panties I worked in all morning. "These have got to go," I muttered and stepped out of them. Everything had to go. Go lean, I told myself. No more storing Miles' discarded t-shirts emblazoned with the names of unknown rock bands. I tossed a load in the dryer and pushed the start button.

I sorted through clothes bundled in a basket. My favorite caftan, well worn and beyond weathered, begged for reprieve from the "to go" pile. I slipped the caftan over my head and sighed at the comfort of the all cotton garment. Everything was warm, except the gold cross dangling against my belly. I gathered the chain and cross in my fingers to remove them. I decided to leave them on. The cross brought me comfort, provided closure to my life with Phillip. Memories of teasing Phillip about his rapper's bling made me smile. It was the only piece of Phillip's jewelry I intended to keep. The rest, clunky gold, diamond rings, tie clips and a Rolex watch, I put away for Miles, who at twenty-five, was not into "old man's" adornment. Miles' idea of jewelry was a braided leather wrist band straight off Telegraph Avenue.

A buzzer went off. I checked the dryer. It was still running. I closed the door on the dryer and inhaled the clawing scent of fabric softener sheets. Every smell, good or bad, was intensified by pregnancy. The buzzer sounded again. Maybe it was the doorbell. Hilton must have forgotten something, I thought. I tiptoed down the hallway. If it was a solicitor, I was not home.

I pressed one eye to the peephole. Renard Broussard's distorted face loomed large. I turned, tiptoed back down the hallway.

I flopped on the bed and sighed. I would not deal with him who would label me a hoochie for being pregnant. He would point the finger, "I told you so" about the lover who was not my lover at the time. There would be plenty of time next week for Broussard's jaundiced eye. Rhonda Madison did not have the nerve to ask, "Is it your husband's baby?" Broussard was a different story. He "got off" on other people's shortcomings. He would not get the satisfaction of poking at me this weekend.

The seduction of sleep, the promise of peace closed my eyes.

47

SLEEP, SLEEP, SLEEP

AUBREY

The rain came in sound scapes-plinks and trickles of New Age music, cymbals crashing in a slate sky. Inside a cocoon of twisted dreams I floated. In Serenity Sanctuary plump babies hung by their feet like inverted flowers. I was in the back room of our rented house in Vallejo, the crumbling 1940's bungalow. Silvery blue faded wallpaper with petite white flowers circled the room. My feet, clad in new white sandals, one size too large, dangled from a tall bed. I was spellbound by my wriggling toes painted tomato red.

In radiant, blinding light thirteen year old Phillip Sampson appeared in a dingy white tank top and flooding jeans. Phillip's lean, muscled arms motioned me, "Let's go." I sprang from the bed, skipped behind Phillip to an open door. He abruptly stopped. "Be still, Aubrey," he directed in a commanding voice. I squeezed my eyes shut, not wanting to wake up and lose him again. Suspended between dreams, my arms reached for Phillip's receding image, racing with open arms into swooshes of slanting rain and frigid air.

My exposed toes teetered on the threshold. I called after him, "Where're you going?" He never looked back. Phillip dissolved into a pinpoint of lavender, soothing light.

The damp coolness of twilight intruded. A grinding pressure threatened to explode my bladder.

My eyes unsealed to harsh reality. At the foot of my bed a man gathered unseen objects. I recognized the back of his head, broad shoulders expanding into muscled wings. In his left hand, he wielded a serrated hunting knife. The thick blade glistened in candle light.

Athletic shoes squeaked. John Bogan turned toward me.

I squeezed my lips together to stifle a scream. My left quadricep jumped uncontrollably. I breathed, willed my body, be still. A tear squeezed from one eye. I prayed Bogan would not notice. "Help me, Jesus. Help me Lord," I prayed silently.

It was déjà vu. Silk lined curtains blocked gray, stormy sky. Menacing shadows zigzagged bedroom walls. This time the body lying perfectly still was mine. My next conscious thought, "Where is he?" He was at my feet sprinkling twigs resembling brown and black potpourri.

A circle of burning candles dropped wax on the walnut dresser. Gray tails of smoke choked my shallow breath. My fiery throat commanded me to cough. One cough meant instant death.

John Bogan's knees braced against the mattress. His stringy breath fell like acid rain on my clammy skin. His electric fingers skimmed millimeters above the roundness of my belly. He gathered the caftan in one hand, split it in one clean slice.

I clutched Phillip's cross nestled in the valley of my bosom.

John Bogan raised the serrated knife above my exposed belly.

My eyes popped open. I tensed what remained of my ab muscles, lifted my back and buried the cross in John Bogan's neck.

Blood spurted like an open hydrant. Bogan grabbed his neck. The hunting knife bounced to the floor.

I rolled to the opposite side of the bed, sprang to my feet pumped up by Holy Ghost adrenaline. Bogan staggered behind, tackled me. I hit the floor, face first. I groaned, pushed to my knees. Bogan latched onto the hem of the caftan. I crawled on all four. The caftan unraveled in his hand. Bogan shackled my left ankle, raised his bloody face and taunted, "Beg."

I remembered Trent's training. "Use your glutes. Kick with your heel." I flipped to my back.

I raised my right foot, hammered my heel into his nose. I nailed his head to the hardwood floor.

On wings of angels I mounted up, raced through the laundry room and into the garage. I pounded the garage door opener and sailed into the street.

———— ((●)) ————

TRUDY

"So I'm talking to my sister in New York when I see this lady running down the street, naked." I gesticulated wildly to Investigator Renard Broussard. "Imagine the horror when I realize, it's my neighbor, Aubrey. She collapsed, right up there." I led the officer from the street, congested with squad cars, to my front door and pointed to the spot where

Aubrey crumpled. "So I hang up on my sister. Open the door. Then I see this guy stumble out of her garage. He's drenched with blood, holding his neck, like this," I demonstrated. "He takes a couple of steps, wobbles, then keeps coming. Oh my God. That's when I come out of my fog. I dial 911. I'm dialing and screaming, screaming and dialing. Glen, Glen. Get down here, quick. Grab the gun. But he's upstairs on the friggin' computer. Watching porn.

"Then I heard an explosion. At first I thought it was thunder. Then I realized it was gunshot. I thought for sure he would kill us all. Thank God it was you."

My words hit hard, a fast ball colliding with unprotected skin. Tremors possessed my hands. Breathless, I panted as if I was the one running naked down the street. "Will she be all right? Aubrey's the only decent neighbor I have. These stuck up bastards care more about their dogs than people. Hmmph."

Renard Broussard scrutinized me, unraveling before his eyes. He fastened his Uni-ball pen to his clipboard and lay his hand on my shoulder. "Ma'am, I'm not in a rush. You don't have to tell the story in one breath. If you don't mind, we can sit on the porch. Take your time. Is that okay?"

I brushed past Glen, hanging in the shadows, afraid to make eye contact.

The normally placid street, dead ending in a cul de sac, was cordoned off. Behind police barriers a handful of curious neighbors craned their necks, ear hustling for clues to this latest incident. In the space of one year the Sampson family had brought screaming sirens and unwanted attention to the high end of town. Their multi-millionaire faces wore "That's what happens when..." expressions. The E.R.A. "For Sale" sign was a welcome addition to the lush Sampson front yard.

Aubrey

A single light lifted darkness from the somber room. His back was to me. Broad shoulders, a narrow waist tapered to a "V". He stood with his legs apart, arms folded across his chest. I could not see his face, but angry thoughts bounced off the walls.

The voice emerging from my scratchy throat was foreign. "I need to pee."

Trent raced to my bed, kissed my hand, then searched for a safe place to kiss my battered face.

"Thank God you're okay," he said.

My hand went to my forehead. "Except for my pounding head. It wants out."

"I'll tell the nurse you need pain meds."

I grabbed his wrist. "No, don't go." I remembered why I was there, in the hospital.

"I'm not leaving. Ever." Trent pulled a plastic chair up to the bed and rested his hand like a feather on my deflated belly.

I felt the pinch of an I.V. needle in my wrist. "What's this for? Is the baby okay?" I asked, afraid of the answer.

"He had to take the baby," Trent calmly explained.

Visions of my baby in the hands of a mad man ripped my brain. I remembered the struggle, running for life, collapsing when my legs would go no more. Did John Bogan catch up with me, use the hunting knife to take my child?

"Noooo," I screamed. My arms flailed, tossed flimsy

hospital cover aside. I tried to sit up. Severed muscles betrayed me. Pain shot from my neck, down my back and radiated in the sacrum. My feet felt paralyzed.

Trent pinned me down with his chest. "It's okay. Dr. Stamper did a C-Section. The baby was in distress. They decided to let her come early. Ella's fine. Seven pounds, six ounces. She's got all her fingers and toes. They'll bring her in when you're ready."

My breathing slowed from one hundred miles per hour to seventy. "I want to see her now." I pleaded.

"You have to lie still. The nurse will bring the baby to you."

"Feels like I drank a gallon of vodka."

"The doctor gave you something to relax. He said you might feel a little loopy."

"Please help me up."

Trent went to the restroom and returned with a bed pan.

"Don't do that to me."

He turned me on my right side and slipped the pan beneath me. Momentarily, I held out. Nature got the best of me. Sweet release.

"Now what were you saying?" He asked, oblivious to my humiliation.

"That was the un-sexiest moment of my life."

"I shouldn't have let you come here alone," Trent lamented, holding my hand.

"You had no way of knowing that sick bastard would attack me...Is he dead?"

"Unfortunately not. But I'll take care of him."

I slurred, "What do you mean? Look at me, Trent Davis. Pull up the jacket." He pulled up the hem of the navy blue workout jacket with fluorescent yellow letters "Team Davis".

I was relieved to see that he was weapon free. "I don't want my Baby's Daddy in jail."

"Your mama and I took the first flight out of Oakland. Otherwise, you know me."

"Mama's here? Where is she?"

"The cafeteria. Pearl hadn't eaten all day. When she called me, I swooped by the crib, picked her up and we headed to Oakland."

A walking ball of nerves, Pearl swept into the room, dropped the white carry-out bag at the foot of the bed. "My baby. Look what he did to you."

Pearl got her cry on for a quick minute, then pulled back and examined my battered face. I saw a flash of anger that I had not seen since Betty Jean Washington and another thunder footed girl, too ugly to remember, ganged up on me in sixth grade.

"I must look rough. Somebody hand me a mirror."

Stricken glances bounced between Pearl and Trent.

"Help me to the bathroom Trent. Please."

"You're hooked up to an I.V."

I gave Trent the look.

"I'll see if the nurse will unhook you." Trent bounced to the lobby.

Nurse Torres, sucking food from between her teeth, entered the room,. "Mee-ces Samp Song. You must take time to heal. Doctor Stamper says, you are to stay in bed."

"With or without your help, I'm going in there," I threatened. I raised up on my elbows, in serious trouble. Rubbery legs looped over the side of the elevated bed. The room was a spinning carousel.

"I'll bring the mirror to you," Nurse Torres offered.

Moments later, an alien stared back at me. She wore a two-sided mask. The left side bore some resemblance to

Aubrey Sampson. The right was a red and purple Halloween scream mask with a black bulls-eye circling the swollen eye-ball that was on fire.

I broke out in cold sweat, a tropical down pour.

Trent squeezed my hand. "Don't worry, baby. It will heal. And nobody will mess with you again. My brother's are headed this way."

Pearl piped in, "Yorba Linda ain't ready for dem…" Pearl caught herself mid-sentence.

Trent finished her sentence. "Damn Davis Boys".

We all laughed, especially me, clutching my stomach with every breath.

My laughter morphed into giant tears. "He tried to kill me and take our baby."

Trent's knuckles strained against balled fists.

I held my hand out to Trent. I felt tension pulsing in his hand. "Promise you won't do anything foolish."

"Shit like this is worth going to jail," Trent responded.

"Everybody calm down," Pearl demanded. "I'll kick that red neck bastard's ass."

I rolled my good eye and shook my head. "Okay, Bonnie and Clyde. Let me rest before they bring the baby in."

Trent

Ella Joy's introduction to Dem Damn Davis Boys (minus Wallace Jr.) came at two in the morning. We lined up like stair steps outside the nursery window. I was the tallest and the youngest of the four. We had identical shape to our heads, long with the hint of an egg below the crown.

Inside the neonatal intensive care unit where she was housed as a precaution due to the special circumstance of her birth, Ella Joy Davis rested content in an incubator. A yellow knit cap was cocked to the left side of her head, a female knock off of Dem Damn Davis Boys. Her skin was peachy clear, not blotched like a newborn under stress.

Rick, the heftiest of the quartet hunched me with his elbow, "Look, man, she's opening her eyes."

I beamed at my first born child. My face was a universe of pride. It had taken forty-one years to find the greatest love of my life. I bit my lower lip, staunching raging happiness threatening to turn into tears of joy. Arms crossed, I squeezed my biceps. This was real.

"Look at her. Fists balled up, ready to rumble. She's a Davis, all right." Rick reassured me. I had no doubt.

Ella's eyes were focused. Her flower blossom mouth was set, matter of fact. She was hyper alert, scanning the ceiling, walls and the rows of incubators. She reminded me of a dated, black and white photograph of my mother, sporting a mop of seal black, straight hair and charcoal eyes penetrating to the soul.

"She's your Mama's twin," Rick chimed in. "I hope the hell she don't act like her," Raucous laughter erupted from the Davis clan.

At the far end of the corridor, a nurse backed up, peeked around the corner. She pinpointed the source of loud laughter in the normally placid hospital.

My laughter evolved into a bottomless, peaceful sigh. One by one, my brothers, Anthony (aka Squirrel), Cedro (aka Pretty Boy) and Rick, bumped fists and hugged little brother. Their hearts traced my long journey through a brutal childhood, failed early marriage, no fruit born of my seed until my improbable union with Aubrey, who gifted me with the lightness of joy.

With my jacket sleeve I dried overflowing tears. "I know I look crazy."

"You aw-ight," Pretty Boy responded. "Now who we got to fuck up tonight?"

48

ISN'T SHE LOVELY

AUBREY

Who is this person with cat like eyes following every move of my lips and bend of my neck. Who is she, burrowing into my skin, changing my life, I mused as I held my baby for the first time. Ella Joy was an old soul with a story to tell before she breathed her first independent breath. I double checked the baby's wrist band circling folds of fat. "Ella Joy Davis, 7lbs., 6oz." the wristband read. I shook my head in amazement. Ella would have been a whopper in another month.

Ella shuddered, heavy eyelids drooped. From deep inside her warm belly, Ella exhaled. The sweet smell of mother's milk escaped from her breath. The baby's eyes flitted, long lashes fell as she lost the battle with the sandman.

I shifted to a more comfortable position. Holding the baby was a feat. Pain from the caesarean came to life once the anesthesia wore off. Dr. Stamper offered more serious meds (Vicodin) for the pain, I resisted. "I want to breast feed my baby, without the toxins."

"Okay. Don't play the hero. I'll leave an order for the big boy. For now, I'll have them bring you Tylenol."

"Twenty dollar aspirin." I laughed.

The doctor flipped my chart shut. Dr. Stamper was not a new fangled doctor, taking notes on a computer while making no eye contact with the patient. "Otherwise, you're doing better than expected under the circumstances."

Stamper squeezed my hand. "Check on you in the morning. If you need stronger pain medication, ask the nurse." He turned to leave.

"Doctor...There's something I need to say."

Stamper turned toward me, rested the chart beneath his belly.

I knew that he already knew. "Ella is not Phillip's baby."

"I figured as much. The last name on her chart is a dead give-away." He let out a mini version of his bellicose laugh.

"I owe you and the church an explanation."

"You owe nothing. My job is not to judge, but to help. If anybody gives you grief, tell 'em to call me."

He placed his index and middle fingers on my forehead, as if to absolve me. "You are blessed." Dr. Stamper rolled away.

It felt good speaking truth to the universe. The information was out there. I could not take it back. For months I held it in, avoiding people, especially church people, who are quick to judge other people's behavior. I skated in the shadows when there was nothing to be ashamed about.

I gave Trent directions to Target in Anaheim Hills. I yearned for a cotton nightgown to replace the backside baring hospital brand, for a proper shower, clean hair and to feel fresh again.

Ella stirred again. Lips tooted out, sucking air feverishly. Contrary to Nurse Torres' warning that breastfeeding might take time, Ella clamped her gums onto my breast and drained the river. It had been twenty-six years since I had tits of steel, pumping out milk like an Enfamil factory. I was quickly reminded of the downside, sensitivity and soreness, accompanying being the milk of human life. Baby girl was more aggressive than Miles, who took his time figuring out the protocol. Ella swigged and slurped like a seasoned veteran.

Aiiee, yiii, yiii. I wondered what I had gotten myself into.

Nurse Torres marveled at Ella's alertness. "She does not look newborn. Baby follows with her eyes."

"That's the same thing I thought," I replied. This child was no mistake, no fluke. She had a starring role in Act Two of my life.

"Time for Mommy to rest." Nurse Torres held out her hands to take the baby. I hesitated, recalling the anguish from the day before.

"Her belly is full and you are tuckered out," Nurse Torres reminded me. I was exhausted, but still afraid to let go.

"Keep her safe," I pleaded.

"This is the safest baby in the world. Your husband's brother stands outside the nursery. Another brother stands outside your door. Such protection. "

To Nurse Torres it seemed like overkill. I was comforted that someone watched over Ella at all times. Who knew whether John Bogan was the last threat to my family? Until yesterday everyone, including me, believed Donovan Upchurch acted alone. The memory of Bogan presiding over a failed deliverance of Donovan at the church reeled in my mind. Hopefully, one day the fear would subside, but it would never die.

Nurse Torres pulled up short at the door. Male voices boomed in the corridor.

"I don't give a damn if you're Jesus Christ. You ain't co-min' in this room." Pretty Boy's voice exploded.

"You're interfering with an officer of the law." Renard Broussard's unmistakable baritone roared back.

"Nurse Torres, ask Pretty Boy to step inside," I called out.

"Pret-ty Boy?"

"Cedro. Trent's brother."

The gaggle of voices pared down to one. "Y'all wait right here. I'll see if the lady is up for this?" Pretty Boy instructed.

Pretty Boy strolled in fresh as a peach eaten straight from the tree. He wore cream colored slacks, alligator shoes to match and a melon hued sweater. Soft facial hair was sculpt-ed to his handsome face. Pretty Boy's wavy hair, thinning at the top, was pulled back into a perennial pony tail and slicked down with generous product. Gold hoops dangled from each ear. Except for a tiny tube of fat around his midsection, Pretty Boy looked almost the same as he did in high school.

"You up to seeing this clown? Calls himself Investigator Renard Broussard? He got a white girl wit' him."

I nodded, "Might as well get it over with."

Amber entered grinning. "We saw the baby. She's gor-geous. You must be overjoyed."

I barely recognized Amber. She looked a foot taller in stilettos, taupe pencil skirt and an acqua silk blouse that plunged between petite breasts. Bone straight, formerly long, corn silk hair was cut shorter into an asymmetrical bob that bounced with each springy step. Amber's freshly ap-plied makeup accented turqoise eyes that came alive when her partner appeared.

Renard Broussard strolled in. "Mrs. Sampson, we need to ask a few questions about yesterday," he said, still strictly business. "All of this might have been avoided, if you had answered my phone calls and texts. Or answered the door."

From the side of her pink glossy mouth Amber shushed her partner, who deserved an "F" in bedside manner. "Officer Broussard. May I handle this please?"

Broussard nodded his head. "Proceed, Officer Mitchell."

I was astonished that Broussard let Amber take the lead.

My near death experience spurted out between stark realizations. Someone else might be telling my story in an autopsy report or a page one feature in the Orange County Register. Within days we would have been forgotten, edged out by the latest breaking news, just as Pastor Sampson had been forgotten by the outside world.

"Thank you is in order from what I understand. My neighbor, Trudy Jarvis, told me what you did."

"There wasn't much left to do. We pulled up. Bogan stumbled out of the garage. That cross put a hurting on him. How were you able to do that? I mean, pregnant and all." Amber asked.

"It was God who did it." I decided not to elaborate on Phillip's warning from the spirit world, "Be Still". They would not understand or believe.

Broussard looked puzzled.

"I had a good personal trainer," was all I added.

Amber jumped in. "We apologize for the way that we..." She turned a dead eye on Broussard. "Were a bit of an ass at our initial meetings. The good news is, we had Delia Upchurch under surveillance for the past week. She met up with the assailant at the Doubletree Hotel off MacArthur. One night we were watching BET..."

I knew it, I knew it. Amber's riding Black Stallion. It was hard not to react.

Amber rocked on without catching her breath. "A church commercial came on. Guess who flashed on screen? The dude at the bar with Delia. We paid him a visit at the church. He's a slippery guy. Sneaked out before we could tag him. We sent his prints to Alabama, where he claimed to be from, but nothing came back. Then Renard...Excuse me, Investigator Broussard...he is super smart...decided to listen to the commercial again. We stayed up all night waiting for it to come on again."

Broussard's eyes rolled to the ceiling. Amber was telling all his business.

"And there he was. Talking in that Southern accent, with a French twist. Rennie jumped up. BAM. He's not from Alabama. That's Louisiana French patois, if I ever heard it."

She turned to Broussard, "Isn't that what you said?"

Faking a smile, Broussard nodded.

"We rushed the prints to Louisiana and they came back a match."

Broussard took up the narrative. "John Bogan's real name is Johnny Tillotson. He's from Shreveport, Louisiana. Served ten years in prison for manslaughter. Killed a man with a hunting knife for sleeping with his wife. Tortured him first. Sliced his face, hands and severed his genitals. Then plunged the knife into the victim's heart."

Amber's mouth flew open in horror. "TMI, Officer. Mrs. Sampson doesn't need that much detail."

"Should've been first degree, but the jury was charmed by him," Broussard added.

"So were a lot of other people," I responded. Flashback. The knife poised over my belly. Bogan's bloody grip on my ankle. Color drained from my face. Why did God save a sinner like me?

"I spoke with the lead detective in Tillotson's case. Said Tillotson came to court every day carrying a Bible. The female juror's loved him. One juror was dismissed for trying to slip him a love note. In prison he became a minister. Built up quite a following. They called him Prophet. Should've called him executioner."

Broussard paused to take a breath. "We put out an APB. Unfortunately, he got to you before we could. When you didn't answer the door, we hoped you were some place safe. But I couldn't shake the feeling that Tillotson was looking for an opening. Few hours later, we circled back to the house. Saw you running in the street. Seconds behind you, Tillotson stumbled out the garage. Unrecognizable. Bloody from head to toe. We jumped out of the car. Ordered him to stop. He kept coming forward. We both fired. Johnny Tillotson died this morning. He can't hurt you anymore."

I should have felt relieved, happy or a sense of closure. Instead I felt flat. Someone pulled the plug on overflowing emotions draining to the torpid beat of fear backed up for months.

"What about Delia?"

"Under arrest," Broussard answered. "After last night's attack, we questioned Donovan again. The truth spewed out like vomit."

Amber rolled her eyes at Broussard.

"Sorry," Broussard said. "Delia met Tillotson in Detroit at a revival. She brought him to the house, introduced him to Donovan and her other kids. He convinced Donovan that Pastor Phillip needed to atone for his transgressions. Donovan swears he knew nothing about Tillotson's plan to shoot Phillip. Says all he wanted was his father to accept him. After Phillip was shot Tillotson convinced Donovan that Donovan was the prime suspect. Told him to run. Against his mother's advice Donovan returned to Orange County for the funeral. Tillotson gave him the gun, said Donovan needed protection. The Prophet, who had his eye on Phillip's ministry, planted incriminating evidence, and financed Donovan while he was on the run. Tillotson paid for Donovan's room and the locker where the quote "evidence" was convenient-ly discovered. It was too neatly packaged. Not even a naïve young man like Donovan leaves that much evidence lying around."

Amber picked up the story. "Whether Delia had any-thing to do with the attempt on Phillip's life, we don't know yet. We do know she lied to Donovan about Phillip being his father. We know she conspired with Tillotson to bring Phillip down and take over the ministry. As a co-conspirator, she gets charged with the whole enchilada. "

I shook my head. "What kind of woman uses her own son?"

Broussard's shoulders hunched. "A desperate, envious one."

"She must *really* hate me," I surmised.

"You were collateral damage. Your husband and his church were the main targets. They didn't care if they de-stroyed your family in the process."

Amber brought the conversation to a close. "We'll get out of here, Mrs. Sampson, and let you rest. Congratulations again on the baby. She's a doll."

To me all sound, including Broussard's goodbye, escaped into a tunnel. "We'll be in touch."

My life. My baby's life. Collateral damage?

49

HAPPY

AUBREY

A balm of tranquility suffused the atmosphere of the Vallejo Marina. The unusually lukewarm breeze tickled my cheeks as I faced ruffling, green water of the Carquinez Straits. Trent's sparkling eyes cast shadows of love upon his child, swaddled in a maize colored cotton blanket. Six week old Ella Joy, floating on a drifting cloud, slept as if the world was in retreat.

Trent screeched his black wrought iron patio chair closer to me.

"Don't wake her up. Please."

"Maybe we should. So she'll sleep tonight."

"Five more minutes. Just five minutes of peace."

He leaned in and kissed my forehead.

I gazed beyond anchored boats to the façade of deserted brick buildings that were once home to an active naval ship-yard. Filmy, smoky gray windows blotted the sun. My breath came easy, slower than before Trent's home became my home and our lives danced to the rhythms of a newborn child.

"What're you thinking about?" Trent whispered.

"Daddy. He worked on the Yard most of his life. When they shut down the Yard, he became a different man. Getting up every morning, riding to work with the same men. Everybody talking smack. That was his life." A wan smile played on my lips and died in remembrance of a bittersweet past. "He was relatively young when the Yard closed. He didn't know what to do with himself. " I exhaled audibly. "Whew...Where did the time go?"

"Yeah. I remember when every man who wanted a job, had a job. Slingin' dope was not the best option. Back then, living in the Crest carried a certain amount of pride," Trent added.

"I never thought..." My voice trailed into oblivion as I watched two middle-age Black men walking snow white Pomeranians down the trail behind Zia Fraedo's restaurant.

"Never thought you'd live in Vallejo again," Trent finished my sentence.

"It's all good. I'm close to Mama, you're here and I'm getting a ton of writing done. It's like the World Book Encyclopedia gushing out, all at once."

"Going from Orange County to Vallejo. That's culture shock. Pearl is in her element, having you and the baby here... But not in the same house."

I laughed loud enough to wake up Ella. The baby jumped, settled back into her snooze.

"You two kill me, competing for HMIC."

"I conceded the title. Mama's the strongest woman I have ever known. Yesterday she told me how much she missed Daddy, dragging around the house and gettin' on her nerves. But she said, the Lord told her to go on."

"I hope her daughter will do the same. Donovan's sentencing was this morning."

"I know. That's why you came home early."

"Wanted to make sure my lady is all right. Donovan got five years, credit for time served."

"Rhonda called this morning. She's pissed, thought five years was too light. But that was the plea bargain. He agreed to testify, which means his evil mama will be on lock down for a long time. Still feels like somebody else's story. God tricked me. Changed the script, just like that." I snapped my fingers.

"He tricked me too. I never thought I'd have a baby this beautiful and a woman fine as you." Trent sensuously stroked my trembling thigh. "Six weeks are up." He eased me into a deep, tongue tangling kiss. "Ready to christen that boat again?"

"How're you folks doing? Ready for dessert?" Bad timing. Franco, Zia Fraedo's head waiter, waded in.

"I am, but my sweetie, fanatical trainer won't allow it," I joked.

"Go ahead. I'll wake you up at five, instead of six, to burn it off."

"No thanks. I'll pass." I dryly responded.

Ella jerked awake. Her reddening face threatened a high pitched squeal.

"Thanks Franco. I'll take the check before my baby clears out all your customers," Trent offered.

Trent scooped Ella from the stroller and patted her on his shoulder.

"You're spoiling her. Don't pick her up every time she whimpers." My argument was lost before it began. Trent was mush in his baby's hands.

In her favorite spot, slung like a rag doll across her father's shoulder, Ella resumed her nap, guaranteeing a long night ahead. Maybe we could sneak in the "christening" before she woke up.

We crossed the median dividing the waterfront from wood frame houses built in the 1950's. The sinking sun illuminated the balcony of the gray bungalow I now called home. A warm breeze cooed to furling wind, fluttering kinky coils of my freshly washed hair. My breasts swelled with the milk of life that Ella would greedily devour once the door to the world closed and her family was safely inside.

50

PREACH

SISTERS IN SILENCE.COM
JANUARY 9

*T*here was a time I existed only as a reflection in my husband's eyes. How my condition came to be was no one else's fault. Just mine. By being the good preacher's wife I elevated his position. In the process I diminished myself and surrendered my once raging confidence. In the end it was a big lie, a masquerade perpetrated on the public, the church and most importantly me.

Ministers often say that pride is a sin. If that is true, they are all sinners. I witnessed too many pulpit parties, preachers crowing their own virtues. Ministers are capable of gargantuan sin due to their elevated positions. They carry the burden (Yes, it is a burden and a blessing) of being shepherds. Sometimes their brains turn into bricks housed inside heads too thick to take criticism.

When my husband passed away, my reflection died along with him. I had to be born again, figure out my purpose minus a man. That ain't easy when you defined yourself *by someone else's title for half your life. I no longer worry, "Is my dress too short? Am I showing too much cleavage? I quit trippin. If "damn" or "shit" slips out of my mouth, every blue moon, so be it. I adopted my father's mantra, "What's this shit about?"*

To my son who had it rough as a preacher's kid, I beg forgiveness. He was held to unrealistic standards. Still, he managed to become a good man. When my son shared with me, "You have been the best mother," it made the years of living in shadows almost worth it. Almost.

I am a good woman. I was a damn good wife. There, I said it. Let the hypocrites crumble at my reclamation of pride. In the name of the Father, the Son and the Sisters In Silence I reclaim me.

One of my favorite lines in the 2011 movie, "The Help", is when Viola Davis has her young charge repeat affirmations of self worth. I reaffirm myself every morning. My hair needs washing, teeth need whitening and the thighs are not as smooth as they used to be. When I was twenty-five an older man gazed at my thighs and sighed, "Thighs so smooth, looks like you're wearing stockings." Well, at forty-five, I'm still wearing stockings. They just have a few runs in them.

As you might have guessed, I am not done with men. It is not their fault they are missing the "third element". Glad you asked, "What's the third element? " The third element is the ability to see beyond two tits and a twat standing over your face. Once Outside Woman has your man looking at life from that perspective, it's all downhill.

Peace

ABOUT THE AUTHOR

Photo by Grant Romancia

Amanda G., a graduate of the University of California, Berkeley, School of Law, is a practicing business attorney. Her previous novels, *Arms of the Magnolia* and *Beyond the Fire*, were published by a division of Random House. *Confliction* is her first edge-of-your-seat thriller. Amanda resides in Southern California with her family.